THE LIFE & TIMES OF GERRIT DE WAAL

THE LIFE & TIMES OF GERRIT DE WAAL

A QUEST TO THE GREAT SOUTH LAND

PETER PURCHASE

Perth Western Australia

The Truth And Reconciliation Trilogy
Book I   The Glass Cenotaph
Book II   The Life And Times Of Gerrit de Waal
Book III Alicia

Cataloguing-in-Publication data is available from
The National Library of Australia

General acknowledgement is made to the following for permission to reprint previously published material: Use of the Australian Aboriginal *Malgana* language, permission courtesy of Ben Bellottie of Denham, Shark Bay; Photographs of the *Zuytdorp* wreck site, © Fremantle Shipwrecks Museum, permission granted by photographer Pat Baker, courtesy of Fremantle Shipwrecks Museum; Photographs of Jandamarra's Rock and the *Zuytdorp* Cliffs © Adam Monk Art Photography, courtesy of Adam Monk.

ISBN: 978-0-9756216-1-5 (paperback)
        978-0-9577364-5-0 (epub)

Other photos from Alamy (JMW Turner – Fort Vimieux) and Dee Browning (from iStock)

This book is dedicated to those who perished in the Zuytdorp disaster in 1712, those who made it ashore and to the Aboriginal Malgana First Nations people who rescued them.

1 WIELINGEN 1 AUG 1711
2 HELLEVOETSLUIS 3 AUG 1711
3 WAGENSPOOR OR WAGEN WEG: 'CART TRACK'
4 SAO TOMÉ ISLAND 13 DEC 1711–4 JAN 1712
5 CAPE DE LOPEZ GONSALVEZ 10 JAN–16 JAN 1712
6 CAPE TOWN 23 MAR–22 APRIL 1712
7 ZUYTDORP CLIFFS JUNE 1712
ZUYTDORP & KOCKENGEN

The de Waal family tree (1575–1712)

(and the connection to the Currie family)

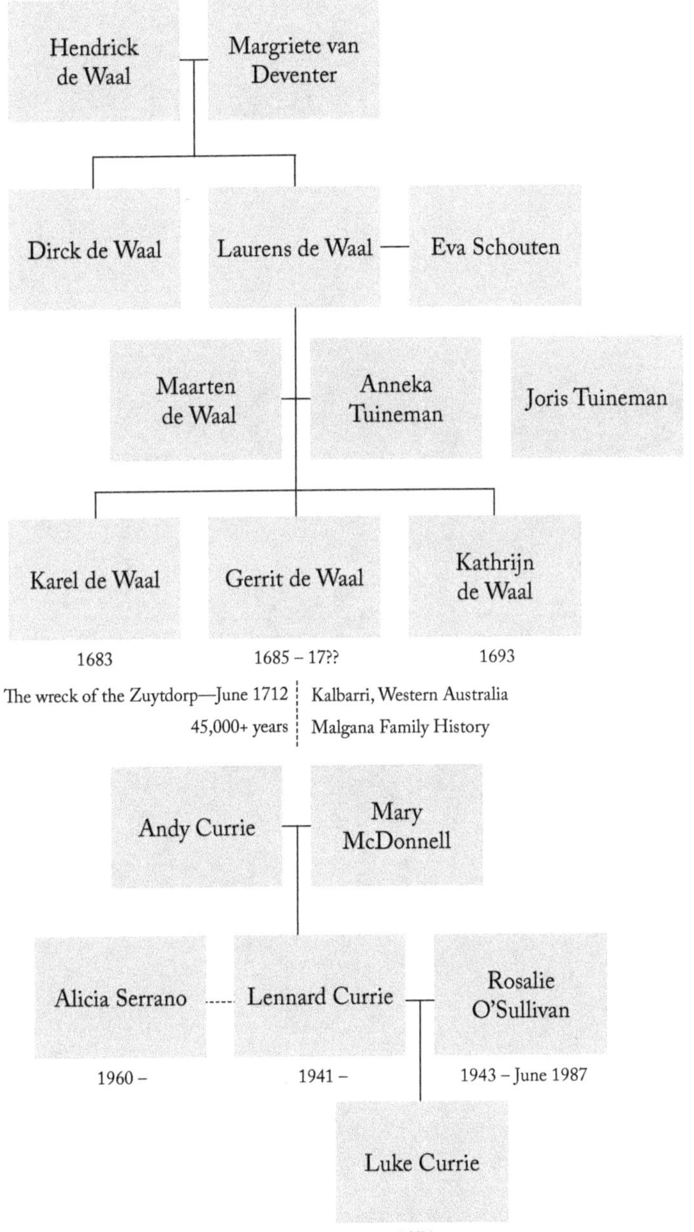

She—the craft—had all the qualities of a living thing: speed, obedience, trustworthiness, endurance, beauty, capacity to do and to suffer—all but life. He—the man—was the inspirer of that thing that to him seemed the most perfect of its kind. His will was its will, his thought was shaping this feeling into the soundless formulas of thought. To him, she was unique and dear, this brig of three hundred and fourteen tons register—a kingdom!

The sea has never been friendly to man. At most, it has been the accomplice of human restlessness.

Joseph Conrad—*The Rescue, A Romance of the Shallows 1920*

Part One
Stefan

30 DECEMBER 2000
in the converted boathouse at Fishing Point on Lake Macquarie

STEFAN NOVAK WOKE TO the screech of the smoke alarm. He reared up, entangled in the sheets. Stunned, he squinted at skeins of smoke snaking across the ceiling, confusion spiralling into shock. *Am I dreaming? Am I cornered in another fire? Have the arsonists tracked me down and set my work ablaze again?*

Heart racing, he steeled himself and peered across the room.

The laptop was open on the table, his files and papers scattered beside it as he'd left them. Beneath the table lay the box where he stored the latest edited revisions, along with Lennard's collection of research notes, photographs, etchings and copies of hand-drawn maps and sketches.

There were no flames. The novel was safe.

Eyes smarting, his throat raw, he scrambled from the bed. He pounded the alarm with a broomstick, then staggered across the floor to slide shut the plate glass doors. Beyond them, cinders swirled from a lurid yellow sky, ash and charred leaves settling like black snow on the veranda and the lawn between the boathouse and the lake. He stared out for several minutes. No live embers flashed among them.

He glanced at his watch. Sunrise. He looked across the hazy foreshore for seabirds. Saw none.

He switched on the television, reassured the power supply had not been cut. He flicked the dial across the channels, then watched Watagan State Forest and the slopes of Mt Warrawalong kilometres away going up in flames, a raging fire-front spurred by swirling winds roaring across the trees. Now and then, two giant yellow helicopters swooped through the smoke discharging bursts of water that turned to plumes of steam as they hit the ground. On one crest he saw flames writhing from a fire tower, its watch house flaring like Sydney's Olympic torch above a field of smouldering tree trunks glowing orange as wind gusts reignited them.

The news presenter confirmed a weather change was on the way. The possibility of rain would give the firefighters a chance to regroup. There were no reports of deaths or gutted homes reduced to buckled ruins, but Stefan imagined charred koalas wedged in the upper branches and panic-stricken sugar gliders leaping from tree to tree, their fur alight, as they tumbled to the forest floor in balls of flame.

He reached beneath the bed for his empty backpack and threw in some clothes and toiletries from the shower recess. *Just in case.*

Then he sat on the bed and picked up his mobile phone. There was a two-hour time difference between Fishing Point and Perth, but he decided to ring the hospital anyway. *Lennard may be awake*, he thought, *or a nurse might take the call.*

As he dialled, he recalled the haunting vision of his friend, Aboriginal glass sculptor Lennard Currie, staggering from the inferno of the Fremantle glassworks three months ago, dragging the red-hot oxy-acetylene tanks behind him, hurling them onto the lawn before they could explode. Stefan had turned the garden hose on him writhing on the grass, the back of his T-shirt in flames, his singed hair a sparking crown of thorns as though he'd set himself alight in an act of self-immolation for his people.

There was no answer. He recorded a brief greeting, 'How are you, Ace? In case you're watching the news, the fires here are a fair way from the boathouse. You get well. I'll call back later.' He hesitated, then added drily, 'Don't you die on me, bro. We've got too much work to do. And remember, Ace—you are a de Waal!'

He rang off and sat staring down at the phone.

Garla! Fire! Lennard saved the glass cenotaph and lit the flame of remembrance for his ancestors, but it almost cost him his life. The shocking memory brought a wry smile. *What if that had been me? How far would I have gone?*

Shaking his head, he reached across the bedside table to pick up Gerrit's abalone shell pendant. Lennard had insisted he wear it while working on the book—the *banduga,* the albatross would give him the inspiration he'd need to ward off writer's block if it struck him, he'd insisted, and it might inspire the ending.

'Guaranteed, bro. Guaranteed. It's never failed me.'

Stefan had looked down at him, lying on the hospital bed swathed in gauze and spray-on skin. He'd sent him an ironic smile. 'I'll believe it when I see it, Ace.'

He straightened the leather thong and hung the pendant carefully round his neck before examining the shell in the palm of his right hand. He ran his fingertips across the albatross cameo carved into its nacre, wings spread, as it swept across the lucent swirl of sea-blues and greens as if far out in the Southern Ocean.

At home there, he thought. *Much like Gerrit.*

He spent the morning editing the script on the laptop. The smoke and ash settling around the boathouse were reflected in the scene he'd decided to revise—a description of the sea battle off the mid-Atlantic island of St Helena and the capture of the Portuguese carrack *Santiago* by the Dutch in mid-March 1602, its decks slippery with pools of blood despite the sand bucketed across them, the air blasted by cannon fire and reeking of cordite, shattered body parts lifted to the deck rails and flung overboard.

He worked through several pages and, as always, lost all sense of time.

When he finished late in the afternoon, the wind had

swung onshore. Cooled by the Pacific, it cleared the smoke. Showers sweeping in across the coast turned the ash to slush. While there was still sufficient light, he stripped down to his bathers, walked out into the rain, checked the damage and began the clean-up. He hosed down the veranda and did what he could to sweep the lawn, which he'd spent an hour mowing the day before.

The tide was out. He swept the muck over the embankment and onto the narrow beach, where it was easier to shovel into the wheelbarrow. He deposited it on the flowerbeds. He did the same to the jetty, spraying the pier and the two yellow kayaks there before scrubbing the matting on the farthest pontoon afloat in deeper water.

He took a breather when the light faded and the showers eased, squatting at the end of the jetty to watch the sludge drift towards the shore, buffeted by the breeze.

He was due to pick up Tania from Belmont airport in three days' time. It was four years almost to the day since he'd last seen her. The prospect of reconciling excited him, but he was wary. There were issues yet to surface. *How much has she changed?* he wondered. *Is she on the rebound? How long will we spend treading on eggshells, feeling each other out?* He frowned at the thought of misreading the signs. *I can't lose her for the second time. Not again.*

He recalled her voice on the telephone a month ago, when she'd contacted him after the opening of the glass cenotaph, and her terse first words echoed in his memory, 'It's me, Stefan. I'd like to see you. Can we meet on neutral ground?'

While the four-year separation was still acutely painful, he had come to terms with it more or less, blaming the failure of his business and threat of bankruptcy for the rift, though he was still uncertain exactly what had tipped her over the edge. When he'd heard that she'd resigned from the Wirruwana

Aboriginal Dance Company and accepted an invitation to choreograph for a dance company in Brazil he was convinced he'd never see her again.

Now he sat with his feet in the water, as they'd done each afternoon last time they'd been here on holiday from Melbourne in October 1996, three months before she'd left him. They'd polish off the wine left over from the night before while he'd improvised on his guitar or played the latest flamenco piece he'd mastered. If she had her nose in a book, she'd occasionally glance across at him, her dark brown eyes alight with teasing hints she dared him to interpret, or distant, as though she was considering something she'd just read, returning to her book before he could ask what she was thinking.

She'd been engrossed in *The English Patient*, he recalled. She'd occasionally place it face down on the pontoon to search for a passage from a well-worn copy of Herodotus she'd bought second hand in Newcastle. She'd been excited about the film version, due for release in a month. Juliette Binoche was among her favourite actors and she'd been keen to see her play the Canadian nurse.

They'd brought the video *Three Colours: Blue* with them on that visit. Each time they'd watched it, she'd raved about Binoche's sensitive performance as the principal character, Julie, and the subtlety of the filming techniques.

When they'd returned to Melbourne, he'd surprised her with a glass chandelier of blue crystals he'd created, identical to the one in the film. It was the only memento Julie had saved after the death of her husband and daughter in a car crash in the opening scene, removing it from her daughter's room and hanging it in the flat where she'd relocated. A shimmering mobile of multifaceted blue diamonds, spheres and cubes suspended beneath a circular mirror, its eye-catching beauty and delicate tinkling when Tania had walked past and set it swinging in the bedroom had delighted her.

Now, staring out over the lake, he remembered the first time they'd watched the fatal opening car crash scene together, both his arms around her, leaning back against him on the sofa. 'I couldn't bear to lose an only child,' she'd said. 'To lose the one thing that completes you. Can you imagine that?'

'And a husband,' he'd replied.

'A *husband?*' She'd given him an ironic nudge. 'Nice try, Stefan.' She was thoughtful as the horrific scene unfolded. 'But a *child?*'

He remembered how they'd slip into the lake when the urge took them, swimming to the nearest buoy and climbing aboard the yacht to stretch out on its deck or sometimes ducking beneath the canvas canopy, the intimacy of their lovemaking on the cushions of the cockpit concealed from the shore and their sated laughter barely audible.

A passing kayaker had almost surprised them once, the splash of paddles warning them. On that occasion Tania had suppressed her sighs and slowed the rhythm of her movements as she'd leant over him, challenging him with a quotation from the video, 'Now try coughing!' she'd whispered in his ear. He had simulated a cough, and the prospect of imminent discovery and her involuntary contractions as she broke into laughter had added spice to their excitement.

Three months after they'd returned to Melbourne that last time, Tania had walked out on him without explaining why, and everything had changed. He looked out across the lake as a familiar rush of anger and regret flooded through him. *On Christmas Eve, for God's sake… and without warning!*

When her sister Alexa had arrived on Boxing Day to collect Tania's belongings, she'd been business-like, impatient and distant, maintaining a hostile silence except when she'd informed him that Tania wanted the blue mobile kept safe for her. He was not to include it with the crystal ware to be auctioned as part of the liquidation of his business. That was a strange request from someone determined to end the relationship, he'd thought at the time, but he'd done as she'd asked. Now it lay packaged under the bed in the boathouse. He intended surprising her with it for the second time. *If things work out well.*

He wanted the boathouse shipshape to welcome her for this meeting. It was their favourite retreat—an L-shaped room converted into a self-contained single bedroom with a kitchenette and spa and a wide glass frontage at the base of a cliff, overlooking the lake. It belonged to the couple who ran the boarding house above them, and they'd climb the flight of concrete steps to join other guests for meals when it suited them.

The sound of lapping water and the blue and purple perennial geraniums in terracotta pots lining the veranda gave the boathouse a Mediterranean feel that had never failed to enchant her.

'We could be holidaying on Lake Maggiore,' she'd said once, 'without the mountains for a backdrop.'

She loved the gardens surrounding it and, in particular, admired the Stanhopea orchids flowering in hanging baskets attached to the veranda eaves, their wax-white blooms suspended like winged insects with a camouflage of vermilion freckles, so much so that he'd struck a bargain with the owners for cheaper access to the boathouse in exchange for manicuring the lawns and caring for the collection of plants. The line of highly scented blue and white Brunfelsias at the base of the cliff held a special appeal for Tania. 'These are Kiss-Me-Quicks,' she'd told him once, turning to face him and placing a finger on his lips. 'Why don't we take the opportunity?' They did, and each time they'd emerged from swimming after that, they'd done the same.

He was anxious for the meeting to go well. There was still

a chance she wouldn't make it, though. The fires had disrupted flights and considering the heatwave and warnings of further outbreaks, she might decide against it.

Would that be for the best? he wondered, then drove away the part admission. He needed her on side if he was to agree to Lennard's latest proposal they'd discussed in July—that he stay on in Fremantle and assist him in preparing the landscaping installation he'd been invited to create for the Quai Branly museum planned for Paris.

A curtain of rain smothered the peak of Coal Point opposite. It churned across Kilabin Bay and lashed the shoreline, rattling on the kayaks. He stood, arms outstretched and face to the sky, the cold sting of rain beating at his skin. By the time he reached the boathouse, the gutters were overflowing, sluicing the remains of the slush across the lawn and over the embankment.

THE NEXT MORNING, he awoke early. The smoke had cleared. The lake's reflections changed from gunmetal to silver as the sun rose over the Pacific, piercing the clouds and scattering shafts of light across the water. The breeze raised waves in diagonal ridges, each racing to leapfrog the next before they reached the jetty.

He was gazing at the shimmer of the headland opposite, floating in the watery haze like a Japanese aquatint, when a pied cormorant broke the surface ten metres out. It splashed up and perched on a channel pylon, shook itself, held its wings out to dry as if pegged to an invisible line and, with a quick double twist of its tail, added another squirt of guano to the black and white streaks collected like barnacles on the timber.

'Hey, cut the crap, my feathered friend, like I have to!' Stefan laughed, as he opened the glass doors to the veranda and placed the laptop on the table.

During the past four years while working on the glass

cenotaph, Stefan had spent most of his spare time sifting through Lennard's research material, developing his distant Dutch ancestor's storyline and character.

It was his first attempt at a novel. His previous writing experience was restricted to informative factual reports on research and development in the manufacture of glass, but Lennard had brushed that aside. 'I've broken all the ground. I've done the research. Now I need his story written. And guess what?'

He had gazed intently at Stefan, eyebrows raised.

Bewildered, Stefan had taken several moments. And then, '*Me*? Write Gerrit's story?' He'd given an embarrassed out-breath. 'I don't think so.'

'Why not? I've read the articles you've published. You've got a way with words.'

'For a scientific report, maybe. But a full-length novel? There's a big difference. Writing up the findings in a glass experiment and ghost-writing a biography are poles apart.'

'Writing the biography of a ghost, you mean,' Lennard had replied. 'I reckon you could bring him back to life if you put your mind to it.'

Stefan had shaken his head. 'What about Alicia? She's a linguist. I'd be a hack compared to her.'

'She doesn't have the time… she's too busy working with the Yamaji Language Centre up in Geraldton. Tell you what, though, I'm sure she'll do the editing. Give you some tips. Maybe even coach you, if you ask her. She wants to see it written as badly as I do.' He had chuckled meaningfully. 'I reckon she'll jump at the chance to crack the whip.'

'Oh, terrific! I can feel the sting of Madam Lash already!'

When Lennard's partner Alicia had agreed to collaborate, Stefan had committed himself to the writing.

He had a wealth of detail relating to Middelburg and

Zeeland during the seventeenth century to draw from—names and family trees, records of births, marriages and deaths, charts and copies of etchings produced at the time, and records Lennard had drawn from the VOC[1] archives detailing Gerrit's service after he'd joined the company as a teenager. Born into a wealthy burgher family in 1685, Gerrit had lived at the height of the Dutch Golden Age during the period of European enlightenment and expansion across the globe.

While he'd been able to compile a linear narrative of Gerrit's life without difficulty, Stefan had found it challenging to create his character, steeped in his family history and shaped by the rapidly changing social and cultural worlds in which he'd lived.

Hesitant at first, he'd felt his way, often seeking Alicia's advice.

'Put him to the sword,' Alicia had suggested one evening as she'd answered him across the dining table, her jet-black hair framing her broad face with its accentuated cheekbones and olive skin, her dark intelligent eyes touched with humour. 'Check his resolve in a crisis. Observe his reactions to new experiences when you put him through the wringer and his resilience and resourcefulness are stretched.' She'd given him her characteristic wide smile, a dimple creviced in her left cheek, her Australianised Mexican accent lending the occasional vowel an extra syllable. 'Force him to live with the consequences of his moral and ethical decisions. As we all do.'

---

1 On 20 March 1602, the *Vereenigde Oost-Indische Compagnie* (VOC)—the Dutch United East India Company, was formed by government decree. The company amalgamated six previously rival Dutch trading companies based in Middelburg (Zeeland), Amsterdam, Delft, Rotterdam, Enkhuizen and Hoorn. Delegates selected from these chambers convened as the *Heeren XVII*—the seventeen lords who ran the company. They were selected from the *bewindhebber* class, the merchant class, who were shareholders.

When he'd dreamed up such scenarios, he had asked himself, *What will Gerrit do when he's confronted with this dilemma? Will he surprise me by reacting unpredictably and out of character? How will he think when he's challenged with this circumstance? Will he have the tenacity to stay the course once he's made up his mind? Or will he regret his choice when it's too late, then fight the yearning to retrace his steps?*

'One question you must always keep in mind,' Alicia had said at another time, when they'd been sitting together on the back veranda steps on a pure blue day, enjoying a morning coffee and looking out over Fremantle and the ocean. 'How do you make Gerrit sufficiently believable across three centuries to interest a modern reader without losing his historical authenticity? From what I've read so far, I think you're finding that an interesting dilemma,' She'd grinned and nudged him with a sharp elbow. 'Remember, I'm here to slash and burn! So don't leave too much of yourself on the page. You're writing Gerrit's story, not your personal running commentary on his life.'

Most of Lennard's notes were scribbled in a barely decipherable scrawl, but here and there he'd discovered passages Lennard had expanded into narratives of remarkable vividness when he'd allowed his imagination to run free. Those episodes made it easy for Stefan; he'd barely changed a word. When he'd inserted them into the novel, he felt that he and Lennard were co-authors, unravelling his friend's European family tree and grafting it onto his Malgana Aboriginal ancestral roots, as though he was seeking out his future in the past.

In Stefan's mind, their collaboration in bringing Gerrit back to life—recreating him as a living ghost—had brought the construction of the glass cenotaph into sharper focus. It had given the project an extra dimension, highlighting its meaning as a memorial to the twenty thousand Aborigines killed during the frontier wars.

Now the novel was finished—except for the ending, the critical final scenes. While grappling with them a month ago, he'd asked Alicia to edit the first draft up to that point. A week later, he'd come close to regretting his request, baulking at her forthright recommendation of a radical revision. Cutting passages that, in his view, lent the book atmosphere was a big ask, but he'd followed her advice and now the latest draft was almost complete. He intended presenting it to her for the final edit on his return to Fremantle.

He fired up the laptop and retrieved an episode he'd revised the day before—*the lion hunt during the* Zuytdorp's *stopover in Cape Town, Wednesday 20 April 1712.*

He printed the pages and stapled them. Then, thinking nothing would irk him more than a grammatical mistake or spelling error he'd missed, he read through part of it.

> *Slung upside-down on a stinkwood trestle, its clawed feet lashed to a cross-pole, the lion's carcass was paraded in an open wagon through the streets of Cape Town. Its thick-necked, black-maned head was flung back. A grotesque coil of tongue lolled from slack jaws. The tail had been shot away, its stump dark with flies above the furred pouch of the scrotum. A cluster of bloated ticks was dug in behind an ear, like polished grey pearls.*
>
> *A group of local Khoikhoi children trotted alongside the wagon, awestruck at the gold glaze of its bloodshot eyes and the vicious curve of teeth that one of the dragoons seated alongside the carcass revealed to them, peeling back its lip with the barrel of his musket and bellowing with laughter at their shrieks.*
>
> *The gleaming, raw-muscled carcass hung from a beam in the abattoir when Sunil and Gerrit went to inspect it. The flayed hide was stretched head-down*

on a frame beside it, leaning against the wall, scraped clean and packed with salt.

They knelt to peer into the jaw, now empty of bone and teeth. They tested the thick sharp claws and inspected the skull that lay on a side-bench, a handful of misshapen lead shot alongside it, dug from the flesh. A thong of lion skin was threaded through a drill-hole in the centre of each bullet—beads of lead on necklaces the dragoons would wear as a testament to their skill.

For Ensign Olof Bergh, who'd led the hunt, the scrotum would carry his snuff and the bullet-severed tail would make him a smart fly-swat.

They left the abattoir and returned to the Strand along the lane that ran between the stockyards of fat-tailed sheep penned for loading aboard the Zuytdorp and the Kockengen.

Sunil was plaiting a bracelet of several shining strands of black and gold hair he'd cut from the lion's mane. He twisted the ends of the threads into a pair of slip-knots he tightened, then threaded the bracelet around his arm above his left elbow and adjusted it there. It was designed to bring him strength and luck, as the elephant hair bracelets had done for him when he'd been diving for pearls along the Mannar sandbanks in Ceylon, or for coins tossed down to him by sailors aboard ships anchored in Galle Bay.

'My Vedda bracelet—for courage,' he said, looking back towards the door of the abattoir and removing his hat. 'I thank the lion for it.'

He withdrew more strands from his pocket and fashioned a second bracelet for Gerrit as they made

> *their way towards the jetty to be ferried in a longboat
> back to the Zuytdorp.*

Stefan was still undecided about retaining the passage. It lent atmosphere, but he knew it detracted from the narrative flow. To his mind, its relevance related to the men's bracelets. They were magical talismans that would bring them courage when they needed it most—such as six weeks later, fighting to survive the storm off the cliffs at Kalbarri.

Besides, he thought, *the lion is the symbol of the United Netherlands.* And it was Gerrit's grandfather, Laurens, who had carved the snarling red lion with its yellow mane and glaring eyes bolted beneath the bowsprit of the *Zuytdorp.*

He placed the pages on the table and looked up at the lake, shards of reflected light striking through the glass doors he'd left partly open. He decided on a morning swim. He picked up a towel and walked across the lawn towards the jetty.

Reading over his work sometimes so obsessed him he was unable to distance himself from it. As he headed for the lake, he seemed to cross a boundary and enter the scene. He heard the musket shots and the clicking of the reload, smelled the creosote stench of burnt gunpowder and felt his heart thumping in his chest as the enraged animal charged the semi-circle of riflemen before a second volley dropped it to its knees in a bloodied spew of clawed dust.

As he passed the yellow kayaks, he felt the wet seat of the longboat slam against his buttocks, the sea's chop jarring his teeth as they brought the boat alongside and Gerrit reached for the *Zuytdorp's* iron ladder rungs, transferring the pewter canister he was carrying to his left hand as he began the climb, the butterfly chrysalises within it rattling as he reached for the deck rail. The tarry smell of fresh caulking on the open decks was overpowering.

He reached the floating pontoon and thrust the images from his mind.

The wind had risen, carrying a fine spray from the crests of breaking wavelets. He slid into the water, inhaled deeply and swam beneath the surface out into the lake as far as his breath took him.

Swimming strongly, he imagined himself alongside Sunil Dewaraja diving in Galle Bay for coins tossed from the decks of the *Zuytdorp* rearing above them. He chased the sunlit flash of a *stuiver* or a *schelling* or a battered Spanish half *reale* as it sank, before snatching it up and adding it to coins already retrieved and held in the pouch of his cheek. Still underwater and desperate for air, he looked down at the blurred shadow of a patch of weed in the sand below, imagining the ominous glide of a tiger shark rising towards him before he barrelled to the surface and sprinted back to the pontoon.

Back at the boathouse, he set the pages of the lion hunt to one side and opened up a manila folder he'd taken from the box beside him. It held a collection of photographs of Middelburg, along with hand-drawn sketches and charts.

He selected a photograph he'd taken of the engraving hanging on the wall in Lennard's lounge. It was by Mattheus Smallegange, dated 1699. It showed a view across the inner harbour towards the Middelburg *dokhavn* shipyard. In the foreground, an old man and teenage boy were pictured beneath the archway entrance to the VOC Company headquarters.

'I like to think that's Gerrit and his grandfather on their way home,' Lennard had said when they'd inspected it through a magnifying glass four years earlier. 'I like to think he's called into the carving shed after school to join the old fella for the walk home.'

The boy was not elaborately dressed. He was wearing a collarless shirt, the v-neck laced to the throat, and long trousers beneath a knee-length coat, an open leather satchel displaying several books slung across his shoulder. Examining the tilt of the boy's head and jut of chin as he spoke to his grandfather, Stefan saw a sturdy, square-shouldered dark-haired teenager whose animated expression suggested someone learning to stand his ground, perhaps downright obstinately on this occasion.

'If it is them,' he'd glanced up at Lennard, 'the young fellow may respect his grandfather enough to walk home with him but he looks like he's got a serious streak of the larrikin in him.'

'Could be. Take a look at the old man's face, though. Whaddya see? A patient frown? Someone who knows the young fella takes shrewd handling?'

'He looks one tough old bloke. I wouldn't like to cross him. I reckon he'd rip the kid gloves off to put Gerrit back in his place when he's crossed the line.'

'For sure, but I can see he has a softer side. Comes with the wisdom of old age, they tell me.'

Stefan leant back and looked thoughtfully out across the lake as he closed the folder. Then he lifted the lid of the laptop and, with his finger on the touchpad, he opened up the novel at the first chapter and began to read.

Part Two
Gerrit

Chapter One

*M*IJN VOORNAM IS GERRIT, *en ik ben de Waal—* My Christian name is Gerrit, and I am a de Waal. I am an only child, if you discount the two stillbirths my Mama Anneka suffered late in her pregnancies. My older brother Karel and younger sister Kathrijn are buried beside each other in the apple orchard.

I spent the first twenty-six years of my life in Middelburg, in the Dutch province of Zeeland. I lived in the attic of the three-storey house my *overgrootvader*, my Great-Grandfather Hendrick built using timbers salvaged from the *Santiago*, a Portuguese carrack loaded with spices his ship had captured off the mid-Atlantic island of St Helena in March 1602.

His full-length portrait hung on the wall beside the stairway to the first floor. In one of my earliest memories, I was playing on the mezzanine when my Papa Maarten appeared. Towering over me, he stooped, took my hand and guided me down the stairs, one careful step at a time. He stopped beside the portrait and swept me up without warning to straddle his shoulders. Gripping me there with one hand, he turned to face the painting.

'This is Hendrick,' he said. 'He is my *opa* and your *overgrootvader*.'

I remember looking into a pair of grey eyes so piercing they seemed to stare right through me. His austere square face frowned beneath the black leather peak of a sun-bleached red cap pulled low across his forehead. A tracery of wind-burned lines fanned from the corners of his eyes. He wore a salt-and-pepper goatee and his lips were compressed. There was no hint of a smile.

He was wearing a simple pale blue uniform jacket silver-buttoned to his lace-collared neck. The sleeves were rolled back halfway to the elbow. His large hands, with fingers linked, rested across his lap… then I saw the lurid tattoos of tiger salamanders on the backs of each, their dark blue scaly tails coiling round his thick forearms, their fire-breathing open mouths casting red and orange flames across his fingers.

I froze.

I stifled a scream, locked my legs against Papa's chest and dug my fingers into his throat. *The dragons in the stories Opa Laurens has read to me are real!*

'That's enough of that,' Papa rasped as he staggered down the stairs.

He tore my hands loose, put me on the floor and squatted beside me. He held me at arm's length and I sensed his impatience when he saw how confused and terrified I was. 'You'd better get used to him, Gerrit,' he said before he let me go. 'You are the latest de Waal, so he'll be watching over everything you do.'

When I glanced back through my tears, I saw Hendrick's eyes follow me as I stumbled across the tiles towards the safety of the kitchen.

That was in 1688, when Papa was home for a year between voyages to the East Indies. He had returned the day before after a three-year absence and was a stranger to me. Apart from the incident with the dragons, I have only the faintest memory of him at that time. All I can faintly recall is the eerie sensation of hovering in the air over smiling faces when he threw me skywards before I plummeted into the safety of his waiting arms. Was it terror I'd felt then or exhilaration once I'd become accustomed to it? Was I too young to feel either?

I was three years old.

It took me several years before I could look up at Overgrootvader Hendrick's judgemental gaze and fiery hands without feelings of fearful awe as I passed up and down the stairs.

I met Papa again when he returned from Batavia aboard the *Ridderschap van Holland* in October 1692. The day he reappeared, I remember we gathered in the dining room to watch him lift from one of his leather bags two male birds-of-paradise, each separately mounted on polished wooden carvings of a leafy tree branch.

'Rosewood,' Opa Laurens said, reaching out to admire the timber and the sculpting of the leaves. 'Beautiful work.'

The taxidermist had done a perfect job. Their glossy dark brown wings were spread as though launching themselves into flight, their brilliant golden tails stretching down beneath them.

To accompany them, Papa had brought with him a marvellous etching on vellum he'd discovered in Cape Town—two more birds of paradise, one above the other, copied from a pen and wash drawing by Rembrandt van Rijn. Opa Laurens framed it, and we hung it in the *kunstkamer*[2] art collection alongside the crude sketches of exotic animals I'd been producing since Mama had given me a box of pastels on my previous birthday. A lion, a tiger, black and polar bears, even a hyena I'd copied from a children's picture book at school, depicting animals kept in the royal menagerie in the Palace of Versailles.

I got to know Papa for the first time in my life during the nine months he was home. I was seven years old, turning eight.

It took me some months to get used to him, this tall, deep-voiced stranger who had invaded my space and seemingly compromised my relationship with Mama. I found it daunting to look up at his tanned angular face, with his eyes as blue as mine. Their bemused expression was difficult to meet. I wasn't used to his teasing and had trouble understanding it at first, no matter how gentle. I thought his words reflected his disapproval of me. He often

---

2 A room housing a family's personal natural history and curiosity collection.

delivered them with a questioning look I later recognised as irony, his eyebrows raised during a watchful pause that left me bewildered and abashed. He may have meant me no harm, but I felt he had expectations I wasn't living up to and I was disappointing him.

'I'm toughening him up,' I overheard him explain to Mama the first time she asked him to desist during the first week. I was hidden on the mezzanine behind the balustrade, secretly observing them in the *voorkamer*[3] below.

'He's not familiar with you yet. I can see he thinks you're bullying him. And you are.'

'It's a challenging world out there. Things are changing. You have to be resilient.'

'Let him get to know you first,' she replied. 'And give him time to grow up. He's resilient enough for his age.'

'Not in my book. Not from what I've seen so far. He has a lot to learn.'

'He's not one of your crew.'

He gave a quiet chuckle. 'Not yet, but I'll work on him and he soon will be. We have boys his age on board.'

Then I heard her mutter, 'Over my dead body.' Twice. And then, 'God willing.'

He smiled and put his arms around her. 'Over your dead body? No, no, my dear. God *forbid*, of all things, that.' There was a long silence as he looked into her eyes. 'He's a de Waal, remember. A Zeelander. He has a reputation to live up to.'

'And a Tuineman. He's a Tuineman. Don't you forget that,' she retorted.

His smile broadened. 'Ah, his sensitive artistic side. The painter. That goes some way to excusing him.'

'He needs no excuses. Leave him be.'

---

3   The front room or parlour.

Unsure how to respond to him, unaccustomed shyness and feelings of rejection sometimes overtook me and I'd seek out the company of Opa Laurens instead or excuse myself and retreat to the sanctuary of my attic bedroom to bury myself in the book Papa had handed to me the day he arrived—*Gerrit in Nova Zembla*, a children's book, the latest best-seller by Jan Mijsters; or I'd examine the prized globe Opa Laurens had bought for me, spinning it for hours to see how often the island of St Helena appeared before me when it stilled.

I liked Papa's thoughtful gift though and, as the months passed, he softened, or I became used to his ways and felt more accepted by him. He no longer mocked me for playing an imaginary violin when Mama was practising on the clavichord, gave me a bemused sidelong glance I took for ridicule when he inspected my primitive drawings, or shouted confusing nautical instructions in Danish or German from the garden below when he saw me seated on my attic window ledge three stories up, sailing the house across the Atlantic and Indian Oceans as though it was the *Santiago*.

I especially appreciated the time he took to help me make my kite. We spent an afternoon cutting up one of Mama's discarded scarlet and green silk skirts for the panels and shaped several flexible strips of whale baleen for the spine and crosspiece. He taught me to fly it on the beach at Domburg on a blustery day, the racing sand yachts swerving around us, spraying us with sand. And he sometimes took me fishing for herring from the Oranjedijk sea wall in Vlissingen during a spring tide, preparing for bait the maggots of bluebottles gorging busily on a stinking bucket of dead eels from the week before.

After New Year, he took me to a secret beach at Westcapelle. It used to be ankle-deep in coloured pebbles when he was a boy, he told me. All the colours of the rainbow. It was a special place, a hidden Roman ruin, an ancient harbour buttress deep beneath the dunes. The confluence of tides and currents there had gathered glass and porcelain fragments jettisoned from passing ships, grinding them into smooth jewel-like fragments of various sizes over the centuries.

'I came here for the first time when I was your age,' he explained as he led me to the tunnel entrance concealed among windswept reeds and grasses.

I followed him into the sloping passageway that angled down through crumbling limestone brickwork to a man-made cavern, an ancient warehouse for Roman galleys fronting the beach. It was filled with the overpowering smell of brine and seaweed and echoed with the smack and hiss of breaking wavelets. The cove was accessible at low tide, and it was on the turn that day, the water shin-deep. Our bare feet scrunched the fragments and I marvelled at the multicoloured pieces I sorted in my palm, selecting various colours, shapes and sizes and filling both my pockets for the kunstkamer—polished glass and shining porcelain pebbles, a treasure Papa and the sea offered up.

He found a marvellous oval stone, smooth and rounded, the size of his palm. 'This looks like Mexican fire opal,' he said as he inspected it. When he held it out to show me, I could hardly believe my eyes. The deep transparent greens and blues flecked with red and polished by the seawater reflected the faint light in the cavern like a dark flame.

'It must be the remnants of the base of a vase or wine cask or some such, made by an imaginative Roman glassmaker, perhaps. A nice addition to our collection in the kunstkamer.' He turned it over. 'Think of the centuries of experience that's gone into it. Man's creative reason and technical skill, drawn from his observations of the natural world around him over time, is concentrated in this artefact that nature has perfected and preserved for us.'

With an enigmatic smile, he handed it to me to carry home.

Even though I was mystified by what he'd said and was too shy to ask for an explanation, I was pleased he'd assumed I'd understand and had entrusted it to my care. Holding it in both hands, I said I was surprised at its weight and found its colours amazing.

'That's something for the Tuineman in you to think about, Gerrit,' he commented.

I thanked him but wondered if he was teasing me. In two minds, I made certain there was no change in my expression.

THE DAY BEFORE his departure in July 1693, Mama and I spent the day in Vlissingen watching him oversee the transfer of four chests packed with newly minted gold and silver coins along with Spanish bullion of inestimable value to the *Ridderschap van Holland,* riding at anchor out in the Wielingen channel. They were destined for the councils in Cape Town and Batavia, Papa told us. Eight armed security *schutter* riflemen accompanied him. A team of sailors staggered under the padlocked, canvas-covered chests they carted from the red-and-black brick blockhouse of the Admiralty Arsenal to the company yacht moored alongside the breakwater.

Before we returned to Middelburg, he introduced us to his new *schipper,* Dirk de Lange, promoted after the resignation of *Schipper* Jan Ammanszoon, under whose command he'd sailed home.

Rangy and hawklike, the *schipper* looked down his long, sunburned nose at me and ruffled my hair. I flinched and gritted my teeth.

'So, Gerrit. Are you going to follow in your papa's footsteps?' he asked. His prominent Adam's apple caught my eye, sliding up and down his throat between cordlike tendons.

'There's no mistaking you for anyone but a de Waal. How old are you? We still have vacancies aboard for a number of boys with your good breeding, if you're interested.'

I looked up at Papa, who nodded encouragement. 'Thank you, sir,' I hesitantly replied, 'I'm only eight, but I already have a job. On a ship.'

'You have? And what's your rank? Are you the schipper?'

'No, I'm the *opperstuurman*[4], like Papa.'

'And your ship? Do I know it?'

Mama, who was then eight months pregnant, interrupted him, gesturing with open hands. 'It's the *Santiago*. He sails the house.'

'Ah, the *Santiago*! So your next destination is St Helena Island?'

'No, it's Eendrachtsland. In Nieuw Holland.'

'*Eendrachtsland?* Why Eendrachtsland? There's nothing there. Except a few blacks, I understand.'

I explained that we were learning about Dirck Hartog at school. We had recently retraced his journey from Amsterdam to the Great South Land aboard the *Eendracht* in 1616, and we'd all copied a chart of that stretch of western coastline with its empty interior and coloured it in. Our maps were hanging on the classroom walls. I had used a pale blue pastel.

He listened intently, before bending to peer sternly at me, his hands on my shoulders. 'Interesting. Then here is my advice. Keep your eyes peeled. Look out for Houtman's Abrolhos Islands. You don't want to end up stranded on a coral reef like the *Batavia*.'

'That was good advice,' Papa said as we walked away, his arm across my shoulder. 'Whatever you do, don't you forget it.'

---

4   First Mate and helmsman.

I WILL NEVER forget the day Papa boarded his ship. That gusty early dawn on Friday morning 10 July in Vlissingen is forever branded into my memory. I remember sunlight streaming across the estuary lighting up the waterfront and throwing my shadow onto the whitewashed bricks of the newly opened mill as I stood beneath its unfurled sails.

I watched them crank slowly into life. They quickened and I placed the green and scarlet silk kite I'd been struggling desperately to launch down on the grass before walking across to the mill. The drumbeat of the giant wooden cogs driving the grinding stones thudded through my hands when I placed them against the wall, prompting me to turn and lean back into the building, my head and chest vibrating.

Laughing, I waved at the group gathered beside the outer breakwater thirty *roeden*[5] to my right. Papa's tall figure stood out among them in the starched and laundered light blue officer's jacket and lace collar I'd observed Mama sweating over for an hour the evening before. He abruptly raised an arm, summoning me back to join them.

With the westerly blowing directly in from the open sea, I lined myself up, held the kite at shoulder height before running forward and releasing it, only to see it lift overhead for several promising seconds before it slackened and zigzagged back to the grass. Determined to send a signal to the two ships on the horizon, I tried again, with the same frustrating result.

After my fifth unsuccessful attempt, a workman from the team loading bags of barley from the horse-drawn dray onto the mill hoist for de-husking walked across and offered to help. Embarrassed, but not defeated, I thanked him and this time sprinted into the wind with the kite soaring behind me, the string sliding out across my palm between thumb and forefinger.

---

5   One Rijnland roede is 3.767 metres, so approximately 110 metres.

I ran along the uneven brick path on the Oranjedijk sea wall towards Papa, hauling on the kite string as it rose, my shouts obscured by the crash of waves sweeping up the embankment. They ricocheted in bursts of spray the length of the waterfront, wrenching the moorings of boats in the inner harbour, sending them bumping and grinding together beneath jostling masts, snapping halliards and whistling stays. I remember pockets of herring gulls stirring and shuffling on the lip of the *dijk* lifting in succession to manoeuvre weightless on the gusts as I tore through them, screaming encouragement at the gyrating kite swooping and swerving across the sky, tugging at my arm.

When I looked back, I saw the messenger-key Papa had attached to the cord spin slowly up towards the kite's thrashing tail. I followed its flash as it lodged itself hard against the split baleen of the cross splice. A stronger gust caught the kite and shook it violently, the panels flashing in the sun as though in flames. In my mind, the kite had reached the borders of the sky and sent a signal to the ships. When it stilled again, as Papa had predicted, the key turned the lock and swung open a rhomboid door to the brightening blue, beckoning me into a world of exploration with infinite horizons.

'You can go anywhere through it,' I heard Papa shout as I got closer. 'Anywhere you choose.'

'I want to go everywhere with you, Papa! *Everywhere!*' I shouted in reply.

Eyes streaming, I ran along the narrow path as though crossing a bridge to the horizon. When I reached Papa, I tripped and lay on the bricks at his feet, panting with joy and laughter, the cord tugging my outstretched right arm as though I'd hooked a struggling herring.

Papa leant across and caught the string. He lifted me to my feet and hugged me, the silver buttons on his officer's tunic digging into my ribs.

Out in the Wielingen channel lay two sunlit silhouettes bedecked in departure flags flickering blue, silver and orange—the *Lands Welvaren* and the *Ridderschap van Holland.* In the inner harbour, the owner's yacht prepared to cast off, her bell sounding, the last group of officers boarding via her bouncing gangplank. I recognised the figure of Schipper Dirk de Lange shaking each by the hand as they boarded.

Papa lowered me to the grass. He cupped my face in his hands and bent to kiss my forehead, murmuring a farewell that I acknowledged before turning away to disentangle the kite string snagged painfully around my fingers.

Mama and Opa Laurens waited for me further along the path. I began winding in the kite, watching as Papa turned to board the yacht. He sent the three of us a final backward wave before he disappeared.

Mama's jaw was clamped, her eyes slits beneath a heavy frown. I could see that she was fighting back tears, ducking against the wind, shanks of dark hair whipping about her cheeks as she struggled to tuck them under her cap. She must have been steeling herself for the year's absence before hearing from Papa, who had promised her a bundle of letters from Cape Town sent home on a ship in the first return fleet. And worse than that, I knew she was preparing to see out a two or three-year wait until his return.

Looking back now, I realise Mama's expression spelled out her loathing for the sea. It had robbed her of Papa's companionship for most of their married life. She must have felt abandoned—pregnant once again—left behind to care for the family and the household.

I never heard her complain, but she must have been overwhelmed by dread when he departed, the premonition that he would not return running through her mind. I imagined her expressing her terror to no one except her God in silent prayer as his departure grew imminent, believing that if she said anything to Papa or her friends, she'd place a curse on the voyage.

And Papa? He was free to take his place aboard his ship, a figure of authority in a tight-knit, structured society of two hundred men heading for the Indies.

Together, the three of us watched the yacht scud towards the anchored ships as the kite descended, rattling and bouncing away from me as it struck the bricks.

WHEN WE RETURNED to Middelburg and the coach was crossing the central square, I stared at the scatter of people stirring in the grounds of the circus which had been set up there for the Pentecost celebrations a month before. The gaudy tents were steeped in dew and the tightrope and flying trapeze were still strung high across the square from a turret below the *stadhuis* city hall clock tower to a building opposite.

One afternoon two weeks before, I had strolled through the jostling crowds with Papa and Opa Laurens, enjoying the laughter, the banter and the raw energy of the entertainers.

Opa and I shared a smile across the carriage compartment as memories of that afternoon flooded my mind. So I craned my neck, knelt up on the seat and peered through the back window.

I caught sight of the solitary mournful dancing bear asleep in the corner of its cage, and in the cage beside it the technicolour mandrill baboon that had fascinated me as it strutted in a tail-lifted, blue-scrotumed half-circle the length of its jangling chain, responding aggressively to the commands of its keeper, brandishing his boathook.

Beyond them were the two mangy lions Papa told me were 'doing a roaring trade', pacing their cages when the crackling fireworks were lit.

There was no sign of the stilted jugglers, though. And the clowning dwarves, the tumbling Italian acrobats in dazzling silks, and the wandering Ashkenazi street musicians coaxing laments from their haunting violins, they were nowhere to be seen.

But *there*, seated outside his stall, was the Egyptian magician who had, with subtle moves, materialised a yellow chick from my nose and then an egg from my ear.

I remembered Opa chuckling as he pointed out, 'The chicken first! Your magician has got the order right, *jonge*. He has answered the riddle for you.'

I glanced back at the lions and saw one of them yawn, its head raised, eyes closed, its monstrous pink tongue curling out between its curving lower teeth, its mouth cavernous.

I looked at Mama, about to ask her to stop the carriage so I could take another look at the baboon to check its features and draw it from memory when I got home, but her eyes were closed. She seemed distant and unapproachable, constantly shifting uncomfortably in her seat, both hands spread across the swell of her belly. The sorrow written across her features dissuaded me.

The carriage followed the creaking wheels of a horse-drawn milk cart crossing the Binnenhaven canal bridge, churns clanking, red and yellow cheeses glowing in the net of shadows thrown by the tall, narrow buildings. The clatter of our crossing resonated among the shipyard warehouses beyond the bridge, where I glimpsed the upright hull of a new ship on the dokhavn slipway. The water was brown and still, multicoloured wooden sledges lined along the embankment waiting for the next winter freeze.

At the house, Opa paid the coachman, and I helped Mama descend from the carriage and walked her to the front door as the coach drove away. I went up to the attic to return the kite to its shelf.

When I returned, Opa Laurens was waiting for me on the *stoep* beside his workshop. He was settled comfortably within the arms of his hand-carved oak chair, smoking his favourite long-stemmed Gouda pipe. As I ran towards him, he blew a series of smoke-rings, through which he thrust a finger, before he spread his arms wide to receive me. He gave me the reassuring embrace I was used to.

'I have something special for you, *mijn kleinzoon*,' he whispered in my ear as I sat down on the stoep beside him.

Reaching into a side-pocket, he withdrew a small lacquered walnut box and handed it to me. Its sides were intricately dovetailed, the brass clasp and hinges highly polished—sure signs of his faultless workmanship.

I looked up at him. 'Shall I open it?'

'Of course, what else?'

I lifted the lid. Encased in purple velvet lining lay a two-piece silver spyglass. I carefully lifted it out, surprised at its weight. On the barrel was etched the label 'Lippershey & Sons' and beneath it, in barely legible print, '*Kalverstraat* M.Z.—*Gemaakt* in 1690'.

'A special instrument to add to your collection. Take good care of it. It will help you navigate those reefs you tell me sometimes threaten your ship. You can use it when you travel up the rivers in America Oom Joris is always telling you about. Remember, close your left eye and use your right to look through it.'

Speechless, I extended the two barrels to put the spyglass to my right eye, but before doing so, I deliberately turned it the wrong way round. I gave a burst of laughter when Opa Laurens clicked his tongue and took it from me. He reversed it and carefully aligned it once again.

'Very funny.' He smiled, before reassuring me. 'But if by chance danger ever does get too close, you can look at it the other way round as you did, to put yourself at a safe distance!'

I swept the spyglass around to peer at the magnified apple trees and the gigantic trunks of the elms across the road. When I focussed on the cemetery beyond them, across the canal, I could almost make out the blurred inscriptions on the mossy gravestones.

'Is this for me to keep?' I asked.

'It's yours, to help you track your papa's voyage to Batavia and home again.'

THAT EVENING AFTER dinner, when I was propped up in bed beneath my polar bearskin rug and reading in the colza-oil lamplight, I heard Opa Laurens tap with his walking stick on the bottom step of the ladder leading up to the trapdoor in the floor of my attic bedroom.

'Come on up, Opa,' I called.

His face soon appeared, his sky-blue eyes wickedly alight. He gave me an angelic smile, which I returned, pointing at the chair beside the window.

He looked like a *huiskabouter*—one of the silver-goateed gnomes we had in the garden—much taller though, with his thinning white hair, his lean patrician's face and aquiline nose, his back permanently stooped after a lifetime working at his wood carvings. He was a captivating and canny storyteller I adored. Animated and astute, he possessed a wealth of tales and provocative parables handed down through the family, along with a seductive knack for telling them when he was in the mood. I rarely had to prompt him.

He climbed into the room, limped to the chair and hoisted himself into it. 'So what are you reading this time?'

I closed the book, a finger between the pages, and showed

him the title—*Gerrit in Nova Zembla*. 'The book Papa gave me. I'm reading it for the second time.'

'Ah, the story of Gerrit de Veer, the carpenter on Willem Barentsz's ship. Or was he the first mate?'

'The mate, I think, but I like the cabin boy, Jakob.'

'Are you enjoying it?'

'I can't put it down, Opa. Some words I can't make out, but I can't wait to read about their journey home again.'

'It's all true. The story's taken from Gerrit's diary. How far have you got? Have they built their *behouden huis*[6] yet?'

I looked down at the enlarged print. 'I've reached October 19.'

'In 1596?'

'Yes. The ship's stuck in the ice. A black bear is looking for food around the ship. Most of the crew are in the *behouden huis* with Willem Barentsz. Only Jakob and two sailors are on board, collecting firewood. They've thrown some chunks of wood at the bear, but it wasn't scared off. It has attacked them and they've run for shelter. Jakob has climbed the mast and he's hiding in the rigging.' I looked questioningly across at him. 'Do you remember that part?'

'Well done, *jonge*. That must be a long way in. You're an excellent reader.' He smiled and held my glance. 'It's a pity your namesake, Gerrit, had to leave his girlfriend Catharina behind, eh?'

'He couldn't take her with him.'

'Hardly. It's no life for a girl up there in the Arctic. Oom Joris can vouch for that. Better she stays home with her father, Pastor Plancius, and waits for Gerrit's return.' He gave me a knowing chuckle. 'I'm sure she misses him playing his flute for her.'

---

6 A 'safe house' built from ship's timbers and driftwood in which the crew survived the Arctic winter on Novaya Zemlya after their ship was stranded and crushed in the ice during their search for the Northeast passage to Asia.

'Would you read some to me?'

'If you'd like me to, of course I will. You're not too tired?'

I shook my head. He took the book open at the page and began reading aloud, his gravelly voice a growl. I was soon half asleep and, as he read on, he lowered his voice so that I could barely hear him or keep my eyes open. After several further minutes I heard:

> *'The 27 October. The wind blew north-east and the snow so heavy that we could not work outdoors. That day our men shot a white fox, which they skinned, and, after roasting it, they ate thereof, which tasted like rabbit's flesh. The same day we set up our clock, repairing the striker so that it sounded on the hour and we hung up a lamp to light our nights, wherein we used the fat of a bear we killed, which we melted in the bowl of the lamp...'*

Opa stopped reading. I knew he was checking to see if I was asleep, so I tightened shut my eyelids to give him the impression that indeed I was. It was a game we sometimes played when he was reading to me—he would end the reading with a riddle or a joke. I was not disappointed when he resumed.

> *'While there was still sufficient light, I reached for the marvellous book I was then reading. It was titled* Gerrit in Eendrachtsland, *a fable describing the imaginary explorations of young Gerrit de Waal in the Great South Land. When I opened it at the page I had reached, I was truly amazed to read the next passage in which young Gerrit describes his opa reading to him this entry for 27 October from my diary, in which I describe myself reading the same passage from his fable.'*

I half-opened one eye and suppressed a laugh when I saw Opa lick a forefinger and pretend to turn the page before he continued.

> *'I was so astonished at the circular coincidence, I turned to the covers of his book as the lantern was flickering out to check the date of its printing. I could not give credit to what I read there— 10 July 1693, almost a century into the future. Therein, I saw the miracle of the meeting of minds across time and space, truly a thing of dreams… so much so that it seemed to me we had both partaken of the roasted fox at the same meal, and agreed that it did indeed have the flavour of rabbit.'*

Then I heard Opa close the book and murmur, 'Whereas now, *jonge* Gerrit, in your case, it's lights out.'

He reached across, covered me with the bearskin, then stretched to snuff out the lantern before shuffling across the floor.

As he descended, I wished him, '*Welterusten*, Opa,' in a whisper. 'Sleep well, Opa.'

'*Zoete dromen, mijn kleinzoon*, sweet dreams, my grandson,' he replied, as he closed the trapdoor behind him.

Chapter Two

LATER THAT NIGHT, a dreadful commotion in the passageway below suddenly woke me. I sat up, alarmed by the clatter of running footsteps and frantic voices I could barely make out. In the background someone was wailing, the sound changing in pitch and volume so that it seemed inhuman until I recognised Mama's voice. Shocked, I climbed down the ladder, the hairs on my arms and the back of my neck standing on end.

Through the din, I heard the grandfather clock in the voorkamer striking three.

Then I heard the maid Adriana shriek, 'It's time for the midwife. I'll fetch *Mevrouw* Pietersz.'

I was paralysed when she rushed past, her face strained and gaunt, the linen sheets bundled in her arms stained red and brown and carrying a sharp, repulsive smell.

'Go back to bed and stay there,' she hissed as she rushed past. 'Your mama is in labour. You cannot help.'

I climbed back up and squatted beside the trapdoor, peering down at the lamplit corridor, listening and watching. Here and there the left footprint of a shoe had stained the white tiles red among the black, marking where Adriana had run.

The wait was interminable and Mama's groaning constant, until the midwife and her assistant passed beneath me. Then she quietened and the mumble of voices was barely audible behind the closed door of her bedroom, her intermittent grunting punctuated, now and then, by a chilling shriek of pain.

For several hours, I waited expectantly for the sound of a newborn baby's cry that Mama had promised would announce its first intake of breath. None came.

When the house was silent at last, Opa Laurens appeared in the passageway below. Shafts of sunlight pouring through the panes of the attic window washed diamonds of light over his face peering up at me.

'Bad news,' he said. 'I'm sorry, but your mama has given birth to another stillborn. A girl this time.'

His words stunned me and the unthinkable overtook my mind. 'Given birth?' I blurted, as uncontrollable tears began to flow. 'Given death, you mean.'

'Don't say that, jonge!' he exploded. 'Especially at a time like this. You cannot blame your mama. It's not her fault.' And then calmer, 'Come on down,' he said. 'Come on down. Now.'

The unfamiliar severity in his voice struck me like a blow. Sobbing, I stood, closed and locked the trapdoor, then lay face down on the polar bearskin.

A sister for Karel. But for me? Just the memory of my excitement at feeling her energetic kicks probing against Mama's abdomen and across my palms each time Mama allowed me to experience them, miraculous lively movements that filled me with impatient anticipation.

Several hours later, when Opa Laurens knocked on the trapdoor and insisted I go down, I crossed the floor and unlocked it.

'Mevrouw Pietersz would like to talk to us,' he said. 'Come down and join us.'

She was in the voorkamer, seated on the oak bench. She was a plump and stocky lady I'd met before when she'd visited Mama. She had a round face and thoughtful brown eyes beneath thinly pencilled eyebrows. She gave me a quick smile, the filling in her front tooth flashing silver as she invited me to sit, patting the broad red leather cushion beside her. Her legs, with their thick ankles encased in grey woollen stockings beneath her blue smock, barely reached the floor.

I sat awkwardly next to her, distressed at the thought that she could see the effects of my tears. Opa Laurens sat opposite on the stool of the clavichord.

'I am very sorry for your family's loss, Gerrit,' she said, leaning forward and gazing intently at me. 'I have to tell you your mama has given birth to your sister, who has passed away.' Her thoughtful expression wrinkled the skin around her eyes. I saw kindness in them. 'Now then, I believe you are eight years old?' She raised her eyebrows, patted my knee. 'Are you a brave boy? I'm sure you are because Kathrijn is still upstairs with your mama, who would like you to go up to meet with her.'

Kathrijn? Meet a dead baby? I stiffened and did not answer.

'Opa Laurens has seen her,' she reassured me.

'I have, *mijn kleinzoon*. I held her. She has black hair. Quite thick. And she is lovely. Very lovely, like her mama.'

I looked at the floor, confused. The only corpse I had ever seen was a German vagrant caught stealing, his body nailed to the breaking wheel outside the Koepoort city gate, his bones shattered. A group of us from school had chased away the crows with slingshots.

Closing my eyes and shaking my head to clear that image from my mind, I held myself in check before rising. 'Alright,' I nodded. 'How about Mama? Is she alright?'

'She's been through torture, Gerrit, and she will face more pain while she's grieving. It will take some time, but she is strong. She's one of the strongest women I know.' She stood and, with an arm around my shoulder, she looked into my face, her breath carrying the rich smell of drinking chocolate she must have discovered in the kitchen, where I glimpsed her assistant still breakfasting. 'And she has her faith. So with your help, and Opa Laurens here, I'm sure she will be fine.'

'Are you sure?'

'I'm sure. You must not worry.'

As I followed her up the stairs, I asked if Mama had also held Karel.

She looked back as she climbed. 'Oh yes. She gave birth to him naturally, as if he was alive. That was a great relief for her.'

'And you're certain she held him?'

'She did, for several hours. Until she was ready to give him up to your papa for burying.'

'Mama never told me.'

We reached the mezzanine and I tugged her sleeve, bringing her to a halt. 'What about me?' I asked. 'Were you here when I was born?'

'I was. I remember it well.'

'Was she afraid I might be born dead, the same as Karel?'

'Yours was an easier birth, as I remember. No complications; as easy as counting up to three. If she was worried about you, she didn't show it.'

'Was she still sad for Karel when I was born?'

She looked thoughtfully down at me. 'Weren't you born two years after Karel?'

'Yes.'

'You never forget your children, Gerrit, so yes, I have no doubt she was still sad. She may have been experiencing many different feelings, but that doesn't mean she wasn't pleased to welcome you. If she was still grieving for Karel, that didn't affect the way she felt about you. She was filled with joy. I witnessed it. She loved you for yourself, as she loved him.' Then she quickly corrected herself. 'She *loves* you. She loves you both.'

'And Kathrijn?'

'And Kathrijn now. All three of you.'

I looked back down at Opa Laurens, still sitting on the stool. He waved me on, so I followed Mevrow Pietersz along the corridor. I realised that what she'd told me explained why Mama had reacted with such determination to Papa the way she did when he'd first arrived—she was protecting me, just as she protected and cared for me whenever I was sick or suffered an injury. The extent of her concern always surprised me, no matter how mild or trivial the situation.

Then, for the first time, I grinned and asked as Mevrouw Pietersz reached for the bedroom door handle, 'So... which one of us is her favourite do, you think?'

She looked back and smiled. 'She loves all of you equally, Gerrit. Trust me.'

She entered the room, then stepped to the left and gently pushed me towards Mama, who was sitting up in bed propped against several pillows.

The curtains were drawn, but in the orange sunlight filtering through them I could see that her face was worn and ashen, her eyes deep in their sockets with shadows dark as bruises beneath them. I expected her to be wearing her nightcap as usual, but her black hair had been brushed and hung loose beside her face and across her shoulders, accentuating her pallor.

The neatness of her bedlinen and the furnishings surprised me. I had expected things to be in disarray. The crocheted blanket was straightened across the bed, Mama's slippers placed neatly beneath it. A fresh bunch of purple lavender Adriana must have cut that morning stood on the side table, its refreshing fragrance drifting.

In the far corner of the room, I made out the rosewood crib that Opa Laurens had made for Karel, which I had used. It lay empty.

Mama gave me a faint smile. 'Come here, Gerrit,' she whispered.

I looked down at the cocooned bundle that was Kathrijn,

held in the crook of her right arm. Shifting awkwardly side-ways, Mama adjusted her hands before picking her up and holding her out to me. 'Hold her with both arms against your chest, as I was doing. Use your left hand to hold her head.'

I looked at her and hesitated.

'No need to be afraid, Gerrit. She can't harm you.'

As I reached out for her, Mevrouw Pietersz stepped forward to arrange her in my arms. I glanced at Mama, shocked at how light the baby felt. Out of the corner of my eye, I saw that the rim of her bonnet had fallen across her face. I took a deep breath and looked over at the curtains as Mevrouw Pietersz rearranged the bonnet. Then, very gradually, I shifted my gaze and looked down.

She was wrapped in silk swaddling clothes tightened with lace bands, a linen bonnet fringed with cutwork lace on her head, surprising tufts of dark hair curling down beneath it. She too was very pale, her lips faintly blue. She had lace brace-lets on the wrists of both her tiny hands, her perfectly formed fingernails also tinted blue.

After some time, 'Is she in heaven with Karel?' I asked.

'I like to think she will be,' Mama replied. 'We'll both pray that is the case and she will wake up there. She looks like an angel, though, doesn't she?'

'Made in God's image,' Mevrouw Pietersz murmured.

'What do I say to her?' I asked.

'Introduce yourself, Gerrit. Tell her you love her.'

Her eyes were closed. She could have been asleep.

'Hello,' I said. 'I'm your brother. My name is Gerrit.' And then, with my heart thudding through her tiny body, 'I love you, Kathrijn de Waal.'

It would not have surprised me to see her open her eyes and look up as I spoke, and for some irrational reason I was about to urge her to do so, but at that moment I was overcome with confusion as I thought, *You are dead and I am alive!*

It seemed for a terrifying instant that I was someone else observing myself holding Kathrijn. I was an eerily disconnected other self, who clearly understood that she was dead and that the words I had spoken, and what I was about to say to her, were not directed at the body in my arms, but at a disembodied Kathrijn in some uncertain elsewhere.

Feelings of such piercing intensity struck me that I felt I was about to faint—alarming feelings I had never experienced before. Panicked, I stumbled towards Mama and leant across to drop the bundle into her arms. I brushed past Mevrouw Pieters without looking up at her and rushed into the corridor. *She'll think I'm not a brave boy, but I am. I am!*

It took me some time, sitting on the lowest rung of the ladder to the attic, to gather my breath and calm myself sufficiently to return to the bedroom doorway and gaze at Mama in the half-light. When she patted the bedclothes, I walked across and sat beside her.

For a long time, no words passed between us.

Chapter Three

IN MID-FEBRUARY THE FOLLOWING year, Oom Joris came to visit us for a week.

I always looked forward to his visits. He would come home from his spring and summer whaling expeditions in the Arctic or poaching live oak timber from America during the winter, arriving unannounced in his seal or bearskin coats, carrying the strong smell of whale oil Mama couldn't stand.

He'd always bring a satchel of treasures for me to add to the kunstkamer: a variety of seashells, for example, or rocks—quartzite, jasper, tourmaline, fool's gold. A pair of silver fox furs once, for Mama. My polar bearskin bedspread. Whale baleen, some of which Papa and I had used as framing pieces for my kite. And once the preserved skin of a diamond rattlesnake as tall as himself, its rattles collected in a jar. He'd trapped it beneath a forked stick on Cumberland Island off the Georgia coast, and when he'd picked it up by the tail and slit open the length of its belly with a razor, a part-digested hare had slid to the grass. He'd placed its carcass on an ants' nest, he told me, when we later sorted the hare's white bones and reassembled its skeleton. We mounted it on a piece of ebony Opa Laurens carved as a base.

As usual, he appeared *uit het niets*—out of nowhere. We hadn't seen him for two years.

'The Barbarian is home!' I heard him shout.

I leant from the window as he threw his kitbag from his shoulder to the front stoep. Short, broad-shouldered and muscular, he stooped forward to loosen and kick off his knee boots and, standing in frayed black stockings, he rang the *Santiago*'s bell as wildly as only he could.

Adriana was the first to open the door, clapping flour from her hands, a sunflower-patterned orange scarf knotted gypsy-like around her silver hair, the wood and silver handles of kitchen implements protruding from the deep pockets of her apron. She submitted to his vigorous embrace with a shriek of laughter as he whirled her round several times, her feet off the ground. She held her arms rigidly out behind him, fingers splayed, either to avoid leaving floury handprints on the back of his shirt or so as not to clasp him in too intimate an embrace. When he settled her on the pebbled driveway, he kissed her on both hot cheeks and then gave her a surprise kiss on her lips, rendering her wrinkled face scarlet as she giggled with pleasure and embarrassment.

'Now *that* was worth coming home for,' he said, as Mama appeared at the door and Opa Laurens staggered around the corner on his walking stick.

I rushed downstairs to find Mama in his arms. He smiled at me over her shoulder. Except for an unkempt ginger beard, his features hadn't altered since last I'd seen him—his battered red cap was pushed back to reveal a thatch of sun-bleached yellow hair and his face still had the topography of a life lived to the full. Deep lines ridged from the corners of his almond-shaped eyes to his temples and down his cheeks, branded there by laughter and the sun. He looked inscrutable and shrewd and deliberately obtuse, with sly humour in a smile in which I recognised his signature touch of scorn.

He gave me an exaggerated wink before turning his attention back to Mama. He disengaged her and held her at arm's length, his expressive green eyes sparkling. I noticed his faded canvas shirt was badly salt-stained at the armpits and across his broad chest.

'You look remarkably well, *zus*.'

'As do you, Joris,' she returned his smile. 'I am feeling well. All things considered.'

'Yes. I heard. Pieter Penne[7] told me. I met him this morning in Nieuw-en St Joosland. I'm very sorry.'

He hugged her again before she wriggled free. 'Thank you. I've had the time to straighten myself out,' she said, brushing herself down. 'Never mind that. Right now, you need a hot bath.' She nodded at Adriana, signalling with her right hand the act of pouring a jug of water from the boiling laundry copper and pinching her nose shut with her left. 'The hotter the better,' she called out as Adriana disappeared indoors, 'and don't forget the scrubber and the lye soap… and the razor. As for you,' she turned back to Joris, 'you can burn those clothes and borrow a set of Maarten's until we organise a fitting for you.'

'Ah! Here we go! I've been here five minutes and you're already turning me into your *huisdier papegaai*—your pet parrot. Promise you'll arrange for a lace cravat and periwig to go with the silk stockings and the breeches?'

He had arrived in Rammekens aboard the *Amazon* with a cargo of timber from the Georgia and Carolina coasts, he explained later when we were seated around the dining table. His hair and beard were trimmed and he was wearing one of Papa's toga-like nightgowns that reached the floor. I was seated next to him and picked up the faint soapy smell of ammonia.

'It's excellent quality timber this time, Laurens,' he said. 'Especially the red cedar. Pieter Penne and the *mulatten* half-castes are offloading it at the saw windmills as I speak. You and I should go down there to select some for your carving shed before someone else gets their thieving hands on it.'

'Ah, Pieter will look after me, Joris. He better had, or he

---

7 Pieter Penne, master shipwright in the Middelburg *dokhavn*, the shipyard.

won't be getting the carvings he wants for the gallery aboard the *Kattendijk*.'

'That's the latest ship?'

'She's a *fluit*!⁸' I interrupted. 'She was launched two days ago. Opa took me to the dokhavn to watch.' I took a breath. 'She can carry three hundred and fifty *scheepslasten*!'

He turned his gaze on me, eyebrows raised, before slowly nodding. 'Is that so? I'm sure you'd be the one to know, *jonge*.' Then he gave a quiet chuckle. 'I see you got her gender right. That's promising for a boy your age. It's good to see Opa's knowledge is brushing off.'

'He's a quick learner,' Opa said.

'So he should be—he's a Tuineman. That more than makes up for the de Waal in him.'

He reached down to his kitbag and rummaged around in it before withdrawing a small hessian gunny sack. He passed it across to me. 'For you, Gerrit. We called in to Curaçao on the way home. Something I found in Willemstad.'

I undid the drawstring and tipped out two pink-lipped conch shells, one fist-sized and the other twice as large. I picked them up and inspected them. 'Thank you, Oom Joris. They're amazing. What type are they?'

'These are Queen Conches. What sort are the ones you have in the kunstkamer?'

'The ones Papa brought back from Ceylon? They're Triton's Trumpets.'

He smiled. 'I thought as much. Now, what can you see that's different about these?'

'Well, they're a different shape. And different colours.'

'Look again.'

---

8 A mid-range three-masted, 760 tonne Dutch cargo vessel designed to carry a maximum shipment. A *scheepslast* (ship's load) equated to 2.17 tonnes.

I ran my hand over them and noticed that the apex on the spire of each shell had been cut away. I pointed out what looked like damage. He nodded and reached for the larger one. He wiped it with a serviette, placed it to his mouth with his lips over the aperture and, with both cheeks bulging, he emitted an astonishing trumpet-like single note, varying its tone and volume. Then he placed his hand inside the aperture of the shell. He lowered the pitch the deeper he thrust his hand in, then raised the pitch as he withdrew it. The tones and tune were mesmerising.

He grinned and placed it back on the table. 'Something for you to learn,' he said, 'blowing until your tongue bleeds and your facial muscles ache. It isn't easy. I didn't get a decent note out until we reached the Azores. There are musicians in Willemstad who can play tunes on shells like these that are out of this world. Especially when they play together in groups, with the drums going. And the dancing! *Het waait je geest*—it blows your mind.' He pointed at the larger shell. 'This one belonged to the most creative of them. A genius, with lungs like a blacksmith's bellows. The music he produced with it was sublime. Here,' he said, leaning across and holding it out to me. 'Listen to it sing, even when it's not being blown.'

I held the shell to my ear, as I had with others in our collection, and, as usual, heard the sounds of the wind and sea… but these sounds seemed deeper, more sonorous and somehow hypnotically enticing. 'It is different,' I said. 'Is that because there's a hole in the top?'

'That's something for you to wonder about when you make your own music through it,' he replied. He smiled as he added, 'Perhaps nature is whispering her secrets to you, inviting you to try it out.' He put the shells back in the bag and handed it to me. 'I'll show you how to blow them later. After that, you're on your own.'

Mama reached across and patted my hand. 'Maybe it's time for you to put away your imaginary violin.'

IT WAS DEVIL-MAY-CARE Oom Joris who alerted me to the challenges of the widening world during my boyhood. He used to say that the risks he took on his whaling voyages, his daring, bordering on recklessness, and his addiction to the wildest seas and remotest landscapes gave him the vitality that thrust him into being. He relished those moments of extreme danger when he was truly tested—when he looked mortality in the eye, exhilaration rushing through him.

None more so than the time he'd snatched up the diamond-backed rattlesnake single-handed, I heard him remind Mama later that evening, when she asked him if he was taking good care of himself. 'I worry about you when you're away,' she said. 'I'd hate to see anything untoward happen to you.'

'You know I love to dance with death, Anneka. I live for those times when I face the greatest dangers! Like the time I picked up that rattlesnake and took my chances. That's the way I affirm my life.'

'One of these days you'll take things too far,' Mama warned him. 'Then you'll be saying your prayers.'

'No need for that. No help from that quarter.'

'That's where you're wrong. You and I think so differently.'

'I trust my own judgement.'

'Exactly my point,' she said, shaking her head with a sigh, before insisting firmly, 'It's not so much *you* I'm concerned about. It's Gerrit, now you're back. You and your stories are a questionable influence. He's far too young to start thinking for himself.'

'My *stories*, Anneka? The boy asks and I respond. He's curious about the Arctic and America, about life on board.' He gave an infectious laugh and I smiled at Mama despite myself. 'Trust me, my dear, Gerrit and I don't debate the pros and cons of religious philosophy or politics. At least we haven't yet, even though the *jonge* is eight going on fifty. I'll wait until he's seventeen or more and has a thinking head on his shoulders.'

'That's good to know. I'd prefer you to leave that part of his education to me.'

'Don't worry. I'll behave. I always do, don't I? You know I go through the motions to keep the peace. I keep up appearances at the reformed church when I'm home, don't I?'

'You only come to listen to me play the organ… and eye off the young unmarried ladies, you always tell me. Never mind the services.'

'That's true.' He smiled. 'You're worth listening to when you get carried away, but never mind the ladies this time. I'm only here for a few days.'

'You're leaving so soon?'

'The *Jacoba* is up at Texel, sailing in three weeks. The coach leaves for Amsterdam on Tuesday.'

'Tuesday next? The sixteenth?'

'Yes.'

There was silence around the table. 'So when will we see you again?'

'In September, most likely.'

'Well, you'll be in my prayers, whether you like it or not.'

He smiled. 'That's reassuring, *zus*, so thank you. I guess every little bit helps. I have to attend the *predikant's* services aboard ship, in any case. No one steps out of line or they're in the brig.' He raised a hand and waved it over his head, the fork extended, a piece of stew skewered to it. 'I'm up to here with his repetitious sermons.' I half-expected the meat to fall to the linen tablecloth or into my lap, but he put it into his mouth and chewed thoughtfully. 'Don't panic. I won't influence the boy, but that's on one condition.'

'Which is?'

'You don't turn him into a choirboy. If you do, all bets are off!'

'A *choirboy*! Have you heard him sing? He's been taking lessons from the frogs in the canal.'

'Then we're agreed,' he said, turning to me. 'Mama, me and the frogs, we'll give you an excellent upbringing.'

HE SAILED IN the spring and summer Arctic voyages deep into unexplored grounds in the Davis Strait and the rugged fjord-bays of Western Greenland, where they tracked pods of giant bowhead and narwhal, or the solitary rogue sperm whales retreating from the over-hunted waters around Spitzbergen.

In the winters when the whaling season ended, he poached the timber of live oak, black oak and cedar from the north Florida and Georgia coasts. Spanish monks and settlers, with their retinues of soldier-slaves, had ambushed him twice in the coastal swamps and dunes where the great oaks abounded. On one occasion, he'd been forced to retreat to his ship when a musket-ball struck the pad of his shoulder. The scar had gleamed on his sunburned skin like a smear in dark wax when he'd removed his shirt and shown it to me.

I found his stories magical. They were a gateway to new horizons that fired my imagination.

Some persistent images overwhelmed me when he was away and I often relived them on my window-ledge when I sailed the *Santiago* of my mind across the world. So much so, that I found myself fighting to suppress the terror that under-scored my excitement each time I manoeuvred the house-ship into the deep river-channels of the Altamaha estuary in search of live oak, for example, the tawny river's surface ribboned with swarming moccasin snakes crossing under the bows.

Or when the ship shuddered to the growl of nearby

pack-ice when I was hunting whales, listening to the thunder of slow-revolving floes grinding together at night, their edges climbing over each other in the luminous dark lit by the glow of low cloud, or when I watched the huge blue icebergs sheered from glacial precipices as they moved majestically southwards, riding the deep currents, booming detonations signalling the parting of the pack ice that cracked and split before them.

Sometimes, when I was sitting on my window ledge remembering Oom Joris's words, I clambered up one of the bergs. While I imagined the *Santiago* lying sheltered in a dock cut into the ice shelf on the western Greenland shore, I collected chunks of ice to melt for water. I revelled in the exhilarating slide on the barrel-stave toboggan carrying the ice blocks down, the slope slippery with melt in the weak spring sun.

Once, as my toboggan slowed at the base of a slope, I was startled to see the tusked snow leopard Oom Joris had told me about, glittering within the ice-wall, savage fury caught in the green gleam of its frozen eye. Trapped deep in the ice, leaping to shake itself free, it was journeying southwards in the berg, an eerie phantasm buried for three thousand years in its glacial tomb.

I think it was that vision that triggered a boyhood nightmare that often used to horrify me as if it carried uncanny warnings of catastrophe to come. Though its context and the characters within it varied, it always filled me with the same choking atmosphere of foreboding that woke me in terror.

Dying of thirst on an unknown cliff, I yearned for my child-hood Zeeland sky of pastel greys and blues, its soft light filtering through raindrops I caught on my tongue as they fell from the leaves of the linden trees. It was a shielding sky I'd been thrown towards by Papa when I'd floated high over the family's smiling faces before falling into the safety of his waiting arms.

But in this dream, I had truly fallen. I lay on a rock shelf, blanketed in pain. Drifting in and out of consciousness, I closed my eyes to the blinding sun and faded into darkness, no waiting arms ready to catch and throw me skywards again.

Below the cliffs, my ship lay on her side, her back broken. Her mainmast hung awkwardly over the shelf jutting from the cliff base, awash with pounding surf. The topmast pennant, caught by the breeze, fluttered like the orange, white and blue feathers of a broken-winged bird.

One of the survivors shattered another empty gin bottle, the explosion of breaking glass drowning out the murmur of voices.

The signal fire roared…

WHEN OOM JORIS visited us again the following November, I barely recognised him. I heard the bell ring and, when Adriana opened the door, her cry of fright echoed up the stairwell. By the time I reached the top of the stairs, she had ushered him into the voorkamer and I saw him seated on the bench, a pair of crutches leaning against it beside him.

Mama, her hands on her hips, looked down at him, dumbstruck. The tips and lobes of his ears were missing and what appeared to be a brand-new prosthetic nose concealed his nasal cavities. He had lost weight. The skin on his face seemed fleshless, the bones of his skull and cheeks protruding. Were it not for the challenging gleam in his green eyes and the characteristic way he slowly broke into a sarcastic smile, I would not have known him.

'Relax, *zus*. It *is* me,' he said, his voice unchanged, thankfully. 'Handsome, hey? *Of heb ik jullie allemaal doodsbang gemaakt*—Or have I frightened you all to death?'

'Oh, *Joris*! What have you done to yourself?' Mama cried out, kneeling in front of him and weeping, her arms around him.

A mix of emotions surged through me as I ran down the stairs, my gaze fixed on him. Apprehensive dread at first, fascination, then overwhelming joy at seeing him again as he reached out his right hand and pulled me in to Mama, sobbing against his chest.

After several minutes, she stood and straightened her dress before reaching out to stroke his cheek. 'My God, your bones! We have to fatten you up. Can you walk?' she asked. 'Shall we go into the dining room?'

'Yes, with crutches, in answer to your first question. And why not? I'm starving, to your second.'

Mama nodded at Adriana, who disappeared into the kitchen.

When we were seated around the table, Oom Joris turned to me. 'Is Opa Laurens in the dokhavn today?'

'He's working on the carvings for the *Noordgow*. She's a frigate, I think.'

'You think? You don't know? *You*?' He smiled.

I nodded. 'She is.'

'That's better.'

He turned to Mama and pointed with a forefinger at his face. 'Obviously frostbite, *zus*. I'm very lucky to be standing.' Then he chuckled. 'Your prayers have come in handy, even though I don't believe it and you didn't know it.'

He had suffered frostbite in March, he told us, in the first month of the whale hunt.

'The *Jacoba* was temporarily moored alongside the fast ice off Greenland where we were flensing and processing the latest catch. I was assigned to go hunting with Willem Verbeek, remember him?'

'Esther's son?'

'That's him. A good shot. The best among us, especially at close range. We were looking for arctic foxes. They'd circled the campsite during the night. We found tracks everywhere, but the smart little devils had avoided our traps.'

They'd tracked and shot two, he said, when a blizzard had separated them from the ship and each other. 'We saw it coming, but we'd sighted a third fox and thought we had time to get close enough for a shot. Bad judgement on our part. The storm came up quicker and much worse than we expected.'

He had spent two days in the blinding snowstorm in a hole he'd dug in the snow before his rescue, the red scarf tied to his musket barrel signalling where he lay buried.

'They recovered Willem's body days later. They buried him deep enough to protect him from polar bears.'

The extremities of his ears and the septum of his nose had been surgically removed aboard ship when gangrene had set in. The ulcerous toes of his left foot and the fore pad of his right had been amputated in Amsterdam on his return. A week ago, he'd received a prosthetic nose styled in an alloy of copper, gold and silver designed for him by a silversmith in Delft, where he said he now lived.

He laughed as he tapped it. 'You like it, *zus*? It's the latest fashion in nasal surgery!'

'How does it stay on?' I asked.

'I glue it on with a paste an apothecary prepares for me. It's brand new. I tried it on for the first time in public last week.' He gave a burst of laughter. 'Before that, I spent months frightening the life out of people on the street, catching them off-guard.' He turned to me. 'You want to see me with it off? You want to see your oom looking like a ghoul?'

'Don't you dare,' Mama shrieked as Adriana came in with a plate filled with slices of buttered bread covered in chocolate *hagelslag* sprinkles. 'Not while we're eating. Not ever!'

Before reaching for a slice, he stood and adjusted his crutches beneath his armpits. 'Watch this,' he said, balancing precariously on them as he kicked up one leg and then the other, stumbling forward and circling the table. 'No toes and only half a foot and I can still dance the reel!'

I leant back and watched him, enthralled. *He's back! My Oom Joris! Displaying the Zeeland resilience that Papa talked to me about, no matter what the circumstances are.*

Chapter Four

On 18 September 1695, I joined Opa Laurens on the bench beside his workshop shaded beneath the apple trees.

Mama and the two maids, Adriana and Miranda, were in the house. Miranda was a slender nineteen-year-old mulat freed slave Mama was training in domestic duties so she'd qualify for work in the Gasthuis Hospital. They were busy preparing for Papa's return any day.

A year ago, the letters he'd promised Mama had been sent home from Cape Town in the care of Klaas Goelet, a friend of Opa's, who was the carpenter aboard the *Karthago*. We had gathered around the dining table and Mama had opened each letter in turn, reading them aloud to us, as was her practice.

In one of the letters. Papa had indicated that the *Ridderschap* would be departing Batavia sometime in December 1694.

> *The vessel will arrive in Goeree in late July or August the following year, weather permitting, and always provided the VOC does not change the voyage schedules or allocate Ridderschap temporarily or for longer to the coastal trade across the Indies.*
>
> *I am missing you more than I can express. I cannot wait to embrace you once again.*
> *Your loving husband,*
> *Maarten.*

'If Goeree is his home port this time,' Opa Laurens had explained, 'considering the time taken to offload the cargo and travel south to Middelburg, it will take him at least a fortnight to get home. We can expect him in mid-September. At the earliest.'

I found the old man deep in concentration, carving a wooden sculpture. I watched his deft fingers for several minutes, marvelling, as always, at the hand-crafted design within the block as he coaxed it into life with his razor-like tools.

He was putting the finishing touches to a commissioned bust of Pastor Ouderman's wife Edda in walnut, his templates a pair of portraits on the bench beside him, etched by Mattheus Smallegange—one frontal, the other in profile.

Without looking up or interrupting his stroke, Opa Laurens asked, 'Any sign of him yet?'

'No. Nothing.'

'Any time now, then.'

'I can't bear waiting, Opa. I thought I'd come out here and do some work on the wren.'

'Good idea. That'll settle you down.'

For the past two years, Opa had been teaching me to carve. Under his watchful eye, I'd begun with clumsy attempts at basic three-dimensional geometric forms in softwood pine—cubes and spheres, pyramids and tetrahedrons.

'You must learn to crawl before you can walk, and walk before you can run,' Opa had insisted. 'You must learn to imagine the shapes from every angle in the wood before you apply the next stroke.'

When I'd progressed to a slightly misshapen dodecahedron which Opa thought commendable, I'd displayed it on a shelf in my bedroom. Opa's congratulations confirmed that it qualified me to take the next step.

Now, I delighted in crudely whittling my own simple toys—stringed puppets with lozenge-shaped beads for arms and legs, spinning tops, miniature working windmills, and cuboid and polyhedral dice of various shapes and sizes, into the surfaces of which I painstakingly used a stylus to gouge the numbers, marking them in black ink.

Most of all, I enjoyed turning out diabolos on the great wheel lathe in his workshop. Opa had bought the lathe thirty years earlier when he'd found it for sale in a dilapidated state in the Middelburg Abbey courtyard. Once used for turning and drilling rosary beads, he'd adapted it, incorporating a simple treadle system I'd found difficult to manipulate at first, but easier as my strength and skills matured. When the treadle became too tiring to operate, I used to recruit Daniel to assist. He was my best friend from next door, in my class at the Latijn School. Sometimes, Daniel's younger sister, Sara, also helped, as she always seemed to want no other company but ours.

My diabolos had become more and more refined and accurately balanced, so much so they were in high demand at school. I'd sold several for a tidy profit and had more on order, as well as dice and hardwood spherical ammunition of various sizes for slingshots, requested by my classmates. And I was assisting Opa Laurens in selling his carvings on the stalls of the artists' guild of St Luke at the weekend market in the town square, often adding my works to Opa's display.

I retrieved my latest carving from the workshop. It was my most ambitious yet—a wren carved in pine, its wings partly unfolded, about to take flight. I'd almost finished it.

It was my third attempt at a bird. I was determined to carve a bird of paradise next, based on my favourite drawing in the family kunstkamer—that remarkable etching of a pair of birds of paradise, copied from the original by Rembrandt van Rijn.

I held the wren out in the palm of my hand. 'What do you think, Opa? Am I ready for the bird of paradise yet?'

He picked up the wren and gave it a critical inspection, turning it this way and that, before giving me a long, unfathomable look. 'Let's see what you're made of, then, *mijn kleinzoon*. Follow me.'

He led me to the kunstkamer and we stood in front of the etching. It was on the finest vellum, framed and hung in pride of place beside the two preserved and mounted specimens of male birds Papa had brought home from Batavia.

'Look carefully,' he said. 'Absorb it. Thoroughly. Then, when you think you're ready, tell me what you see.'

I stared at the etching, as I had often done before. The two birds, roosting one above the other and facing to the left, appeared to have been swiftly drawn, captured in an instant. They were so still and yet so alert, so filled with life, quivering with latent energy.

'They're roughly drawn,' I suggested. 'They're filled in without much detail. It looks like he drew them quickly, in a minute or two.' I gathered my thoughts. 'But I really like them.'

'Why?'

'Because they're watching me. They're checking to see what I'm about to do before they fly off.'

'They're very shy birds.'

'I can see that.'

'Now look at the real one.' He pointed at the nearest light brown specimen mounted on a carved rosewood branch protruding from the backboard, its brilliant yellow tail sweeping beneath it. 'Can you see the likeness?'

'Well, I can, but it's not exact. I've seen better drawings in the books at school.'

'If it's not an exact copy, what then has Rembrandt captured?'

I looked back at the picture, turning his question over in my mind, unsure where he was leading. Out of my depth, I ventured, 'The bird's… spirit?'

'*Goede jongen*—good boy!' He gave an explosive single handclap, then placed an arm across my shoulder. 'He's captured the *essence* of the bird, the mystery of its being. That's what makes it so marvellous. That's what you must aim for when you're carving things in the natural world, starting with your wren. The life in it.'

The life in it? The mystery of its being? I contemplated the etching for several further moments as he walked back out, still mystified, but determined to study it in private later to better understand the message he had delivered.

I settled next to him on the bench and began working on the wren, smoothing it down with a rectangle of worn shagreen.

As usual, when silence descended for too long between us, impatience got the better of me. 'How about a story, Opa? If it won't interfere with what you're doing.'

'It will, of course. What would you like to hear about this time?'

'Don't you know by now?'

'Let me guess…' He looked down at his carving, rubbing its contours with a thumb. At that moment we heard Mama strike upon the clavichord as she began her morning practice, running through several scales. It galvanised him into action, and I wondered what was coming next.

'Ah, right. Talking of Overgrootvader Hendrick.' He sucked in his cheeks and scratched at his sparse white beard. 'Now there was a Zeelander of the first order.'

Overgrootvader Hendrick again! I wondered which tale he'd tell me this time. I'd heard them all and, as usual, I prepared for him to add another fabulous twist, another unforeseen turn of events to catch me out.

'You know he was a true Calvinist and clearly one of the chosen. He knew where he was going and how to get there, God willing perhaps, but by the force of his own will also. He was a strict one, *jonge kereltje*, not like we are these days, far too easy on you youngsters running wild.'

'Would you rather have us tamed?'

'Disciplined, at least! The way we were, but never harshly

enough to put out the fire in you. He drove me and my brother Dirck hard, but no harder than he drove himself.' He put down the carving, spat on his sharpening stone and passed the chisel across it. 'He was as determined as you can be,' he gave a wheezing laugh, 'and twice as stubborn at times. But it's good to see you've inherited his traits. They'll serve you well.'

'You've always taught me to stand up for myself,' I said.

'So you should, but keep that temper of yours under control. Remember, it works both ways. You must learn to judge when holding your ground will work for you and when it will be to your disadvantage,' he shook the chisel under my nose, 'the way Hendrick taught me. I saw the value of his lessons when I was a little older than you, especially during my first voyage with your *Oudoom* Dirck to the Baltic.'

'Oh *no*,' I interrupted with a groan, 'not again, Opa! Not your famous Baltic voyage. I've heard it a thousand times already.'

'Well, what do you expect? I'm not Scheherazade. You asked for a story and that's the story you're getting today. Take it or leave it.'

I shrugged. 'I'll take it… this one more time,' and then muttered under my breath, 'until next time, of course.'

He clipped me lightly over the ear with an unexpected flick of his wrist.

'Hey Opa, come on! I didn't think you heard that.'

'Hey *kleinzoon*, come on! I didn't think you felt that.'

He rubbed his hands together before inspecting another chisel. He picked it up, then held his other hand out to me, palm up, displaying the lined and work-hardened leather of its skin, before reaching for the sculpture.

'Hendrick left his mark on me,' he said. 'I can remember many a whipping delivered by those hands of his because of stolen apples or apricots, or when I told the slightest white lie, even though he was middle-aged by the time I was born.

His salamanders left a stinging imprint I didn't forget. They breathed fire when he had me over his knee. But I understood it meant he cared enough to keep me in line.' Then he added sardonically, 'Remember what Father Cats has to say. You spare the rod, you spoil the child. On his advice, that goes for the wife as well, but don't mention that to your mama.'

'She'd use your guts for sausage skins?'

'She'd do that… and the rest of me for stuffing them.'

He began in his usual rambling way, describing the spring of 1640 when he'd sailed the Baltic for the first and only time. As he spoke, I pictured skeins of geese scudding in wavering lines beneath sea-reflective clouds on their way north to their nesting grounds and the solitary deer poised on the sheeted snow at the water's edge, alert, breath steaming, before bounding at the crack of a sailor's musket and staggering to the cover of the pines, its blood a trail of holly berries that led to fresh venison.

I smelled the smoke gusting from villages in hidden coves on that coast of dark forests and granite boulders shaped like the distant pods of sounding whales. I heard the shrieks of children at play, their excited voices carrying like bird calls to the ship as she sighed her way towards Riga.

He described how he wrestled with the heavy whipstaff[9] and came to know the strange power in the rudder as the ship responded to the lift and fall of the surge at the stern. As he spoke, I saw the sea as a cauldron of steamy mist each icy sunrise and, in the evening, a black sheet across which stars glittered like shattered glass.

He found himself at the centre of the circle of a dozen

---

9 A vertical rod attached to the tiller of a ship for steering when underway, used in sixteenth and seventeenth-century Europe before the development of the ship's wheel. Sweeping the whipstaff across to the left or right moved the tiller and the rudder attached to it accordingly.

sailors, he told me, comfortable in their easy-going companionship. He learned their bawdy work songs and the sea-doggerel shanties of the sea-beggars, those rousing patriotic chants with their *oranjeboom-dee-ay* references to the House of Orange. He sang with them when they were sail-setting and reefing and sheet-hauling.

He remembered, in particular, another moment when the ship glided across the flooding swell at the Dvina river mouth to its anchorage near Riga and a solitary voice rang out over the water, announcing their arrival, singing the first lines of the '*Wilhelmus van Nassouwe*', their national anthem. The crew joined the singer, their voices reaching the anthem's final descant before fading among the surrounding trees.

I grinned as he warned me, 'Don't you laugh at me now!'

I knew what was coming.

He took in a hoarse breath and, in his cracked tenor, croaked out words he struggled to recall, tapping the bench armrest with his chisel, the tune barely recognisable.

> *'Van al die my beswar*
> *End mijn Vervolghers zijn*
> *Mijn Godt wilt doch bewaren*
> *Den trouwen dinaer dijn*
> *Dat sy my niet verras schen*
> *In haren boosen moet*
> *Haer handen niet en wasschen*
> *In mijn onschuldich bloet…*[10]'

---

10 My God, I pray thee, save me From all who do pursue And threaten to enslave me, Thy trusted servant true. O Father, do not sanction Their wicked, foul design, Don't let them wash their hands in This guiltless blood of mine… Original lyrics (1568) *Het Wilhelmus*, the first European National anthem. Official modern lyrics were adopted in 1932.

Then he broke off and doubled over, coughing a hoarse laugh when I grimaced and put both hands over my ears.

'Word perfect so far!' he said when he'd recovered. 'So what do you think? Should I audition for the Nieuwe Kerk Choir?'

'Stick to your carving, Opa! Get mixed up with those ladies and they'll eat you alive.'

'I should be so lucky!' He rolled his eyes as he wheezed. 'Or unlucky, in some cases, no names mentioned.'

He put the carving and the chisel down on the bench beside him and climbed stiffly to his feet. 'I've been sitting too long,' he said. 'I need to stretch my legs.'

I handed him his cane and supported him by the elbow as he began pacing slowly back and forth beneath the apple trees.

Then the sounds of Mama's clavichord stopped and the creak of carriage wheels and rattling harnesses of an approaching coach carried to us.

'My God, Gerrit!' Opa Laurens called out as I bolted through the trees for the front of the house. 'That must be Maarten!'

I careened around the corner and saw the carriage draw up at the end of the front pathway. The door opened, but Papa did not descend. I froze when Ole Reineus appeared. I knew he was the schipper of the *Lands Welvaren* that had sailed with Papa's *Ridderschap*.

A black skull cap covered his shaven head and his snub-nosed and pugnacious round face was preoccupied. He balanced his corpulent body on the step before alighting gingerly between the flower beds, the carriage shaking. He raised a quick hand in greeting towards Mama, who stood expectantly between the two maids on the front step. He dusted down his blue velvet jacket and turned to assist the senior VOC Administrative Officer, Carel van Caerden, from the carriage, his angular aristocratic features sombre.

They turned and walked up the path.

Uncomprehending, I searched for Papa, peering towards the empty carriage, its door ajar. *Papa has not arrived!*

Mama blanched, consternation written across her features. It dawned on me they were about to deliver terrible news. It was a moment I knew she'd dreaded for years. I watched the scene unfold in horrified confusion, the visitors blurring as they approached the stationary women.

Mama let out a heart-wrenching wail and buckled at the knees, clutching at the nearest of the maids. My heart racing, I took several backward steps and collided with Opa Laurens, who responded to Mama's scream by breaking into a limping run to reach her. He grabbed me to steady himself, gave me a violent hug and leant down to hiss in my ear, 'It's all right, *mijn kleinzoon*. Go around the back and into the house. Go upstairs. I'll see you soon. I'll deal with this.'

Trembling, I could not move, and Opa signalled for Miranda to assist me. She ran across and, with an arm about my waist, led me to the back door, where I heard another harrowing scream, Mama's strangulated '*No! No! No! No!*' cut short when Miranda closed the door behind us.

We climbed the stairs to the mezzanine as the two visitors settled side by side onto the oak bench beneath the window in the voorkamer.

We paused at the top and I knelt to peer down through the railings.

Supporting Mama with his right arm, Opa Laurens eased her into the armchair that Adriana dragged across, before sitting beside her on the clavichord stool.

They contemplated one another before Ole Reineus cleared his throat. 'Anneka, believe me when I say how deeply sorry we are, but we must inform you that the *Ridderschap* did not reach Batavia after leaving Cape Town in February last year.' He placed a finger across his lips, as though unwilling to divulge what was coming next. 'Neither the ship nor any of the crew have been sighted since.'

There was deathly quiet. Then Mama, who had been staring at the floor, lifted her face to him. Distraught, but surprisingly self-controlled, she murmured, 'It's all right, Ole. I've prepared myself for this all my married life.'

She spoke so softly that I could barely hear her. I deliberately forced my forehead hard against the balustrade as though the pain I then experienced would somehow offset the despair coursing through me.

She leant forward, looked back down at the floor and shook her head. 'I know how hard this is for you, so you can spare me your sympathy. You can go on now and give me the details.' Then, before he could respond, she looked back up to meet his eyes. 'But before you do, tell me, have you spoken to Coby de Lange yet?'

'We've come from her directly.'

'How is she?'

'Distressed, as you would expect, married only a month before Dirk sailed.'

'And how many others do you have to see?' Opa Laurens asked.

'Five more wives in all,' van Caerden said. 'Seven of the crew from Middelburg were married men, and we have spoken only to Coby and now you. Time has not been on our side.'

'And others in the crew?'

'Twenty-two were unmarried, some from Veere and Vlissingen and elsewhere. We have despatched people to speak to their families. Others were from the northern provinces.'

Mama began to sob convulsively, her tears falling onto the black and white tiles until Adriana handed her a lace-trimmed handkerchief, bending to wipe the floor with a cloth before withdrawing.

Silence fell, and Mama clamped shut her jaw, the tendons in her throat taut, her hands trembling. Opa Laurens gently stroked her back.

At last, she looked up, her face tear-streaked. 'What else do I need to know?' she whispered.

I strained to listen, picking up only fragments. 'We cannot confirm whether they have survived or perished… In any event, you can rest assured we will continue the financial arrangements on a reduced basis, you understand, until we have further information… for a year… until then, since we are unsure of Maarten's fate, the widow's pension will continue… *Predikant* Ouderman will be conducting a memorial service… arranging a meeting of all the widows to organise the program…'

Dazed, I stared blankly at the glass-fronted cupboard below, my mind drifting to the pressure of the silver buttons on Papa's blue coat against my ribs the day he'd left, the smell of fresh linen in his shirt, the feel of his fingers ruffling my hair, the kiss on the crown of my head, the kite striking the bricks as it fell… and then the majolica pieces and blue and white china plates behind the glass came into sharp focus, and I gazed at the two porphyry statuettes of the shepherd and a shepherdess Mama had won a month ago in a lottery with a ticket I'd selected for her.

'You are my lucky son, who always brings me good fortune!' she'd said when she'd collected them, reminding me that another ticket I'd selected for her in a previous lottery had also won her a prize—a set of Qing porcelain vases decorated in a green and gilt glaze she adored.

Recalling her words, I looked back down at her, my heart thumping painfully as an unfamiliar wave of self-blame overtook me.

'You are my lucky son, who always brings me good

fortune,' I muttered bitterly as the thought struck me. *Am I now the unlucky son who has caused this change in fortune? Am I the reason why the world has turned against us?* 'So much for good fortune!' I hissed.

Miranda looked down at me in alarm. Her grip around my shoulders tightened. 'How can you be to blame, Gerrit? *Dat is gek praten.* That is crazy talk.'

'The company directors will be forwarding an official letter of condolence,' I heard Ole Reineus say as he stood to leave, 'and they have already determined to send out a fleet to search for the *Ridderschap.* She was carrying a fortune in bullion.'

I clambered to my feet as Opa Laurens called Miranda down to attend to Mama with Adriana while he walked the visitors to the door.

A rescue fleet to search for Papa's ship! They must think the crew survived! My mind was in turmoil as the trio descended the step into the garden. *Papa must be alive!*

I watched the maids lift Mama to her feet and lead her to the stairs. About to go down to her, I heard her ask, 'Where's Gerrit? He must not see me in this state.'

Instinctively, I spun around and took the stairs two at a time to the floor above, where I approached the ladder to the attic. When I reached for the rungs, I discovered the wooden wren in my right hand, its wings embedded deeply in my palm. I carefully pocketed it, rubbing my hand against my hip to ease the throbbing.

I would have been so proud to show the carving to Papa, I thought, and imagined his praise at my achievement. 'I never thought you'd already be this skilled,' he'd say, and then he'd smile. 'But then you are my son *and* a de Waal, so what should I expect?'

I felt a sudden unbearable sense of loneliness and aban-donment. *How will Papa witness my progress now?*

In the bedroom, I shifted several carvings aside and

placed the wren in pride of place on the display shelf. Then I slumped across the bearskin and lay staring at the panels in the ceiling as the carriage clattered away, the coachman's piercing whistle loud above the crack of the whip, the straining horses blowing.

I knew that Opa Laurens would soon appear at the trapdoor.

I closed my eyes as a wave of nausea swept over me, breathing deeply until it passed. Then, torn with grief and about to weep, I buried my face in the crook of my arm and bit hard on the pad of skin above the wrist.

I must not cry, I thought. *I will not! Papa is alive. He will be coming home.*

Despite my efforts, the tears began to flow and I was sobbing and tasting blood as the trapdoor lifted.

Five

IT WAS 25 SEPTEMBER 1695, late afternoon, a week after we'd learned that Papa was presumed lost at sea.

I was deeply disturbed by Mama's open show of grief since we'd been advised, especially her conviction that Papa had drowned. I would not entertain the thought. I suppressed the shock and refused to abandon him to oblivion, clinging instead to the idea that by some miracle he had survived.

'They're sending a fleet to search for him,' I kept reminding her. 'They must think he's still alive.'

And I'm keeping him alive, I persuaded myself, *by blocking out any thoughts that he could die.* My belief offset waves of grief that threatened to overwhelm me as the days passed, although there were moments when I broke down and barricaded myself in the attic.

Opa Laurens absorbed the shock of losing his only son with surprising composure. I was especially grateful, finding comfort in his calmness. It did not strike me until much later how deeply he must have suffered, leaving his grief unexpressed for our sakes. I know Mama found his empathy supportive, and sharing her grief with Coby de Lange and the other widows affected by the disaster gave her further consolation.

I was in my favourite position at the helm of my houseship in the attic window, three storeys up. I was seated on the window ledge braced against the frame, my legs dangling against the outside brickwork. Deep in concentration, I held a short length of rope attached to the window latch in one hand, as though it was a sheet and the open window a billowing sail. I had opened it after school, as I always did, then straddled the ledge and entered this imaginary world, sailing the house.

I loved best the occasional summer storms when the winds gusted against the window, powering the house across the thrashing leaf-waves of the rose bushes below, their white flowers foaming. Then the gnarled and knotted rocks of the apple orchard and the limestone stacks of birch trees lining the garden had shown their teeth and I, *abrolhos*, my eyes peeled as Dirk de Lange had advised me, steered the house to safety past the reefs and rocky outcrops, the gales whipping rain across the garden pathways.

But now there was the stillness of early autumn. Not a breath of wind. No ripples in the dark canal. A surprisingly cold mist had settled over the landscape, the far saw windmill sails barely visible, the setting sun gilding moisture on the windowpanes into fern leaves caught in amber.

Becalmed, disappointed, I lashed the rope to the window catch. I picked up my spyglass from among the navigational instruments on the table beside me. To preserve its magic, I'd wrapped it in the diamondback rattlesnake skin Oom Joris had brought home from Cumberland Island. I unrolled the skin and placed it beside me. Then I dusted the spyglass, breathed on the front lens and polished it on my shirt.

I leant out the window and shook the instrument, counting each movement. It had been eight times the previous day, I recalled. *It will be eleven today, twice for good measure*, I decided. Eleven eleven—a pillared gateway—like the three rocky needles jutting from the sea at Cape Paraveles on St Helena Island, through which Overgrootvader Hendrick had heroically steered the *Zeelandia* into battle a hundred years before.

'Overgrootvader, I need you now,' I murmured. 'I need you, for Papa's sake. I need your courage. We *both* need your courage, Papa and I.'

The glass granules inside the tube rattled as I rearranged the glitter of their colours. On the second count of eleven,

I lifted the instrument to my eye and surveyed the street below. As if by magic, in the muted light, radiant colours lit up the beeches and the linden trees beside the canal. The sombre street beyond the house and the silhouette of distant Middelburg came alive in iridescent blues and reds and greens. I found myself in a world whose luminous beauty was mine to invent, alterable by the shake of my wrist.

When Opa Laurens had given me the spyglass two years before, the tube had been empty—a simple spyglass. But at his suggestion, we inserted some fragments of the multicoloured glass I'd collected with Papa in the cave at Westcapelle. He'd polished the inner lining of the tube, glued a split mirror behind the front lens then added a handful of tiny multicoloured pebbles I'd selected for him. The effect was awe-inspiring. Peering through it for the first time, I'd discovered a dreamlike world of brilliant patterns reflected within it. People strolling in the twilight on the cobblestones along the canal had transformed into harlequin acrobats, and swans on the canal had become peacocks in full display.

It was dizzying. Emerald, turquoise, ruby, topaz—I saw in the chance fall of the fragments a jewelled universe through which I could journey to distant destinations of my choosing, illuminated by the light reflected within the highly polished silver tube.

Now it was the island of St Helena I was searching for, to reconnect with my legendary Overgrootvader Hendrick, opperstuurman—first mate and senior helmsman aboard the *Zeelandia*. He was a hero of Middelburg folklore, who had participated in the capture of the *Santiago* in March 1602.

I wanted more than ever to escape the dread triggered by Papa's absence by reliving once again the story I'd heard told and retold by Opa Laurens as far back as I could recall. His ability to bring the characters to life and dramatise the action always held me spellbound, and I knew the story virtually word for word…

I watched in my imagination the sunburned boy standing on the foredeck of the *Santiago*, the blistered caulking tarred to the tough skin of his feet. Screaming gulls cartwheeled in the carrack's wake, as a cry from the masthead announced the cloud-smeared shadow of Saint Helena Island emerging from the dazzling Atlantic distance, where azure sky met azure sea, inseparably blued.

The boy turned the four-minute-glass he was holding and spat into the gliding water. He walked slowly towards the quarterdeck, following the bubble of spittle. He watched the fine-ground eggshell in the glass drain away its measured time in pace with his steps. He climbed the companionway past the helmsman holding the whipstaff and, when the bobbing spittle reached the rudder-wash, he called out the dead reckoning calculation to the mate scribbling on the slate. He showed three fingers and a knuckle on his upraised hand—the minutes and seconds it took the lumbering carrack to sail the spice-and-silk laden waterline of its length.

Duty done, he vaulted back down the stairway. He scooped up a handful of coconut oil seeping from barrels lashed to the rail and spread it over his already teak-brown face and shoulders, before stretching out beside Francesco Carletti's young Korean servant, asleep beneath the canvas awning. The beaten-copper St Christopher medallions dangling around the Korean's neck glinted as he breathed.

The ship barely moved. The lightest of breezes teased worn canvas, the listless sun-bleached flags occasionally lifting to display the Portuguese coat of arms—its red and white shield bearing seven castles surmounted by a crown.

The shout from the lookout brought passengers and crew

to the rails, excited at the prospect of their first landfall since sailing from Goa three months before.

Italian merchant Francesco Carletti was on the deck beside the aftercastle, leaning against the wooden cage holding his last pair of scrawny chickens. He frowned as he took another quick inventory of his personal cargo stacked beside him—two thousand ounces of musk in civet-skin bags, rolled Indian silks and a dozen Persian carpets, a selection of ivory carvings, three boxes of Mexican cacao beans, a dozen willow-green Chinese celadon vases full of preserved pears, and the crate that held his prize—an exquisite Cantonese silk-quilted bed he had bargained for in Macau. He intended to give the bed to his patron, Ferdinando de Medici, Grand Duke of Tuscany, on his return to Florence.

Once he'd run his eye over his goods, Francesco looked up at the quarterdeck behind him, where the carrack's captain, Antonio de Melo de Castro, and two officers stood staring at the distant island. Beside them, Francesco saw the retired *fidalgo* captain-general of Ceylon, Senhor Pedro de Sousa, who was the senior passenger aboard and privileged to accompany the captain at the navigation station.

Mixed fortune had dogged them since their departure from Goa. The heavily laden carrack had narrowly skirted a reef off Kwila on the run down the Swahili coast. Moonlight on breaking water had semaphored a warning seen at the last perilous moment by a Malagasy slave urinating in the heads. His scream, which had saved them, would have woken the dead, let alone the lookout.

They had bypassed Cape Agulhas and Cape Good Hope, expecting a swift run across the Atlantic from the Cimbebas coast of Portuguese Angola, but that plan had changed when they'd run out of wind. They were low on supplies, and Francesco was running out of chickens and patience.

But God, or perhaps chance, had directed the carrack through a shoal of mackerel tuna. Their sleek, silver-green torpedo shapes had broiled the sea around the ship as they'd attacked baits that were thrown, exploding from the water in a sparkling display of aerobatics before smacking back below the surface and flashing vigorously at the lures.

They were exhilarating and arm-wrenching to catch, and the lines had thrummed and twanged across the thwarts as fish were hauled aboard. Their writhing, bloodied bodies had thumped and quivered on slime-stained decks as the whooping crew had slit their throats. Fried, marinated, dried and salted fish had postponed the squawking decapitation of the last of his poultry.

Francesco looked back up at Captain Antonio, broad-chested and bowlegged, his thick calves standing out like house bricks in tight stockings. He stood, gimlet-eyed and granite-stubborn, at the rail. He shouted up at the sailor on the crosstrees, who picked out three ships at anchor in the harbour ahead. Dutch flags hung astern, the lookout yelled back—they must be on their way to Asia or on their return. Their sails were furled. No movement was discernible.

Francesco considered the vulnerability of the vessel. She was an easy target, and he wondered if new hostilities born of shifting alliances in Europe made the situation more perilous. He had spent eight years trading around the world—the last two across the archipelago of the East Indies and along the Malabar and Coromandel coasts, and the news in Goa last Christmas when he'd booked passage aboard the *Santiago* was six months old.

He knew the Dutch were making inroads into Portuguese trade. He'd heard about skirmishes fought in the Sunda Straits. And when he'd been standing with others on the jetty in Tidore two years ago, he'd witnessed first-hand the burning of the *Trouw*—the first Dutch ship to make landfall in the Moluccas. Jealous of their monopoly in cloves, the Portuguese had executed almost the entire crew and imprisoned the rest, forcing them first to witness the gruesome beheading of their schipper, Balthasar de Cordes. His blind eyes had peered eerily up at them through the brown and smoky water as he sank.

The *Santiago* hove to off the breeze.

The crew and passengers were silenced by the ship's loss of way. The rigging no longer sighed and creaked, the decks were still, the wash slurrying against the windward hull. Moments passed as the deck officers surveyed the distant island.

Then, after a terse discussion, the captain gave his command to the helmsman, who leant into the whipstaff to re-engage the tiller. The ship turned, caught the lightest of breezes and began the first long starboard haul on its cumbersome way to round the island's furthest corner, beyond which lay Cape Paraveles. The rocky headland glittered in the dwindling evening light as the Dutch ships faded behind Horseman's Point.

Francesco sensed the mounting excitement around him. He frowned and slowly shook his head at the possibility of losing his cargo. He patted the diamonds and the lustrous white and grey-blue Mannar pearls he carried in a pouch on his belt. He wondered how he'd manage to swallow them if they were captured. Worse than that, how would he recover them? He had dabbled in many things before, but he had never stooped to sifting pearls or diamonds from shit.

He wondered if his young Korean servant could swim. It had never crossed his mind to ask. He'd paid for him in Nagasaki to save him from a grisly execution in a public demonstration of samurai swordsmanship. When he'd exchanged the coins and untied the boy roped to other victims queued up for slaughter, he'd given him the St Christopher medallions in celebration. *They will see him through,* Francesco thought, *or else he'll drown.*

One of the ship's crew, the seventy-year-old Corsican cannon-master Agostini, lit his clay pipe at the brazier beside the mainmast and joined Francesco at the rail. Sweet-smelling smoke billowed around him as if some ancient internal combustion engine was generating wiry energy for his skeletal, sun-leathered body.

He was the only other fluent speaker of Italian aboard. '*Questa e una buona decisione,*' he muttered to Francesco. 'This is a good decision, to sail on to Paraveles and avoid unnecessary trouble.'

But trouble, said the twinkle in his eye, was his brother. Trouble coursed through his Corsican veins.

Elbows on the rail, they leant into the evening wind, the old man gripping his pipestem between his wooden false teeth.

On sunrise the next morning, Francesco watched two Zeeland ships tack towards the *Santiago* across the crimson sea of early dawn—*like two hunting dogs,* he thought, *closing on a scent.* The third ship remained anchored at the landing.

He felt mounting concern as Captain Antonio ignored the shouted warnings of his passengers, who took the pennants of the approaching ships for war flags and the distant sound of rattling drums as a call to arms. He would hold his ground, he bellowed at the crowd. He was committed to a standoff. It was too late to retreat.

Francesco heard him roar instructions at the crew to check the moorings. The *Santiago* was anchored close to the island cliffs, her starboard flank exposed. The Dutch couldn't sail between the carrack and the island without risk. The wind and current were running her parallel to the shore, the angled rudder secured to hold her steady. Open water lay behind.

Dead ahead three rocky pinnacles, the Cape of Needles, reared above breaking water off Cape Paravales. They were standing guard for the *Santiago*, anchored in their lee. They provided protection from that quarter should he decide to flee.

Antonio ordered the gunners to load a precautionary line of starboard cannon but kept the cannon ports closed. The bombardiers stood alert, unlit tapers at the ready. The boy and the young Korean held packaged second charges for the cannon. They were trained to sprint like monkeys to and from the powder room below.

Francesco noticed that the Dutch ships were smaller than the carrack, lower in the water. They ranged swiftly past and, once upwind outside the Cape of Needles, they swung and drifted, their sails flapping windless, backing onto the masts.

A *shallop* was lowered and a group of sailors rowed across, a bugle sounding. A salute of two arquebuses was fired and Antonio signalled his reply.

'*Buen viaje*,' the Dutch officer shouted up to him in Spanish, the lingua franca of the sea. '*Cual es el nombre del barco*? Good voyage. What's the name of your ship?'

'Good voyage. The *Santiago*. We're on our way from Goa to Lisbon. What vessels are you?' Antonio replied.

'We're from Zeeland. The *Langebark* and *Zeelandia*. We've come from Atjeh. Do you need supplies?'

'We don't need anything.'

'Do you have a message for our captain?'

'No, we don't.'

'When are you departing?'

There was no reply. The ensuing silence lasted several minutes, dripping oars at rest.

Francesco peered down at the upturned faces in the boat. Two fusiliers, arquebuses still smoking. The bugler used the gunwale as a footrest, his elbow propped on his lifted knee. Six paired rowers had their oars up, relaxed. A blue-coated officer sat at the tiller, silver buttons glinting down his chest.

It was a deathly quiet moment in which Francesco heard the faint rattle of drums carrying across the water.

'*Volveremos mas tarde. Hasta luego*! We'll see you later. Until then!'

The oars were dipped and the boat pulled away across the splashy chop. The *shallop* was recovered and the Dutch ships caught the wind. Their sails filled and pennants flew as they bore down in line astern. They swung inside the Needles, closing to within cannon range.

Aboard the *Santiago*, Francesco stifled his alarm, but other passengers saw menace in the manoeuvre and shouted confused warnings at the captain. Francesco did not join them. He recognised the danger, but he also knew the ships could be sailing back to join the third, still at anchor at the landing.

On the decks, the pandemonium grew.

The *Langebark* was closing, her sailors visible along the rails. On the poop, blue-coated officers raised their swords in what seemed a mock salute. *Is the flash of blades a challenging farewell, a scornful kiss goodbye or a signal to open fire?* Francesco wondered. He saw deception in the fact that only half their cannon-ports were closed.

The mocking challenge in their kissed swords called for a reply.

Captain Antonio, his face livid, screamed for the cannon ports to be flung open. He seized a taper, which he lit from the coals glowing in the brazier at the mainmast, and shouldered his way through the crowd of passengers to the closest cannon.

He touched off the fuse-powder. There was a roar of flame. The passengers ducked at the recoil as a shower of splintered timber exploded from the *Langebark*'s bowsprit, and the cliffs of Paraveles echoed the thunderous blast.

The Dutch ship veered seaward, showing the broad decorated after-galleries on her transom, where the flag twitched in horizontal stripes of orange, white and blue. She swung upwind, opening a passage for the *Zeelandia*, whose reply was thunderous. Her starboard cannon ports were opened and, as each cannon-sight met the *Santiago*'s flank, it fired in turn, broadside on, a shattering burst of explosions lasting two long minutes. The blasts echoed down the island cliffs and valleys, as though she was firing a sixteen-gun salute.

There was the whirr of incoming balls, chained in revolving pairs that split the air overhead and shattered a topmast and rigging. The bombardiers, harangued by their ancient cannon-master, Agostini, gave their erratic reply. There was silence as the ship passed, turning to windward to follow its partner, ribbons of smoke settling over its wake.

Francesco dived for cover at the first broadside. He watched from behind the poop wall as the boys handed across the second charges and scuttled down the fore-hatch for more. Two crewmen lifted the mutilated torso of a bombardier and heaved it overboard, while a third hurled a bucket of sand into the slick blood carpet smeared with skidding footmarks left by the cannon crew reloading. The smashed foretopmast hung crazy-angled across the port deck. A sailor slumped, head down, groaning, a splintered shaft of wood protruding grotesquely from his bloodied shirtfront.

Agostini screamed instructions at the fusiliers shinning up the ratlines and manning the ramparts of the poop, their muskets and arquebuses primed.

THE DUTCH SHIPS sailed deliberately behind the Cape of Needles. They had time to spare, their flags signalling their intentions as they turned in slow circles, concealed from the Portuguese.

Hendrick de Waal, feet apart, stood at the *kolderstok,* the whipstaff tiller, aboard the *Zeelandia.* He eyed the sails and smelled the wind, revelling in a situation that called for all his sailing skills. Success would depend on his timing, his use of wind and drift and current. Instinct and experience had given him a cold and seasoned confidence, a resolute oaken toughness that showed in his broad face and steel-grey eyes that missed nothing.

The backs of his powerful hands bore the red and blue tattoos of tiger salamanders breathing fire he'd received in Naples in 1594, when he'd spent four years delivering Baltic wheat to famine-ravaged Italy. They came to life as he gripped the whipstaff.

Standing to one side above him on the quarterdeck, the admiral, Kornelis Bastiaansz, looked down and gave him a nod and a wave of his hat.

'*Terug naar doeloefening,* Hendrick! Back to target practice,' he shouted, so that Hendrick could hear him through the protective wadding in his ears. 'In for the kill! We'll give them a taste of Zeeland revenge.'

Hendrick glanced at the shrouds to check the *wimpel* frills and pennants, gauging the breeze. He eased the whipstaff into the sail-tightening wind and shouted quick instructions to the two seamen on the deck below, heaving on the auxiliary pulleys roped to the weighty tiller, as the *Langebark* ranged alongside.

Still out of sight of the *Santiago,* they surged forwards, line abreast.

Using the wind's slingshot, Hendrick accelerated the *Zeelandia* from behind the rocks under full sail. He swung her around the Cape of Needles, angling for the *Santiago's* bow, to bring the ship within range and broadside-on. The *Zeelandia's* cannons roared in turn as she shuddered her way the length of her opponent. He watched the smoke of the return fire and leant into the whipstaff as the poops were aligned and the swivel guns on the deck above him were fired, deafening him, despite the wadding.

Barely underway, he eased the ship out into the wind to begin the first tack back to the Cape of Needles. Fingers of smoke stroked her sides and stern. Behind him, he heard the cannons aboard the *Langebark* discharge, the percussive growl of gunfire echoing in diminishing thunder up the island valleys.

He took a second and third tack, edging in behind the Cape of Needles, and circled slowly as the crew worked to the shout-song orders of the *hoogbootsman*—the bosun—to clear the decks and reload. The *Langebark* reappeared and took her position in the tight circle, the two of them partners in this deadly dance of the sea.

AND SO IT went—a long day's bombardment, the same relentless manoeuvre, slow turn and turn about, until the *Santiago* lay at anchor, crippled, her foremast down and rigging shattered. Charred wreckage littered the greasy, sand-covered decks. Bodies and body parts that had been thrown overboard sank into the waters of the bay, billowing plumes of blood like smoke.

Nightfall brought a truce.

The Dutch ships anchored off the *Santiago*'s beam, line astern, to cut off her escape. Their capstans rattled as chains and hawsers were run out, and the sails were half-furled. Voices echoed as the night-wind lifted and fell, and soon the pungent smell of cordite was overtaken by the oven smoke of cooking.

Francesco and the stunned passengers emerged from the poop and forecastle to confront the captain, who was fuming with his officers at the futility of the situation and the cat-and-mouse advantage the Dutch enjoyed. The foremast was out of action, that much was clear, but there were sufficient yards and canvas on the other masts to get them underway.

Turning to face the passengers at the rail of the quarter-deck above them, Captain Antonio roared for silence.

'We have to set sail as best we can,' he shouted, pacing up and down. 'To remain at anchor here is suicidal. We have no choice.' He pointed up at the yardarms that were still intact. 'As you can see, the crew is already making preparations. The Dutch were at the landing when we arrived, possibly taking on water and exchanging supplies. The third ship avoided the action. It might be under repair. These ships might not, therefore, follow us in the dark. Either way, escape is our only option.'

He leant against the rail staring grimly down at the gathered crowd. 'There is no alternative, and from now on you all have a duty to comply with my orders. Every one of you. I want complete silence aboard! All lights must be extinguished. Right now you must find shelter below decks.'

Watching the passengers gradually disperse, he bellowed after them, 'Whatever the outcome, do not interfere at any time with my actions or the working of the crews.'

Looking out at the dark unseen horizon, Francesco knew their only hope of survival lay in that distant refuge. The irony that he was a neutral foreigner who'd spent so many years accumulating a small fortune and was now committed to the Portuguese in a quarrel that wasn't his, struck him like a blow

As he made his way towards the aftercastle, he met Agostini supervising two bombardiers realigning a cannon trunnion into its groove on the truck.

The old man looked up and grinned, the whites of his eyes gleaming through the grime. '*La resa è impensabile mentre abbiamo ancora armamenti*, Francesco,' he said. 'Surrender is unthinkable while we still have armaments, Francesco. Several of our gunners are dead and others injured, but I promise you we will man the cannons to the bitter end!'

Francesco reached out to shake his hand in both of his. 'That's good to know. I wish you all well.'

The braziers and lanterns were doused and, an hour later, the bower anchor hawsers were sawn through. Two staysails were set and the carrack's hulking shadow drifted from the Cape of Needles on the current, obscured by background cliffs.

Francesco felt his hopes rise as the night-wind picked them up in Manatee Bay and the carrack swung wide around the cordon, heading for open water.

Leaning across the rail the following morning, he looked down and watched the shadows of shearwater and dark-winged petrel skimming the breaking waves in the pre-dawn half-light around the carrack. When he glanced up at the horizon's skyline, he was alarmed to barely make out two sil-houetted shadows—no, it was *three* shadows now—approach-ing down the line of the carrack's phosphorescent wake.

By mid-afternoon, the ships had overtaken the *Santiago* in open water. Bombardment followed bombardment as the two Zeeland ships once again ranged in on either flank, emptying their port and starboard cannon in turn. They aimed lower this time, at the waterline, which was exposed as the stricken *Santiago* lifted on the waves. Her rudder was shot away and she listed deeper in the water.

The retired *fidalgo* captain-general, Senhor Pedro de Sousa, hung a white flag across the rail late that afternoon, despite Antonio's furious determination to fight on.

The surrender came too late for Agostini. Blown to pieces an hour earlier, most of him was scattered overboard. His crews stopped firing and it was over.

My journey was abruptly interrupted by the appearance of Opa Laurens in the garden below. Leaning on his walking cane, he peered up at the window.

He waved his gnarled hand at me sailing across the evening sky. 'Come on down now and eat,' he shouted, 'before you miss your longitude and the winds and currents take you into Eendrachtsland and you sink us all.'

I pointed beyond the canal. 'I'm on the right course, Opa. I've reached St Helena. I've witnessed the sea battle and still have some way to go before Overgrootvader Hendrick meets with Francesco. I can't stop now!'

'Cast anchor all the same. You must be starving after your travels. We're waiting for you downstairs. The *snert*[11] and *stamppot zurkool*[12] are getting cold.'

'Is that all you've got? We've got *hutsepot* stew on board.'

'There's one of your favourites to follow. Blackcurrant tart and custard. Can't you smell it?'

'Then I'll be down in a minute, Opa, but I'm not really hungry.'

'We'll be expecting you.'

'On one condition.'

'Which is?'

'You tell me about their meeting.'

'Again? That will be the second time this week.'

'I know, but I want to hear it.'

Opa looked thoughtfully up at me, before responding at last, 'Alright. We'll talk about Hendrick and Francesco again, but I have one condition too.'

'What's that?'

'You empty your plate. Your mama is concerned you haven't been eating since we got the news. And so am I.'

---

11 Thick pea soup.

12 Stew made of potatoes and sauerkraut, served with fried bacon and smoked sausage.

'I'll try,' I replied, an impatient surge of resentment running through me at this reminder that I accept the news of Papa's disappearance and behave as though things were normal.

'That's good enough for me. I'll race you back to the table. My magic walking stick will get me there first.'

I furled shut the window-sail and latched it against the night. I wrapped the spyglass carefully back in the snake-skin and placed it on the table alongside my other sailing instruments.

Before going down the ladder, I turned the globe so that the broad Atlantic faced me. In the dim lamplight, the island of Saint Helena was etched at its southern centre.

'You *must* try,' Mama insisted as I pushed my food listlessly around the plate. 'We're all suffering since we heard about Papa, but that's no excuse for you wasting your food. It's been a week now. Not eating makes matters worse.'

I looked down at the table, indignation rising, then glanced across at Opa Laurens. 'You've given me too much, Mama. I'm not hungry. I'll eat half and save the rest.'

'You'll do no such thing!' she muttered grimly. Losing patience, she snatched up the plate and returned part of the food to the serving dish. She slammed the plate back in front of me, spots of gravy staining the tablecloth. 'Now finish that.'

Opa placed a restraining hand on her forearm before picking up a napkin, dipping it in the fingerbowl and wiping away the stains.

'Don't be too heavy-handed,' he advised quietly. Then, tapping the side of his nose, he leant across to me, 'Eat, *mijn kleinzoon,* for your mama… and for Overgrootvader Hendrick's sake, if you want to hear his story tonight. Remember our agreement.'

I stared down at my plate then looked defiantly at Mama. 'I'm sorry, Mama. This is as much as I can manage.'

'Alright then. Eat.' She shook her head as she regained her composure, before reaching out to stroke my hair. I flinched, then quickly relaxed. 'I'm sorry too,' she said, 'but we must accept the situation, Gerrit. This time Papa is never coming back.'

I felt my eyes sting but I tensed and held her gaze with an unblinking glare as I muttered forcefully, 'He *is* coming back. I *know* he is. They were *lying* when they told us Papa must have drowned.'

Mama glanced despairingly at Laurens, who gave her a slight nod but did not intervene. She scraped back her chair and crossed the room, hesitating at the foot of the stairs where she gripped the balustrade, her knuckles white. I immediately regretted causing her to leave the room with such graceless impatience.

Have I gone too far this time? Has Opa Laurens's silence upset her?

I watched her begin the climb. She looked back once, clearly on the brink of tears.

Six

After dinner, Laurens settled into his armchair and filled his pipe with his favourite Amersfoort tobacco. He took his time. I sensed his deliberate movements were intended to calm me, sitting cross-legged on a velvet cushion at his feet, and he was right. He lit the pipe using a candlewick he inserted into the glowing coals in the fireplace, the flame flaring and dying with each quick inhalation, before he took a deep appreciative breath and exhaled a stream of smoke, disturbing the canary fluttering in a gilt cage suspended on a pole beside him.

'Now, where do we begin?' he asked.

'Agostini has been hit by a cannon ball... and the Portuguese have surrendered.'

'Aha! So you've witnessed all that?'

'Yes, Opa'

'So the *Santiago* is sinking and Overgrootvader Hendrick is about to meet Francesco?'

'Yes.'

'Right then.' He cleared his throat and lowered his voice a dramatic octave. 'The moment that changed all our lives.'

I listened, enthralled, as the story unfolded.

Confounded by his change in fortunes, Francesco watched Captain Antonio tear the white sheet of surrender from the rail. He hurled it into the sea and unfurled a Portuguese flag in its place, but his defiance came too late. The *Santiago*'s silent cannons signalled their defeat.

He and the captain-general hurled abuse at each other as the first longboat pulled alongside and Dutch officers boarded.

'Treason!' Francesco heard the captain roar, leaning uphill

against the angle of the deck. 'Your cowardice has betrayed Portugal, the king and my command!'

'Don't talk to me about cowardice!' the captain-general shouted in his hoarse treble. Outraged, he waved his flashing rapier to prove his point, nicking Antonio's right ear. He quivered, sweat funnelling down his nose. 'We were outgunned. If we had sailed on two days ago, as I advised you to, none of this would have happened.'

He gathered breath as a group of Dutch officers advanced towards them down the sloping decks through the silent parting crowd.

Enraged, Antonio swung an open palm at the wild-eyed face before him, the sharp smack resounding. The old man recoiled, then drew himself up and glared with unblinking fury into Antonio's eyes. He pointed dramatically at the other cheek.

Fuming, Antonio swung the other hand. There was another explosive smack, then a third, as he responded to the pointing finger. And a fourth, before his anger evaporated and the pointing finger became an accusatory one, shaken furiously under his nose. They turned—one deathly pale, the other strawberry-cheeked—to face the group of blue-coated Dutchmen, one of them slow-hand-clapping his applause.

'*Uma questão de honra*. A matter of honour,' the old man confirmed defiantly, his chest heaving, the tip of his rapier on the deck. 'Senhor Pedro de Sousa,' he added, haughtily jutting his chin as though confirming his rank.

At the senior officer's signal, a second officer stepped up to interpret for him.

Antonio unbuckled his sword at the gesture of the Dutch officer. About to hand it over, he took a deliberate step back towards the rail and flung it over the side. The spinning silver sheath turned end over end before it struck the water, glittering as it sank.

Francesco peered over the rail as it disappeared, then turned back to watch Antonio face his enemy.

'Antonio de Melo de Castro, knight of the Cloak of Christ,' he growled, clutching a piece of wadding to his ear. 'Under what law do you presume to take my ship?'

'Under the same law that applies to you—the law of the sea, retaliation in self-defence. We greeted you in friendship. We offered you our hospitality and fresh provisions. And your reply? You fired the first shot.' The officer looked thoughtfully at Antonio, measuring his words. 'That was an act of war. What's more, you killed one of my officers. You hit the heads and he was there at the time. That constitutes our right, in accordance with the owners' instructions and the licence of the United Provinces, under the seal of Count Maurice of Nassau, Prince of Orange. You responded with hostility. You jeopardised the safety of my ships and crew. You impeded our progress.'

'I fired a warning shot across your bows to keep you honest,' said Antonio. He looked scathingly around the group of Dutch officers, 'But clearly, there's no honesty among thieves.'

The officer did not offer a reply. He led Antonio aft under guard to his cabin to discuss the terms of his surrender. As they disappeared towards the poop, the other Dutch crewmen who had clambered aboard lined the stunned and apprehensive Portuguese passengers and crew along opposite rails.

At that point, Francesco enquired in stumbling Spanish if any of the Dutchmen spoke Italian.

One of the officers stepped forward. 'Hendrick de Waal,' he said, continuing in Italian, '*Io lo parlo abbastanza bene. I speak it well enough.*'

Francesco, shrewd and calculating merchant that he was, caught up in a fight that wasn't his, held out a hand that Hendrick bluntly ignored. 'Francesco Carletti,' he said, careful not to react to the snub. 'Get me out of this mess and I will reward you well. Let me show you.'

He led Hendrick aft to view what remained of his cargo. The silk and musk alone would fetch a fortune on the Amsterdam market, he explained. 'And as a down payment a share of my pearls? Some diamonds?' He retrieved his jewel pouch and spilled a sample he displayed on his palm.

Hendrick did not respond at once. He looked thoughtfully at Francesco. 'Where are you from?' he asked, bending to examine the jewels.

Francesco observed him closely. *I can see he recognises their high quality*, he thought. 'I'm from Livorno and Florence.'

'And who is your patron or are you independent?'

'My patron is Ferdinando de Medici, Grand Duke of Tuscany.'

Hendrick promptly reached out and closed Francesco's fingers over the jewels. 'That's good enough for me.' He pointed at Francesco's fist. 'Put them away. We'll discuss them later. Keep them well hidden.'

Ah! So he recognises the strategic importance of my Italian connections. It seems my commercial network will benefit Zeeland trade.

The bargain struck, they waited for the officers to reappear from Antonio's cabin.

When the senior Dutch officer emerged into the evening sunlight, he was clearly jubilant. Francesco noticed that he was carrying an open salt-stained leather satchel in which were crammed Portuguese maps, sailing instructions and papers that appeared to be bills of lading.

'*De kaarten die ik heb bekeken, zijn een schat die de achtervolging waard is!* The charts I've looked at are a treasure worth the chase!' he said, as he handed the satchel to another officer for safekeeping. 'They'll be a pleasant surprise for Reinier

Lambrechtsz and his cartographers back in Middelburg. They'll give our fleets the edge over those from Amsterdam and Hoorn, not to mention Rotterdam, Delft and Enkhuizen!'

Then he turned to the assembled passengers. 'If she doesn't sink overnight, the *Santiago* is forfeit,' he shouted, his interpreter yelling even louder, 'We claim the carrack as our prize. She's the price you pay for your captain's breach.'

He glanced around the steeply sloping decks, then nodded across the rail at the horizon. 'If she is still afloat in the morning, we will provide one of our ships in exchange tomorrow. You can sail west, to Brazil. You can land at Pernambuco or Bahia. From there, you can arrange passage on to Portugal.'

He looked deliberately around his audience, staring down the gaze of anyone who showed defiance, before continuing, 'So you've got some backbreaking work ahead of you manning the pumps and bailing with any other instrument you can use.' He turned to a florid, silver-haired woman dressed in a gaudy green chintz gown patterned in white hibiscus blooms standing to his left. 'I suggest your captain's chamber pot for you,' he said. 'He'll have no further use for it.'

Then he smiled blandly at the faces around him. 'But before all that, my friends, we have another score to settle. There is the matter of whatever valuables you have on board.'

At the bosun's signal, the Dutch sailors forced the indignant and fearful Portuguese to strip naked and remove any pieces of jewellery they were wearing, women and men alike, at sword and cutlass-point. They piled their clothes in front of them and the Dutch crewmen paraded up and down the lines, collecting the valuables in hessian sacks—the silver brooches, crucifixes and amulets, gold and pearl necklaces, jade and coral rosaries—lifting the clothes on sword-tip to inspect them, exchanging their worn calico, canvas and flannels for the finest silks, linens and muslins.

Hendrick led Francesco to the senior officer. 'Meet my admiral, Kornelis Bastiaansz,' he said. 'Kornelis, this is Francesco Carletti, an independent merchant from Livorno. His patron is the Grand Duke of Tuscany. I suggest we respect his neutrality.'

Kornelis inspected Francesco keenly up and down, before giving Hendrick a shrewd nod. 'Granted,' he said.

'The honour is mine,' Francesco responded with a bow before Hendrick led him aft to join four other passengers similarly exempted from the strip search.

They watched three sailors tear the wooden *retablo* painting of Our Lady from the Catholic altar against the poop wall, staggering to the rail to fling it overboard. Sea-wash spilled over the Madonna's pink face, upturned and framed in sun-cracked gold and blue.

At this point, thirty terrified Malagasy servant-slaves were herded onto the deck from the hold, dusted in pepper-sweat, blinded by the sunlight and trembling. With pantomime politeness, they were led down the lines of naked passengers now wearing less than they. They were offered the remaining clothes and the promise of a ticket of leave. The slaves watched the Dutch crew select random shirts and pantaloons and followed suit.

Evening fell as the Dutch officers disembarked, taking Captain Antonio, Francesco and the handful of Portuguese passengers who had negotiated a tenuous hold on freedom with them.

Crouching in the longboat beside Hendrick, Francesco carried his jewel pouch hidden in his boot. When he looked back at the carrack, he saw his Korean servant among the passengers lining the rail in the last glimmer of sunlight.

As the boats drew away, the crimson dome of the evening sun sank into the ocean, intermittent flashes from the distant Holy Virgin seemingly signalling her distress.

At first light the next morning, Francesco and Hendrick, leaning against the rail of the *Zeelandia,* saw the *Santiago* defiantly afloat. Hendrick suggested that the accretion of pepper packed densely against the shattered hull may have slowed the intake of water in the hold to a seepage, saving the lives of those pumping and bailing, panic-stricken, through the night.

They watched Kornelis send carpenters and caulkers to repair her. The teams shifted the cannon and deck cargo to alternate sides to lift and expose the damage below her waterline, toiling all day with sheets of lead to seal the jagged holes.

In the afternoon, some of the spoiled, sea-soaked pepper was thrown overboard, its dark stain curving away behind the carrack like a fan of coral spawn. Floating ribbons of discarded silk unfolded in a rainbow blaze in the pepper-smear. Scavenging sailors from the third Dutch ship launched two skiffs to retrieve them, hauling them in like fishnet.

'They're not Zeelanders,' Hendrick explained, gesturing towards their ship. 'They're Hollanders from Amsterdam, aboard the *Witte Arend.* They're picking up the scraps. They didn't participate in the capture, so they don't share in the takings.'

The fore and main-masts, and the damaged yards and cross-trees aboard the *Santiago* were reset. The rudder was repaired. The decks were returned to some semblance of order and, by evening, she was seaworthy. Spare yards and mainsails were attached and adjusted overnight.

By the next mid-morning, with the wind rising and swell increasing, she could be sailed.

OPA LAURENS STOPPED talking. He leant forward and tapped his pipe out against the grate. 'It's getting late,' he said, looking down at me. 'Hendrick has met Francesco. That's all you asked for.'

We shared a long look, as though we were aware of each other's thoughts.

He broke the silence. 'It's no good looking at me like that. You know the rest of the story, probably better than I do.'

The silence between us persisted until my pleading look got the better of him.

'Alright… alright. I'll give you a very quick version.' He took a deep breath and when he resumed, he spoke fast. 'They spent a month anchored off Fernando de Noronha Island, repairing the *Santiago* so they could sail her to Middelburg. They cut up two longboats to make a larger boat the Portuguese survivors could sail to Brazil. When they arrived in Middelburg, they dismantled the *Santiago* and auctioned her timbers to avoid a political incident with Portugal. Francesco kept his promise and rewarded Overgrootvader Hendrick, who used the money to buy much of the timber and the land to build the house.' He waved an arm dramatically around the room as he sucked in a second breath. 'You only have to take a look around. The front door. The pillars. The beams. I could go on all night, but I won't. He spent the rest of his reward leasing two *fluits* to carry pine and elm from Livonia and Estonia and iron from Sweden for the dokhavn. Our timber business never looked back…'

'We have much to thank Francesco for,' I said, as he sat panting above me.

'We do. Our stars were aligned. Think about the chance coincidences, *jonge*. Overgrootvader Hendrick learned Italian when he was working on a wheat carrier in 1594, when Italy was in drought. Then he transferred to the *Zeelandia* for a voyage to Atjeh in 1601. Francesco set out to circumnavigate the world on a trading mission in 1594. Then he boarded the *Santiago* in Goa in 1601, to travel home.'

'And they met at St Helena Island in March 1602.'

'As they were destined to, led there by the choices each had freely made.' He laughed. 'Or was it simply luck? Either way, your destiny is upstairs to bed. The Portuguese have hung out the white flag. It's time for you to do the same. My word is final now, no arguments. Tomorrow is another day.'

At that moment Mama returned down the stairs with several sheets of music. I watched her arrange them on the clavichord music stand. Opa pointed upwards and I dragged myself to my feet.

I headed for the stairs, passing Mama, now settled on the stool to begin her evening practice. I put my arms about her and laid my forehead on her shoulder before whispering, 'You won't disappear as well, will you, Mama, and leave me on my own?'

I did not wait for her answer. I was halfway up the stairs before she replied. 'Of course not, Gerrit. What makes you think such a thing?'

I shrugged as I turned to climb the rest of the flight.

'What do we do?' I heard her ask, as I retracted the attic ladder. I released the lever and paused to listen. 'He's not handling the situation at all well.'

'Give him time. He can't be expected to consider our feelings when he's in such turmoil himself. And give yourself time, too. We all need time. He's lost his father, after all… and you a husband.' He was silent before he added remorsefully, 'And I've lost a son. Now I understand the pain of experiencing my son's death before my own.

'We've only had a week to absorb the news, Anneka. Do you remember my advice the day Ole Reineus told us about it? I mentioned each of us would grieve in our own way and should be allowed to do so. Gerrit is experiencing shock and disbelief right now, and that's understandable. He's only ten, remember. He's confused. It's a new experience for him.

'We don't know for certain Maarten is dead. No one saw

the *Ridderschap* go down. He's clearly hanging onto that hope, so we won't push the boy, my dear. We'll support him. We'll help him through his grief. We'll help each other through it.'

'I remember your advice,' I heard Mama reply, 'and we will. Of course we will.' The loud clack of the lid as she threw open the clavichord reached me, and she hissed, 'But no matter what you say, I *hate* the injustice of it. Why *his* ship?' I heard the squeal of her seat and assumed she'd spun around on it to face Opa, then I caught the heart-rending despair in her voice. 'Answer me that! What has he done to deserve it? What have *we* done?'

'You know I don't have an answer,' Laurens replied, 'and there'll be many a new widow asking herself the same question tonight. God moves in ways so mysterious at times he leaves us nothing to rely on but faith and trust.'

'Faith and trust! That's little consolation, Laurens. In fact, none at all.' Then she hammered a single jarring chord that echoed through the house.

A charged silence followed. I imagined her snatching her hands from the keyboard and wringing them, perhaps trembling as she fought to keep her outrage in check.

At last, I heard her rustling through sheets of music and she murmured so quietly I could hardly hear her, 'Forgive me, Laurens. That was childish. It wasn't called for.'

'It's to be expected.'

She did not reply, responding instead by playing with intense sensitivity the wistful *Allemanda* I recognised, from Pieter Bustijn's first Clavessin Suite in D minor, his latest.

Seven

IN THE EARLY MORNING, Saturday, 24 April 1700, I woke to the sound of gravel thrown against the window-pane. 'Hey, Gerrit!'

I stretched, rubbed the sleep from my eyes and heard a second shout. 'Wake up, lazybones!'

Daniel! I threw aside the bearskin, opened the window and looked down.

He stood beside the rose bushes, my unmistakeable neighbour, Daniel, red-haired, olive-skinned, gangly, with his part-Japanese eyes always full of humour. He was about to throw another handful, then he threw it anyway, and I swung shut the window to protect myself.

'You've already wasted half the day! Meet you at the front door.'

I dressed, raced barefoot down the ladder and took the stairs three at a time, my right hand sliding down the banister.

'We're going to clean the nesting boxes of the geese, remember,' he said when I opened the front door. 'You said you'd like to come. We can swim or net for eels afterwards.'

Behind him stood Sara, auburn-haired, a willowy shadow shifting from one foot to the other, her warm brown eyes lighting up when I acknowledged her.

'You're coming, aren't you?' Daniel asked. 'The cleaning won't take long. There may be eggs. And the water's warm enough for swimming.'

'Which boxes? Not *all* of them, surely?' There were twenty in all, spread along the banks of three ponds connected by the brook that ran behind the houses. I quickly calculated that cleaning and scrubbing them all and replacing the straw would take us through to mid-afternoon.

No time for swimming or netting a bucket of eels.

'Just the four in the red-breasts' pond. We cleaned the others when you were away in Zierickzee.'

Of course! The red-breasts, I suddenly remembered. *I did agree to help.*

A week before, Daniel had shown me the dozen rare red-breasted geese his papa had netted in the northern marshlands during their migration. He was preparing them for the taxidermist, Daniel had explained, and several collectors were already clamouring for a specimen. He'd also shown me several wild mallards his papa was fattening for the table and promised he'd set a pair of them aside for Mama and me.

'Oh good, that sounds easy.' Sara giggled as my breaking voice shifted up an octave and back again. 'Come on in while I get something to eat. I won't take long.'

'We've eaten already,' Daniel said before I could ask. He sat waiting on the voorkamer bench while Sara peered into the glass cabinet through her reflection, inspecting the majolica and porcelain display as though checking that nothing had moved since she'd last looked.

The sun was lifting over the linden trees beside the Haven canal and filtering through the orchard leaves, its warmth seeping into us, as we made our way along the embankment to the ponds behind Daniel's house. I counted seven birds in a flock of pigeons, greys and whites that rocketed skywards at our approach before drifting down to the loft on outstretched wings.

I pointed. 'They're exactly like paper darts. We'd win the long-distance throwing contest at school using a design like that.'

'Why don't we work out the shape and folds to make one?' Daniel suggested. 'We can start on it this afternoon, if you like.'

At the first pond, Daniel lifted the netting that caged the

geese. We crawled beneath it, dragging a bundle of straw, while Sara heaved a second and then a third from the hay store. The geese, immaculately feathered in deep red, sooty grey and white, scrambled hysterically across the pond, their wings thrashing at the water until they reached the opposite embankment, where they crowded against the netting, hissing and honking in alarm.

Daniel leant over to lift the lid on the first of the nesting boxes. A solitary goose came storming out, wings flailing. Its feet scrabbled at his chest as it flapped across his shoulder, blinding him with its pinion feathers. He flung up his arms to fend it off, took a backward step and slipped down the bank. He hit the water on his back and I saw his eyes wide with shock as the foam closed over him.

He surfaced at once, throat-deep, struggling for balance and a foothold, stirring up clouds of sediment. Sara subsided in a fit of giggles as he floundered, but I was torn between laughter and panic as Daniel appeared to sink further. *Are his boots trapped between rocks*, I wondered, *or entangled in the leaves and roots of underwater weeds?*

Before I could react, he slipped deeper still, his mouth and nose buried in the foam boiling around him, his forehead and the crown of his head now all that was visible.

Tearing off my shirt and boots, I dived into the pond. Unable to see, I felt my way down Daniel's flank to his boot buried in the mud. Both hands gripping the ankle, I heaved Daniel's right foot free of the boot still suctioned to the bottom. Clinging to the empty boot with one hand, I dragged it free and reached for his left leg with the other hand. It was stuck fast. My breath gave out as Daniel's kicking slowed. As I struggled, I felt Sara's hands close over mine as she reached for Daniel's left boot.

I launched myself upwards and burst into the sunlight, gasping.

I hauled myself to the bank where I flung the boot I'd freed into the grass and crawled out. Sara was head down, her legs kicking wildly as Daniel re-emerged, coughing and gulping for air. He struggled to the bank, propelled by Sara from behind and, with me dragging on his collar, clawed his way to the safety of the grass. He lay on his back, arms outstretched, panting.

I squatted beside him. 'That was no fun,' I said, my chest heaving. 'That goose nearly prepared *you* for the taxidermist!'

I retrieved my shirt from beneath Sara's abandoned dress. Then I reached out to help her clamber from the water, before settling on my back beside Daniel to dry off in the sun.

Sara picked up the solitary boot, washed it out in the pond and placed it at Daniel's feet. Then she leant over him, her long hair falling about her face as she wrung the water from it. It ran down her arms and splashed onto his face. He shook his head about to avoid it.

Then she flung her hair back over her shoulder and stood over him, arms spread wide, her chemise clinging to her lean body, ribs and budding breasts in contour. She broke into a carefree smile. 'Daniel, you should see yourself—one boot on and water weeds in your hair. Like you're dressed for the *kermis* ball! Will you promise me the next dance?'

She nudged me aside and stretched out between us, looking up at the sky. After a moment's silence she began to giggle, before breaking into peals of laughter that had us following suit—laughter with no sense to it but joyous all the same, reaching a hysterical crescendo that brought tears, before subsiding again into panting silence, followed by another fit of laughter.

When we were calm at last, I heard her sigh. 'Such a sky. Have you ever seen a blue so beautiful?'

'Only the sea,' I responded. 'It has blues of many shades.'

'But none to match the sky.' She turned, leant on an elbow and looked down at me, 'Except your eyes!' she whispered. 'They're the colour of the summer wind.'

Surprised and wary of the intimacy in her whisper, which I was concerned Daniel may have overheard even though his eyes were closed and he appeared to be falling asleep, I asked, 'What do you mean, the summer wind? How is the wind coloured blue?'

'All the winds have colours, don't you know? Lime green and silver in the winter, sometimes grey. Yellows in autumn, like the leaves. Shades of violet and pink and cherry red in the spring. And *blue* in summer! *Oma* Ramika taught me.'

Then, for the first time, she bent compulsively to brush her lips against my cheek. She pulled back, gazed at me with a teasing smile and, before I could turn away, placed her lips lightly on mine, the only sound my sharp intake of breath and an intimate click as our teeth met.

Without waiting for my reaction, she was up and running barefoot towards the house as though her life depended on it, trailing her white dress in her upraised hand like a streaming banner.

I glanced across at Daniel who seemed to be asleep until one eye opened and he squinted at me. '*Now* you're in trouble, my friend! You've always known she worships you, surely. Wait till they hear about this at school.'

'Come on, Daniel. She's like a sister to me.' I wiped my cheek and ran a finger rapidly across my lips, before adding scornfully, 'Coloured winds! Mention this to *anyone* and you'll have me to reckon with.'

Daniel closed both eyes and, after a few moments, conceded, 'I owe you both a favour, so your secret's safe, but Sara's going to get some teasing.'

I shook my head. 'I wouldn't risk it. You can't match that tongue of hers.'

'Maybe you're right, but I'll enjoy trying.'

We lay in silence, our wet clothes drying, then Daniel explained, 'Our Oma Ramika believes the winds are coloured, like everything you see through your spyglass.'

'But there's a reason my spyglass works that way. And you can't see the wind through it.'

'Well, Sara sees the winds in colour. You've seen that in her paintings.'

'That's true. They're strange, her paintings.' I sat up to contemplate the geese, before adding, 'But I like them.'

I recalled the sketches Sara had once shyly shown me—naively drawn landscapes of the fields and farmhouses around Middelburg and Westcapelle over which she'd washed watercolours in a mix of unexpected pastel shades. *So it was Oma Ramika who'd taught her the technique*, I realised. *That old lady still has her memories of Japan intact beneath her wrinkles.*

I lay back and the sun glimmered red through my eyelids. I felt its warmth skin-deep, then a deeper inner glow radiating through me as I recalled Sara's voice, felt her lips on mine and conjured her fresh smell and, with the spreading warmth, felt my groin stir, the insistent pleasure of it bringing panic so that I raised my knees and sat up again, staring across the pond. I watched the reflections shiver on its surface and the iridescent patterns in the geese, now quiet, until the pressure eased, my emotions calmed and my breathing gradually slowed.

Then I reached across and shook Daniel by the shoulder. 'Come on. We have work to do and eels to catch.'

I put my boots back on and picked up Sara's shoes, buckled them together and slung them at my belt before walking across to the first of the nesting boxes and lifting the lid.

I glanced back at Daniel, who was putting on his boot. Then I looked at the patch of grass where Sara had lain. And when I handed back her shoes two hours and a bucketful of writhing eels later, the silence between us was charged and I knew that those moments of unforeseen tenderness and all that had followed would be engraved on my memory to the end of my days.

THAT NIGHT, PARTWAY through dinner, Mama turned to me with an unexpected frown. 'I've had word from school you've put your name down for an apprenticeship at the dokhavn.' Her voice cutting, she raised a hand to silence Opa Laurens. 'Is that true?'

'Yes.'

'Why in God's name, after all the discussions we've had?'

I looked down at the half-eaten meal on my plate. 'You know why.'

'And you know why I won't allow it! I want you to be worthier than that. I told you I've spoken to the apothecary in Aagtekerke who'll be looking for an apprentice next year.' She fixed her eyes on mine, her expression fiery. 'If you must leave school, the position is all but guaranteed.'

'Don't I have a choice?'

'Of course you have! You know you do. You can study law if you get down to some serious revision and improve your school results. That's your other option.'

'That's not what I meant.'

Her eyes flashed. 'Well, that's what *I* mean, as you well know. I want you to make a responsible contribution to society, not avoid it. I want to see you make your mark,' she lowered her voice, 'on the *world*, not on chunks of wood.'

I stared back at her, unblinking, as the silence lengthened. About to point out that it was chunks of wood that had given the family its prosperity, I held myself in check. I sensed in her anger her fear for my future and the prospect of losing me, yet, for the first time in my life, I experienced an unaccustomed sense of empowerment as I faced her across the table. The sensation was different from the stubborn, childish petulance with which I'd sometimes reacted to her when I was younger.

So I stood my ground, before granting her, at last, a conciliatory shrug. Despite this new and heady defiance, I knew I shouldn't push her too far. Not yet. I took a mouthful of the stew. 'Have it your way, Mama,' I said as I chewed, 'but you know I want to work among artisans in the open air, not hidden away in an apothecary's backroom or a courthouse wearing a wig and lace collar. That won't suit me. I want to get my hands dirty instead.'

'Show me some respect, Gerrit, and give me some credit. I won't have this. I won't have you going to sea like your father and, if you don't drown, ending up in some godforsaken shipyard in the Indies to die of smallpox or elephantiasis.'

'*Elephantiasis?*' I gave a burst of mocking laughter. 'That's a new one! You think I'll catch some tropical disease that will turn me into a sciapod?[13]' Aware that my reaction was offensive, I glanced quickly at Opa Laurens. His face was impassive. 'At least I didn't apply for a position as a VOC cadet, like Papa.'

Outraged, Mama smacked a palm against the table. 'Sciapod indeed! Don't answer back. You're not a man yet! You can't decide to take whatever direction pleases you.' She reached for her glass and drank some water, glaring at me over its rim. 'If your father was here you wouldn't be so disrespectful. And swallow your food before you talk to me.'

'But surely I can let you know my preference and there's only one,' I said. 'I'm not running away from my responsibilities, I'm running *towards* them. And if Papa were here, I know *he'd* listen.'

---

13 One-legged mythological figures often seen on early maps of Africa, their single foot large enough to use as a sunshade when lying on their backs.

'How can you be the judge of that?' Mama shrilled. 'You knew him when you were eight and then for less than a year!' She drew a sharp intake of breath. '*I'm* the one who's been father and mother to you for most of your life.'

I turned once more to Opa Laurens, this time for a sign of his approval, but the old man leant forward in his chair and reached out to place a reassuring hand on Mama's forearm.

'I want to become a carpenter and then a senior carpenter—or shipwright perhaps, in the dokhavn,' I continued, raising my voice, 'and when I reach that position, I can decide on my future. That will take me a good ten years, Mama. I know you don't want me going to sea. I won't until then, if I decide to at all. I'll be home for at least that long.'

I could see that she was surprised and hurt by my outburst and I could hear how offended she was when she replied, her voice strained, 'You've shown so much promise up till now, Gerrit. Live up to your potential. Make us proud. Fulfil yourself. Don't lower your expectations or our standards.'

'*Lower my expectations?* What about Opa? He works in the dokhavn and sees nothing wrong with it.' I clamped my jaw and shook my head. 'I'm not changing my mind about this. Never!'

'I'm your mother! I have a say. In fact, I have the final word.' Trembling now, she deliberately removed Laurens's hand, threw her serviette on the table and stood. 'This is *not* over, Gerrit. This is unfinished business. At the very least do me the honour of letting me know next time the school wants that sort of information. Talk to me about it first.'

She swept from the room and into the kitchen.

Opa Laurens gazed at me in silence. After long moments, he murmured, 'Time for an apology, I think.'

I pushed back my chair and walked around the table to help Adriana clear the dishes. 'I'm always expected to apologise.

Well, not this time. This time I've done nothing wrong.'

'For not telling her you'd applied through the school.'

'Ah, that. I should have explained. They took us by surprise, asking us if we wanted to enrol in the Illustere School when we qualified or if we had other plans. I had no time to talk to her.'

'That was days ago. You should have had the good sense to face her at the time. You should have shown her some respect. You knew it would upset her. You shouldn't have let her find out through someone else.'

I nodded. 'True, but now she knows. I'll talk to her when the time is right.' I sat back at the table. 'Whose life is it anyway, Opa? If I do what she says, whose life will I be living? Hers, not mine.'

'Remember, she's lived a lot longer than you. I don't need to remind you that she knows all about risk and the consequences of unfortunate decisions, the tragedies that can follow. She doesn't want you to do something you may regret.'

'I'll be doing that the moment I walk through the apothecary's door or into the admiralty courts.'

He reached out, placed a hand on my shoulder and looked into my eyes. 'My God, you are both so headstrong! She's gifted you with her Tuineman determination and her… well, I have to say, sometimes unbending obstinacy. We've talked about this before. You need to control it or it will lead to self-indulgence you can't afford.

'So my advice is to back off for the moment. Apologise and give her time to get used to the idea. Sweet talk her into accepting it. Be subtle, my boy, not pig-headed, and you're sure to bring her round. And don't forget, you're still young and she's a mother with a mother's instincts. She's protecting you from what she sees as a dangerous world out there *and* from your impetuous self. She's standing by her values—the values she taught you. I wouldn't expect any less.'

A knowing smile quietly spread. 'And as for you, *mijn*

kleinzoon, don't let self-pity lead you to think she's punishing you by insisting on science or the law for not doing as well as she expected at school. You spend too much of your time in the carving shed with me.' His smile became a sympathetic laugh. 'Getting your hands dirty! I liked the sound of that. She's aware of how talented you are. *Everyone* tells her—everyone. Perhaps she doesn't like being reminded so often, but I'm sure she's as proud of your work as I am, even if she rarely shows it.'

Calmer, I patted his hand on my shoulder, removed and held it. 'She certainly didn't like my comment about the sciapod.'

'No, it was your tone. And I believe she was thinking of Maarten and what may have happened to him. Not a day goes by.'

'Not for me, either.'

'Not for any of us.'

Back in my attic bedroom before dousing the lamp, I wondered at the way I'd stood up to Mama. I'd put my case without deferring to her to keep the peace, as I had before when my future was discussed and she'd laid out her plans for me. *This time I've been reasonable and persistent under fire*, I thought, and that surprised and pleased me, despite the qualms I felt at hurting her feelings. But my mind was made up. And I knew why. *Ships. The sea. And Papa! I have to find him!*

I looked up at the thick squared roof beams exposed above me and the *Santiago* immediately came to mind. I opened the drawer of the bedside table and retrieved the polished silver medallion struck in 1603 to celebrate her capture.

I ran my forefinger across the embossed images of the two Dutch ships and the carrack during the engagement. As I did so, my mind ranged over all the timbers in the house that reminded me of Hendrick. The oaken window ledge. The narrow teak stairway with the four mermaids carved in ash in its balustrade. The rosewood dining table from the officers' mess. The oak and walnut sideboard from the captain's cabin on which Mama displayed the Qing vases she filled with fresh flowers. The full-length ebony-framed Venetian mirror in the hallway.

But most obvious of all, the thick oak-panelled front door the family had refused for a hundred years to paint the traditional green. Studded with the *Santiago*'s blackened bolts, it stood in contrast to the doors of the neighbouring houses in the cul-de-sac and further down the canal. And my favourite—the carrack's bell fixed into the brickwork beside the front door.

All these and more, within the framing of the house and roof, were from the *Santiago*. For me, the house I sailed *was* the *Santiago* and, when I sailed at night, she was my ghost ship, a Portuguese Flying Dutchman navigating moonlit skies under a Zeeland banner—*not doomed to sail the empty oceans forever, according to the legend, but coming into port triumphant, with me at the helm.*

As far back as I could remember, I had admired the immense ships that towered above the buildings of Middelburg during construction. I would often sneak into the dokhavn to visit Opa Laurens and his team of craftsmen in the carving shed after school to watch them work, and two or three times a year I'd watch the launching of the latest hulls.

I observed the ships from my window seat, those on their maiden voyages and others long in service, as they moved majestically down the Haven canal, towed behind crews of chanting rowers or teams of horses straining along the embankment. They floated past the house, bunting flying from sheets and mastheads—and my ambitions had been born.

True, I *had* seen myself at first as a navigation officer, training as a VOC cadet, following in Papa's footsteps, but later, as my woodworking and carving skills had developed under

Opa Laurens's tutoring, I imagined myself as senior carpenter aboard, promoted from the dokhavn.

I leant across and spun the globe, my eyes turning to the broken curve marking the west coast of Eendrachtsland and the Abrolhos Islands, wondering if that was where the *Ridderschap van Holland* had met her end and Papa may have been marooned.

I reached up to snuff out the lamp.

Before drifting to sleep, I recalled that Mama had insisted the decision was unfinished business.

Well, I thought, *it will be resolved when I walk through the dokhavn gates next year, my VOC apprenticeship indentures in one hand and a bag of tools in the other, but with her blessing. I have eight months to win her over.*

The memory of Sara crossed my mind and my heart glowed. *But for that goose, she would never have given me my first kiss! Tomorrow, I'll select a piece of ebony and carve a goose for her to remember the moment or, better still, my favourite, another bird of paradise so perfect she'll never forget me.*

Eight

3 JANUARY 1701. UNACCUSTOMED to carrying a weighty bag of tools, my shoulder was aching as I walked through the gates into the dokhavn with Opa Laurens, six months after my fifteenth birthday. Even though I had regularly visited Opa in the carving shed as a boy and knew many of the teams of workers, I felt I was crossing the threshold for the first time.

Mama's words as she'd embraced me when I'd left the house that morning were burning in my mind, 'Remember, you are a de Waal and Maarten's son, Gerrit, and we never do less than our very, very best.' I was grateful and relieved that she had relented and wished me well, but I knew her smile hid her deep disappointment. *I must succeed beyond her expectations,* I thought. *I will not fail her… or Papa.*

My heart hammered at my throat, my excitement at that moment tempered by foreboding. I was aware of the strict traditions of the Shipwright's Guild and acutely conscious of the testing ceremonies I would undergo during my initiation. There were frightening surprises in store, not least the tiered pyramids of rough-squared oak logs I knew I could barely lift in the drying shed. They spelled out the backbreaking work that lay ahead.

It had been an unexpectedly cold winter. A light snowfall drifted, obscuring our footsteps. In the forecourt of the saw windmill, we stepped into the shadows of its giant sails angled across the yard.

Secluded among chestnut trees at the far fence-line lay the hulk of the *Onrust*[14] propped in a cradle of angled chocks. She stood preserved and tarred in her dry-dock stockade,

---

14 Cargo ship *Onrust* (*Restless*), built in 1614, in New Amsterdam (later New York) and subsequently decommissioned in Middelburg.

where she served as a mess hall and boarding house for several journeymen and senior apprentices, sleeping three to a cramped cabin on her fore and aft decks. Smoke from her galley chimney drifted, carrying the aromatic whiff of lard and frying ham.

To our left, the ice-sheeted water of the canal edged the flagstones on which our footsteps rang. A pair of hardwood slipways was embedded flush with the bricks that angled down towards the ice. Above each slipway lay two massive rails of oak, worn smooth and darkly scorched. They were the bilge-way skids that carried new ships into the canal when they were launched.

I'd been at the dokhavn a month before to watch the launching of the latest ship, the *Gouden Phoenix*. As we crossed the courtyard, I glanced towards the Kinderdijk quay beyond the trees, where she glinted, green and gold, bright with fresh enamel.

I recalled the ship's hull high on the skids and the synchronised swing of the axemen slicing through the ropes anchoring the skids to two disused cannons buried upright in the ground. The cables had whipped apart with an explosive *crack* and the skids had slid slowly down the tallow-greased slipways to the raucous hollering of the crowd. The skids gathered speed, screeching as the grease burst into flame, extinguished as they struck the water and sank, releasing the hull, which had surged across the canal before settling on the backwash, fragments of broken ice lifting and falling around it.

On the first of the slipways, I saw the two-and-a-half roeden[15] oak stem and sternpost of a new vessel arching up from its immense elm keel. I counted six separate lengths of timber in the keel, a patchwork of beams scarphed and

---

15 The stem and sternposts were approximately ten metres tall and the keel forty-five metres long.

copper-bolted together to form a solid backbone I knew was twelve roeden long. Stem and stern had been raised a fortnight before. Tenoned to the keel and perfectly aligned, they were held upright by a web of block-and-tackle ropes dark with melting snow, a cat's cradle lashed to straining sheerlegs anchored to the frozen ground.

Several barn swallows were roosting on the ropes, stray birds wintering in the eaves of the warehouses. I nudged Opa when I saw them, the sheen of their feathers a silky blue-black, a splash of ivory across the chest. 'Looks like they're dressed for the occasion, Opa, lining up to welcome us. Blue cravats and all.'

'They must have missed the autumn migration. Or they're setting off late.'

'Where do they fly to?'

'They've been seen in Africa, I believe… some as far south as the farms around Cape Town.'

The birds took off as we approached, gliding and looping between us. I flicked out an arm to capture one that evaded my hand with fluent ease.

The towering stem dwarfed a group of red-coated workmen warming their hands at a glowing brazier, waves of heat rising, their breath in steamy plumes as their conversations seemingly went up in smoke.

We crossed the flagstones to join them.

Moments later, the duty overseer struck the iron barrel-ring hanging at the entrance to the saw windmill workshop. His shout, '*Kom op, u luie mormeltjes*! Come on, you lazy mongrels!' echoed over the shipyard.

The group shuffled to the first task of the day, straining at the capstans to shift the turntable foundations of the saw windmill into the light morning breeze. As the mill shuddered around, the soaring sails began to ripple and the gears cranked slowly into life, snow that had gathered on the sails overnight slumping across the forecourt.

Two other new apprentices joined the dokhavn that morning—Nikolaas Haysen and little Axel de Vos. Both were inmates of the city's *Abdij*[16] orphanage and I knew them from school. They had mentioned their selection to me months earlier, and the strange coincidence that the three of us were fatherless had struck me then. I was pleased to see them.

The overseer directed us to the windmill workshop where the clerk-of-all-trades crammed us into his cubicle to sign us on.

He sharpened his quill as though paring a fingernail, then introduced himself, 'I am Alois Brinkman.' His broad accent sounded Flemish. 'You will call me "sir" at all times. I'll be looking after you today and you'll be seeing me once a fortnight for your pay and for your timetables. I allocate you to different workstations once the *meister*, the master, decides where to send you. Have you got that?' We gazed at him in silence. 'Have you got that?' he shouted at the top of his voice. We responded at once in a chorus.

He wrote our names in painstaking copperplate into the leather-bound payroll ledger, which we signed in turn. We paid our Shipwright's Guild dues—I carefully counted out the coins I'd accumulated from the sales of my wooden diabolos and dice.

Alois explained the nature of our indentures and the terms of our contracts. He ran through the rates and frequency of our pay and outlined the contributions that we could choose to make into the *scheepstimmerman beurzen*, the mutual benefit fund that took care of us in times of illness and accident. He discussed the bonuses we would share with all the journeymen and shipwrights for completing projects ahead of schedule

---

16 The Abbey of Middelburg.

and for shaving costs.

'And the shavings will be yours, too,' he said, gesturing across the forecourt. 'You can sweep them up with the rest of the woodchips and sell them as firelighters for pocket money. You earn twenty percent. In fact, you can start today. Clean the place up last thing before you leave tonight. That's a duty you'll share for the next five years. You'll be rostered to deliver them around the city with the peat carriers.'

He pointed his quill at a faded drawing pinned to the wall behind him—*Be content with your wages*, its title read. *Luke 3:14*. Above the slogan was a rough-sketched cartoon of himself as *predikant*, his scrawny pastor's body enveloped in a tattered black robe de Calvin, his face unsmiling beneath a lopsided halo. He held a leather moneybag tight in one hand, offering a meagre *stuiver*, a shilling, in the other to a group of caricatured carpenters begging around him. I smiled when I recognised Opa's crestfallen face among them.

'There's no point smiling about it, de Waal,' he said. 'Read that and don't you forget it because that's all you'll be earning. You're lucky to be earning anything at all. Most guilds don't pay their apprentices until they qualify, so count your lucky stars and thank the VOC for their generosity. You'll be learning the trade for the love of it and your pittance will be reward enough. So don't come bothering me for a pay rise until you turn twenty.'

He raised the back of his quill to probe his ear canal, checked for wax, which he wiped on the sleeve of his red work coat, then grinned. 'By the way, none of you is Jewish, are you? Or illegitimate? Or God forbid, *female*? Because if you are, own up to it now,' he doubled up with laughter, 'and I'll record it here, even though the guild's gone soft these days and may allow you membership.'

Master shipwright Pieter Penne's boots appeared through

the trapdoor in the corridor ceiling as he descended the ladder from the upper gallery, where the two giant circular saws began their rasping grind into the first run of oak logs, their gears wrenched by the mighty wooden cogs driven by the wind-sails. He stopped halfway down the ladder to watch the first bite of the blades and roared parting instructions to the sawyers on the log-feed. Then his face appeared beneath his upward-reaching arm and he smiled down at us. He grunted a Russian '*Dobraye-ootro!*' good morning, his long salt-and-red-pepper moustache parting like a theatre curtain across tobacco-stained, tombstone teeth.

Tall and spindle-shanked, he stood just under seven *voeten*.[17] 'More *mast* than master,' I recalled Opa had mentioned once, as I looked up at him.

I had observed him for years, running his yard with an infectious, energetic urgency. He was always on the move between his teams of carpenters and caulkers, sawyers and rope-makers, surveyors and painters. He kept them on their toes, standing out amongst them because of his beanpole height and his extraordinary uniform—he wore a black velvet knee-length Cossack coat, its white lapels of snow fox fur, on his head a grey mink fur cap.

He was wearing them as he jumped from the last ladder rung and bowed, removing his cap with a theatrical sweep of his arm, his flaming hair tumbling around his face, beetling eyebrows accentuating the keen glance he swept over us.

'See this cap,' his voice rumbled at us in a deep bass as he held it out, 'It's the mark of my seniority around here. Do you know who presented it to me? That Russian prince, Peter the Great! Three years ago. In Amsterdam. When we collaborated with him and his underlings in building the frigate *Peter en*

---

17 A *voet* equals 31.4 cm, compared with 30.48 cm for the English foot.

Paul. He had to visit our shipyards to find out how it was done. What do you boys say to that?'

We stood in front of him, stunned and tongue-tied, glancing nervously at one another. 'He knew we were the best shipwrights in the world—second to none! *That's* what you say to that. And now *you*,' he pointed a long, bony finger at Axel, then at Nikolaas and I, 'and *you* and *you* are here to join us. You have a lot to live up to. Make sure you don't let us down.'

Then he ushered us out to the slipway and led us to the newly laid timbers of the latest ship.

'This is a ship of the new design, *jongens*,' he said, his eyes a piercing blue under the burning bush of his hair, his face as passionate as an Old Testament prophet. 'She's a design of the First Rate, her structure decided on in 1697. She'll be the first this century for the VOC and the first of her type for Middelburg.

'The design is still hotly debated. I've been sceptical ever since it was agreed on. Take the stern, for example. Should it be square or rounded or a bit of both? Well, I prefer rounded, but they outvoted me for square. They decided to keep to the *spiegel*, flat as a plate glass mirror.

'Why? Because it enables the hold to carry more cargo… and it's cheaper!' He waved a hand before his eyes as though erasing the memory and growled, '*Cheaper!* Accountants will be the ruin of us. Money is all that matters these days. Good design is a thing of the past.'

He rapped his knuckles against the sternpost, sending us a triumphant smile. 'Well *jongens*, let me tell you, in *my* shipyard, not quite! Not while I'm the *meister* here. There are *spiegels* and there are *spiegels*, that's the long and the short of it. And in our case,' he tapped the side of his long nose, 'the shorter the better.

'See the transom over there?' He pointed at the giant square frame of the transom, the after-end of the ship that would be lifted into position on the sternpost some weeks later. 'It's a *spiegel*, yes, but it's short. That's the secret. It will give us a chance to sneak in a set of curving garboard strakes from the keel below the waterline to just above it. That will give the rudder some extra bite, with more stern wash to manoeuvre in. She'll be shaped like a fish.' He looked around us with an expectant grin. 'So what do you *jongen*s have to say now?'

There was another embarrassing silence. We glanced nervously at one another for several long moments.

'*What*? Youngsters your age stuck for words? Come on, speak up! Surprise me.'

'Like a whale,' I murmured, seeing through Oom Joris's experienced eye the sleek flanks of a whale curving to tail flukes powering through blood-and-oil covered water as he steered the whaleboat, with the watch officer leaning into the killing harpoon, the crew oars-up at the moment of the deadly final thrust.

'*Exactly*, Gerrit. She'll be streamlined like a whale. She's of the First Rate, and we'll make sure she *is* first-rate.' He gave us a conspiratorial wink. 'You boys have joined us at the right time. We're testing another new technique in her construction. We'll be building her frames first. Up to now, we've always started with the outer planking of the hull and *then* installed the frames inside the shell.'

He reached inside the left lapel of his coat and withdrew a sheet of vellum which he carefully unfolded. He held it out, bending to protect the inked sketch from the powdering of snow. I saw the skeleton of a ship, a cage of fourteen ribs pointing skywards. Indecipherable formulae were scribbled across it.

'This time we're following naval architect Cornelis van Ijk's advice; this is a copy of his latest drawing. Frames first, outer planking last. He's a ship's architect after my own heart. It should save us a month in construction time, at least.'

THE NEXT MORNING, we travelled two *mijl*[18] south to the timber yards and ponds beside the Haven canal at Nieuw-en Sint Joostland for six weeks of induction.

'You'll be working with crews offloading timber delivered from the Baltic, boys,' Alois advised us as we clambered aboard the carriage, 'so be prepared. You'll be sweating blood, especially whichever one of you gets tangled up in a circular saw!'

With a burst of dry laughter, he pointed a forefinger at each of us in turn. '*Anne, manne, miene, mukke*, make sure it's not... *you.*' He tapped Nikolaas on the chest. 'Mind you, you have paid your insurance dues, so I'll arrange a memorial service to end all memorial services for you, one *we'll* never forget.' Still laughing as the carriage pulled away, he shouted, 'And you won't be the first, young Haysen.'

Separated from home and family for the first time, a shiver of anticipation ran through me as we approached the yards, rattling across the wooden bridge over the waterway that led from the Haven canal on our right to the two ponds in the yards on our left. I noticed with relief that there were no ships loaded with timber moored at the jetty.

Two doddering old men identically dressed in funereal black frock coats, who looked as old as Methuselah and must be twin brothers, opened the gates to allow the carriage through. They climbed onto the foot rail and clung on as we rode on to the barracks. When we alighted, I read the cardboard labels hanging around their necks, 'Cain', one read in sprawling red ink, and 'Abel' the other.

They led us up the steps to a communal dining room lined with pinewood tables and benches. I ducked as we entered to avoid the iron ring and striker hanging on a chain beside the door. I took it to be the timber yard bell.

---

18 A *mijl* (mile) was about five kilometres.

Abel held up his label. 'In case you think our names are a practical joke, that's how we were baptised, Cain and I, by our Papa Adam, and our Mama Evelyn,' he said. 'We're Puritan English gentlemen. As you can hear, our Dutch is rudimentary, but we do our best to get the message across. We're retired professionals from Norwich. And I'm the chef here, as you'll learn to appreciate or you go hungry.'

He snapped a finger several times and the door beside the servery hatch opened. An extraordinary figure appeared, one I'd seen many times around the city, had stared at and commented on among my friends but had been too fearful to approach.

'Meet Otello,' Abel continued, smiling as he observed our surprise. 'If you want to eat well, he's the one person in the camp you want to show special respect.'

He was a tall, broad-shouldered, white-skinned and heavily freckled albino Afro-Zeelander mulat. His receding, tightly curled hair, caught in parallel shafts of winter sunlight slant-ing through the slatted window, was tinged a fiery orange. His eyes were pale blue, so pale I noticed that his irises had a faint pink colour at certain angles, as he turned to look at each of us in turn. He had a massively muscular right arm, the tendons and sinews writhing like snakes beneath his skin as he moved. His left was missing at the shoulder, the sleeve of his white jacket pinned to his chest.

He stepped forward. 'Otello Ferreira,' he growled. He reached forward and offered Nikolaas his broad hand. 'Welcome,' he said, and I saw Nikolaas wince as he took it. He turned to me and did the same. 'Welcome,' he repeated, crushing the bones in my fingers, and 'Welcome to you too,' he said to Axel, who wrung his hand when Otello released it.

'Now then,' Abel said, 'before you start work, we have a small test for you. Follow me.' He led us towards the kitchen door, stopping at a red line painted across the floorboards, dividing the room in two. 'You see this line? No one crosses it. It's as close as you come to the servery hatch at mealtimes.' He pointed down with dramatic emphasis. 'This side—your territory. That side—Otello's and mine. And never the twain shall meet!'

Then he gave us a mysterious smile. 'Unless of course, you can get past Otello here. You have two chances to try. Once now and once again the day you leave. That way we measure the progress you've made.

'Let me explain. When he was younger, Otello was taken to Dejima Island in Nagasaki to work as a family cook for the VOC administrator. He was there for seven years and, during that time, he learned how to arm grapple the Japanese way. Show them, Otello.'

Giving each of us a curt bow, in turn, Otello stepped up to the line. He turned sideways to face us, feet apart, his left braced against the wall, his right pointed along the line. Then he extended his arm, cocked slightly at the elbow, tensed the muscles and tendons, and cupped his hand with the fingers together.

I found the suggestion of threat and obvious power in his posture alarming.

Abel chuckled as he placed a small hourglass on the servery ledge. 'Now I'll give each of you one measure on the timer to shift that arm and claim some of our territory. Like this.' He stepped forward, took up an identical stance facing Otello, and placed his right hand in Otello's fist. For several moments he strained unsuccessfully to shift Otello's arm towards the kitchen, before relaxing with a frustrated gasp. Otello's face was impassive.

Abel stood panting, gathering his breath, before pointing at Axel. 'You're the smallest,' he said. 'So you try first.'

'But I'm left-handed.'

'Then we'll handicap Otello. You can use both hands and take up any position you choose.'

Axel walked up, placed his left hand in Otello's extended hand and his right on Otello's forearm. When Abel turned the timer, Axel stretched forward and struggled to push the arm, his feet scrabbling on the floorboards until Abel eventually called for him to stop. The arm did not budge.

It was my turn next. I positioned myself as Abel had done. Otello's fist closed over mine and I tensed, waiting for Abel's call. When it came, my body convulsed from head to toe as I exerted all the strength I had, leaning forcefully in, my shoulders rotating awkwardly into the thrust. I gave a long, grunting outbreath. Gasping for another, I felt my face reddening, the veins in my neck pulsing, before I groaned again. And then again, with another desperate and violent effort. It was like pushing against a rock, against a statue, while time seemed to extend unbearably. The longer I struggled, anxious that my energy was deserting me, the more agonising it became.

When Abel at last called 'Time!' I glanced up at Otello, breathless. His face was expressionless or was that a glimmer of quiet satisfaction in his eyes?

'Now I know how Sisyphus felt,' I murmured, rubbing my hands together.

Abel smiled in surprise at my comment. 'That is a commendable reference indeed, coming from an apprentice. Sisyphus. He personified the idea of persistence. You boys can learn a valuable lesson from him.'

Nikolaas was the last to face the test and the result was no different.

'As I said, you get to try again before you leave,' Abel reminded us as he pocketed the hourglass and walked back to the kitchen with Otello. 'We'll see you boys when you come back in for lunch.'

'*Ik ben je baas terweijl je hier bent*, I'm your supervisor while you're here,' Cain explained as they disappeared, 'and I carry out the clerical and accounting duties for the mill. That includes handing you your fortnightly allowances and assigning you to your duties. Come with me.' He led us rapidly through a rear door into the dormitory, rising on his toes with each stride in a quickstep walk we could barely keep pace with.

He showed us to our beds at the far end of the room, where we deposited our bags and tools.

'I see you're dressed for work,' he said. 'That's good. As for your tools, you won't need them here. We have enough adzes and draw knives to go round, not to mention shovels and axes. You bring along your muscle power.' He gave an unexpected knowing grin, as though forewarning us. 'We start early and finish late, especially when we have a fresh shipment to clear. We're expecting a consignment from Riga within days. And by the way, I report back to the *meister* on your progress when you return to the dokhavn, so keep your noses clean and do what you're told!'

Then he directed us out to the veranda to familiarise us with the yards.

We stood at the rail, our breath vapourising in the freezing air. I noticed some fifteen workmen scattered at different stations. Two close at hand used scythes to slash at weeds infiltrating the fence line. The yard itself was surprisingly clear—not a blade of grass or a weed to be seen. The neat, semi-circular marks of rakes sweeping up whatever debris may have been there had scored the gravel. Two parallel lines of whitewashed bricks indicated a laneway running the length of the yards.

Cain pointed at several men in waders knee-deep in the first pond, its surface steaming. They appeared to be clearing sludge. I saw that they were Afro-Zeelander mulatten, one very dark-skinned and others with skins of lighter shades. 'They're the hardest men you're ever going to meet, those blacks. And the least friendly,' he said. 'They'll drive you with fists of iron, *jongens*, so be prepared. Never take offence, not under any circumstances. Follow their instructions and their example and you can't go wrong. *To the letter*, now!'

An unexpected wheeze gave way to a racking cough until he turned aside, cleared his throat and spat a gob of phlegm across the veranda rail. 'They've been here for two generations, as you know, but the fear of exile is still in their blood. They stick together so no privateer gets the wrong idea and tries to kidnap them again to ship them off to Brazil.' He sucked in his cheeks. 'If they do let you in and you get to know them, you'll find they have hearts of gold.'

I saw one, lighter-skinned than the rest, stand and look across at us, a hand raised to shade his eyes. My heart missed a beat when I recognised Miranda's father, Sebastiao. He raised his shovel in a wave, which I returned, only to see Cain beside me wave back and I wondered with some embarrassment if I'd misread his signal.

We stepped down to the laneway and began walking, with Cain pointing out and explaining the processes.

To our left was a line of six saw windmills and, at the end, a seventh smaller mill. The third of these was slowly turning, the sawblades within it grinding and screeching irregularly as we passed. The laneway separated them from the two brackish ponds on our right. In the second of these, I counted three rafts of logs I took for trunks of yellow pine or maybe larch. They were debarked and lashed together, their backs exposed to the pale sunlight. A labourer was balancing carefully across them, bucket in hand, filling it and tipping water over them.

Beyond the ponds against the distant southern fence was a cluster of wooden cottages, blue smoke spiralling into the still air from brick chimneys. Colourful washing hung from lines between them, and several small children were playing in the yards between beds of vegetables. They were the married quarters, Cain explained.

'They're out of bounds to the likes of you three,' he added with a warning glare.

We reached the seventh windmill at the end of the row, smaller than the others. It was also slowly turning. I saw beside it a light spray of water showering from outlets along a pipe that ran above logs and planks piled neatly in tiered pyramids. They stood on a raised brick platform, the wastewater leaching down into a wide drain, its grill lid visible at the base of its foundations.

'This is our little miracle,' Cain told us. 'She's our water pumping windmill—the beating heart of the process here. We're in trouble she ever breaks down.' He tapped Axel's head with the knuckle of his forefinger. 'Touch wood she won't and we don't run out of wind.'

Beyond the mill lay a spectacular wetland surrounded by reeds and willows, its shallows edged with thriving water plants, a thin crust of ice shimmering here and there between them. It was teeming with birds, domestic ducks diving beneath the glassy surface and black moorhens scooting busily across it. Three years before, Daniel and I had gone bird-nesting there, looking for eggs, until the gamekeeper had screamed a warning and fired two salt-packed shells from his *donderbus*[19] over our heads as we ran for our lives. I looked for the gamekeeper. There was no sign of him.

We stood and admired the lake as Cain explained that it was the sedimentation pond, purifying the run-off water drained from the sprinklers, as well as brackish water pumped from the ponds, which the pumping mill then recycled. I estimated the lake to be a Waterlandse Morgen[20] in area.

---

19 Blunderbuss shotgun, just coming into common use.
20 *Waterlandse morgen* equals 10,700 square metres of wetland.

'We run the sprinklers to avoid the timber drying out. You'll find out why once you start work.'

He pointed at the pyramids of wet logs. 'Logs piled high like this can be dangerous, especially when they're wet. So remember one thing, boys, above all else. Think safety first! Everything you do here will have an element of danger attached to it. Take your time. Watch how the others approach their work. Do *not* rush in headfirst.'

He reached out and tapped the closest pyramid with his rake handle. 'Let Otello serve as a warning. I'll tell you how he lost his arm. Five years ago, he came down here from the kitchen one morning to take a shower. Three labourers were building a pyramid, similar to these. They were halfway through the task when the labourer at the top slipped and the logs began to move. Had they fallen, the two below him would have been killed, no doubt about it. Let alone himself.

'As it was, Otello jumped forward without a second thought. His upraised left arm was caught between two rolling logs that wound it in up to his armpit like a wet sheet squeezed through a box mangle. But with the strength of his right arm and the bulk of his neck and shoulder, he stopped the movement in the logs in time for the three labourers to escape and come to his rescue. So did every worker in the yards. He was trapped for almost half an hour while they dismantled the pile. His arm was crushed beyond repair. Sebastiao amputated it right here while he was unconscious. The rope that Abel tied round his arm saved his life. I helped him wind it tight enough to stop the bleeding, using a stick tied through a loop.' He gazed at us as the story sank in. 'He was in the Gasthuis Hospital for several months. We thought we'd lost him.'

We found the story both horrifying and fascinating, especially when he asked, 'What colour do you think his blood was?'

'Is that a trick question?' Nikolaas asked.

'Do you think it is?'

'No.'

'Then why do you ask?'

'I don't know. Red?'

'You're not sure?'

'Red. It must be red.'

'And what colour is yours? Also red?'

'Of course.'

'If you remember anything from your time here, make sure you remember that.'

'What? That my blood is red?' Nikolaas was incredulous.

Cain did not reply. He was silent as he led us across to a workman debarking a pine log balanced on trestles at either end. When we reached him, Cain turned to us. 'That we all share the same red blood, no matter the colour of our skins or nationalities.'

He nodded at the labourer who was panting and lathered in sweat despite the cold, holding a broad two-handled draw knife ready for the next stroke. 'This is Konrad, from Hamburg. He doesn't speak Dutch. *Zeigen Sie ihnen, wie es gemacht wird.* Go ahead, show them how it's done.'

'*Es ist einfach.* It's simple,' Konrad muttered, taking a step back and stretching out his arms to engage the blade against the next strip of bark at the top. He dragged it towards himself, peeling the bark away deceptively easily, chunks showering over his boots. He reached out again, this time to the side of the previous stroke, with the same result. After several similar swift strokes, he rotated the log, grunting with the effort, and debarked the opposite side. Then he shaved the knots in the wood with special care, passing the palms of both hands over them to make sure the surface was flush, before stepping aside and smiling blandly at us.

'You boys got that?' Cain asked. When each of us had

nodded, 'Konrad is in charge,' he went on. 'You each have a trestle and five spare logs to get on with. Remember, it's not a race. Make sure you work as a team. You're equally responsible for getting the whole job done by this evening.' He signalled a thumbs up at Konrad as he turned to leave. 'When you hear Otello ring the mess hall bell it will be time for lunch.'

Cain stepped back and stood with his arms folded across his chest. Frowning thoughtfully, he contemplated each of us in turn. When he gazed at me, he resembled an old and wrinkled Calvinist predicant about to deliver a sermon of fire and brimstone. Instead of that, the concern in his voice surprised me.

'Welcome to your next two months, boys,' he said. 'It's going to be tough, but I'm sure you're made of sterner stuff than your appearances suggest.' He smiled gently at Axel, reaching out to pinch his bicep. 'Especially you, my son. Learn all you can. Work hard. Follow Konrad's example and heed his instructions.' Turning to leave, he reminded us, 'I'll see you at lunch, but you don't get dinner this evening until this job is done. Not until it's completed to Konrad's satisfaction,' he kicked at the pile of scrap bark beside his foot, 'right down to clearing up the rubbish… even if you have to work into the night.'

About to go, he turned back on his heel and barked, 'Young Gerrit here mentioned Sisyphus. Be as persistent as he was pushing that rock uphill. But make sure you also remember *Icarus*. Get too carried away with yourselves and *I'll* be the one trimming your wings, never mind the sun melting the wax.'

At the end of that first day, I was in a state of collapse when I reached the boarding house dormitory. It was a far cry from the Latijn School I'd attended until the previous November and I felt an unexpected wave of nostalgia for the two-storeyed redbrick building I'd been so pleased to leave, now wryly recalling the comfort of its blazing fireplaces lit in the depth of freezing winters, its twin chimneys smoking.

Lying in my bunk after a late dinner, unable to sleep, disturbed by the snores and frequent farts of the workmen around me, I amused myself by comparing these new and unfamiliar noises with the drone of teachers instilling Latin rhetoric, logic and poetry selected from Seneca, Horace, Ovid and Virgil; the sudden snap and creak of wooden bunks as sleepers turned with the crack of the cane; and the smells of sleeping bodies with the overpowering stench of pickled herring, cod, plaice and eels that had sometimes wafted across the school grounds from the fish market two streets away.

As I drifted into sleep, I ran my mind through the proverbs of Jacob Cats I'd memorised, bemused by the irony of my homesickness for an institution from which I previously couldn't escape fast enough.

My last thought was of the ship we would be working on in two months, *Will I soon be assisting carpenters to install planks of yellow pine sawn from the logs I debarked today?* That thought brought with it a deeply satisfying feeling of elation. *My backbreaking, muscle-tearing work here will form part of its construction!*

We woke at dawn when Otello's hammering at the iron ring dragged us from sleep. It was a deafening warning that we were about to face a second day more brutal than the first. Our bodies with their aching muscles, joints and tendons were barely responsive, until Cain appeared, rake in hand, thumping at our bedclothes with its handle.

Once we were up, he shepherded us out onto the gravel and down to the water pump, where we had to strip and take a freezing open-air shower before breakfast.

'That'll wake you lazy donkeys up!' he insisted while we were dressing again, shivering violently with the cold.

So began our second day, also spent labouring at the debarking trestles with Konrad—a routine we followed for the rest of that first week. It was a nightmare that left us fatigued beyond belief each evening, grateful for the scant comfort of the straw-filled mattress and the sleep of the dead through the night.

Our duties varied after that, and periods of welcome respite were infrequent as we worked among Danish, German and Belgian labourers—vagrant immigrants who spoke little Dutch, who had left their home villages in search of a better life in Zeeland.

We offloaded trunks of spruce, pine, oak and larch from the *Zwaarte Leeuw* when she arrived in the third week, manhandling them onto the davits and pulleys of the mobile crane at the jetty before carting them to the ponds. We removed and chopped up logs stained blue with fungal infestation, brown with tannin, or ruined by beetle attack. We painted the ends of the dry-stored logs with a wax-based sealer to prevent them cracking and checking, and we cleaned and greased the great wooden cogs of the gears and machinery in the saw windmills, sharpening each of the saw blade teeth to a polished razor-like keenness. And once, for five claustrophobic hours, Nikolaas and I assisted poor Axel, the smallest of us, with the filthiest job of all—crawling into the water drain leading to the sedimentation pond to clear it when it was clogged, bucketing out the mud and rubble he shovelled back to us.

During the fifth week, at the beginning of February, I felt that an extraordinary change had come over me. I felt strong. Fit. Broader in the shoulders and deeper in the chest. My sixteenth birthday lay ahead in June and I sensed I was maturing, able to hold my own in the teams within which I worked. Able to look my co-workers in the eye, respond to their teasing, give as good as, or sometimes even better than I got. All this without losing sight of the fact that I was an apprentice, available at Cain's beck and call and dependent on him for a good report.

That week, he directed me to work for the first time with the Afro-Zeelander group of eight senior lumbermen—the terse, muscular mulatten he'd warned us about the day we'd arrived.

I knew they were descended from a shipment of 130 Angolan slaves aboard a Portuguese caravel from the island of Sao Tomé, captured while on its way to Brazil by the Dutch privateer *Eenhorn*. The story was legendary. They had landed in Middelburg in 1596. As soon as they had been baptised as Christians in the Reformed Church, they had been granted their tickets of leave. Overgrootvader Hendrick had known the Dutch schipper who'd captured the caravel, but his name had escaped Opa Laurens, who'd passed the story down to me. That was all I knew; the barest outline of their history. I was keen to learn more.

The supervisor, Sebastiao, instructed me to assist two of his lumbermen working on saw windmill number five that memorable first day. I was to help them remove the worn hemp cloth sails, replace any rusted bolts connecting the sweep-spars to their stocks, and repair sections of the lattices that had rotted through. It was dangerous work but I found it exhilarating, perched high on the scaffolding, a safety rope about my waist. For seven glorious hours, I passed different tools, new bolts and fresh battens of larch to the lumbermen when they required them. I had time to spare while they were working and, just as I had on my window ledge at home when I was younger, I felt once more that I was sailing free across the oceans.

Back in the mess hall that evening, Sebastiao invited me to join them at their table during dinner. It was an unexpected privilege and, when I was welcomed by the group, who shifted along the bench to make room for me, I was overwhelmed. But not for long. They treated me as though I belonged there, a brief nod from each sufficing for a communal greeting before they turned back to their lively conversations while they enjoyed the stew piled high on their plates, washing it down with *roemers*[21] *of local Drie Tonnen bier* —Three Barrels beer.

They were talking in Dutch, which surprised me. Earlier in the day, I'd heard the lumbermen I was working with talking in a mixture of what I thought was Portuguese and a language I'd never heard, its intonations and pronunciation strangely musical.

I sat listening in fascinated silence as I ate, amazed at what I took to be their tacit acceptance of me. *Or is it in acknowledgment of Mama's kindness in offering to train Miranda, who is now qualified and working in the Gasthuis Hospital?*

After dinner, the darkest-skinned among them, who had introduced himself to me that morning as Serafino, *de Zwarte Prins*, the Black Prince, gave me a surprise sideways nod of invitation as they made their way to the end of the veranda, as they'd done each evening after dinner throughout the time we'd been there.

I trailed after them, despite my fatigue, and squatted outside the circle they formed. Several had thumb pianos with upturned tines they began to quietly twang, one had an empty metal canister he drummed with the fingers of both hands and, when Otello later joined the group, he had a worn tambourine he rattled against his knee. I found the sounds and cadence hypnotic, its background hum and the occasional quietly singing voice accompanying rather than interfering with the talking. Whenever the music stopped, there was a complementary silence, the conversation resuming as soon as it was taken up again.

---

21 Large drinking glasses.

I should have brought my Queen Conches, I thought. *I wonder what they would have made of the sounds they produce.*

At one point in the evening, Serafino stepped across to join me.

'*Je hebt het goed gedaan vandaag, jonge kerel,*' he said when he'd squatted and leant back into the veranda railing. 'You did well today, young fellow.'

'I didn't know you were watching me.'

'I wasn't. Lourenco and Marais both vouched for you. They've asked for you to work with them again tomorrow.'

'Will that be that all right with Cain?'

'It will. Sebastiao has influence.'

'Thank you. I'd like that.'

'Good. That's settled. Now, I have observed your interest in us.'

He looked askance at me, eyebrows raised, as though wondering if I had anything to ask him, but I was uncertain whether he'd posed a question or made a statement.

Then he broke the silence. '*Ebuê?*'

The expressive way he'd voiced this strange new word, accentuating it as though it was the musical sound of a question, prompted me to reply, 'You are right. I am curious.'

'About?'

'Well, you, to begin with. Are you a prince?'

His teeth flashed in the lantern light. 'No. But I am *ya makala.* I am black… the blackest here. I am *Muene ya Makala,* the Black Prince. That's my nickname.' He smiled broadly again. 'And you see Otello over there? He's *Ndundu Dibanga,* Albino the Rock! You'll surprise him if you call him that.'

'What language is that?'

'*Kikongo ya munu kituba…* Kikongo is our language. Our *bambuta bampika*, our slave ancestors brought it with them a hundred years ago. None of us speaks it well now. Portuguese, a little. Dutch, yes. But Kikongo-kituba?' He shook his head, his mouth drawn down and his bottom lip protruding slightly in a grimace. 'We are second generation, as you know, so a few of us have only slight memories of it.'

I observed him with interest as he rubbed his palms together thoughtfully before giving me a keen look. 'You understand that the language you are born with ties you to your country and your people? Without it, you no longer belong. You cannot truly communicate. You are someone lost at sea. You are someone carried into slavery. As we are. Or were.'

He gave me a thoughtful smile in which I saw sadness, but sadness tempered by what? Determination? Resoluteness in the face of ill-fortune?

'Imagine landing in a place where no one speaks your language and you have to learn theirs to communicate.' He gazed at me as though wondering if I could comprehend a situation I had yet to experience and possibly never would. 'You lose part of yourself. You lose your spirit. It vanishes with every new word you have to learn. You become someone else.'

After a brief silence, he added emphatically, 'That may be us, but we are survivors and above all else, *free*.' He closed his fist and struck his chest above his heart. 'Free to choose not to brood over our history, *jonge*, but to acknowledge it… and to use that knowledge to work towards a future that is safer and better for us.' He raised his eyebrows and gazed keenly at me as though ensuring I was following him. 'That way we keep hope alive, especially for our children.'

'You have children?'

'Not yet. Some others do.'

Then he opened up his palm and showed me his extended thumb fractionally separated from the tip of his forefinger. 'We may be partly Dutch, but only by *that* much. Just *one* drop of white blood. With me, it doesn't show! I am *Muene ya*

Makala, a true Angolan man, a fisherman from the Kisolongo coast!' His teeth flashed again as he broke into triumphant and ironic laughter. '*Eé!* I am *ya makala mulat*, married to a blonde and blue-eyed beauty from Friesland—my perfect Severine! *Beto ke ebene mpi ivuari.* Together we are ebony and ivory. A perfect match!'

When he'd gathered his breath, he asked abruptly, 'Anything else?'

I responded at once. 'Cain suggested you were all afraid of being sent back into slavery.'

'Ah! *Now* we get down to the heart of the matter! What do you know about us?'

He listened intently as I told him what I knew of his origins.

He did not comment for some minutes. He appeared to be concentrating on the music playing beside us, gathering himself, before he turned abruptly towards me, his expression intense. He confirmed that all I'd said was true, but that I only had half the story. Yes, they were descended from slaves brought to Middelburg aboard a Portuguese caravel captured by a Dutch privateer in 1596.

'That was the *Gouden Eenhorn*, the Golden Unicorn,' he said, before draining his glass, 'and we haven't forgotten the name of the schipper. It was Melchior van der Kerckhoven. And yes,' he went on, placing his glass carefully upside down on the floorboards beside him, 'there *were* one hundred and thirty of our ancestors led ashore—men, women and children, who were granted their freedom by the Zeeland courts after they were baptised Christians. What you clearly do *not* know, is that the owner of the *Gouden Eenhorn*, Pieter van der Haegen, whose name we *also* remember only too well, appealed to the Supreme Court in The Hague. Three months later, the judges there tore up our tickets of leave and handed our ancestors back to him.' He threw up his hands. 'To do as he pleased.'

He rocked back and forth against the railing, frowning. The lantern light caught the muscle in his jaw shifting as he appeared to grind his teeth. 'And what did he do? He rounded up our ancestors and shipped them off to Bahia in Brazil. He made his fortune after all, selling them and slave trading for years after that!'

I waited for more, but he had turned away again to listen to the single thumb piano that was then playing.

When it stopped, I pointed out, 'But all of *you* are still here.'

He stood as the group started to disperse, then looked down at me, nodding. 'We are, what's left of us. The people of Middelburg at the time insisted that the men who had already found work, along with the women and children who wanted to stay, should be allowed to remain in Zeeland. The local magistrates agreed. We've been working in this timber yard ever since.'

He hesitated as he turned to leave. 'Nine of our ancestors died when the decision was made, the week before they were due to be loaded back on the ship. They're buried in a corner of the cemetery close to your house.'

Close to my house? He knows where I live?

He saw my surprise. 'Of course you didn't know. Why should you? We often visit the grave to pay our respects.' He looked me directly in the eye. 'Was it suicide, do you think? Or grief?' He gazed at me, his eyebrows raised, then went on, 'It was both, of course. When we gather there we're meeting on *African* soil. It's our special place. It's sacred to us.' He reached down to pick up his empty roemer. 'We bring their bones back to life when we remember them, *jonge*. When we celebrate their act of defiance, their *escape*, we celebrate our own.'

I stood and dusted myself down, unable to respond.

As though sensing my discomfort, he smiled and nodded. 'We used to see you sitting in your window when you were a boy.'

See me in my window? That was years ago. Ah, they must have been looking out for Miranda. 'Do their graves have markers?'

'Only one—a large piece of limestone carved by Lourenco's grandfather. They were buried beside each other in a common grave.'

'Is it a cross?'

'No. An open book. One page lists their names, the other is blank. It's the book they carry when they go to meet *Nzambi a Mpungu*, the Divine Judge—the book that is supposed to tell the story of their lives.' He began walking away down the veranda, following the group. 'In their case, the blank page represents the life they were unable to fulfil, the life that was stolen from them. On the other are their names. Lourenco does his best to preserve them.' He slowed and looked back at me. 'Reading them brings them back to us.'

I caught up with him.

'You asked if I have children and I told you not yet,' he said. He patted his stomach. 'I should have said I will, soon. My Severine is carrying. We expect our first in May.' He gave me a sudden brilliant smile. 'With his or her birth, *Angola* will be reborn and in future, share the best of both our worlds!'

'That's excellent,' I congratulated him as we reached the dormitory door. 'Thank you for talking to me. I have learned much.'

He turned to descend the steps and join several others who were waiting for him to walk across to the married quarters.

'Thank you for listening.' He placed a hand on my shoulder. 'We have a saying in Kikongo. See if you can memorise it. *Tosali menga mosi.*'

'*Tosali menga mosi.*'

'*Ya mboté*, very good.' He went down the steps, looking back at me. 'We may all be separate individuals, but *we zijn van één bloed*, we are of one blood.'

THE SIXTH WEEK working with the crew flew past and, on the day we were due to leave, all the workmen in the yards came to the dining hall to watch us face down Otello for the second time. They lined the veranda as we approached with Cain.

Then he surprised us. 'Wait here,' he said and disappeared inside.

Moments later he reappeared with a donderbus and spent several minutes priming and charging it. He leant it against the veranda pillar when he was done and then he drew a line in the gravel across the laneway with the handle of his rake.

'Right. Follow me.' He led us in silence the length of the yards to the pumping windmill.

'This is something we didn't warn you about, boys. It's a race from here to the line I drew at the dining-room door. To warm you up for Otello. You can run in your boots or barefoot, as you choose. Make that decision now.'

Axel bent to remove his boots. He handed them to Cain.

'Right, now I'll walk back to the finish line. When you hear me fire the donderbus, go for your lives. After that, you face Otello. Good luck.'

When the gun fired, Nikolaas took off and left me in his slipstream, beating me by at least three roeden. We turned to wait for Axel, who limped across the line. The gravel had grazed the soles of his feet, and he painfully levered them back into his boots.

Axel was again Otello's first challenger. He took up the same position as he had before, but this time he was less strained, the intensity of his effort protracted, his outstretched legs taut and his feet, despite the pain he must have felt, steady on the floorboards. He laughed aloud at the applause that met his effort, even though Otello's arm had not moved.

Otello looked across and nodded at Cain, who was marking up a report card.

'*Eé,*' he said. 'Yes, he has improved. We should allow him

a score of *makumi zolé*, twenty. *Ana madungu ya nzawu*! He now has the testicles of an elephant!'

I was the next to face up to him. As I gripped his hand, I grinned and looked him in the eye. '*Wa faso*? How are you, *Ndundu Dibanga*? This time I am ready for you.'

He raised his eyebrows and gave me a barely perceptible challenging twitch at the corner of his lips.

Abel yelled for the start and, as I had on the previous occasion, I took a deep breath and exerted all the strength I had. Concentrating from the core, I felt my face redden and no longer heard the cheering of the crowd. I felt strong, unyielding, as though I had an endless store of stamina and energy. Otello's arm did not move, though I sensed a tremor run through it as he increased his effort. Then, for a split second, I deliberately relaxed, before immediately resuming the contest. Otello's arm responded by swinging fractionally across my territory before I forced it back and applied all the reserves of strength I had. To no avail. The outstretched arm was rock-solid and did not budge. When I heard Abel call time and applause erupted, I exhaled and stood panting. I hadn't taken a breath throughout the contest.

Otello smiled, gave me a second slight nod of acknowledgment, and turned to Cain.

'*Eé*,' he said. 'Yes, this young man has improved as well. We should allow him *kumi na uvua*, nineteen. *Tokoi ni mubaku kibakala*. He is a courageous young fox.'

Nikolaas fared no better than either of us, also scoring nineteen. However, he was awarded a pendant that Sebastiao hung around his neck for his win in the sprint—a miniature lion carved in ivory strung on a leather thong; the Zeeland symbol.

On my first day back in the dokhavn, I was handed two buckets and a long-handled brush from the paint shed. I was assigned to whitewashing the inner walls of the moulding loft above the ropewalk.

'Two coats,' the painting foreman informed me. 'I want it done by the end of February and don't leave any brush strokes visible.'

I mixed the lime-wash in a barrel, filled the buckets to the brim and lugged them up the steps to the first storey, where I ducked through the doorway, placed them on the floor and wrung my hands.

There was no one there. I saw several wooden ships' models hanging on pegs on the wall to my left and walked across to look them over. They were arm-length pine block carvings of different hull shapes, painstakingly sawn, whittled and filed to the traditional designs of the last hundred years. I ran my eye over them, counting nine in the row.

Nearest to the door I recognised the latest in the series—a model of the *retourschip* of the First Rate, the new ship on the slipway outside. Laurens had carved it the year before, taking meticulous care of its line, sheer and displacement, and I'd watched from the carving shed when it had been tested on the canal. When Pieter Penne had been satisfied, he'd marked the positions of the fourteen mainframes from stem to stern with shallow vertical saw cuts. Then Opa Laurens had sawn the model into five horizontal planes, each two centimetres thick, to provide mini-templates of the ship's dimensions at different heights above the keel. A single vertical bolt had held the planes together loosely at the stern.

I lifted the model from the peg. The five segments separated as I did so. I realigned them and carried the model to the window. I held it at eye level, sighting along it at the sky. Then I fanned the panels left and right in turn, following the contours of each.

I'm taking aim with a fantastical instrument spanned across my palm, I thought. *A crossbow, firing arrows at any coastline of my choosing… including Eendrachtsland!*

I was returning the model to its peg when one of the mould-makers entered—Solomon Benitez, an old and irascible *conversos* Sephardic Jew, who I had seen in the yard since I was a boy.

He glared at me from beneath bristling eyebrows, the pupils of his eyes glazed blue-grey, like an old dog with early blindness. Silver hair sprouted beneath the rim of his greasy leather skull cap. Opa had warned me about his fearsome rages. It had earned him the ironic nickname of 'Torquemada the Inquisitor'.

'Whenever he loses his temper,' Opa had told me when I was younger, 'his tongue is sharper than the razor-edged adzes he uses.' I had been naïve enough to believe him when he added, 'When he has finished with his victims, he leaves them bleeding.'

'Drop that and you'll be dropped yourself, *jonge kameraad*,' Solomon screamed. 'You'll be crucified by me and not by Romans. Those carvings are out of bounds! You want to get sacked on your first day here?' He snatched the model. 'Next time ask first. Now, follow me.'

Carrying the model, he led me to the pile of planks and battens used to make the moulds for the ship's frames. They lay beside one of the far windows.

'We've got three more moulds to make.' He leant forward arthritically, holding up the model to point them out. 'These ones here I'm talking about. Towards the bow. Once they're done, we'll have the whole set. Then the sailmakers will take over the loft and you and I will be back out with the boys in the yard,' he laughed drily, 'in the wet. You'd better have a strong back. That's when the work really begins.'

He pointed down through the window at several adze-wielding hewers rhythmically hacking curved oak logs into shape. '*That* is where the real art is. We make the moulds up here and they use them as templates to carve the main-frames down there. You need a good eye, a strong forearm and the patience of *God verlaten* Job!'

When he looked back his gaze unnerved me, his milky lenses opaque as fish scales. 'The frame makers, they're the kings of the dokhavn, as you already know, and if you don't, you'll soon find out. They rule the roost. Get on the wrong side of *them* and you'll know all about it. I used to be one myself,' he pointed at his eyes, 'until these went on me.'

At that moment I vividly recalled Opa's advice when he had been teaching me to whittle. He'd insisted that I draft my ideas, visualising them clearly on paper then in my mind's eye, before committing to the first knife stroke. He'd drummed into me the message Overgrootvader Hendrick had earlier impressed on him, 'If you don't know where you're going, how will you know when you've arrived?'

I glanced back through the window. Beyond the frame makers, I could barely make out the slogan Opa had carved into the lintel above the entrance to his carving shed. I couldn't read it, but I knew it by heart, '*Ik zag de Griekse sphinx in de eik en ik sneed tot ik haar vrijgaf,*' I recalled aloud. 'I saw the Grecian sphinx in the oak and carved until I set her free.'

'Michelangelo may have seen his angel trapped in marble,' Opa had once explained, 'but for me, it was the Grecian Sphinx.'

I spent each day whitewashing the loft walls and helping Solomon heave the segments of the last three moulds into the yard where they were assembled.

Eleven mainframes were now almost complete, the frame-makers chiselling and planing them into their final form. Now and then they lit smoky flares at the brazier to scorch their outer edges, preserving them at the point where they'd meet the ship's external planking. Then the overpowering smell of charred timber drifted and, during that first week, I twice looked out with concern, relieved to find no shed going up in flames.

I also took time out now and then to look down from the loft window at the slipway as I painted. I was fascinated as each mainframe was installed and the ship's outer curves became more defined. The shouts of '*Op met het kader van het schip! Op! Op! Het kader! Op!* Up with the ship's frame! Up! Up with the framework! Up!' brought all hands to the pulleys to raise the hefty floor piece and first futtock into position, where it was slotted and bolted to the keel. Teams on the outer scaffolding assembled the rest of the upper framing pieces— the next two futtocks and the top timber—before they braced the completed frames with temporary crosspieces.

And I listened to the discordant mix of dokhavn sounds as I painted, some I'd become familiar with during previous visits to the timber yards. The rustle of the saw windmill sails and the creak of their axles, the thump of the great cogs spinning the gears that turned the circular saws, for example. Others I was less used to were now louder and more persistent. The hammering, the intermittent sigh and squeal of planes, the screech of drills and augers driven from the gut or shoulder of carpenters grunting and swearing as they worked the bits into the seasoned wood of keelson and frame-futtock and top-timbers.

By the end of February, when I'd finished the first coat and was applying the second, the ship looked like a gargantuan rib cage on an outstretched spine. Each frame was supported by angled props tenoned into chocks on the bricked slipway and suspended in a web of ropes and pulleys. A massive inner keelson ran the length of the ship over the floor pieces, scarphed in its turn into immense supporting knees behind the sternpost and the stem. It was an inner walkway, along which I observed labourers wheeling barrows to deliver buckets of treenails to journeymen carpenters working the length of the ship. Impatience began building as I rushed to apply the second coat. *How soon will I be helping them do that?*

When temporary ribbands were pinned outside the frames in sweeping curves the full length of the ship, I was amazed at her immense dimensions. The first of the external bottom planks were fitted, their edges set in grooves along the keel and their ends curved into slots in the stem and sternpost. Whenever I went down to refill the buckets, I felt an overpowering sense of awe as she towered above me and dwarfed the workmen busy on the three-tiered scaffolding that surrounded her.

On the first day of March, when I only had half a wall to complete, I watched Pieter Penne supervise the raising of the subtly shortened stern frame—the fifteen-ton transom. It was a challenge lasting two full days. Every workman turned out to assist or watch as the *meister* straddled the structure, screaming instructions as it was inched off the ground, his judgement ensuring the manoeuvre didn't distort the transom's shape.

I found the delicate precision with which the teams laboured on the mobile capstans that lifted the huge frame intriguing. I held my breath as it rose, inch by inch, until it hung vertically between guyed sheerlegs. They winched it into position, its rear recess guided into the stern-and-inner posts by a team of carpenters heaving overhead, their agitated yells of warning and instruction echoing. Locked into place, at last, the two crosspiece transom timbers at the height of each deck spread like gigantic wings across the stern, the upright frames of the after-gallery windows spanning the width of the ship.

She looked magical to me.

LATER THAT WEEK we experienced an unseasonal cold spell, with three days of freezing sleet. The canal iced over, its surface covered with a thin layer as clear and reflective as glass when the weak sun broke through on the first fine day.

That evening, when I went down to the carving shed to meet Opa for the walk home, he was nowhere to be seen. I called out for him, peering into the shadows where the rows of blocks and carvings stood. When I stepped across the threshold I was caught from behind, a pair of arms pinioning me despite my struggling.

A sack was dragged over my head and pulled below my waist. A lanyard threaded through the sack's seam was lashed tight and knotted beneath my hips and around each leg. I couldn't dislodge it.

I stood shocked and shaken, unsure what was coming next, when my legs were knocked from under me. I fell winded to the floor. My boots were removed by two pairs of hands, then my trousers, leaving me in woollen workers' long johns. I was picked up and carried by feet and armpits across the shipyard and tipped headfirst into an empty barrel. Someone hammered home the lid, locking it against the soles of my feet.

I heard a roar of laughter as the barrel was tipped on its side, rolled some distance and stood on end. Dizzy, barely able to breathe, coughing from the dusty residue in the sack, I found myself upside-down. Unable to move and in semi-darkness, I could see through the hessian that pale light was filtering through holes drilled into the lid beneath my feet. I heard the echo of barrel staves and iron hoops on flagstones and what I thought was Axel's muffled shouting, as other barrels rolled towards me.

I caught the unmistakable sound of the shipyard carthorse hauling a timber dray alongside on its iron skids. My barrel was the last to be hoisted aboard and the dray shuddered forwards, screeching on the paving.

I listened to the impact of hooves as we crossed the Buitenhaven Bridge, then heard the odd shout of the cart driver to passers-by. The distant clang of the *stadhuis* bell sounded six o'clock as the cart clattered on the cobbles of what I took to be the Houwerstraat along the inner canal. The raucous sound of singing from taverns along its embankment carried to me and I smelled the rich odours of Three Barrels beer and the reek of pipe smoke.

The skids hissed across the wooden Langeviele Bridge, then the horse stopped abruptly beside the Kloveniersdoelen building, home to the *schutters*, the Guild of Riflemen. I heard one barrel clatter to the sidewalk, a single furious shout of complaint coming from Nikolaas.

Ten minutes further along, my barrel was rolled to the end of the cart and dropped onto the grass, thankfully the right way up.

The cart driver slapped the lid twice and shouted, 'Time for your second birth, *jonge kerel!* Time to make your way back into the world,' he gave a coarse laugh, 'without the help of a midwife's forceps! No good crying for your mama's nipple now—you're on your own! And make sure you're at work on time tomorrow. There's more in store for you there. You don't want to miss the fun.'

The cart ground back onto the bricked road and skidded away.

I could not budge. There was no response to my shouts for help. Within half an hour I was suffering excruciating cramps in both legs, the barrel lids compressing the back of my neck and the soles of my feet. Waves of panic ran through me. I was freezing.

Crouching in that confined position, I strained to listen for passing voices and the clunk of clogs on the embankment. I heard nothing for what seemed hours until the distant rattles of the curfew watchmen reached me at ten, and I caught the last faint calls of revellers emptying from the taverns across the canal. My only visitor was a sniffing dog that urinated against the barrel staves, as I was forced to do moments later inside the barrel.

Then I recalled the shock, self-blame and grief I had experienced the day Papa had failed to return. Certainty and security shattered, I'd felt exposed to forces beyond my understanding and control. And yet, despite my grief and confusion that day, I'd known I must endure, must struggle to overcome the terror and the dread.

Trapped in that suffocating space, I was overtaken by rage.

I rocked the barrel until it rolled slowly sideways, corkscrewing down an embankment I didn't know was there. When it came to rest, I pounded my feet on the lid, my head forced into the far corner, my neck rigid. I attacked the lid for several minutes, my determination intensifying as I heard the screech of nails giving way. At last one foot burst through the cracking timber. I kicked at the shattered panel until I was able to crawl free and then lay on the grass gulping the icy air.

I could not remove the sack, though my arms were free inside it. I couldn't see until the broken branch of a blackberry bush penetrated the sack's weave, scratching my face. I enlarged the hole and, peering through it, climbed the embankment. I took my bearings and then began the long walk home along the southern embankment of the Heerengracht Canal to avoid the empty taverns and the city centre.

I crossed the bridge at Kuiperspoort close to home, my feet numb, my mind fixed on banking up the embers of the peat fire, anticipating the warmth of fresh clothes and Mama and Opa's greetings when they answered the sound of the *Santiago*'s bell.

That thought brought on a spasm of coughing and laughter. *I'll be ringing it with my head!*

Opposite the Kloveniersdoelen building, I passed Nikolaas's barrel. It was overturned and empty. There was no sign of Axel's.

When I reached the front door, I leant in and struck the bell with my forehead. The ringing sound was so dull I realised neither Opa nor Mama would hear it, so I stepped up to the door, stretched back and head-butted it. Twice. I was about to strike it for the third time when the door opened and I saw Opa silhouetted against the lantern light.

He stepped back to let me in, stifling a burst of laughter as he led me to the full-length mirror in the voorkamer. I peered at my reflection through the hessian and grinned. *I look like someone at a hanging or, better still, after one, dishevelled, covered in hessian and reeking of urine as I do.*

Opa turned me round, cut the ties, and lifted the sack over my head. This time he was unable to contain himself. 'I knew it,' he roared, 'they used the indigo sacks! Anneka, come take a look. We have a Moorish Arab visitor. You won't recognise your son.'

In the mirror, I saw Mama's reflection rush from the kitchen and stand behind me, a hand over her mouth as she began to shake with laughter. I joined her when I saw that my hair and face were streaked with blue dye, along with my clothes and hands.

When I glanced back at Mama in the mirror, I saw her gazing at me looking into her eyes and, in that uncanny recursive moment, it seemed my mind opened up to hers and I was flooded with the joy I saw there. Or was it love?

'Oh, *Goede Heer*, Good Lord.' She giggled, looking closer. 'What are we going to do with you? You look like one of those Tuareg nomads we've heard about. Even your eyelashes are blue!'

'You're a young Viking,' Opa suggested, 'wearing woad for war paint.'

As I peered back at my face, the strangest memory crossed my mind. *It's the same shade of blue I used to colour my map of Eendrachtsland at school years ago! Now I really belong there.*

Mama led me to the kitchen where the fire was banked high and a pan of *hutsepot* stew was bubbling on the stove. The zinc bath beside the far wall was filled with water, steam rising. She handed me an ash-handled scrubbing brush and a bar of lye soap, then cut me a slice of rye bread and ladled me a plate of stew. Opa had already placed a brimming roemer of beer on the kitchen table.

'Eat first. The bath will take you a long while.' She smiled. 'Enjoy the beer while you're in the tub. I'll leave Opa to scrub your back. I'll be the maestra playing the clavichord.'

No MATTER HOW hard I scrubbed, I couldn't remove the blue from my skin. While it faded slightly, my efforts simply spread the stain more evenly across the affected parts. The backs of my hands carried the circular patterns of the scrubbing brush, as though I'd applied henna, and my scalp and hair were an intriguing pale blue tint.

The cart driver had mentioned that there was more in store for us. When I asked Opa, he raised his eyebrows and placed a finger across his lips. 'For me to know.' He took a silver *daalder*[22] from his pocket and flashed it mysteriously to and fro before my eyes. 'And for you to find out.'

When I joined Axel and Nikolaas at the dokhavn, I discovered they were both stained as blue as I was, though Axel's shade was still a deeper blue.

I described how I'd broken out of the barrel and rung the bell with my head.

'I can go one better, Gerrit,' Nikolaas responded. 'At least you were wearing long johns. I wasn't, so I'm blue all over.

---

22 Dollar—worth thirty *stuivers* or thirty shillings.

Even my bits and pieces and my legs. They're as blue as the rest of me.'

I smiled at him. 'Like a mandrill baboon?'

'Exactly like one!'

He explained that a canal ferryman who overheard his shouts had released him as the curfew was sounding.

'I was only wearing my shirt and jacket, so I borrowed the ferryman's knife to cut holes in the corners of the sack to put my bare legs through and cover my *zaadballen*, my tackle. Then I ran the gauntlet through the streets. *Jongens*, were they crowded! You should have seen me go. I was so fast I must have been a blue blur.' He pulled the lion pendant from beneath his shirt. 'Reckon I deserved to win a second one of these.'

Axel told us he'd endured the entire night choking in his barrel until a passing milkman had rescued him as the sun was rising. He'd ridden home among the churns in the back of the dairy-dray under wet canvas for warmth.

'I haven't had time for good wash yet. I came straight here from breakfast,' he said, and then, with a slow shake of his head and a disenchanted smile, 'I felt like a cat-in-the-box waiting for the mallet. *De hele bloedige nacht*, the whole bloody night.'

'Nice comparison,' Nikolaas commented, patting his shoulder. 'A *kat-in-de-doos*.'

'That's for sure,' I agreed.

I thought his image of a captive cat in a wooden box strung from a tavern beam as a target for crushing cudgel blows was apt. I had felt the same—like a yowling animal about to leap from the smashed box as all hell broke loose until an accurate blow crushed its skull, the panting winner waving the dead cat in triumph overhead by the scruff of its neck, his reward a night of free brandy.

When we reported to Alois, as we always did at the start of the shift, he cackled with laughter. 'Don't look so upset, *jongens.* The colour suits you. And there's plenty more where that came from.' He grinned. 'They're all waiting for you, every last one. Follow me.'

He led us across the yard to the paint shed. Everyone was there. The shed itself was packed, with standing room only inside, and those who couldn't get in were gathered at the three open windows.

An ironic cheer erupted when Alois led us through the crowd to an open space at the centre, where he lined us up at the end of what looked like a runway three roeden long. He placed me between Nikolaas and Axel, so that our heights descended, tallest to the left. My boots, I noticed, were sticking to the floorboards in a thick carpet of treacly foam.

Alois reached down, put his right forefinger into it and lifted it to his lips. He took a quick taste and nodded as he addressed the room. 'A perfect blend, gentlemen. Three parts linseed oil, a fistful or two of red ochre and an *aam*[23] of pitch… with a splash of vinegar for extra flavour.'

Then he reached into the pocket of his overalls and withdrew three silver spoons. 'See these?' He fanned them and showed each of us the engraving in the bowl. 'You each have one—you see your names? And you *push* them,' he said, bending to lay a spoon at our feet with one hand, tapping his nose with the other, 'with *this!*'

He pointed at the spoons. 'From here…' he pointed at the far end of the foam, 'to there. And *fast!* It's a race, *jongens,* and may the best among you win. Because the last of you will receive a longer beating from your jockey!' He took out a large silver *rijksdaalder,* holding it up to each of us in turn. 'There's money on it, *jongens.* The room is full of gamblers, so I wouldn't want to be the one to lose!' He put the coin back in his pocket.

---

23 A measure used in the wine trade—approximately one hundred and fifty-five litres.

'But I don't put my money on you. I'm the handicapper and the referee. So remember, don't let your backers down.'

Three large carpenters stepped towards us carrying blindfolds and riding crops custom-made from flat lengths of batten. My heart sank when I saw Erasmus Klinkhamer among them, a *beelsnijder*, a woodcarver from Opa's workshop and the fattest man in the dokhavn. The crowd roared advice as they inspected us. It was deafening. They checked the width of our backs and the strength of our arms and, above all, the length and breadth of our noses, giving them a vigorous tweak between thumb and forefinger.

Of course Erasmus selected me and I had no doubt Opa had put him up to it. *I'll have words with him later!*

Then Alois declared the odds and last-minute bets were traded. I was down at five to one, Alex an outsider at ten to one, and Nikolaas the favourite at two to one.

We went down on all fours. Erasmus blindfolded me and engaged my nose in the bowl of my spoon. Starter's orders sounded and, for several forcibly-steered, hard-ridden, foul-tasting minutes I nose-pushed the spoon through the foam, carrying Erasmus towards the finishing line. After what I was later told was a promising start when I led the field, I momentarily lost my spoon. I recovered it too late, halfway down the straight.

'You lost me five dollars, *mijn kleinzoon*,' Opa complained after the race.

'*Wraak is zoet*, Revenge is sweet.' I smiled triumphantly.

After the race, which Alex won, Erasmus dusted me with oakum followed by a bucket of itchy sawdust before unmasking me. I imagined the whites of my eyes standing out in my face stained blue from ear to ear, as Alex's and Nikolaas's were.

Then Erasmus, clutching my collar, hauled me across the dokhavn paving and up the steps to the Maisbaai embankment. We were accompanied by the crowd. Erasmus and another carpenter picked me up foot-and-wrist and swung me backwards and forwards for momentum, to the crowd's deafening count of five, before they hurled me into the freezing Buitenhaven canal. At the last moment, I saw Nikolaas and Alex flying through the air behind me, their arms and legs wildly windmilling.

I crashed through the sheet of ice on my back and clawed my frenzied way back to the embankment, where several workmen reached down to haul me out.

The crowd was raucously applauding, and I knew the induction was over. I was a full member of the Shipwright's Guild at last, symbolised by the baptismal spoon that Erasmus was waving at me.

Now Erasmus and his partner lifted me onto their shoulders and carried me back across the shipyard through the cheering crowd. I read my name engraved along the handle of the spoon and saw a fully rigged ship flying downwind etched in the bowl. The VOC insignia, with the Z for Zeeland brand across it, was inscribed on the back. I brandished it triumphantly overhead.

The challenge of those tests gave me a new sense of maturity and power. I had overcome my helplessness in the barrel and for days I relived the wave of confidence and relief I'd experienced when I'd emerged from it onto the blackberries. No longer a victim, I faced the world with an invigorating sense belonging. Reborn. Fiercely *alive*.

The Zeeland motto enamelled on the shield on the front door of the house took on new significance for me. *Luctor et emergo*—I struggle and I emerge.

During the next three months, I was in my element. I'd completed the painting of the sail loft and was allocated to different teams working on the hull. I could not get enough of it. I learnt new skills I'd looked forward to acquiring since I was a boy, soaking up all the advice and practical wisdom the tradesmen around me passed on.

And I was participating in building what I considered a great machine, a brilliant craft newly designed to explore the vast and empty spaces opening up to us across the globe.

The excitement was intoxicating and I discovered my energy was boundless. I climbed over the hull delivering tools to the carpenters—awls or file-toothed saws, chisels and plane blades I'd sharpened, augers and drills I'd cleaned and oiled. I loved vaulting monkey-like from one level to the next, a leather bag slung over my shoulder, climbing the diagonal braces installed crosswise from floor to beam, or shinning up the central stanchions that ran down the middle of the ship, supporting the decks above.

I filled barrows with oak treenails I'd learned to cut and turn, upending them into buckets I topped up for carpenters working at different stations along the framework. I assisted as the crossbeams of the two decks were installed and worked with the teams placing the hanging and lodging knees that reinforced them. I helped manoeuvre the filler frames into place, ribbing the ship between the fourteen mainframes, or I leant into the weight of the curved and bowed knee pieces as the carpenters bolted them into position.

As the ship neared completion, Nikolaas, Alex and I worked together to carry weighty carved chunks of deadwood oak to the carpenters to reinforce the uprights. And we walked the full length of the ship when called on to remove the slender ribbands pinned outside the frames from stem to stern, used to guide the carpenters installing the outer planking.

I sailed through one of my early exams and was exhilarated by my result. Blindfolded, I successfully recognised different timbers from the scent of their sawdust and shavings despite the pervasive background tang of pitch and turpentine. There was the fresh resinous smell of yellow pine that sometimes gave me a touch of hay fever, the oily spice of cedar and the pungency of elm, the bittersweet smell of the larch bowsprit, the charred whiff of white oak frames scorched to cure them and the tell-tale almond scent of reject white pine, with its pale red heartwood that I recalled sniffing as a boy when Opa had brought home off-cuts for me to whittle. I was reaping the benefits of a boyhood spent in Opa's carving shed and his workshop at home.

When the clanging of the metal hoop signalled the end of the day and I walked home along the embankment towards the house with Opa, the saw windmill sails still turned in my mind and the pounding of their cogs beat like a hallucinatory timepiece, punctuating his conversation and reminding me, it seemed, that my time was coming. I was, at last, a fully-fledged apprentice carpenter, the talismanic spoon hanging from my belt like a commemorative medallion.

Nine

BY EARLY JUNE THE shell of the ship stood solid on the slipway, two storeys tall. The lower sills of the gunports on each side were in place, the upper timbers of the deck frames marking her greatest height. To my eye, she was impregnable and sure, and I felt I was familiar with every piece of timber in her construction, right down to the treenails and the placement of every bolt.

I was growing impatient for the launch. The external planking was complete. The caulkers were hard at work, packing oakum and pitch into the seams and preserving the timbers with coats of Swedish tar, the stench filling the dokhavn.

At times I worked beside the smouldering braziers, helping to assemble the massive lower blocks and deadeyes to which the mast stays and lower shroud lanyards and cables would be lashed, bolting them to the outside of the hull. My clothes reeked and Anneka ordered me to offload them into the boiling laundry copper every evening and stir them in lye soap myself, to save her arthritic arms.

On the evening of 21 June 1701, Pieter Penne climbed the scaffolding to announce to us gathered below him what we already knew. 'She's ready for a taste of water, boys. We baptise her tomorrow.' He grinned across the crowd. 'We're a month ahead of schedule, by my reckoning. You've earned yourselves a bonus!'

He read out his instructions for the following day—a dozen labourers to assemble the enclosure of floating pontoons into which they would haul her after the launching for the installation of the bulkheads and the superstructure and deck machinery. Crane operators would then move the town's capstan-crane down the Kinderdijk quay to lift aboard the lower segments of the main and fore and mizzen masts, and to slide the bowsprit in over the beakhead.

I listened intently as he named the teams selected to complete her, listing their duties—the painting, the setting of the stays and the cables, ropes and yards, the installation of the upper and lower capstans and the pumps, whipstaff helm and rudder, the assembly of the giant wood-stock bower anchors, and the construction of the bricked kitchen with its woodstoves and chimney-pipes. To my dismay, he did not call out my name. *Has he forgotten me? Don't I qualify for work that complex?*

Then I heard him roar, 'Where is young Gerrit?' I promptly raised my hand as he searched for me in the crowd. 'Yes, you. You can help Opa Laurens with the figurehead. We don't want him having a heart attack or falling in the canal. We need him for our next assignment. Speaking of which, the rest of you can start work on the *Suikermolen* on the second slipway. We want her launched by Christmas.' He pulled off his cap and waved it, releasing a messianic blaze of red hair. 'And now I can confirm she'll be named after the town of Zuiddorp!'[24]

A solitary cheer rang out. It was Klaas van Breen, with both fists raised.

'As for you, Klaas,' he called, pointing at the paint shed where the kegs of beer were stored, 'you can pour for us while we toast our achievement.'

The *meister* waved his cap across the crowd in salute, congratulating us once again, thanking us for our efficiency and the quality of our workmanship. Then he joined those jostling for a foaming roemer of beer, the first of which was passed ceremoniously overhead to him. He downed it in seconds and called for a second, wiping froth from his unruly moustache.

---

24 Cargo ship the *Zuytdorp*, named after Zuiddorp—*South Town.*

WORK ON THE launching began at sunrise the next morning. It was going to be a cloudless, hot day. Alex, Nikolaas and I greased the oak slipways with wads of thick tallow from the bow to the water's edge.

The ship was still chocked in place, timber stays angled against her outer shell. We assisted the carpenters working through the morning fitting a line of short, thick perpendicular props to the outer timbers, low on each side of the ship. The props carried a row of planks tight to the hull, forming a cradle. The rope makers worked feverishly for hours, lashing each pair of props together, passing hemp cables beneath the keel and tightening them with mobile capstans.

By mid-afternoon the cradle planks had taken the weight of the ship, lifting the keel fractionally off the line of oak sleepers that had carried it for the past six months. We helped drag the sleepers away and then the rope makers lowered the cradled ship onto the skids.

She was ready for launching.

I heard a group of spirited children aboard, whooping it up, and noticed Pieter Penne's flame-haired twin girls among them. They were busily attaching red, orange and green streamers and pennants to her sides and stern in between tumultuous games of hide-and-seek as they sprinted wildly along the decks and pelted shrieking through the echoing holds. The mass of tangled ribbons snapped and fluttered in the gusting breeze, a giant Zeeland flag filling and emptying at the stern.

When all was ready, the children gathered with us on the flagstones. We took up a shouted chant when Pieter Penne and Klaas van Breen stepped forward on opposite sides of the stern, with sharpened axes raised. They swung together at the restraining cables and we roared at the detonation as they snapped apart.

The released skids shuddered and began inching down the slope. The groan of timbers echoed bell-like through the ship, drowned out by our cheering as she came closer to the water. The skids gathered pace, the tallow smoking as the bow struck the water in bursts of spray. The skids sank, their density taking them deep into the canal, their retrieval ropes hissing out as they uncoiled and whipped across the paving.

The ship heaved forwards on the surging wave of her massive displacement, a raft of barrels lashed across the canal slowing her momentum. A series of waves followed her across to the far wall and washed over the embankment as she turned majestically side-on in the spray, tangled wet ribbons stuck to her sides and stern as she moved to a slow lift and fall.

I felt an overwhelming sense of achievement at seeing her afloat; excited at the prospect of her journeys across the globe.

The *meister* and the surveyors boarded a raft and poled their way out to her to check her waterline and compare her internal measurements with those taken before the launch to determine how true her keel ran. His beaming smile and the triumphant twirl of both ends of his moustache signalled success.

I raised my green-and-gold glass roemer of beer and, before drinking, held the glass to my eye. The ship, blurred through the amber, floated on a foaming sea of gold.

Ten

O N MARTINMAS EVE IN November, Opa Laurens and I crossed the Kuiperspoort Bridge after work to meet with his friend Klaas Goelet. He was the senior carpenter aboard the chamber of Amsterdam *hoekboot*, the *Zilveren Leeuw*.

'You last met him seven years ago,' Opa said, 'when he delivered Papa's letters from Cape Town to Anneka.'

My memory of him was so vague I could barely remember him.

'Did he meet Papa when he picked up the letters?'

Opa put a hand on my arm. 'I believe so, and he served aboard the *Nijptang* in Willem de Vlaming's fleet.'

A shiver of excitement ran through me. *He sailed aboard one of the three ships sent out to search for Papa's* Ridderschap *in 1696!*

'Then I can't wait to meet him,' I said.

The walkway along the embankment was lit with celebratory bonfires, the air carrying the appetising scents of roasting almonds, apples coated in cinnamon and dried rosemary fed to the flames. Smoke misted through the linden trees, the dancing shadows of townsfolk flitting between the trunks. A young blonde girl in white petticoats circled me at one point, a bunch of flaring rosemary in each hand. She whirled them overhead like sparklers lighting up the delight on her face as she teased me, her braided hair swirling like golden snakes.

When we walked past the *Zuytdorp*, we stepped carefully around two dozen bronze bells lined on the quay, destined for farms in Paarl and along the valley slopes of the Drakenstein Mountains at the Cape. When I looked up, I saw she was almost ready for the sailing of the Christmas fleet, a month away. Her three masts were set, each capped with its circular crow's nest platform from which ratline ropes ran in taut triangles to the line of deadeyes at the rail. The capstan crane towered beside her, its pulleys hooked to the first of ten oak-trolleyed, long-snouted twelve-pounder cannon lining the walkway for loading the next day.

She looked glorious to me—business-like, powerful, especially at the bow, where I turned and took a few backward steps to admire the red lion figurehead jutting from the prow that Opa and his team had carved. It snarled out over the beak head below the bowsprit, its yellow mane flowing around black and white eyes and exaggerated fangs. Below it ran the scroll boards and splashboards, intricately sculpted in oak leaves and acorns. The great bower anchors hung lashed to beams at the prow, their thigh-thick hawsers of plaited hemp coiled through the hawse ports.

The *Zilveren Leeuw* lay further down the quay. Several crewmen leant at the rail. I assumed it was the end of the day's shift and waved as I passed. Spark-ridden smoke coiled up from her kitchen chimney above the smoke sail. I left Opa talking to one of the sailors and walked the length of her, admiring the flow of her lines. The polished heraldic insignia of the Amsterdam Chamber with its vertical column of three black crosses on a scarlet ground and silver lion rampant gleamed under the lantern at her stern. I read the motto beneath it, translating it aloud to myself, '*Vigilate! Deo confidentes*. Be vigilant! Put your trust in God.'

A sailor was there, squatting on his haunches against the trunk of a linden tree, quietly smoking. He tapped out his pipe on the heel of his shoe and walked from the shadows.

'Gerrit?' he asked.

'That's me.'

I shook the hand he'd extended. 'Klaas,' he said, smiling. 'You've matured since I last saw you, and I've aged some since

1694, but I haven't forgotten you. I think I'd pick you out in a crowd, even though you're now a teenager. I'm good with names and faces. And places. Even dates. It's a gift. For some strange reason, I never forget.'

We turned and strolled back down the quay towards Opa Laurens and made our way to the house.

When we reached the garden and were passing the smoke-house, Opa turned to Klaas. 'This you have to see. I think you'll appreciate it,' he said as he opened the door.

We had slaughtered the winter pig earlier that month and its barely visible carcass was hanging in the shadows, curing in the smoke of apple-wood shavings.

'Now *that*,' Klaas commented when he'd admired its plumpness, 'is what I call a pig! It must have been a boar?'

'No, a sow this time.'

'Ah, right. That does surprise me, but I notice you raise them big in Zeeland.' He grinned wickedly. 'Sows after my own heart! All the tastier and better for breeding.' Opa suppressed a laugh as Klaas patted the thick-thighed limb and set it swinging on the hook.

At the dining table, Opa Laurens filled three roemers to the rim from a bowl of fiery liqueur he'd concocted using Rhenish wine, immature must and a dash of Schiedam gin, in which he'd floated a raft of mint and pears fermented for a week. He poured a smaller sample into a roemer for Mama, who was busily carving the goose. He removed the pears for Mama to mash into a dressing to accompany the apple stuffing. She filled the plates and Adriana handed them around.

At the start of the meal, I raised my glass and the others did the same. 'To you, Klaas, we wish you a safe voyage. And the same for the *Zuytdorp*.' We touched glasses and swallowed down the toast.

During the meal, we raised and drank innumerable other toasts in refilled roemers. I recall another two that I proposed, both surprising Klaas. One to Eendrachtsland, the other to Dirck Hartog.

'Why Eendrachtsland?' he asked. 'That's a godforsaken place. Nothing but cliffs and wind and the wildest seas.'

'I'm drawn to the empty inland spaces on my maps,' I replied. 'Since I was a boy. They're unexplored. And I often wonder if that's where Papa may be living.'

'I hope not, for his sake. If he is alive that's the last place I'd wish on him.'

'No ifs about it, Klaas,' I interrupted him. 'He *is* alive. *Ik voel het in mijn botten.* I feel it in my bones.'

He looked intently at me. 'If that is the case—excuse the 'if'—then he may have been marooned in the Abrolhos Islands. Like the crew and passengers aboard the *Batavia*. That would be my guess.'

Mama abruptly excused herself from the table and cleared the dishes with Adriana. I noticed with concern that her face was drawn and tired. Several minutes later, she was quietly playing the clavichord, the music barely reaching us from the voorkamer.

Once the table was cleared and we settled around the fire, the liqueur and his pipe brought out the raconteur in Klaas. He came to life, his gesticulating hands energised, particularly when he mentioned Gerrit Colaart and the *Nijptang*.

'Now *there* was a schipper worth his salt, that old man. If you wrote down everything he didn't know about seamanship you'd be left with an empty page.'

I fixed my gaze on his grizzled and sunburned face beneath his shaven skull. The ravages of smallpox and scurvy had left their mark on his scarred cheeks and missing teeth. I sensed we were in for a long night and was keen to hear stories told by someone with the miraculous memory he claimed.

Will he bring my maps and globe to life more realistically than my imagination can? I wondered. *He saw Papa in Cape Town and picked up his letters. What did they discuss? He must have seen the* Ridderschap van Holland *depart. And Eendrachtsland! Did he step ashore there?*

'Twenty-third of April 1696,' he began. 'It was a Monday, I remember, the weather mild, the Zuiderzee so calm it seemed a laundrywoman had starched and ironed it flat. Two *waterschepen* towed us across the Pampus sandbar, their rowers bending their backs like they'd never bent them before. I can still hear *de ongelukkige klootzakken*, the poor bastards chanting away in unison as they strained at the oars.

'We picked up some wind the next day and made it to the Texel Roads, where we waited for the *Wezeltje* and the *Geelvink* with de Vlaming aboard.

'For ten days we waited. Ten. Then on the third of May, the following Thursday, we were out in the channel and on our way.' He looked sharply at me. 'A *jacht*, a *hoeker* and a *galjoot*. That was our fleet, Gerrit. Do you know the difference? Has Pieter Penne taught you anything in the dokhavn yet?'

'Do you want them in that order?' I responded immediately. 'One hundred and ninety… fifty… and thirty-five *scheepslasten*. The *jacht* a three-master, though that can vary. The other two most likely single masters.'

'Very good. Not bad for a fifteen-year-old.'

'He's a sponge,' Opa said.

'Sixteen,' I corrected Klaas. 'You want the rigging designs?'

Klaas laughed. 'Now you're showing off!'

He reached into his pocket for his tobacco pouch and refilled his pipe. When it was lit, he took several quick puffs. 'We made it down to the equator in no time, and one night when there was no moon and we were in the *wagen weg*[25], we separated from the other two.

'We were the first to reach the islands of Tristan da Cunha. The seas were wild when we arrived. And the drop-off into the Atlantic… it was a black and bottomless abyss, even close inshore. The full length of the lead line was carried away in the currents. It never touched bottom. Trust me, it was no place for the faint-hearted.'

The mountainous main island was tipped with blizzards and its nearby smaller sisters were threatening through the mists, he went on. Unable to put ashore, they charted the inhospitable shorelines as best they could during breaks in the weather while waiting for the other ships.

'You should have seen Mandrop Torst trying to sketch them! He may have been the ship's surgeon, but he fancied himself an artist. He set his drawing board on the foredeck and ran for cover each time it rained or when the waves broke over the decks. He was a raving lunatic; needed a straightjacket and locking up. Why the devil he didn't draw through the window from the shelter of his cabin I'll never know.'

He raised his glass. 'Ah, but Cape Town! Now *there's* a town I won't forget—the tavern of the two seas! Did I say tavern? *Streets* of taverns, I tell you, filled with sailors from every country you could name. I remember my favourite, *Het Laatste Stuivertje*, The Last Farthing. Coins from around the globe covered one wall. You name it, not a single coin was duplicated. From China to Peru! I studied them while I was

---

25 The 'cart track' sea lane that stretched south of the Cape Verde islands to the equator. This three-hundred-mile corridor led ships through the fickle calms of the doldrums and between powerful currents that could drag them eastward towards Africa and into the Gulf of Guinea or westward into the Caribbean. Once safely through, they swung in a westerly arc towards Brazil and then south into winds that swept them along the latitude to Cape Town.

sober and added a coin they didn't have—a double *stuiver* from Surinam.' He glanced across at me. 'That's where the landlord handed me your papa's letters.'

I gasped. 'You mean you didn't see him?'

'No. We missed him by a month. But he'd lodged at the tavern when he was on shore leave.' He reached out and squeezed my forearm. 'The landlord assured me he was in fine spirits when he left. Not quite the same high spirits as I am in right now, perhaps, but high spirits all the same!'

He went on to describe the cloud-spilled backdrop of Table Mountain, the windswept hillsides of the Devil's Peak and the Lion's Rump running down into the green waters of Table Bay marbled with foam—names on my maps that had intrigued me all my life.

A month after their arrival, he had assisted in the rescue of the *Vosmaar*, he said. Six months out from Middelburg and in sail-tattered distress, she'd barely negotiated the reefs of Robben Island when she'd arrived.

'One hundred and four of her crew died on the voyage out,' Klaas went on. 'Only four of the sailors were strong enough to work her sails. You should have seen them, *jonge kereltje*. Seventy were suffering scurvy and dysentery. Lying all over the decks they were, half dead. A ship crewed by skeletons. The stench was like a damned charnel house.'

He'd helped carry the sick from the stinking below-decks to the shore hospital, and when that was full the coasting *jacht* the *Windhond* was converted to a hospital ship for the others.

'When I was back in Cape Town on my way home two years later, I heard that the *Windhond* broke free of her moorings and foundered during a storm. She ended up on the rocks at Bloubergstrand. You can imagine the chaos. She was still filled with the sick. They had no crew to help them man the ship except the trainee surgeon and his hospital orderlies. They wouldn't know *aars van elleboog*, arse from elbow. Besides, we'd moved all her sailing gear to our fleet when she was converted to a hospital ship.

'There's no escaping the rocks and surf on that *van God verlaten* stretch of coast in a winter storm, let me tell you! Thunderous waves, *jonge kereltje*. Thunderous! They had to burn the corpses on the beaches when they washed ashore. It's a beach haunted by ghosts, by the spirits of many a Jan Maatroos.[26]'

He took a long draw on his pipe and thoughtfully exhaled a stream of smoke before turning to look me in the eye. 'It's a common story, *jonge*. One you want to remember. Give it careful consideration before you ever set foot aboard one of our ships for a voyage out. They can be death traps.' He gave me a quiet smile and a shrug of resignation. 'Me, who cares? Look at me. I'm a toothless old sea dog who knows no better and never had anyone give me good advice when I was your age. But you? You have your life ahead of you.' He drew on his pipe again. 'Think carefully, is all I'm saying. Don't make the wrong choice you can't go back on.'

Then he gave a loud burst of ironic laughter. 'Hah! Don't listen to this old fart, sounding like your counsellor. Listen to your gut,' he looked across at Opa, 'and Opa Laurens here, of course, and you won't go wrong.'

The fleet had departed Cape Town five days after he'd worked aboard the *Vosmaar*, he said. 'We headed out into the Indian Ocean on the twenty-seventh of October. A Saturday, unless I stand corrected.'

They landed on St Paul and Amsterdam Islands while crossing the Southern Ocean but found no signs of wreckage or marooned sailors.

Then, at last, they had their first distant sighting of Nieuw

---

26 Jack Tar, sailor.

Holland, far to the southeast. They saw the faint haze of rocky headlands north of Cape Leeuwin on Christmas Eve, the tantalising vision appearing and disappearing as the ship rode the long, rolling swells. The celebratory pennant was raised as the sighting faded in the twilight.

When he mentioned Nieuw Holland I leant forward, mesmerised.

'*The Cape of Scents!* I would never have believed it, but you can smell that cape before you sight the land. It's strong, like sweet peppermint. Lemon-scented, but headier, like musk. It haunts you when you're standing off at sea. Think of the finest roses with a pinch of cinnamon.'

Four days later, they'd anchored off Fog Island, which de Vlaming renamed Rattennest when they discovered knee-high, rat-like animals hopping among the pines and scrub when they landed.

'We buried a good friend of mine ashore there,' he said. 'He was a Belgian, Bauduyn Ganesvoort. He fell from the crosstrees during the night and broke his neck. I dug his grave at the edge of an inland lagoon. It had a clear view of the ocean I knew he would have appreciated. He'd have thanked me for it.

'I'm wearing Bauduyn's necklace. He carved it in Cape Town and I bought it at the auction after his burial. It cost him his life, but me a single silver lion dollar.'

I watched with interest as he reached inside his shirt and withdrew a sweat-stained leather thong, an oval of blue and green whorled abalone shell dangling from it. He lifted it over his head and laid it in his palm, stroking the thong to straighten it.

He pointed at the cameo carved into its surface. 'See the albatross there? See the wings? Never mind the superstition. It was meant to be a charm to save his neck, but he ended up breaking it instead. It may not have worked for him. For me, it has worked miracles.'

He lifted the shell and kissed it. 'So far, at least. We were true *heeren van zes weken*, men who stayed six weeks in Cape Town, while Bauduyn was carving this. Six weeks? Those ladies of the night, they treated us like royalty. We needed the seventh week to sober up!'

I reached for the shell. I looked down at the blues and greens marbled like the surface of a shallow sea, the wings of the albatross sweeping across its surface. 'May I try it on?'

He held it up and I put my head through the loop in the thong. The pendant fell across my chest. I admired the patterns swirling through the nacre, identical to the abalone shell we had in the kunstkamer.

'We collected samples of pine on Rattenest,' Klaas continued, 'and some other trees I've never come across before or since. We stripped the bark and used the poles to shore up the goat and sheep enclosure on the *Geelvink*. It's interesting wood, tough and hardy and salt-resistant with a strange smell to the leaves when you crush them. They made my eyes water.'

He reached his empty roemer out to Opa, who refilled it. 'You're looking tired, Laurens,' he observed. 'Am I boring you with all this?'

'No, no. It's been a long day, that's all. You've got Gerrit's full attention and it's good to watch.'

'You can't stop now,' I interrupted.

Klaas raised his eyebrows. 'Eendrachtsland?'

'Exactly.'

'We are almost there.' He smiled and turned back to Opa. 'That timber would have interested you, Laurens. It's a hardwood, ideal for carving, I would say. A couple of the *jongen* made fishing spears from it and caught some lobsters in the shallow reefs there. Very tasty.

'We got the cooks to distil the bark and the spiny leaves of another shrub there. It was also very aromatic and we extracted

two phials of oil. It was hot when you rubbed it on the skin…
and vile to taste. We delivered one phial to Chairman Nicolaes
Witsen in Amsterdam when we got back. God knows where
the other ended up. My guess is the perfumers got their hands
on it.' He leant back and beamed at us. 'Maybe they prepared a
new scent for the whores on the Peperwerf—a perfume to bring
a crocodile tear to their eyes when they're seeing one boyfriend
off on a ship before sprinting back to town to satisfy the next.'

'Never mind the perfume and the whores in Amsterdam,
Klaas,' I broke in 'Did you land on the continent?'

'I did.'

'So how was it when you went ashore?'

He cocked his head to one side and shook a knowing
finger at me. 'It's an unfriendly coast, inshore from Rattenest.
In the mornings, the seas are calm, but in the evenings, the
winds come in and blow you about. We went ashore in two
longboats, dragged them over the sand bar at the river mouth
before rowing upstream. We spent three days on the river,
going ashore now and then. It was stinking hot.'

'Did you see any natives?' I asked.

'No, but they were there, sure enough, the savages. They
never showed their faces. Not a single one. We assumed they
were black, as they were to the north, where we saw them in
the dunes—black as the swans we shot and ate. You've never
seen the likes of those birds, Laurens! Feathers like blackbirds
and beaks dipped in blood. I should have brought you one
for your kunstkamer. We baked a couple and ate them. Or
tried to. Nothing like tonight's goose, I can tell you. They were
tougher than sea biscuits baked from boot leather.'

Then he talked of their chart-making voyage up the coast.

'So now you've reached Eendrachtsland?'

'We have.'

'At last!'

They'd weaved their way through the reefs, recording regular soundings and landing several times on the four-hundred-*mijl* ribbon of beach and on waterless islands close inshore.

'We saw signs of the savages. There was signal smoke everywhere. We went ashore at one place where we explored some huts. We found the ashes of fires still smouldering and the bones from a recent meal. And some dead fish.'

Further north, they coasted along a spectacular stretch of cliffs as steep and white as those at Dover, sloping away to rolling dunes, where they discovered a narrow inlet and shallow river estuary, its water running red with silt that stained the sea.

'From out to sea we saw a strange haze rising behind the dunes. It had a pink tinge to it. The very air seemed discoloured, so the schipper sent a crew ashore to investigate.'

They'd anchored outside the reef off the estuary, where they'd launched two dories. The oarsmen rowed across the outgoing river flood to an inland lagoon, its claret-coloured waters brackish and its shores encrusted with salt. At the base of a tall bluff in the hills along its inland eastern edge, the sailors found fresh water bubbling through creviced springs in the limestone.

'We calculated that this must be the place Francisco Pelsaert marooned the two *Batavia* mutineers seventy years ago. You remember that story, Gerrit? Pelsaert exiled them beside those freshwater springs.'

'Wouter Loos and Jan Pelgrom de Bly?'

'That's them! Your memory is as good as mine. We half-expected two mad Dutch lunatics with beards to their knees to come wandering down to us. But we saw no one, even though many pathways led across the hills. God alone knows what happened to them. It seems they got their just deserts. Mandrop Torst had a field day sketching there.'

They'd replenished their freshwater supply and coasted

along another spectacular line of rust-coloured cliffs, he said, before rounding the sheer burnished face of *Roede Hoek*, Red Bluff. There, the line of reefs had curved into a shoreline of dunes, where they'd discovered another river mouth.

'We saw savages on those dunes as we passed. I watched them through a telescope, but I had to share it, so I only had a brief glimpse. Stark naked they were, arms waving as they loped across the sand, following us. The interpreters we took on board in Cape Town, Jongman the Balinese and Mangadua from Makassar, they were chattering away in their excitement. Mangadua told me he'd dived for trepang when he was a boy in the waters of a coast some distance to the south of his island. He told us these people looked to be the same.

'It took us half an hour to sail along that stretch before we reached another line of cliffs. Very rugged they were. Very threatening. They ran to the horizon for two days' sailing. I remember how de Vlaming described them, *"Helemaal hoog en kaal, zonder groen alsof afgehakt door een bijl*, altogether high and bare, without any green, as if chopped off by an axe."'

The ocean had shown its teeth at the base of the cliffs, he told us, the roar of breakers heard for *mijl* after *mijl* north to the Dirck Hartog Roads.

'The compass needle misbehaved along that coastline. God knows why. It deviated so much we sailed well out to sea until we reached the entrance to the Roads.' He looked at me, his pipe in hand, and shook his head. 'Eendrachtsland, *jonge*! Believe me, those cliffs are more like the end of the earth and the gateway to hell. There's no place for a landing. And like I said, we stayed well offshore. You would have done the same. As anyone in their right mind would.'

The *t'Weseltje* was the swiftest in the fleet, he went on. She had anchored overnight and was waiting for them in the lee of Dirck Hartog Island, moored beside a beach when they rounded the point the next morning.

Four of the crew of the *t'Weseltje* had climbed the cliff face to the summit the evening before to signal the other two ships. At its northernmost point, they'd found a weathered pewter plate left there by Dirck Hartog in 1616, on which he had engraved the record of his arrival. It lay at the foot of a splintered pole.

'When the commander came ashore from the *Geelvink* and read the plate, he handed me one of his dinner bowls and ordered me to print a similar message recording our landing. So I did. I hammered his plate flat and stamped it with the names he wanted printed on it. Took me half a day. I squatted in a longboat beside the beach using its seat as my workbench.' He looked at me and grinned. 'You want to know the date, *jonge*? The fourth of February 1697, a Monday, to be precise.'

He'd nailed the plaque to one of the Rattenest pine poles, he explained, and de Vlaming had erected it with great ceremony the next day on the clifftop in the fissure of the original. A volley of musket shots marked the occasion.

'I was up there for the ceremony. My plate, going down in history! It must still be there.'

The gunfire had echoed northwards, powder-smoke drifting across the channel. Klaas said he saw the distant outline of Dorre Island there, a shadow against a blood-red sky, sharing the westernmost point of what I was astonished to hear him call the '*het ellendig Zuidland*, that miserable South Land.'

That miserable South Land? My Eendrachtsland—the unexplored area I so carefully coloured in? And spent so many years peering at through my spyglass from the quarterdeck of my houseship? Miserable? I refuse to believe him!

After a week of inshore exploration, they'd changed direction and angled away from the continent. The wind had lifted the *Nijptang* on growing seas and their cannon echoes had signalled a change of course nor'westward for the Sunda Straits.

They'd reached Batavia with the *t'Weseltje* a month later, the *Geelvink* three days behind them.

After dinner, Opa and I accompanied him unsteadily along the embankment back to the ship, bonfire embers still flaring among the linden trees in the fluky breeze.

Klaas told us that the *Nijptang* had remained in service in Ceylon and he'd transferred to the *Karthago* for the journey home a year later, the same ship he'd served aboard years before when he'd brought the letters to Mama.

'After that voyage, I joined the *Zilveren Leeuw* on the coastal run,' he said. 'I've been with her ever since.'

When we reached the ship, a fine mist was settling across the canal; a curtain through which he disappeared up the rocking gangway. He was partway up when I remembered the necklace. I felt for it through my shirtfront and called out to Klaas, who came back down and put a hand to my chest.

'No, it's yours now, *jonge* Gerrit,' he said. 'Look after it, and I trust it will look after you, as it has me.' He grinned. 'Never mind my good friend Bauduyn, God rest his soul!'

I gripped his hand in both of mine and squeezed it gratefully. 'Thank you. I'll take good care of it. I'll remember you gave it to me and where it was made… and especially the story of its journeys.'

He placed a hand on my shoulder. 'As for your future journeys, I hope I haven't ruined your vision of Eendrachtsland.'

'You've given me food for thought, but I'll get over it, Klaas. I'll have to go and see it for myself.'

'To discover how biased I may have been? Wherever you go, *jonge*, the albatross will keep you safe.' He gazed down at me, his expression thoughtful. 'Even so, tread carefully.'

After Christmas, while I was working on the *Suikermolen*, the *Zuytdorp* slipped from her moorings beside the Kinderdijk quay. She was hauled down the Binnenhaven canal by three longboats, the oarsmen chanting, as she glided midstream.

Two barges loaded with heavier cargo delivered by the *Zilveren Leeuw* followed her. I watched them as they passed, the inventory Klaas had mentioned to us during dinner running through my mind. Rolled sheets of lead for Batavia, Swedish iron and copper ingots destined for Surat on the Gujerat coast, sacks of charcoal for the Stellenbosch blacksmiths and granite building blocks and red kiln bricks for the Salt River flour mills near Cape Town. They would all be loaded aboard the *Zuytdorp* when she was in deeper water in the Westerscheldt Estuary off Fort Rammekens.

I climbed the scaffolding for a better view. There was a break in the squalls, and I saw members of her crew moving about the decks. Her flags and bunting hung damp and still. Her schipper, Kornelis Jorissen, was at the poop-deck rail, his arm raised now and then in salute as the houses slipped past.

When she reached the turn and swung into the Haven canal, her masts moved away above the trees and she faded from view. I felt an unexpected emptiness for several minutes before determining that I too would sail one day, to explore the expanding horizons of my world in my search for Papa and on my quest for self-discovery, despite Klaas's pessimistic advice.

Eleven

I VIVIDLY REMEMBER THE day I met Magdalena.
It was a Saturday morning in September 1698, market day in the Middelburg town square. I was looking after Opa's stall, helping him sell his carvings. I had some of my toys, dice and birds among them.

Trestle tables were lined end to end in five rows on the cobblestones the length of the square. Opa's stall was in the middle of the row closest to the *stadhuis*, the town hall. I remember bands of passing cloud casting shadows over the tables, the sun intermittently flashing from the freshly painted red and white triangles on the *stadhuis'* window shutters and washing the slate roof tiles grey-blue.

I was sitting on a stool among other artists, sculptors, woodcarvers and silversmiths licensed by the Guild of St Luke to sell their work there.

Opa had taken the morning off to collect a batch of ebony off-cuts someone aboard the *Karthago* had promised him, brought back from Ceylon.

The crowd was quiet and slow-moving and trade had been slow. I was thoroughly bored. I distracted myself with one of the games I'd carved—tossing up a bright yellow wooden ball and catching it on a cylindrical rod with a cupped end, the loud click of each unsuccessful throw disturbing bright-eyed sparrows hopping beneath the tables. I had succeeded only twice that morning.

Deep in concentration, at first I didn't notice a young couple at the stall inspecting the carvings on display. I gave a triumphant whoop as the rod and ball connected for the third time and I held it there.

'*Goed werk, jonge kerel.* Great work, young fellow!' the

man congratulated me. I looked up, unsure whether he was referring to the carvings or my success with the rod and ball. I had never seen him before. I recognised his Nordic accent and foreign-sounding intonation. *He's Danish, or Norwegian, perhaps.*

The fair skin on his broad forehead was peeling and his cheekbones, unprotected by his thick blonde beard streaked with grey, were badly wind-burned. His hair was a mass of curls. His neck was thick and his brawny bulk filled his worn blue mariner's coat and breeches. The seams had a threadbare look and I noticed three ships' names embroidered on the left breast pocket in gold thread, one above the other, like a row of war ribbons. The latest name, *Zandloper*, was brighter than the rest.

He must have arrived home from Batavia aboard the ship the month before, in company with the Karthago, Schellag *and* Ijsselmonde, I guessed.

'It's not as easy as it looks,' I replied.

'May I try?' the woman asked.

She was a slender Eurasian of startling beauty, her flawless brown skin tinted copper in the sun, her expressive eyes a deep olive green of a shade I had never seen before. She had an eye-catching gap between her front teeth, which I found surprisingly alluring. She was wearing an ankle-length black skirt and a revealing sleeveless white blouse, a multi-coloured semi-circular band of flowers embroidered across the low neckline.

Transfixed, I handed her the toy and she turned her back as she began to toss the ball, attached to the cylindrical rod with a length of string.

Her dark hair, flowing down her back, was pinned by a broad tortoiseshell comb inserted at the nape of her neck, around which a fine gold necklace flickered. I watched the sinews glide across her shoulders as she tossed the toy.

After several unsuccessful throws, she turned back to me, 'Here, show me how it's done.'

I took the toy and placed it back on the table among the others, painted in different colours. 'It takes a lot of practice. I've been trying for hours this morning and only succeeded once or twice.'

'Then we'll make do with the success you had.' She smiled.

I glanced at her forehead, expecting to see the cherry red or vermilion dot that appeared on many of the pictures of Indian women I'd seen. She seemed amused by my scrutiny and withdrew her necklace with her long tapering fingers, the manicured nails polished deep henna maroon. She dangled a pendant cross before me. 'I'm from Goa,' she said. 'I'm not the Hindu everyone expects me to be.'

'Vasco da Gama,' I mumbled, then ducked my head in embarrassment at the obscure reference.

'That's right. I'm partly Portuguese, but no relation to Vasco, as far as I know.' She gave me a brief, conciliatory smile as she turned to the man. 'And now I'm married to a Dane. Tell me that makes sense!'

'Don't confuse the boy, Magdalena,' he said, his bass voice sonorous, his fluency in Dutch barely passable, 'or he'll never talk to us again. We were admiring these birds of paradise. Did you carve them?'

'Yes.'

'Without assistance?'

'Yes.'

'What, you taught yourself?'

'No, my opa has been teaching me since I was six.'

'Well, I think they're very, very good. Did you copy them from Javanese wood carvings?'

'No, we don't have any. I copied a picture by Rembrandt van Rijn.'

The man raised his eyebrows as he inspected the carving. 'Very ambitious and very successful. So much so I'll buy one and have a Rembrandt of my own. How much are they?'

I named the price. The man dug into his pocket and carefully counted out twelve *stuivers*. 'So you don't have any Javanese wood carvings?'

'I've seen a few. That's all. My opa hasn't bought any.'

'Then you haven't seen the real thing or you'd spend your last guilder for it. I have a collection at home. Would you like to see them?'

Beside us, the woman had picked up another rod and ball, a red one this time, and as she began tossing it, I heard her frustrated and bemused 'Oh! Oh no! Not again. *This* time. Now. *Now!*' in the background as we conversed.

'Do you have Javanese birds of paradise?' I asked.

The man looked down at the carving, 'No, no birds of paradise. Not until this one now. I have herons, a pair of sea eagles, parrots, a hummingbird and what they call over there in Ambon an antique bird—a bird from their mythology. Sitting in a cage.'

Intrigued, I asked, 'What sort of wood do they use?'

'Teak, I think. Some others. Hibiscus. Chinaberry maybe. And sandalwood, of course, when they can get it. But mostly parasite wood.'

'Parasite wood?'

'Ah, parasite wood has a special quality. I doubt if you'd see it here. It's formed by a kind of mushroom that grows on the bark of a chinaberry tree. It leaves behind a solid lump that's perfect for carving. They're all different shapes. And colours too, mostly shades of white and yellow-brown.'

'Like ripe corn,' the woman added as she placed the rod and ball back on the table. 'At least ours are.'

'That sounds interesting.'

'Listen, *jonge kerel*, you're welcome to visit us and take a look. We have a kunstkamer on the second floor where I store them all.'

'I'll mention it to Opa.'

The man turned and pointed beyond the *stadhuis*. 'We live around the corner on the Lange Noordstraat, fourth house along. Magdalena has hung a tile with a red tulip on it above the door. You can't miss it.' He extended a hand. 'I'm Leif, by the way, Leif Morgensen,' he gave a slight bow, 'new bosun aboard the *Zandloper*. I've transferred from the Danish merchant navy and moved here from Aarhus three months ago.' He raised a hand to the woman. 'And this is Magdalena.'

'My Christian name is Gerrit,' I responded, 'and I am a de Waal. I'm pleased to meet you both.'

'As are we to meet you, Gerrit,' Leif replied.

'You haven't sailed with the VOC before?' I asked as they turned to leave.

'No, first voyage.'

'Don't you like the Danish navy?'

Leif cocked a thumb at Magdalena. 'This one hates the cold. Your winters are much warmer here, they tell me, and I like the idea of coasting Ceylon and India... and the Arabian Sea, which is our next assignment.'

Magdalena returned to the table and picked up each rod and ball in turn, inspected the colours, tested their weight and gave each a trial throw. She selected the yellow one. 'And I'll take this. I'll have time to practise while Leif's away. It's the one we saw you succeed with, so it should bring me luck.'

Leif paid for it and, as they turned away, Magdalena looked back. 'We'll see you when you decide to come around,' she said.

'I'll talk to Opa.'

I watched her walk away, drawn by the silken sway of

her lithe hips, and when a delicate tinkling carried to me, I followed the contour of her left leg and saw an anklet of tiny silver bells above her heel.

Opa and I visited them one evening the following week. When we reached the house and Leif ushered us inside, Opa remarked, 'This place used to belong to Schipper de Haze from the *Moerkapelle*! I've been wondering who'd bought it after he died.'

Leif showed us into the parlour where we found a glassed atrium filled with luxuriant greenery competing for the light. There was a kitchen to the left, where Magdalena prepared chocolate drinks for us, which we enjoyed seated at an extraordinary round rosewood table. It had a tropical village panorama carved into its surface, a river running through it, and people in sarongs and head cloths going about their business among palms, dogs, tusked pigs and a horde of chickens running wild.

Then Leif led us up the stairs to the kunstkamer, located between two bedrooms.

The wood carvings on display were impressive real-life reproductions. They were exotic, polished and elegant, particularly the birds carved in parasite wood, exactly as Leif had described them—a hummingbird hovering above a ripened fruit filled with seeds and nectar, a pair of herons facing each other over a clutch of eggs, a diving eagle impaling a fish in its talons.

Two unfinished part-carved elephants in ebony, still emerging from the blocks, caught my eye. Leif was using them as bookends, several volumes between them. I pointed them out.

'They're from Galle in Ceylon,' Leif said. 'I found them in the carving shed of a Buddhist temple there.'

Then he reached for a basilisk lizard sculpted in silver. 'What do you think of this? It's my favourite piece, from Brazil.'

Every scale was exquisitely etched, its dorsal fins and the crest on its head raised as it sprinted on long talons across a sheet of polished tin, as though across a rainforest pool. I found it marvellous as I handled it with great care, noting its solid weight and meticulous accuracy, before returning it to the stand.

The rich smell of chocolate still wafted from the dining room when we stood at the front door about to leave. Opa told Magdalena as we made our departure that Francesco Carletti had introduced the cacao bean to Middelburg a century before and his mother, Margriete, following Carletti's instructions, had concocted what may have been Zeeland's first chocolate drink.

NEWS OF THE *Zandloper*'s capsize with all hands lost did not reach Middelburg until 8 March 1702. I was in the second year of my apprenticeship, three months before my seventeenth birthday.

I had kept in touch with Magdalena during Leif's absence, when Alois regularly rostered me to deliver bagged woodchips for fire starters around the city, including a consignment for her. I delivered them on foot, leading one of the dokhavn horses hauling a cartload, accompanied by the peat carriers.

Whenever possible, I'd leave her delivery to the last. I'd tether the horse to the spiked wrought-iron railings in front of her house and heft the sack into the parlour where she always had a glass of water, or lemon when she had them, ready for me.

When she didn't have other visitors, we'd spend a short time together. She'd quiz me about the progress of my relationship with Sara or listen to the latest gossip I'd pass on from the dokhavn or Cape Town and Batavia. Sometimes we'd compete with the now battered yellow rod and ball, my departure timed to coincide with the first successful toss. I often wondered if Magdalena ever correctly suspected that I'd deliberately fail in order to extend my stay.

The day we heard that the *Zandloper* had capsized off Trincomalee with all hands lost was also a catastrophic day for the nation. On that very day, news that the *stadhouder*[27], William III, had died filtered through to Middelburg. His death threw the republic into political turmoil.

I did not visit Magdalena for a fortnight after receiving the tragic news. Then I called on her one evening after work, privately, to convey my sympathies.

When she opened the door, words deserted me. An unforeseen wave of grief overwhelmed me and I struggled to control upwelling tears. I stood in the doorway at a loss, tongue-tied and awkward, until she stepped forward and put her arms about me as if to reassure *me*.

We stood in that close embrace for several minutes. We did not move until she began to weep silently, her shudders running through me. I willed them to subside, my heart pulsing uncontrollably.

Then she disengaged herself. Holding me at arm's length by the shoulders, she assured me that she knew all would be well, given time.

'I have done much of my grieving,' she said, as she turned and led me to the table beside the atrium, where we sat facing one another, our hands clasped. I found her drawn face and

---

27 Stadhouder (political leader) of the Dutch Republic, member of the House of Orange-Nassau, founded in 1544 by William I (William the Silent). William III became heir in 1650 but was not officially recognised until 1672. Married to Mary II of England, he was crowned Co-Regent of England, Ireland and Scotland in 1689 and died on 8 March 1702, without heirs. In 1815 the Netherlands converted to a monarchy.

the faint smile she attempted haunting. 'If you'd heard me the day I received the news and the day after that, you'd have thought it was the end of the world. But it was such a relief, Gerrit, all that wailing. We do things a little differently in Goa. We don't hold back.'

She leant in and took me in her arms again across the table, stroking my back and whispering, 'Thank you for coming. It means a lot to me. I know Leif would be grateful.'

Then she released me. She stood and led me by the hand to the door. 'I know this has been hard for you, but I am stronger than I look. Your visit and the visits of others make me stronger still.'

'If there's anything I can do for you, you only have to ask,' I assured her as she held the door ajar. 'Anything at all.'

'I know that, Gerrit,' she said as she closed it. 'I won't forget. Thank you.'

As I walked home, I realised there was something I could do for her immediately, and she did not need to ask. *For the rest of this year, while I'm still rostered to make firelighter deliveries, I will not charge her for them.*

I privately rearranged my rosters with Alex and Nikolaas so that I'd deliver all her consignments, and I paid for them on her behalf from my pay packet. Alois never suspected what I was doing or if he did, he did not comment. As far as I knew, neither did Magdalena.

I made my first free delivery to her a week later. When she reached into her purse for the payment, I put my hand over it and closed the clasp. 'You don't need to pay. Not anymore.'

'I don't? Why is that?'

'You're entitled to a free issue now that you're a widow,' I lied.

'Is that the VOC policy?'

'It is.'

'Thank you, Gerrit,' she called out as I led the horse and cart away. 'And thank whoever is responsible in the company.'

By November that year, fierce political rivalries across Zeeland surfaced, with frequent demonstrations in Middelburg threatening to develop into riots and tear society apart. William III had left no heir, so pro-state Republicans and Orangist royalists opposed each other with worsening threats of violence.

There was also an economic downturn throughout the republic that affected the VOC, one that impacted us in the dokhavn, with sackings reducing numbers to an essential workforce. Opa and I survived 'By God's good grace,' according to Mama.

Others were less fortunate, and I was devastated the day I sat with Daniel and Sara in the garden eating ripening Gravenstein apples we'd picked in the orchard.

'Papa Jakob has told us we're leaving,' Daniel said through a mouthful. 'He has sold the house.'

My heart lurched and I was speechless. Then I blurted, 'You can't be. You are joking.'

'We are leaving, Gerrit. He has sold the house. He told us yesterday afternoon.'

'Sold the *house*? I didn't know it was on the market.'

'Neither did we. He has made a private deal with someone in Leiden. In exchange for a wine importing business there, apparently.'

Shocked, I looked at Sara. She was pale and clearly distraught. I reached for her hand. 'When?' I asked Daniel.

'We aren't sure exactly. He has his business affairs to settle.' He took another crisp bite. 'But it may be as soon as a fortnight.'

'A fortnight!' I squeezed Sara's hand. 'I don't believe it.'

'That's what he estimates. Oma Ramika and the maids started packing this morning.'

'Just before we came over to tell you,' Sara murmured.

'But *why?*' I asked.

'He says the political situation in Leiden is not as bad as it is here. He thinks it's going to get a lot worse in Middelburg.'

I sat there stunned. *A lot worse? Not for your family, surely. You're the Miermans, related to the Veth family. Your relatives have power and prestige on the council.* Then it struck me—*That may be precisely the reason you have to leave. You're vulnerable.*

'And he has arranged places for us in Leiden University,' Sara added.

'Doesn't your Oom Gabriel and his family live there?' I asked.

'Yes, the one with the estate. You've seen the picture of it on the drawing-room wall,' Sara replied. 'We'll be living there at first.'

'Until Papa Jakob finds us our own house,' Daniel explained.

I tossed away my half-eaten apple and shook my head. 'What am I going to do without you?'

'Don't ask that,' Sara said. She laid her head against my chest and I placed my arm around her shoulder. 'I don't want to think about it. I don't. I don't.'

That fortnight turned into three weeks that raced past.

My mood was bleak the morning they left, despite brilliant sunshine spilling through the silver birches. Standing to one side of the group clustered around the scarlet coach, I gave Daniel and then Sara a last embrace.

When I looked down at her she reached up to stroke the v-shaped scar on my forehead. 'Your reminder of the miracle of your escape. My reminder of the miracle of you,' she whispered and pressed her hot cheek to mine. I felt it wet before she gave me a brief kiss and broke away to follow Daniel and clamber aboard.

She turned on the top step, waved and ducked into the cabin. I craned my neck to search for her among the shadows. She was nowhere to be seen.

Frail and palsied Oma Ramika was the next to climb aboard, assisted by Jakob and the coachman. She seemed uncharacteristically fearful and silent, perhaps because she was exposed beyond the familiar confines of the house. She blocked my view.

Then Jakob climbed the step and, with a last backward look, he pulled the door shut. I remember sunlight striking the gold-enamelled Veth family coat of arms emblazoned on it, momentarily blinding me. The four restive horses, necks arched, leant into the clinking harnesses at the coachman's signal, and the coach slowly creaked away.

I sat for hours on the top step of the Mierman house in despair after they'd gone. At one point I reached up and ran my fingers over the scar that Sara had stroked when she'd told me it reminded her of the miracle of our relationship. A miracle, because the day I'd received the injury two years before, I had escaped death by the narrowest of margins. She had cared for the wound while it had healed.

For the rest of that month, I was torn. Their absence was unbearable at first. I experienced moments of piercing unhappiness when memories of Daniel's lifelong friendship and my deepening affection for Sara resurfaced. In those moments I often wrote to her and her replies were no less expressive, but, as the months passed, her letters became less frequent and her responses shorter and, I sensed, less enthusiastic.

The day she enrolled at Leiden University, I received the last letter from her. I reread it several times, undecided whether to keep it with the others or not, before going down to the kitchen and committing them all to the fire in the ovens.

Unexpectedly, I felt a weight had been lifted. Months of

conflicted feelings were over. On one hand, I knew Sara was beyond my reach—we were living separate lives, developing in different directions and I must forget her. On the other, I conjured poignant images of her, swearing in moments of bittersweet nostalgia that I would seek her out one day and re-establish our relationship. This became an obsession offset by a despairing sense of futility and frustration. All that was now ended.

Thankfully, during that time, I had my fortnightly visits to Magdalena to look forward to. I used to read Sara's letters to her… except for the last one, and she'd empathise and allow me to express my disappointment and confusion.

Then in April, she told me she was returning to Goa. 'The company has offered to repatriate me home, Gerrit. I have a berth aboard the *Huis ter Boede*.'

The Huis ter Boede! We launched her last October.

I was taken aback. I had always known she'd leave one day, but I was unprepared for that moment to arrive so soon. 'When? Have they decided on a departure date?'

'In June some time.'

'You'll be sailing on her maiden voyage.'

'I know. It's time I went home,' she said. 'It's no reflection on you, but I'm lonely here. I haven't seen my family in seven years. I miss my older brother, Filip. I want to taste a ripe mango straight from the tree and eat it down at Anjuna beach when I'm sitting in the sea. My God, I even want to smell a Durian fruit in Batavia to know I'm almost home. And peel a chikoo. And chew betel again at sundowners… *with my friends!* Thinking about it makes my heart race, Gerrit.'

She gazed at me, then gave me a blazing smile that took my breath away. 'You should pack your bags and come with me!'

'I wish I could,' I replied, the painful surge of regret I experienced a contrast to her happiness.

Twelve

O PA AND I WERE sympathetic to the rebel Republican cause, but we weren't active in the movement. When pamphlets were delivered to the house deriding the older, long-serving Orangist Party members elected to the *Vroedschap*[28] City Council in the 1670s by the *Stadhouder* William III, accusing them of all manner of corruption and calling for immediate resignations, Opa and I consigned them to the fire. We refused invitations to participate in Republican meetings held in private houses and then in public open spaces across the city.

'We'll let things work themselves out,' Opa said. 'Take the wisest course. We don't want to get caught in the crossfire.'

Month by month, growing numbers of Orangist councillors bowed to pressure, resigning their positions, but a hardcore group stubbornly refused to budge.

Towards the end of 1702, when the rebel leadership crystallised under Daniel Fannius and his deputies Johan van Reygesberge and Martinus Veth, the pamphleteering became an avalanche.

'Now we're heading for real trouble,' Opa said when he heard. 'Young Fannius is a firebrand we can do without.'

When we were walking home from work late one afternoon in mid-December, we stood aside to watch Fannius lead a group of chanting marchers carrying a strident red banner along the Kinderdijk that read, '*Majestas penes populum*'—'Sovereignty belongs to the people.'

Opa gave me an ironic glance and nodded. 'Of course it does,' he muttered, 'but who takes charge after that?'

---

28 The name given to city councils across the Netherlands—selected groups of 'wise fathers'.

Early one morning later that week, the day overcast and threatening rain, we were on our way to work when two Republican organisers, Gillis Dekker and Otto Bijland, both from nearby Arnemuiden, barred our way at the Segeersweg Gate. The previous day, Pieter Penne had thrown them out of the dokhavn and banned them from re-entering when they'd been soliciting for recruits to the cause during working hours.

Tall and lean, Gillis stepped forward, a no-nonsense glare in his pale blue eyes, his receding chin camouflaged beneath a sparse black beard. The ammoniac smell of horse sweat, manure and liniment from his father's stables clung to him.

'Your time please, gentlemen,' he said, brandishing a petition. 'We're gathering signatures endorsing a Republican takeover.'

'My time is precious, Gillis,' Opa grunted, 'and I won't waste it signing that. Now move aside, if you don't mind.'

'I do mind, *oude man*. We need to know the numbers of those who are for us. We have fifty-seven so far and we believe you de Waals agree with our agenda.'

Anticipating our compliance, Otto stepped forward carrying a list of signatories in one hand and a state-of-the-art ink-loaded double quill in the other. The open palm Opa raised halted him in his tracks. 'What makes *you* an expert on de Waal family politics, *jonge kerel?*'

'Ah, come now, Laurens, everyone knows where you stand,' Gillis said. 'You work for the VOC, not the West India Company. You have no time for the privateers. You don't mix with the regents or the councillors. Do I need to be an expert? Or have I added a pair of twos and totalled five?' He brushed a length of lank hair from his forehead and turned his baleful stare on me. 'Besides, Gerrit here gave the game away at school.'

He turned away, spat across the sidewalk and wiped his mouth. 'Judging by the choices you and your friend Daniel

Mierman made backing my brother in the gang fights after school I'd say I'm on the right track. You remember, don't you?'

'How could I forget?'

'So you'll sign?'

'I won't sign for either party, Gillis. I know your brother, Asmus. I remember what happened to him and I don't want a repeat. I'm done with all that.' I looked him steadily in the eye. 'So move aside and let us pass.'

'We have a plan of action, Gerrit. Those last few stubborn old fools in the *stadhuis* won't budge, so we're taking things to the next level. If it takes force, we'll give them force. We have most of the militia on side. Now we want at least a hundred *burgher* citizens, especially young ones your age. It's only a matter of time.'

'Judging by the number of agitators you've dragged in from Domburg and Koudekerke I'd say you already have twice that many,' I said.

'I'm talking about able-bodied Republicans from Middelburg, my friend. We want as many local citizens as we can muster. Cleaning out the *vroedschap* is an issue for this city.'

'Are you deaf?' I shouted. 'What part of "I'm done with all that" don't you understand? I'm not interested. I won't sign.'

'And neither will I,' Opa said bluntly. 'So go and find your hundred *burghers* in the coffee houses where I saw you operating last weekend. Failing that, try the taverns you haven't already visited. That's our last word. Now stand aside! Let us through.'

After a charged silence, Gillis unwillingly signalled Otto to allow us to pass. 'If you're not for us, you're against us,' he yelled as we walked down the laneway to the Korendijk, ducking for shelter close to the walls of the houses as a light rain began to fall. 'Don't expect any favours when we're in power.'

We strode along the Binnenhavn Canal, the distant

clanging of the signal to start work faintly echoing.

'Poor Asmus,' I said as we increased our pace. 'It's out of order for Gillis to bring him up and pressure us like that, don't you think?'

'When did it happen?'

'Three… no, four years ago. In the summer of 1698 at the end of the school year.'

'That's not something you'd easily forget.'

'No, never. It was a miracle for me,' I frowned, 'and almost fatal for him.'

We turned from the Kinderdijk into the Compagnie Plein, where we had the dokhavn in view.

'How exactly did it happen? I vaguely remember Mama panicking when you came home covered in blood. Wasn't it something to do with one of his father's horses?'

I looked down at the cobbles as vivid recollections of Asmus flashed through my mind.

'There were thirty of us, on the last day of school,' I said. 'An organised battle, fifteen a side, Republicans against Orangists.'

Opa smiled. 'Even then, as it is now?'

I nodded. 'We were all well-armed, us Republicans. So were they. Slingshots, with wooden balls as ammunition. Cudgels. Wooden grenades in the toes of wet stockings. Asmus was our leader, carrying our black and red banner riding bareback on his Gelderlander grey.'

'You meant business, then.'

'All was fair in sport and war when we were that age, Opa.'

'Not much has changed then. But I'd question the word "fair".'

I explained that Asmus had won the toss and chose to attack. We'd given the Orangists ten minutes headstart to defend the circular mound we used to call the 'Muiderslot' fort after the ancient castle. There was a ring of poplars there, and a line of trenches dug years before.

'Asmus was behind us on his stallion. He was waving our banner when we heard him scream out to us to charge.'

I told him about the chaos of running bodies emerging from the undergrowth, missiles filling the air, screams and laughter and the clashing of sticks and groans and howls as the wounded went down.

'And then I felt the earth shake, Opa. I flattened myself to the ground, and when I turned, Asmus's horse was thundering straight for me.'

I described the swollen knots of pectoral muscle bulging in the arch of its broad chest above me, the front legs out-stretched. The rear pasterns and hooves appeared between them, striking the ground with unbelievable force on either side of my face directly before my eyes, spraying me with mud and rocks. The front legs had lifted again and I'd tensed for the blow before the horse had sailed over me and pounded on towards the trees, casting up great clods of turf beneath powerful hindquarters.

'Asmus jerked around to peer back at me,' I said. 'His body slid to the left across the horse's withers, his legs flung skywards and both hands torn from the reins. He flew in a slow-motion cartwheel into a poplar sapling that smacked across his back.'

Those fighting closest to him heard the simultaneous crack of wood and bone and watched him thud to the ground at the base of the tree.

'There I was, untouched by the horse. Frozen with shock.' I pointed at the scar beneath my hairline on the left. 'My face and jacket were blood-soaked from this wound. There were deep hoofmarks in the turf on each side of me, the earth bared as though someone had torn it away with a shovel.

'We thought Asmus would die there and then,' I said, 'but he was our general, he told us when he recovered… and he still tells us now, when we meet. He had to set his foot soldiers an example!'

'An example in courage is exactly what he is,' Opa said, 'getting around on that home-made cart of his. Can you imagine looking up at the world from ground level now he's paralysed? He's a fine example of someone accepting the *ongeluk pech*, the bad luck that life deals out.'

'Like Oom Joris?'

'Exactly like Joris.'

WE SOON LEARNED that Daniel Fannius had mustered seventy-two signatories in all, the Orangists ninety-four on their rival petition.

Opa and I looked on with concern as the situation took a brutal turn.

Infuriated with the result, the Republicans immediately mustered militia reinforcements and undertook a full-scale assault on the *stadhuis*. By evening the following day, they'd evicted all the occupants, despite fierce resistance and hand-to-hand fighting across the square.

In the aftermath, they enjoyed several months in office unopposed. The city returned to relative calm, but it did not last.

On 1 April 1703, in the early afternoon, I was working on the rigging of the latest *jacht*, the *Schonewal*, penned in the dokhavn canal. The mainmast had been stepped and I was slung high in a safety harness installing the backstay clamps for the topmast.

It was mid-afternoon. I had been working on the clamps for an hour, my fingers cramping, when several volleys of musket shot rang out in quick succession, followed by sporadic single shots.

Silence descended across the dokhavn.

'What in God's name was that?' someone shouted, as

figures appeared from different workstations and gathered in the forecourt of the saw windmill.

Opa Laurens called out, 'What can you see from up there, *mijn kleinzoon?*'

'It's coming from the *stadhuis*,' I shouted back. 'It must be the Duvelaers and the Orangists on the attack. We know they've had something brewing.'

A waft of smoke two streets away spiralled to rooftop level where the wind dispersed it across the buildings. It rapidly developed into a dense grey column charged with sparks. Scraps of burning paper and torn pages whirled skywards, drifting down in charred debris that settled on the cobbled laneways and in the canals.

A rectangle of burning paper caught my eye as it soared past. It coiled in on itself before gliding down to the dokhavn canal where the flames were doused. When it came to rest floating face-up, I recognised in the scorched remains a Republican poster that had recently appeared around the city—a gruesome, crudely drawn torso of William III, his head severed.

'We have another book-burning on our hands, Opa,' I yelled as I belayed down the mast. 'Maybe I should check on Magdalena to make sure she's not caught up in it.'

'That would be for the best,' Opa Laurens replied. 'If this is a repeat of the recent violence it could go on for several days. I'll let the *meister* know you've gone.' Then his eyes lit up, a wide smile engaging all his wrinkles. 'Give the widow my greetings and make sure you're at work on time tomorrow morning. We need that masthead finished. We're waiting to install the bowsprit.'

'I'll be home tonight,' I called back as I took off at a sprint, dodging around householders emerging from doorways along the Rouaansekai to investigate the commotion and threading my way through citizens streaming away from the uproar.

Halted by three armed militiamen blockading access to the market square, I hurdled a fence and ducked down several back alleys past the Latijn School to the Blindenhoek crossroad, where I turned into the Lange Noordstraat. I rushed towards Magdalena's house, rocks and fragments of broken glass littering the cobblestones, the smell of smoke hanging in the air.

I jumped over shattered wooden chairs vandalised from the coffee house opposite Magdalena's front door and circled two men kneeling beside the body of a labourer from Vlissingen I recognised, lying prostrate in the middle of the street, a purple contusion across his forehead. They were rifling through his pockets.

Further up the street and closer to the fighting, I could see rocks flying through a pall of smoke. Marauding groups were engaged in a wild melee, their howls and screams deafening, the commotion punctuated by occasional musket and pistol shots.

I bounded up the steps and called for Magdalena through a jagged hole smashed in a front window. There was no response. I called out once again and the door opened a fraction before she pulled it wide, stepping back as I burst in. I slammed it shut and slotted the security bar home, before walking towards her, my footsteps crunching shattered glass.

'Now they can't break in,' I said.

'Thank God you're here,' she replied, her voice shaking as she held out her arms. We clung to each other. 'I was hoping someone might come,' she said, her voice drowned out by yelling and the clatter of running footsteps in the street beyond. 'I'm glad it's you.'

'I couldn't leave you on your own.'

She took my hand. 'Come, it will be safer upstairs. I was up there when I saw you cross the street. I was halfway down the stairs when you called.'

She had arranged an armchair beside the window in the kunstkamer with a clear view of the street, the curtains partly drawn. I dragged a second chair across. When I took her hand, I found it freezing, so I reached for the other and held them in both of mine, breathing on them now again to calm her and for warmth.

'Such violence!' she said. 'It's far worse than it was last time! They've been tearing down the street to the hospital, their carts loaded with God knows how many of the wounded. I can't believe my eyes, Gerrit. They even ripped the door from the coffee house over there. Right in front of me. To carry away what looked like a corpse they'd dragged this far… covered in blood! Look, you can see the trail. It's been unbearable.'

I pointed down at the man staggering to his feet on the cobbles below, the pair who'd filched his belongings now gone. 'It doesn't look good. I don't know how long it's going to last.'

'Were you at work or caught up in it when it started?'

'I was up the mast. I had the best view in the house.'

'Are you expected back?'

'Not until tomorrow. I can stay for as long as you need me.' I glanced around the room at two large trunks placed against the far wall. 'I see you've started packing?'

'Yes, my departure date is getting close. I have so much to do.'

'Then let me help you.' I gestured beyond the window. 'There's no point in watching what's going on outside. We can leave them to sort things out between themselves.'

She drew shut the curtains. 'Help me pack? That's nice of you, Gerrit.'

I walked to the closest of the chests and peered in. It was part-filled with linens. 'What else goes in here?'

'More of my clothes and the sheets. I was in the middle of packing when the fighting broke out and I've done none since. They're stored down in the laundry and I have some boiling in the copper right now. I need to hang them out and wash the rest.'

'Then why don't we get it done?'

I followed her down to the washhouse at the back, where I stoked the fire beneath the copper with peat from the stack in the outside shed. She swirled the clothes in the simmering water with a paddle, before I made comical sport of winding them furiously through the table mangle and into the rocking rinsing tub, into which I pumped fresh water from the underground tank.

Red-faced, the sweat poured off me in the steam. For the first time since my arrival, I was gratified to hear her laughing at my clowning.

'You're privileged!' I shouted as I slowed the winding. 'I learned how to do this for Adriana and her arthritis. I used to wonder if she was feigning to keep me at it.'

Evening fell as the last batch was put through the wash. Both silent now, we hung the linens on lines across the yard, intent on getting everything up before dark.

When we re-entered the house the sounds of skirmishing were more distant and sporadic.

Magdalena moved into the kitchen. 'Should you go now it's quietened down? Or shall I prepare a meal for the two of us first and you can go after that?'

Her expression seemed to indicate that she was hoping for a yes but was not expecting it. When I made an eating gesture with my fingers, she broke into a smile I took for relief.

'Alright then, but while I cook you can warm some water and wash those enticing dokhavn perfumes off yourself.' She pinched her nostrils with thumb and index finger as she stepped to the stairs. 'I'll get you one of Leif's shirts. It'll be too big, so it should cover you to your knees.'

She returned, holding out a faded red shirt while I was

filling the tub. She turned me around and measured the shirt across my shoulders. 'It is too big, by several sizes, as I expected. That makes it a perfect fit. I'll see you in the kitchen when you're a new man and dressed for dinner.'

When I walked self-consciously back into the kitchen, Magdalena was placing on the table two steaming bowls of a thick pea soup she'd reheated. She'd added bacon cubes and thinly sliced smoked sausage. Two crusts of white bread lay beside them.

Choking back a laugh at the sight of me wearing what was more a nightgown than a shirt, she pulled back a chair for me and then sat opposite. 'You look as though you're dressed for bed already,' she said. 'Red is definitely your colour. It matches your cheeks.'

'I think it suits me,' I said, 'and I don't mind the style. Do you think the fashion will catch on?'

She did not answer at first as we broke the crusts and sipped the soup, and then, 'Do you know, I think it might. The legs might do the trick. They'll give the girls ideas. This is the first time I've seen yours bare. They're so much *whiter* than I expected. And *hairier!*'

I heard one of her slippers clunk to the floor and moments later her big and second toe slid up my calf, gripped the hairs and gave them an excruciating upward tug. My spoon clattered to the table and I gave a yelping burst of laughter, begging for mercy. At the same time, an unexpected glow of excitement rushed through me, momentarily intoxicating.

'You submit? Too much to bear?'

'Yes! *Yes!* I submit! *Pax!*'

'That is all I need to hear.' She released me, and I retrieved the spoon and regained my composure.

After dinner, Magdalena pointed out that my clothes needed laundering, and I could hardly be expected to wander through town half-dressed. I reconfirmed that Opa Laurens had suggested I stay until the following day.

'That's settled then. You can use the second bedroom. It's cramped in there, but we can make room. I'll make up the bed for you. We can have an early night if you like. I for one need the sleep.'

She prepared hot chocolate and I followed her up the stairs carrying the mugs, placing one in each bedroom. Once she'd prepared my room, we stood gazing uncertainly at one another, Magdalena biting the corner of her thumbnail. Then she stepped forward and took both my hands in hers.

'Look,' she said, 'I know this is awkward for you. I know you're wondering where this will lead, but this is me saying goodnight.' She leant in and kissed me on the cheek, her breasts brushing my chest before she turned away. 'I'll go down and run your clothes through the wash. I can hang them to dry before the fire. No.' She raised a hand as I took a step towards her. 'I won't need your help and I've got one or two other things to do down there. I'd prefer it this way but thank you anyway… for everything you've done for me today.' She stood at the door, shaking her head as our eyes met. 'This is not the time, Gerrit,' she said quietly. 'It has to be special for you. Now you go to sleep. I'll see to your clothes before I do the same.'

She turned away and closed the door.

I woke with a start in pitch darkness to the deafening sound of multiple rattles as a group of nightwatchmen patrolled the street below. I turned over, half-asleep, listening to them pass on towards the Penninghoek Singel embankment.

My blood ran cold when the curtains shifted and someone murmured from the shadows, 'The fighting stopped about an hour ago.'

I sat up alarmed before I recognised Magdalena's voice. 'My God, you gave me a shock! I thought someone had broken in.'

'They must have agreed on a truce or one side has surrendered.'

'I doubt that. Sunrise will tell the story.'

'It's past midnight. It's strange to see the night watch and their dogs on the street so late. I usually go to bed hours earlier when I hear them pass.'

'What are you doing up at this time?'

'I couldn't sleep for the noise so I came in here for the company.'

My eyes adjusted to the dark and I watched her shift from her seat on the windowsill and move towards the bed. I shuffled aside to make room for her. She sat, reached forward and smoothed my hair, her fingers cool. 'I've been here a while, watching you sleep. You looked so peaceful. And you're very quiet. You don't snore, not the way Leif used to on some nights. You give a slight puff now and again as if you're halfway through smoking a pipe. It's entertaining.' Her teeth gleamed. 'I half-expected smoke rings.'

Unsure, I reached out and stroked her cheek with the back of my hand, felt the heat in her, and was immediately aroused. Taking my hand, she moved my fingers to her lips, then stood. 'Come,' she said. 'I have something to show you downstairs.'

In the drawing-room she had built up the fire, two large kettles simmering above it. In the orange light and wavering shadows, I saw my clothes on a drying frame and on the floor a wide travelling mattress, unrolled, with sheets and two pillows laid out.

'What do you think, Gerrit? This is more comfortable, isn't it?'

Fully erect, confused, my heart beating at my throat, I was speechless as she led me to a side table on which she had a glass phial. She released my hand, removed the stopper and sniffed it before raising it to my nose. 'Lavender concentrate,' she said, placing it back on the table and then lifting her nightdress smoothly over her head. 'We only need a drop or two. Come, take off your shirt and give me your hand.'

Both naked, she poured a drop into my palm and then another.

I was trembling.

'Relax, Gerrit. Don't be afraid. It will come naturally to you. Now, rub your hands together until you have a film of perfume on both your palms. Then you can explore my body in any way you want.'

Her eyes filled with tenderness as she moved close to me, her groin to my thigh. 'Nothing is forbidden.' She smiled up at me. 'I know you're ready for me, but you must enjoy me first and the best will come later.'

Breathless, I ran my fingertips across her shoulders and down her back, following the fine ridges of muscle to the base of her spine, and moved my palms across her flanks. Then I stepped back to look into her eyes, reaching for the sides of her slender neck, stroking my fingers beneath the fine gold chain of her necklace.

Seemingly aware of my hesitant uncertainty, she reached for my hands and guided them to her breasts, then down to her vagina where she clamped them between her thighs. Sighing, she backed towards the mattress, leading me there. Lying with her back tensely arched, she guided me into her, the movement of her hips pulling me deeper still, until minutes later, ecstasy overtook us both.

Thirteen

Middelburg, 19 July 1710

ON A SERENE day under a clear blue sky, four carthorses hauled the *Zuytdorp* along the Haven canal into Middelburg, straining to make the turn to port from the Binnenhaven waterway and bring her alongside the Kinderdijk quay. She was home after her third voyage.

I left the shipyard to join the townspeople crowding the quayside between the bollards over which the dockside *garbuleur* labourers were looping her mooring ropes. Her foot-stamping crew manning the deck capstans winched her in from mid-canal.

I looked up at the masts, now cracked and weathered. I saw the caulking dislodged from between the side planks and noted the coat of slime at her waterline. Opa's lion figurehead had been freshly painted red and yellow for her arrival, but the rest of her was in disrepair. I nudged the carpenter, who had joined me for the inspection, indicating on the fingers of one hand the four months it would take us for her refit.

The decks swept away above me, a line of expectant faces at the rail.

As she moved closer, one sailor clambered onto the rail and, with a warning scream, leapt across the narrowing gap between the ship and the quay. He landed, overbalanced and somersaulted into the crowd, where he lay and kissed the quayside brickwork.

The crowd roared as a second figure and then a third hung outstretched in mid-air before falling to the bricks. I knew that all three faced a penalty for preceding the ceremonial disembarkation of Schipper Jan Akkerman and his officers, for whom they should have lined the decks as the drums rolled, but for them, I guessed it was a fine worth paying to be the first ashore. Besides, they were back on Zeeland soil and the provoost's lash would be aboard ship, hanging in his cabin.

Scanning the line of faces above me, I saw someone who looked like an Indian among the faces.

Where's he from? I wondered. *Goa, like Magdalena? Ceylon? Or is he Indian as I first suspected?* I looked closer. *He may be from the Moluccas perhaps, though he hasn't quite the features, and his skin is definitely darker than the three Javanese crewmen I met yesterday aboard the* Vaderland Getrouw *when she docked.*

On his arm, he carried a startling green-feathered parakeet of a type I'd never seen. Its red beak was tipped with yellow and its black neck ring stood out against a pink band across its throat. I made out a loose drawstring connecting its leg to his wrist, beneath which stretched its long, narrow blue-green tail, splashed with yellow.

Particularly interested in the bird, I nodded up at him and saw him nod in return. He wore a grey felt hat with a wide loose brim, mottled with splashes of paint and tar. He removed it and ran his fingers through his hair, which looked as if it had regrown after being recently shorn. The parakeet flapped and shrieked in alarm as he did so.

I surveyed the faces of the disembarking crew and recognised several old school friends among them.

The blue-coated, red-braided, lace-throated officers already ashore were distinct among the crowd. Then I caught sight of Opperstuurman First Mate Joost de Vlieger. He detached himself from the group and strode back up the gangway. He was a close friend of Opa Laurens. Our eyes met when he was partway up and we acknowledged one another.

I walked further along the quay to watch the *Belvliet*, the third and final ship in the returning fleet, glide past under tow.

The labourers who had completed the *Zuytdorp*'s moorings kept pace with her to man the bollards as the foreman swung the knotted lariat up to the *Belvliet*'s deck. Stragglers who had wandered down to watch shouted and hooted up at those they recognised at the rails.

Beyond the *Belvliet* lay the recently commissioned *Berbices*, the latest sister ship to the *Zuytdorp*, her freshly enamelled surfaces gleaming. An eight-pounder cannon was swinging inboard on the crane's straining pulleys, the black snout of its barrel ranging across the quayside houses. A team of riggers waited alongside to sling the next cannon onto the crane.

When I got back to the *Zuytdorp* and was about to board for a closer inspection, I had to wait as Joost descended the bouncing gangway. The Indian was behind him, shouldering his roll and carrying the parakeet in a bamboo cage.

Joost shook my hand as he stepped ashore and asked after Opa Laurens, who was now retired and confined to the house.

He turned to the Indian and then held his arms out to both of us. 'Sunil, meet Gerrit de Waal, senior carpenter in the dokhavn.' He turned to me. 'This is Sunil Dewaraja, one of our sailors. He joined the crew in Galle… in Ceylon. This is his first assignment and his first visit to Middelburg. I've arranged lodgings for him in the *Onrust*.' He turned back to Sunil. 'You'll come across Gerrit in the dokhavn, no doubt.'

When he mentioned Ceylon my interest quickened. I had a copy of a book of illustrations by Baldaeus at home, his evocative tropical sketches and paintings unforgettable, and Sara and I had once borrowed a copy of van Spilbergen's diarised voyage to the island from her papa. We had read some striking passages together on the bench beneath the apple trees.

Looking into the frank openness of Sunil's face in the shadow of the hat's brim, his dark and quizzical eyes examining my own, I sensed friendship with an immediacy of feeling

I knew I could trust. I'm not sure whether it was the humility and simplicity I saw there, but his sincerity and honesty, yes, for certain. And all that in a single glance. It seemed someone I'd known in the distant past and missed for years had walked back into my life.

As I stepped onto the gangway, I promised to look in on him at the *Onrust* during the coming week.

ON A WINDSWEPT day the following month, I invited Sunil to join me on a visit to the wide, hard-packed beaches at Westhove, to the north. They lay beyond Domburg and Oostkapelle, where timber groynes jutted at right angles into the channel from the sand flats and the dunes, protecting the coastline from consistent onshore gales that lashed the chartreuse shallows into foam.

Papa had taught me to fly my kite there years ago. Once again it was the wind I was after—this time to experience the thrill of riding the *zeilwagen* sand yachts, which I often sailed with others from the dokhavn.

We rode out of Middelburg on borrowed horses.

'We used donkeys used for pulling hay carts,' Sunil assured me when he surprised me by ignoring the stirrup and springing into the saddle. 'Vesak and me used to race them with other boys in the fields beside the village. This little horse should be no different.'

'Vesak?'

'My brother.'

'Younger than you?'

'Two years younger.'

The wind was gusting as we heeled the horses to a trot and headed down the Haven canal embankment. We rounded the three grain silos marking the southern edge of the town, where summer wheat supplies from the Baltic were being transhipped from a *fluyt* anchored in mid-canal. Rats and field mice swarmed among the silos, a pack of yapping terriers busy ferreting them out. A pair of red-coated kennel-maids whistling their commands to the dogs gave me a distant wave as we passed.

'Your friends?' Sunil asked, when I waved back.

'We used to help them with our slingshots when I was at school. The Wheat Merchants' Guild paid us a florin for every thirty rats we killed,' I smiled. 'Enough for a piece of buttered bread and a slice of beef washed down with a roemer of beer for each of us!'

We turned the horses northwards directly into the wind, Sunil's hat flapping, the occasional solitary bee striking our faces.

We crossed wooden bridges over irrigation channels interlaced between green fields of madder, kohl and beet, experimental tobacco and taller clusters of maize grown for fodder, their russet seed-heads rippling with the gusting wind. We passed gabled whitewashed farmhouses sheltered among elms and dark stands of cypress, their dense green foliage spiralling upwards. Here and there, farmers ploughed furrows behind teamed oxen, flocks of pied wagtails flitting across the fields as the black soil was turned.

When we passed through Aagtekerke, an unexpected cannon roar marking midday alarmed the rearing horses. I dismounted to coax my baulking roan back into a nostril-flaring walk along the cobblestones, Sunil calming his grey with clicks of his tongue and by stroking its neck.

An hour later, we skirted Domburg on the coast, pausing at the Black Bear Tavern for a taste of costly *Roote Leeuw bier*, Red Lion beer, recently imported from the one surviving Dutch brewery in New York.

We sat and drank from the bottle in the garden on a bench built around the trunk of an immense linden tree, renowned for its age.

'Nehalennia, the goddess of navigation and seafarers,' I said, pointing at two ancient granite sculptures on display in the landscaped shade. 'Opa copies them in oak occasionally, to decorate the after galleries on the ships.'

'I haven't seen anything that looks like them on board.'

'No, his template for the *Zuytdorp* gallery was the Grecian sphinx—his favourite.'

He walked across to inspect them. Each showed a goddess in a flowing toga seated in a rocky grotto, carrying a basket of apples, a dog reclining alongside. He knelt and ran his fingers over one of them.

'How old are they?'

'This used to be a Roman province, so they may be Roman, but some people think they're originally Germanic—Batavian, that is. The Batavi were our tribal ancestors.' I flexed my arm and pointed at my bicep. 'They were fierce! True Zeelanders. We're very proud of them.'

'Like you de Waals?'

'Like us de Waals!'

The enticing splash of the sea rolling up the sand beyond the buildings reached us, the faint smell of drying seaweed announcing the outgoing tide.

'Joost de Vlieger told me you're a good swimmer. He said you were diving for coins beside the *Zuytdorp* in Galle Bay the first time he saw you.'

Sunil did not comment, but when I added, 'In fact, you amazed him,' he stood, balanced his bottle of beer on the sculpture, crossed his arms and gazed thoughtfully across at me.

'I was diving for pearls at Mannar when I was twelve,' he said quietly. 'So yes, I can swim.'

'You were twelve? How old are you now?'

'Twenty. I turned twenty the day we crossed the equator.' He took off his hat and tugged at a fistful of his spiky hair.

'They gave me this hat after the ceremonies. To protect my shaved head.'

'The crossing ceremonies are an old tradition,' I said.

'I learned the hard way.'

'He told me you stayed underwater for almost four minutes when they threw you in after the ceremony.'

Sunil smiled. 'They thought I'd drowned.' He lifted his bottle, peered through the green glass then slowly drank the dregs. 'Did he mention anything else?'

'The shark attack.'

For a moment he seemed shocked, and then, 'What did he tell you?'

'Very little. He said you climbed the hawser onto the ship after the attack. You were injured and they took you to Galle Fort hospital.'

'The skin on my chest was torn open.'

'When you healed, Schipper Akkerman offered you a position on board.'

'As a *jongmatroos*[29].'

'So that's how it happened.'

'That's why I'm here.'

Sunil gathered himself for several hesitant moments, as though preparing to tell me about the shark attack, before asking instead, 'So, Gerrit, where are your sand yachts?'

We refilled the bottles from the cheaper barrel of local Three Barrels beer and stowed them in my saddlebag for the ride through the dunes that led to Westhove.

The line of trees marking the limits of Domburg ended abruptly in a row of steep dunes. The horses struggled up and then cascaded down their seaward slopes to the sand flats of the Westhove foreshore. Powdered sand whorled in the horse's

---

29 An apprentice deckhand

footfalls as we galloped, Sunil's shouts of glee whipped away as he waved his hat, while I gritted my teeth with my head down, scarlet scarf and tears streaming in the wind's blast.

When we reached the first scatter of houses at Westhove, we dismounted and led the blowing horses over the embankment to tether them at the tavern.

'You're back again, young Gerrit,' the publican said when I called him out to unchain the yachts. 'It's been a while.'

'It has, Andries. It has.' I raised a hand and waved it over my head. 'We're up to here in the dokhavn at the moment, but I'll more than make up for it now.'

I paid for three hours' sailing and he led us to a dozen sand yachts standing ready for hire, their ropes clattering against thin pine masts that seemed disproportionately tall for the bodywork. The streamlined hulls were constructed of light pine, low-slung and painted in garish barber's pole racing stripes of orange, white and blue, their cushioned box-seats low in the carts. Each wood-spoked wheel was rimmed with a wide circle of iron to track the sand.

We selected our yachts then uncorked the first of the two saddle-bagged bottles. The beer erupted and we ducked to catch the foam, open-mouthed and roaring with laughter as it splashed over us.

We wheeled our yachts over the embankment to the beach. I showed Sunil the workings of the steering-rope controls, the front wheel bridle and the way the gaff-sail caught the wind.

'It's simple,' I told him. 'These steering ropes control the front wheels. Like so.' I dragged the wheels to the left and right, then showed him how to raise the gaff sail. 'You know how the sails work aboard the *Zuytdorp*. This is no different. Keep your eye on the peak and adjust the shape of the sail to accelerate or tack. Always remember your steering's at the front, not the back, and avoid the sand close to the dunes. It's too soft. Follow my tracks if you can.'

We raised and rigged the sails, the ties loose so that the canvas whipped and cracked, then settled into the seats and hauled in the rope laced to the sail's boom. We wound it around the side cleat as the canvas filled and the yachts edged slowly forwards, then canted away from the wind as we steered them towards the sand swirl hurled along the beach.

Then the bellying sails opened up to the wind's full bite, and we accelerated away.

I slid full-length to the floor, resting my head on the seat. From this angle the sand flashed past at vertiginous speed, the craft swerving as I fought to bring the front wheels back towards the hissing edges of incoming waves, the sail lifting me in the opposite direction. I felt the play in the wheels and the tug in the sail rope, the spinning off-side wheel spokes stinging me with jets of loose sand as they bit and lifted, bit again and reared to bite once more. The screech of spinning metal, the wind's roar and the surge of shallow breakers sweeping up towards me and sliding away ran through me like ice fire.

I yelled with excitement. I had speed at my fingertips, each subtle switch in direction and each swerve in the sail's knife-edge giving the craft more power. I looked up and, with each kick of the gaff boom swaying against the blue silk of the sky, felt myself soaring on effortless wings.

When I looked back at the sand it blurred into an undulating glass carpet on which I seemed airborne. I was afloat, spinning through the immensity of space, hurtling into a void. I had often experienced the sensation before—but this time, for some uncanny reason, it conjured deep within me the intensely vivid thought that if my older brother Karel had been alive we'd have been racing across the sand beside each other, shared exhilaration streaming through us both. The image lasted for an astonishing split second before I looked back to see Sunil's yacht bearing down on mine and the black wooden piles of the groyne at the end of the beach less than twenty roeden away.

I immediately released the sail so that the craft canted sideways and swerved to a stop at the sea's edge, where I sat up and watched Sunil fly past. I held my breath as he swerved at the last moment, his yacht lifting dangerously onto the front offside wheel, the other three airborne, before righting itself and ploughing into the shallow sea beside the piles.

By the time I reengaged the wind and reached him, Sunil had hauled the craft back onto the sand and was sitting on the coaming. I stifled my laughter when I saw tears streaming down his face. I took them at first for the effects of the wind, but was concerned when it became clear he was unable to control them.

His wet shirt was open, the last tie connected at his waist. I was shocked to see the healing welts of horizontal scars ridged down his brown chest from neck to navel. He disengaged the last of the ties, opened the shirt wide and ran his fingers down his chest. 'These are my scars,' he explained, wiping his cheeks, 'the day I lost Vesak. I couldn't save him.'

Ah, so the tears are his own… and he lost his brother.

I leant forward, my elbows on my knees, my chin in my hands. 'Joost told me about the shark, but he didn't mention you lost your brother.'

He looked away. He did not reply as he manoeuvred his hull around to tack back up the beach, to rescue his hat and start the next run downwind.

The deeper scars are in his mind, I thought, as his craft caught the wind. *He must be tormented by feelings of piercing intensity similar to those I experienced when I looked down at Kathrijn in my arms, feelings I could not understand or put a name to until years later when I looked back and forgave myself for responding with guilt and remorse to a situation in which blame played no part.*

I watched him tack away and knew I had to let him know, somehow, that grief was one thing and self-blame another, as though he was my younger brother.

Was it Sunil's hint that he'd lost his brother to the shark that prompted me to ask Joost the next time he visited the house, 'Would you do the same for me as you did for Sunil?'

'Do what the same for you?'

'Sign me on aboard the *Zuytdorp* if I could convince you I had good reason to do so?'

'With your skills, I'd sign you on without you needing to ask,' he replied.

Mama peered round from the clavichord, slamming shut its lid. I saw her look of shock when I said, 'I'm asking all the same. I believe it's time and I'm certain Papa would agree if he was able.'

'Agree to *what?*' Mama called out. She upset the stool as she stood and rushed towards us. She thrust aside Opa's outstretched arm. 'Agree to what exactly?'

'To me taking one voyage to the Indies aboard the ship I helped to build. I've been preparing for it all my life. And I need to.'

'You need to why?'

'To follow in Papa's footsteps, if not to find him if he's still alive, at least to pay him the respect a son owes his father.'

Mama did not reply, her eyes glistening. She slowly shook her head as she sat beside me. 'So this is the day,' she murmured. 'This is the day I've been dreading.'

I reached out and took both her hands. 'We've always known that I would go. The time is right and what better vessel could I choose? I know every piece of timber in her structure, from the topmast to the keel.'

As I gathered my thoughts, I lifted my right hand and

smoothed away the tears on her cheeks that she seemed unaware of. 'If Papa is dead, then the least I can do is mark the places he visited before the end, to retell the story none of us knows concerning the last months of his life.'

The image of Sunil clinging to the forward anchor hawser with one hand and perhaps clutching his dead brother in the other rushed across my mind. 'If Papa is dead, then we need to give him a voice by telling his story to its end so that we can make sense of his life.' I released Mama's hands and raised my own, palms up, unable to find the words for the idea I was searching for. 'It's the only way I'll be able to imagine Papa telling me the story of his life himself,' I stammered. 'To pass on all he knows.'

Fourteen

WHEN I ARRIVED AT the Kloveniersdoelen Building where the VOC had set up its team of recruiters, there was a crowd already squatting on the steps.

I saw that some were immigrants from neighbouring Flanders, Westphalia and the Rhineland, ragged would-be soldiers who had heard about the recruiting drive and travelled from Bergen op Zoom and the south Bevelandt mainland to try their luck, exchanging the last of their money and possessions to be ferried across the Scheldt.

Others were locals I recognised who had followed the bugler and drummers as they'd paraded in VOC blue silks and black tricorn hats through the streets, announcing the opening of the recruiters' registers.

A dozen others were clearly homeless paupers brought along by one of the city's *zielverkoopers*, soul sellers, crimps who ran the Eagle and Rabbit Tavern and supplied the VOC with vagrants offered lodging at inflated prices in their premises, subsequently paid for out of their salaries once they signed on. They were often indebted for years. They were lying on the grassed embankment of Pottenbakkers canal in the shade of the linden trees waiting for the call from the contractors seated at desks inside the door.

I made my way through the crowd and climbed the steps towards the open double doors. I leant over the table to read my contract, prepared for me at Joost de Vlieger's request.

I checked the details. I'd been out of indentures since 1706, I read, and was now a senior carpenter in the dokhavn. I was signing on for three years as *oppertimmerman*, senior carpenter, sailing for Batavia aboard the *Zuytdorp* under Schipper

Marinus Wijsvliet. The scheduled departure was a fortnight away, at the end of July.

In the east, I could choose to remain aboard the *Zuytdorp* as she plied the Indies or I could work in Batavia's dockyards on Onrust Island or seek reassignment to another posting offered by the VOC officials there. At a salary of forty-five guilders a month, this was equivalent in rank to the opper-stuurman or the *koopman* under merchant, with an officer's privileges. It was a senior role with a satisfactory salary and I arranged for part-payments[30] to be made to Mama and Opa Laurens before I signed the document and countersigned the register. Then I signed the *bentcontract*, a voluntary sickness, accident and life insurance scheme that covered me for any adverse eventuality.

As I stood to leave, I felt a tap on the shoulder. I spun round to confront a grinning Karel de Reus, a labourer I had occasionally supervised in the dokhavn. Sporting a sparse moustache around a sensuous mouth and the flap of his left nostril split as punishment for vagrancy in Amsterdam, Karel had a deceptively whimsical look in his pale blue eyes—eyes in which apparent innocence could turn devilish in an instant. It was a look I had come to recognise as a warning of irre-pressible misbehaviour simmering below the surface. The lines that marked his devil-may-care smile were a seismograph signalling trouble.

I nodded to him, picturing his antics aboard ship if he was given too much slack. Schipper Marinus Wijsvliet and his

---

30 The VOC allowed crews to authorise *maandbrieven*, or 'monthly letters', allowing family members to claim the equivalent of a month's salary to a maximum of three months' salary a year while the crew were in the East Indies. The company also allowed *transportbrieven* or 'transfer letters'—IOUs authorising the payment to nominated family members of between one hundred and fifty to three hundred guilders, according to rank.

officers were in for a testing time and the provoost would have full use of his whip. As I walked away, I smiled with relief, knowing that Karel would not be a member of my team of carpenters. *Good luck to the other officers,* I thought. *Better still, he may be allocated to the crew aboard the Belvliet, the other ship accompanying us.*

When I walked back out into the summer sunlight, I knew I'd committed at last to a course of action I'd long dreamed about. I leant on the balustrade and looked across the canal at the houses curving the length of the opposite embankment and the shops lining the streets towards the centre of Middelburg. Beyond them, the *stadhuis* cupola and gold-painted quarter-moon spire towered over the gabled rooftops.

Now I saw them all with an unaccustomed sense of nostalgic finality. The secure feeling of place, of home, that I had so long taken for granted, had been altered by the scratch of the inked quill at the recruiter's desk into something unexpectedly insubstantial. The canal-side buildings seemed to float on their own reflections in the brown water as though transforming into imagined recollections.

I walked down the steps and across the bridge, determined to absorb the city and its streets and buildings, to capture them in my mind's eye as if for the last time.

I strolled along the Langeviele, before winding my way through the maze of streets towards Wijngaardstraat and Sint Sebastiaanstraat, soaking up the smells, sounds and colours of each successive market.

I slowed first at the street of butchers' stalls. Cuts of meat were suspended beneath the awnings and lesser slices of heart, liver and kidney lay on smeared marble under netting that kept persistent flies away, headless chickens hanging from ceiling hooks, their necks protruding like severed fingers.

Beyond them, I paused to talk to some of the fishmongers

with whom Daniel and I had often traded eels writhing in black and olive knots in buckets, the tang of salted *hareng* hanging in the air.

Further along, I passed the tailors' shop-front windows glowing with unfurled linen, calico and gauze. Expensive chintz and silks billowed across the dark recesses of the shops' interiors, where rolls of materials lining the walls were piled to the ceilings.

Then I browsed among the three bookshops ranged along the Lange Noordstraat, their foxed and battered second-hand volumes displayed on pavement tables. A fortnight before, I had bought a journal there to record the voyage. Bound in green leather, the letter 'G' was elaborately embossed in gold on the front.

I had also been amazed to find a second-hand copy of John Thornton's atlas on display, *The English Pilot*, published in 1703, which I'd promptly bought. I had pored over its pages that night and each night since, marvelling at the precision of the Englishman's updated copies of the charts of the VOC cartographers.

I glanced at the bakers' and pastry makers' shops along the Potten market. The warm scent of freshly baked bread and honeyed almond carried until I turned into the central market square fronting the *stadhuis*, where the aromatic cinnamon and coffee smells of the teahouses lined up around it filled the air.

I ordered a cup of Carletti chocolate and sat to watch the townsfolk stroll by. Some acknowledged me as they passed, others gathered at the far end of the plaza to inspect rows of flower stalls ablaze with marigolds and white and yellow chrysanthemums. An old gypsy couple caught my eye, bent under willow baskets overflowing with early sunflowers in a brilliant display of green and gold.

I experienced an outpouring of feeling for the lively scene, a sense of deep connection.

Beyond the flower stalls, I saw the wares of the St Luke's Guild artists laid out for sale. On the nearest of the displays, I noticed the latest still life paintings of Adriaen Coorte. From my cafe table, I could make out a series of exquisitely depicted seashells on rectangles of paper pasted on wood.

Leaving my drink, I wandered over to admire their detail more closely. They were miniature oils and pastels, executed with astonishing precision. I examined them, recognising among them peach pink angulate periwinkles, spotted cowries and white lace murex, each accurately patterned in coils and spirals of rose and rust. But the picture that particularly caught my eye showed two conches identical to those in my bedroom, painted in pale coral with orange veining. I couldn't resist buying it before returning to the teahouse to finish my drink.

Sipping the chocolate, I admired the intricate depiction of the shells. Coorte's superb draughtsmanship had pared them to their essence, capturing the subtleties in the grain of their surfaces and the intricate mottling in their colours. To my mind, the only feature the artist had missed were holes drilled into them, through which I used to play basic three-note tunes and sound warnings from my window ledge.

I finished the chocolate, picked up the picture and resumed my walk homewards.

I wandered through the arched entrance to the monastery of the *Abdij*, its wing of cellars-turned-prison cells and its farthest corner housing the city's orphanage, the cries of children at play echoing in the grassed courtyard. Halfway across, I stopped to allow a young girl to sprint past chasing a purple hoop. She was breathless, her cheeks scarlet and her hair streaming black above the bounce of starched white lace in the collar of her dress of grey and turquoise stripes.

The shouts of the children faded as I passed through the doors at the far end of the courtyard and out into Sint Pieterstraat. I followed the line of houses to the domed octagonal building of the Oostkerk church, where Mama played the organ. Steps led up on each side to its polished plain-glass windows, faintly lit by candles glowing inside. I halted before the pillared front doors, above which a macabre skeleton lay on a bed of nails sculpted into the granite, its knees up and its skull resting on a bedroll. Chiselled into the brickwork beneath it I read a dire quotation from Corinthians warning of the fleeting nature of the human condition.

I contemplated it. Like both Oom Joris and Opa Laurens, I was not religious, though I used to accompany Mama to the services there for her sake… and to privately admire some of the younger women in the congregation. Nor was I an atheist, preferring to keep an open mind to mysteries beyond my understanding.

As I reread the inscription, I recalled Opa Laurens admonishing me once, 'An *open* mind? Keep an open mind and you risk everything you think you know with any certainty flying out of it. Remember the riddle we pondered once? Is your mind in the world or the world in your mind? Or is it both?' He had spluttered with laughter. 'When you make up your mind that you know the answer or your mind makes itself up and convinces you, I want to be the first to know!'

And Oom Joris, who had been with us at the time, had added dryly, 'Always remember, *jonge*, your only certainty the more you experience the world around you and rationalise its nature is the revised extent of your uncertainty. Take a good look at me and learn.'

I strode on up the Breestraat. Partway along, I reached the house that had once belonged to Overtgrootvader Hendrick and Overgrootmoeder Margriete before he'd built the house on the canal. Oudoom Dirck—Great Uncle Dirck—had been born there and Francesco Carletti had lodged there when he'd landed so long ago.

The paving blocks beyond the picket gate were scrubbed clean. Red geraniums filled window boxes each side of the front door. Behind the panes of one window, a pair of pale grey cats with charcoal faces peered between the net curtains, studying me as I passed. They were so still I took them for porcelain ornaments until one flicked an ear as though repelling a fly, eased itself from the ledge with a flick of its kinked tail and disappeared as I walked on.

A harpsichord played behind the closed windows of the last house in the Breestraat. I recognised composer Pieter Bustijn's latest suite. I'd first heard it at an open-air concert in the *stadhuis* square a month earlier. It was now all the rage. The music grew fainter as I turned towards the Rotterdamse quay. I paused there to listen through to the end, even though Mama was intent on learning the same piece on the clavichord at home, her repetitive practising driving Opa and me mad.

I walked on down the embankment past the Middelburg Mint. The presses rattled as the batches of coinage ordered by the VOC for the coming voyage poured out. It was a fortune that the mint *meister*, Adolf de Groene, would sweat over until it was safely lodged in Schipper Marinus Wijsvliet's cabin beneath his bunk. Word was out that the *Zuytdorp* would be carrying an order from Batavia for more than one hundred thousand *gulden*-worth of coins, so security around the presses had been trebled.

I quickened my stride as I passed, the clinking of the bridle chains of the sentries' horses following me down the embankment.

I passed through the Segeersweg gate and turned at last into the garden. I walked around to the back door of the house. Opa Laurens was sitting in the last slant of sunlight beneath the apple trees. He raised a hand in greeting and I reached out and held it.

The moment became another farewell. I was turning away at last, relinquishing a communion I'd shared with Opa Laurens all my life, concentrated now in the feel of the old man's arthritic fingers between my own and in the vision of his short-sighted eyes peering up at me.

And I was leaving behind Opa's latest carving on the green slats of the garden bench—a part-finished block of white oak. It was a carving of my face, the cheekbones and beard half-emerged from the wood streaked with a flame-shaped fault line of dark tan.

My face in white and brown oak, the thought struck me. *When will I return to Middelburg to see it finished?*

Fifteen

Monday 27 July 1711 on the Rouaansekaai quayside

Mama gave me a desperate hug, clearly as reluctant to release me as I was to let go of her. She sobbed silently, tears running down her cheeks. I felt her shoulders shake with each inrush of breath. She looked up at me, ashen, managing a broken smile. 'Remember what we have always told you, Gerrit. You are a de Waal.'

I saw that she could not continue, so I put my cheek to hers and whispered, 'And a Tuineman. I am Maarten's son and yours. I will do the best I know how, the way you've always guided me.'

After a moment, she added as she always did, 'The *very* best, my son.'

'Yes, the very best.'

The silence enveloping us after we'd spoken was so charged the crowd surging around us melted away.

Opa Laurens, standing beside us, didn't say a word.

I looked across at him and understood that words were superfluous. I released Mama and embraced him, holding his frail skeletal body to mine for several minutes. I did not let him go until I saw him slowly nod and felt him pat me on the back.

I held him at arm's length with both hands on his shoulders.

'Opa, if there is no trace of Papa, at least we will have done him the honour of searching for him. And if that is the case, when I return, I would like us to carve the gravestone you've been wanting for him in the cemetery. An open book, with his name on one page.'

'And on the other?'

'That's up to you.'

He gazed at me for a long moment before his face softened. 'He was a de Waal. As are you.' Then he reached into his coat pocket. 'I have something for you.' He surprised me by withdrawing a brand new spyglass. He gave me an understanding smile as he handed it to me. 'You no longer have to look through it the wrong way around to put the things you were once afraid of at a distance. You don't need to transform the world through coloured glass anymore. Not for this journey.'

My childhood days are over, when I saw the world through a blaze of colour with a magical shake of the wrist. I will no longer be setting out on my daring voyages and confronting my fears within the secure walls of my house-ship and in the safety of my imagination. I have truly emerged from the barrel!

I turned back to him. 'Thank you, Opa.' I leant forward and kissed him on the cheek as I pocketed it. I could not resist smiling as I did so, whispering to him loud enough for Mama to overhear, her eyes softening as I quoted, 'When I was a child, I spake as a child, I understood as a child, I thought as a child—but when I became a man, I put away childish things.'

Then I stepped back and looked at them both. 'I will send letters home to you from Cape Town. I'll also send you the pages from my journal so you know exactly how the first part of the voyage went. I trust it will make a good story for you to tell your friends, Opa.'

He smiled. 'I look forward to telling it and I'll add it to the library. Take good care of yourself, *mijn kleinzoon.*'

I reached across and held Mama's face in both hands. She placed hers over mine and we gazed at one another before I lifted my bag and climbed aboard, unable to look back.

I stacked my gear in my cabin. When I returned to the rail, Mama and Opa Laurens were gone. It seemed for one lurching moment when I looked for them that the space where they'd been standing a moment ago had transformed into a void from which they'd been physically erased. I stayed at the rail, ridding myself of that gut-wrenching feeling, until the ship at last cast off and I was grateful they'd had the good sense to leave rather than go through the agony of watching us depart. I knew they'd watch her later as she moved down the Haven canal beside the house.

I imagined the mix of emotions they'd experience as the ship disappeared from view, after expending so much love bringing me up in the sanctuary of the house. Anxiety on my behalf, considering the fate that befell Papa; satisfaction, hopefully, at the way I'd matured with their guidance; bewilderment at the prospect of their lives continuing without me until my return, and perhaps anguish at the length of time it might take.

She glided at last from the dockside, the widening gap soon unbridgeable. Anticipation surged through me as I gazed down at the canal, but beneath the exhilaration, I felt a rush of what I can only describe as anxious regret as time seemed to slow and the water between the hull and the quay mirrored longer and wider reflections of the algae-stained bricks and wooden protective dolphins of the wharf, the linden trees lining its pavements and behind them, at last, the red-brick facades of warehouses beneath a pale blue sky streaked with cloud. As the ship drifted further, a dizzying uncertainty engulfed me, my departure marking an unnerving disconnect between the unknown future and my past.

I gripped the rail to steady myself, then looked up at the mainmast, gouging its track across the blue like a sharpened stylus. When I looked back at the houses drifting past, the unfamiliar sensation of vertiginous weightlessness passed and my focus shifted to the hoarse chant of the rowers in the two *waterschepen* towing the ship, the click-clack of their oars in the rollocks regular as clockwork.

The mainmast is my mapping stylus, I thought, *marking my track on my voyage across the globe to whatever the future holds in store.*

LATER, WHEN WE'D made the turn to starboard past Fort Rammekens and entered the broad Westerchelde estuary, I went back to my cabin in the forecastle. My subordinate carpenter had thrown his gear onto the top bunk. I read his name painted on the canvas—Evert Silkens. We had never met, but Joost had informed me that he was an old hand from Batavia who had transferred from the *Vaderland Getrouw* to return to Java, where he intended to retire.

I stretched out on my lower bunk, testing its length and comfort, once again checking the cabin I was so familiar with. I smiled to myself. *Are any of these yellow pine planks in the bulkhead among those I stripped in the saw windmill yards? I should have marked them in some way.* I rapped my knuckles on the bulkhead, pleased to hear it thump so true.

The quarters were cramped, though. An eight-pounder cannon lashed sideways to rings in the framing took up much of the space. Evert would be using it as a step to clamber into the upper bunk.

The ship's movements took on a special magic when she gradually picked up the wind in mid-channel. For the first time, I felt exultant as she began creaking and swaying on her way to the Wielingen anchorage. She was my ark, and her timbers, so familiar to me, were committed to my care.

When we passed the place Papa had taken me down through the Roman ruins into the cavern with the glass pebbles, I peered through the spyglass to see if I could pinpoint it, but that corner of coastline was pockmarked with the shadows of caves and overhangs in the cliffs and I was unable to recognise it. As I closed the spyglass, it struck me that my experience with Papa that day was a colourful fragment among so many in my memory. *I must hang on to them or the cross-currents in the oceans of my future will contrive to sweep them away.*

Thankfully, Opa had agreed to me taking the glass stone from the kunstkamer display that Papa had found that day. I'd packed it along with larger of my Queen Conch shells. There was something reassuring in having the stone and the shell with me. They held such strong and long-lasting connections with home and family they'd taken on the characteristics of sacred objects to me.

An hour later, we reached the anchorage where we were due to wait for the *Belvliet* to join us, and for the winds to pick up for the journey into the channel and on to Rotterdam. The rest of the fleet was gathering there.

I heard the port bower anchor released, the chains rattling out and the rope hissing through the hawse port, when the cabin door opened and Evert peered in before stepping around it.

He was short and wiry and, at first glance, deeply sun-burned. Then I noticed his features were East Asian and guessed he may be part-Javanese. His high forehead carried a web of fine lines that deepened when he smiled, his eyebrows lifting. I thought he was bald, before noticing a circle of grey stubble running round the back of his skull from ear to ear. The seams and panels of his unusually styled sun-bleached blue overalls were badly worn, the leggings very bowed. He was wearing wood-soled sandals.

'Evert Silkens, *agan*,' he said, extending his hand. 'Happy to meet you.'

His Dutch is fluent. But 'agan'?

'Gerrit de Waal,' I replied. 'Me too. I heard you transferred aboard to get back to Batavia.'

'I did. I want to get home. My family is in Serang.'

'Ah.' There was an awkward silence, before I asked, 'So that's why you called me "*agan*"?'

He ducked his head to one side. 'From *juragan*,' he laughed, 'you get *agan*. It means boss. Or I could use *tauke* if you prefer.'

'What if you don't use either? What if you use Gerrit and I use Evert?'

'That's good with me… *agan*.' He grinned. 'That's the last time I'll use it. But if my tongue forgets, you'll know the meaning.' Then he turned back to the door. 'Time for me to eat. I hope the food is better on board this ship than it was on board the *Vaderland Getrouw*. It should be. One of the cooks is a friend of mine.'

'His name is not Karel de Reus, is it? I've heard he's working as a messmate in the galley.'

'No, Santoso. Second cook, from Atjeh. He's a good man.'

'He'll need to be, with Karel working for him. You'd better warn him. There won't be much left for the rest of us with Karel working there. We have a trainee *timmerman* with us, by the way, Laurens Voort. He's been working with me in the dokhavn for the past two years. He's young, just nineteen, but he already has good skills.'

'Where is he now?'

'I've arranged a bunk for him in our tool store, up on the starboard side.'

'So he's not down on the orlop deck with the others?'

'No. It's more convenient to have the three us up here together.'

FOUR DAYS LATER, in the late afternoon of 1 August, favourable winds rose from the south-west, a bank of dark, lightning-lit clouds low on the horizon threatening thunderstorms. I watched Schipper Marinus Wysvliet, on his first full command to the East Indies, relay orders through his officers on the quarterdeck to raise the anchors and set the sails. Beside us, I saw the *Belvliet* do the same.

Schipper Marinus had advised us during an officers' meeting that morning that we faced a considerable risk in leaving at that time. We were too late to join the *Paasvloot* April Easter fleet and too early for the October and December *Kerstvloot* fleets that avoided the worst of the doldrums in the *wagen weg*, north of the equator. He confirmed that he and Schipper Dirck Blauw aboard the *Belvliet* had agreed to chance it.

'Even if we run out of wind there, a delay still gives us a good two-month head start on the October fleet. That's good for business,' he said.

I joined the crew lining the mid-ship rails as the *Zuytdorp* eased through the Sluisegat shoals on a north-easterly bearing. She rounded the flare of the Westcapelle beacon, the seas rising. The beaches stretching between Westhove and Breezand were barely visible as Walcheren Island faded behind us. As night descended, I leant far out to catch a last glimpse of the estuary disappearing as darkness fell.

When I felt the deck shudder beneath my feet, an intense rush of exhilaration and relief coursed through me as the *Zuytdorp* responded to the power of the wind and the drag of each wave, rolling up the face of one surge before veering down the back of the next, responding to the thrust of the sails, coming alive.

As she lifted, swerved and settled, then pitched and rolled again to career across the next series of waves, she brought to life my boyhood fantasies at the helm of my imaginary *Santiago*, flying across those wild and empty seascapes into the unknown. *What secrets will the world open up to me now,* I wondered, *as a life imagined becomes a life lived?*

Two hours later, when I was back in the cabin after dinner, eight bells rang in the watch change and I heard the running footsteps and curses of crewmen emerging from the orlop deck below. The bosun struck his baton against the railing as he strode the mid-ship deck, his baritone ringing through the ship as he sang for the relieving *prinsen-kwartier*, prince's four-hour watch to fall to—

> *'Hoort mannen, hoort!*
> *Niemand drinken hem dronken in bier of wijn*
> *t'Zal vanavond prinsenkwartier zijn.*
> *Prinsenkwartier houdt goede wacht…*[31]*'*

For several minutes the staccato beating of the baton echoed against the deck rails accompanied by answering shouts in the companionways, the slamming of distant doors and hatchways and the bellowing of the bosun's voice as the song trailed off and crewmen of the relieved *Count Maurits-kwartier*—Count Maurice four hour watch—shuffled to the deck below.

The smell of pipe smoke, sweat and the tang of brandy carried to me as they passed, heading for their hammocks and mattresses slung in parallel above the cannons on the port side of the ship. It was eight hours until their next four-hour watch and they needed the rest and warmth, sheltered from biting winds coming up the channel and off the North Sea.

At FIRST LIGHT, I was back on deck as we skirted the Slijkgat sandbanks in tandem and turned towards the Hellevoetsluis naval base, where I counted six other merchant vessels lying at anchor, line astern, close to the northern edge of the embankment. Shadowy warehouses lined it, obscured by mist.

Cannon fire from the battlecruisers welcomed us—the *d'Uyno*

---

31 'Listen men, listen!
    Anyone who's drunk with beer or wine tonight
    Is not to turn out for the prince's quarter watch.
    The prince's quarter is an excellent watch…'

and *d'Oranje Galley*, both allocated to protect the fleet on the first leg of the voyage. I watched the *Belvliet* slip past, leading us to our appointed mooring stations. She was close enough for me to recognise old Schipper Dirck Blaauw in full uniform on the poop deck. He was in overall command of both ships.

As we anchored, the VOC supply ship, the *Fortuin*, rounded the northern promontory and sailed past us to take her upriver position. Joost had told me she'd be joining us. She was carrying emergency food supplies to replenish the home-coming Christmas fleet returning from Batavia and Ceylon.

Within hours, departure signal flags were hoisted in the stiffening breeze and capstan songs rang out aboard each vessel as the bower anchors were wound in, oozing estuarine mud. The ships glided into the grey wash of the North Sea under wind-filled staysails and topsails and the last glimmer of the Scheveningen sands faded behind us as the ships pitched into the open sea towards the northeast coast of England.

I watched the wake uncoiling behind us as we set course *achter om*, around the back of Scotland and down Ireland's west coast.

I knew we'd taken this longer course to avoid skirmishes with French fleets in the channel, a consequence of the ongoing War of Spanish Succession. I had also heard that the English fleets, our allies at the time, were not to be trusted either. It had something to do with the recent arrest of the Duke of Marlborough by the Tories in London on charges of embezzlement. I found that impossible to believe. We considered him a military hero in Zeeland after his string of victories against the French Alliance on our behalf.

It took me some time during those first days at sea to settle into shipboard routines I wasn't used to. Joost advised me to be patient. It would take a month or two.

After a breakfast of groats, prunes, bread, cheese and *Princesse Royal* beer, Evert, Laurens and I gathered on the waist deck with the ship's company to attend compulsory prayers and a brief sermon led by the *ziekentrooster*, the chaplain. That was followed by Schipper Marinus or one of his delegated officers giving us various readings from the *Artikelbrief*, the ship's disciplinary rules and regulations, confirming the duties of the officers and crew and the severe disciplinary measures for the slightest misdemeanour.

When the bosun called for the sick to attend the medical team at the base of the mainmast for the *verband*, the bandaging and the administering of potions and prescriptions by the *oppermeester* senior surgeon and his two assistants, we were free to set about our duties. I allocated the tasks and we began work, occasionally as a group, but usually independently.

I spent the mornings stripped to the waist and sweating in the humid holds, despite cold winds sweeping the upper decks. My only company down there was the ship's gigantic black cat, a fiercely independent tom that answered to the name 'Beelzebub' when it chose to. It was kept aboard to take care of rats and, according to the superstition, to bring the ship good fortune.

I inspected the planking and caulking below the waterline, squeezing between crates and rows of casks and barrels stacked to the deck above. I surveyed the ballast and measured the ever-present slop of stinking seawater in the bilges, regularly cleared by the manning of the pumps. The thump and wash of waves thrashing at the bow and the hiss of water brushing along the sides were magnified in the enclosed spaces.

Above decks, my greatest pleasure was clambering each afternoon up the ratlines to the topmast crow's nests on each of the three masts. I'd grown used to their dizzying height when working in the dokhavn. There they had been still, but I soon grew used to bracing myself against their swaying at sea. I inspected the yards and mast lashings and the blocks and pulleys, checking for the slightest evidence of timbers springing, before relaxing on the foremast to enjoy the ship's roll and pitch and the rush of the wind through the sail canvas and slapping pennants.

The sight of the distant decks below was dazzling. Men in miniature worked across the ship or rested between watches, colourful passengers and their children at the rails, the rectangle of sunlit green on the poop where oak seedlings destined for the company gardens at the Cape were boxed and lashed, the squawking chickens cooped beside the kitchens and the pigs in the holding pens, their grunting carrying faintly to me each time the wind dropped.

The foremast swung me out over waves that exploded beneath the forepeak as the ship rolled and settled and surged, the wash ahead of the hull alive now and then with dolphins. On one day of light breezes during that first week, a pod appeared in the glassy thrust, entertaining me with an exuberant display of muscular leaps and somersaults, each re-entry tracing on the sea's surface a sunlit trail of sparks. They disappeared as abruptly as they'd arrived and I wondered if I'd dreamed them.

That particular night, I recorded an incident in the journal I'd maintained since departing Hellevoetsluis.

> *12 August—Mid-morning observed the rapid approach of galjoot Geertruida from the south-east, sent out from Texel to report the returning Christmas fleet from Cape Town arrived ahead of schedule and was already at anchor in the Zuiderzee. Zuytdorp and Belvliet shortened sail, allowing Geertruida to meet with us. The schippers were thereupon presented the opportunity to make free with the victuals aboard Fortuin. Hold number two rearranged for*

fifteen extra barrels of bread/biscuit/water/beer/ sauerkraut and three casks of Burgundy. Two live oxen also loaded. On this voyage, it is certain we will not starve.

We entered the channel between Fair Isle and the rocks of North Ronaldsay the next morning. This was our gateway to the broad North Atlantic and, towards evening, we turned south-west towards St Kilda, still a week away, I was told, and the west coast of Ireland beyond that.

That day the body of a dead soldier was brought out of the sickbay. He was an old German who had died of typhus fever. The senior surgeon had quarantined him six days earlier when the recognisable dark rash had appeared.

'Where did he catch it, do you think?' I asked the day he'd moved him into the sickbay, three cabins beyond mine. 'Not aboard ship, surely.'

'I don't believe so. We have a clean bill of health. I've confirmed he was recruited through the *zielverkooper* at the Eagle and Rabbit Tavern. He must have caught it there.'

'Is he contagious?' I asked.

'There's a chance because we aren't sure how it spreads. We've taken all the precautions. We disinfected him with a mixture of vinegar and gin spirits and we found little evidence of lice or fleas when we gave his clothes a thorough smoking.'

'I hope you're right.'

'We're in trouble if I'm not.'

We attended his burial service with the crew, the first I'd witnessed at sea. We watched the sailmaker sew him solemnly into the canvas of his hammock, weighted with a pair of cannonballs. Four sailors paraded his corpse on a stretcher around the mainmast three ceremonial times to a funereal drumbeat and the prayers of the chaplain, before they slid him over the side down a plank chute. Air-pockets kept the package momentarily afloat on the churning sea before it sank.

Immediately after the burial, I stayed to observe with interest the auction held to dispose of his belongings—two clay pipes and a half-filled tobacco tin, a ragged brass-buttoned worsted waistcoat and wood-soled leather shoes, three full bottles of *Jenever* gin and a battered, red-buttoned squeezebox.

Sunil approached me moments before the bosun began the bidding for the squeezebox. 'I was learning to play one of those in Galle,' he said. 'Should I bid?'

'Your decision, Sunil. Do you have the money?'

'A little… probably not enough.' He smiled. 'Would you back me if I need more?'

'Of course, but only so far.'

'How will I know how far?'

'Watch me. If I nod, you can take it up another guilder. If I don't, that's my limit.' Then I laughed. 'Take care! Don't outbid us both and break the bank.'

At first, Sunil was the only bidder. He was about to claim the prize for his opening bid, but before the gavel came down for the last time in his favour, I was astonished to hear Karel de Reus, of all people, top Sunil's offer. The pair then bid furiously together and, despite my backing, Sunil, to his chagrin, lost out.

A WEEK LATER on 1 September, we turned due south, and the next fortnight saw us in open water. I revelled in watching the blue-black waves, strong winds hurling rain squalls from the starboard quarter, the ship swaying and pitching in the steep hollow seas as she made good time under full sail down the west coast of Ireland. I was often up one of the swaying masts watching the crews occasionally take in the *bramzeilen* topgallants as the wind gusts strengthened.

One afternoon, I noticed the chief gunner and his gunnery crew, busy on the waist deck below, preparing four cannons for firing. I shinned down the mainmast ratlines and joined Joost at the navigation station on the quarterdeck.

'We'll be firing a sixteen-gun salute in half an hour or so. Be prepared, it can get noisy,' he warned me. He held out an hourglass in his right hand. 'We'll be timing the gunnery crew reloading.'

Sharing one of his powerful telescopes, I swept it across the faint blur of the distant coastline. 'That's Bantry Bay,' Joost assured me, as our course kept the distant Irish coast in the glass. 'Cape Clear is up ahead.'

When we swung south-east away from the coast, the *d'Uyno* and the *d'Oranje Galley* turned back towards the north on their return journey to the Zuiderzee.

The gunnery crews aboard the *Belvliet* and the *Zuytdorp* gave them successive full powder broadsides as they glided past. When they both returned fire, I imagined myself back in St Helena alongside Overgrootvader Hendrick, sensing the changes in wind direction off Cape Paraveles, deafened, and breathing the smoky stench of cordite during the battle.

THREE DAYS LATER, we celebrated the crossing the fortieth parallel and, coincidentally, Schipper Marinus's fortieth birthday. We had passed the Berlengas archipelago off the Portuguese coast, and the schipper broke out extra rations of brandy and raw Spanish Marsala for the crew.

'You can also slaughter one of the oxen for roasting,' I overheard him instruct the ship's steward, during the morning meeting. 'I'm feeling charitable now I've reached middle age! Everyone aboard is to enjoy a share, soldiers included.'

That surprised me. It seemed uncharacteristic, given his conversations in the officers' mess which had suggested until then that his nature was more frugal than generous. In fact, I half-suspected he intended to preserve the extra rations we'd loaded from the *Fortuin* to profit from their sale on the black market in Batavia. It was a common practice among senior officers to which the VOC turned a blind eye, according to gossip in the dokhavn.

An extraordinary incident occurred during the celebratory dinner that night.

Karel de Reus was among the messmates serving the two officers' tables. Partway through the evening, he carried a prized ham and large sausage filled with minced tongue and herbs through the swing door. He strode to the schipper's table, the loaded silver tray balanced on his shoulder with his right hand. He placed the tray on the table with a dramatic flourish, caught my eye across the room, gave me an unexpected conspiratorial grin, and swept out. When we did not receive a helping at our table, I gave it no further thought, though Karel's smile had puzzled me. *It must be a special privilege for the senior officers only,* I thought.

The second ham and sausage, which Second Cook Santoso had arranged on another tray for our table, were not missed at first, but when the messmates cleared away the plates, one of the undercooks noticed that only one ham bone was returned. When the provoost and the quartermaster searched Karel later that night, they discovered the second bone, picked clean, in his apron pocket. He should have thrown it overboard.

I was standing beside Evert at Karel's public trial the next day. He was accused of secreting the ham and sausage under his apron and returning the empty tray to the galley. According to the testimony of witnesses, he served them up—with typical bravado, I imagined—to a group of soldiers gathered out of public view below the forepeak. Apparently, he'd used the ham bone to beat a triumphant tattoo on a military drum, while a pair of fiddles was scraped, then threw his energies into producing a series of unpractised notes from his red squeezebox, several soldiers dancing drunken jigs.

'I knew it wouldn't take him long,' I commented to Evert. 'His thieving sleight of hand does not surprise me.'

'But why keep the bone? It gave the game away.'

'As a souvenir, perhaps? To prove how cunning he is. Or as proof of his daring when he outmanoeuvres those in authority.'

He was shackled to the mainmast and we were all obliged to witness the thirty lashes he received, his back bared, his grunts succeeding each crack of the whistling leather. Then the quartermaster held his right hand over his left against the mast, fingers splayed, and the provoost drove a razor-sharp stiletto through the fleshy webbing between the thumb and forefinger, before hammering it home to the hilt.

He hung in half-crucifix for six long minutes, his gasps agonising to listen to, before tearing himself free. The *onder-meester*, the second under-surgeon, later told me that when he was stitching and bandaging the wounds Karel had boasted that 'the scars will be cheap at the price'.

I had to smile. 'That's Karel, through and through,' I replied. 'He used to work for us in the Middelburg dokhavn. We used to call him the "*Waterspaniël*".'

'Why?'

'You've seen the split in his nostril?'

'You can't miss it.'

'He earned it when he was arrested for begging in Amsterdam before looking for work in Middelburg. He'd been imprisoned for a year in the Tugthuis prison, you know the one. He used to boast about his experiences in the drowning cell. He swore it was an experience he'd regarded as a challenge the first time, furiously pumping the water out faster than it came in to drown him, had looked forward to it the second time and had embraced it as an enjoyable routine the third!'

'How so?'

'It gave him the chance to bathe and launder his clothes, he told us. All he had to do to get thrown in there when he felt the need for a clean-up was fold his arms and refuse to go down into the sawpit. They always had him at the bottom of the pit, so he was the one who got covered in sawdust.' I laughed. '*Itch!* Scabies is nothing, according to him… brazil-wood sawdust makes your *bones* itch!'

By the time he'd scrubbed himself clean, I explained, the fast-rising water had been up to his chest. Only then did he slosh his way across to the internal pump handle and work flat-out to pump the water out quicker than it was pouring in. Hours later, he'd overtaken the incoming volume and had the water down to his navel. By nightfall, he'd have the room cleared and they'd let him out, but never before he'd worked his heart out at the pump and come close to breaking point.

'He pounded his chest the first time he told us that story,' I said, 'and he burst out laughing.'

'Why?'

'"They thought they could tame *this* wild animal[32]," he told us. "They might have come close, but I had other ideas!"' I nodded at the under-surgeon. 'It seems he has a point, wouldn't you say?'

Five days later, while I was writing up my journal after dinner and had completed three brief phrases, Laurens pounded on my door screaming for me to come quickly to the

---

32 The Tugthuis prison motto was '*Wilde beesten moet men temmen*'—wild beasts must be tamed by men.

galley. 'Evert is in trouble,' he gasped. 'He is choking. He can't dislodge whatever he has swallowed into his windpipe.'

Rushing with him to the galley, I saw Evert stretched out on the deck, a deathly silent group around him. I forced my way through and found Santoso kneeling over him, head down, his fingers probing Evert's open mouth. Evert was not breathing. He seemed to be unconscious and convulsing.

'Stop!' I shouted. 'You might make it worse. Someone get the oppermeester!'

Santoso jerked his hand away and stumbled sideways as I reached down, turned Evert over and, with an arm around his midriff, forcefully lifted him. His unexpected weight almost brought me to my knees.

'Laurens! Give me a hand!' I yelled.

Together we lifted him, head down, his hands scrabbling on the deck as though he was reaching for his sandals. We shook him violently for several minutes, but he turned at first an apoplectic red beneath his tan and then his lips and fingertips a blue I'd seen before, as his eyes rolled back into their sockets.

At last, shocked and exhausted, I glanced across at Laurens and shook my head. We laid him back on the deck and the senior surgeon and his under surgeons, who had arrived and were watching us, took over.

Half an hour later they carried his corpse to the sickbay, where I witnessed the senior surgeon probe with a pair of silver tongs and remove a grisly chunk of green-skinned apple lodged deep in his windpipe.

When I completed my journal entry the following day during a thunderstorm, it read,

> *23 September—sighted the Madeiras. Closed to within one-half mijl. The rounded peaks of Porto Santo run due south.*

> *Evert Silkens died last night after choking on what was discovered to be a large piece of apple lodged there. Our considerable efforts to save him were in vain. There was no cure in prospect, God rest his soul. He was sent to his Maker in the rain, which his Maker has sent us. Schipper Marinus Wijsvliet agrees that is 'A fair exchange'. I am uncertain of his meaning unless it is in scornful reference to his Javanese descent, which I note here with concern. Or it may be that the rain that saves many lives is measured against the one life sacrificed.*
>
> *I have promoted Laurens Voort to my ondertimmerman.*
>
> *I am now without one timmerman. I am negotiating with the schipper to promote Sunil Dewaraja to the vacancy. It is my belief he will make a fine apprentice under my tutelage. The decision will be made at the schipper's pleasure. Sunil has expressed his interest in the appointment, but the schipper has yet to be convinced.*

We passed the reefs of the Salvages two nights later, lit with the flares of fishing boats from the Canaries. I thought of Venice when I saw them, in particular, the many illustrations I'd seen of gondolas carrying lanterns at carnival time. Our arrival there was a signal for three ships destined for Curacao and Surinam to change course westwards at first light, so that only the *Belvliet*, the *Zuytdorp* and a *galjoot* heading for Brazil remained the next day.

That morning I watched the line of the Canary Islands lift over the horizon.

When we reached them, Joost showed me how to take a bearing on the island of Fuerteventura as we sailed in fluky winds through the passage. We had the island's westerly point to port and Gran Canaria's bleached cliffs infested with flocks of shrieking tern on the starboard beam.

During the evening I sketched Fuerteventura in profile on a blank page in Thornton's atlas. The island's rolling Jandia hills were split by an elongated scimitar-shaped slash of white sandstone in the green, which to my mind stood out like a wind-filled sail so that it seemed the island itself was on a voyage eastwards towards Cape Juby and Morocco.

As usual, I consulted the atlas and marked our progress, then ran my finger south-east to Cape Bojador on the Mauritanian coast, surrounded by the maze of reefs of *Abu Khat Ar*, the Father of all Dangers, and beyond it the dunes of the Sahara. The empty land of the Tuareg! I recalled Mama's comment regarding my blue eyelashes when I'd returned home after escaping the barrel so many years ago.

At dawn the next day, with the winds easing further still, I saw to the west the distant peak of Mount Teide on Tenerife. Morning sun on the snow shimmered like water down its volcanic face.

Joost pointed across the rail. 'That is one of the few landmarks in the open ocean we can use to calculate our longitude against the VOC charts,' he said.

I nodded. 'I know. Opa Laurens explained the principle to me. When I was a boy I often imagined steering my houseship towards St Helena Island to confirm my exact position.'

FOUR DAYS LATER, we crossed the Tropic of Cancer and the wind stilled, as though responding to an unseen signal. The sea smoothed to an undulating sheet of blue silk, its surface haunted by ghostly whorls of breeze that died away, flattening to glass, leaving the ships dead in the water. For days, when I looked across at her, the *Belvliet* seemed a hazed mirage floating to starboard on a sea with a plunging emptiness to it. Beyond her, the *galjoot* destined for Brazil drifted westwards, gradually disappearing into the void of the vast sea-sky.

The eerie silence and the ocean stillness were dispiriting and the heat unbearably oppressive. The mood among the listless crew became tense and sullen and I noted in the journal that scurvy, already apparent in a few before Fuerteventura,

> *…has now spread to many. Eighteen reported sick today at the morning verband and most are showing symptoms. Twelve are ordered confined to the temporary sick bay forward of my cabin. I hear them very doleful and smell them. The senior, second and third under-surgeons work around the clock administering to them.*

THE FOLLOWING WEEK, the Cape Verde islands drifted into view, clouds over them promising rain. In the mid-afternoon, a series of showers fell, accompanied by the lightest of breezes. The crew collected water in buckets and casks from sagging awnings rigged against the sun.

That night my journal entry was still focussed on the sick. I wrote,

> *6 October—I observed the ondermeester bleeding all the sick into a roemer, which he discards overboard. My understanding is they are also given twice daily enemas of chamomile, Venetian soap and boiled seawater. God forbid I should fall sick. They are served a diet of chopped sauerkraut in chicken soup and biscuits softened with olive oil and cheese, in accordance with the 1695 Ordre en Instructie. The schipper presented me with a copy against the occasion that any of my subordinates are struck down with any sickness. This remedy is understood to hold*

the disease at arm's length. I trust it may be so.

THE BROKEN SHADOWS of the Cape Verdes were in sight for two days as we gathered way in the squalls. Sao Tiago faded from view on 8 October as the ships entered the northern limits of the *wagen weg,* our avenue to the equator.

I enjoyed the company of Laurens Voort, who was now living in my cabin. He was young, lively, brash and good-humoured. We got along well and, although he was unqualified, I had confidence in his skills.

'At least the chickens are enjoying this lack of wind,' he'd said the day he'd moved into my cabin, leaning over his bunk and grinning down at me.

'Why?'

'They only have to lay their eggs once.'

He had been amused by my puzzled expression. 'Down the west coast of Ireland every time they had their backs to the howling gales, they had to lay them twice. I can vouch for it!'

MY NEGOTIATIONS FOR Sunil's transfer from the *prinsen-kwartier* watch took two weeks. At last, with Joost de Vlieger's recommendation, the schipper agreed. 'You can have him,' he said, 'on loan. On condition he returns to watch duties and sail handling whenever we need him.'

So Sunil shifted from his stifling quarters on the orlop deck to the bunk Laurens had used, rigged on a converted shelf in our store, which was filled with tools, jacks and timber planking. He was pleased to learn he'd be joining Laurens for meals, his new diet at under-officer level a step up from the peas and salted pork or beef and stockfish he'd faced until then.

The day he joined us, he lifted his lip with a forefinger, pointed at the stub of a snapped front tooth and broke into a victorious jig, his arms upraised, when he heard the news. 'No more tooth-breaking hardtack biscuits! No more cheese you can't chew, smothered in mould!'

Over the coming weeks, he and I worked together throughout the ship. I enjoyed explaining the intricacies in its construction to him, reliving the work I'd done ten years before, frame by frame, panel by panel, plank by plank. I found him to be a quick learner with a surprisingly retentive memory, and I felt both relief and pleasure as he took to the work as though born to it. He absorbed my demonstration of the various tools and soon learnt the qualities of the ship's different timbers that were displaying stresses and wear.

OUR PROGRESS THROUGH the ship over the four oppressive weeks we were becalmed in the *wagen weg* was an absorbing distraction from the disaster developing around us.

On 3 November, the *Breede Raad*—the council of senior officers from both ships—met aboard the *Belvliet* to review the situation. I knew it was dire.

'Seventy-six crewmen on both ships are ill and incapable of working,' Schipper Marinus said after the meeting. 'Seventeen of those are unlikely to survive the next fortnight.'

He went on to confirm that under the influence of the Guinea current, the ships had deviated off course to the eastern edge of the *wagen weg*. 'As you can see, we're about to enter the Gulf of Guinea and we'll be drifting eastwards towards West Africa. It could be worse—we could be heading westwards in the wrong direction to Curaçao. So we have no choice. We'll plot the course towards Africa. There's a chance we'll find stronger winds inshore. If so, we can call in to Sao Tomé and Principe for fresh supplies and water. If not,' he shrugged and raised his hands, 'we'll make the best of it and find an alternative. Annabon, perhaps.'

We sighted the mouth of the Cavalla River, east of Cape

Palmas, three days later. The wind lifted, and we kept the distant shore in view through intermittent rainstorms, past Cape Three Points. There we changed course east-south-east across the gulf for the next five weeks and the eighteen deaths it took us to reach the island of Sao Tomé.

During those weeks, several crewmen showing symptoms of scurvy sought me out. They asked me to prepare their wills for presentation to the *scrijver*, the ship's clerk. It was unexpected and strangely gratifying to discover that they trusted me.

When Laurens noticed them knocking at the cabin door in increasing numbers, he asked me about it. 'Is that part of your job?'

'No. I'm doing them a favour.'

He seemed surprised. 'Why do they come to you? What's wrong with the ship's clerk?'

'I'm not sure. Perhaps they respect my education and think I understand the law.'

'As a *timmerman*? They've seen how practical your technical skills are, but that doesn't make you an expert notary.'

'I guess I speak their language. I've been mixing with men like them for most of my life.' I chuckled. 'I even stoop to talking to the likes of you, Laurens.'

He returned my smile. 'Even though you're a de Waal and a member of the *breede burgerij* merchant class?'

'I don't believe that gives me the right to put on airs.'

'That's probably it.'

'You want to know who drummed that into me?'

'Someone in your family?'

'Partly, but especially an old Englishman called Cain when I was an apprentice in the timberyards. He was a strict old devil, but straight to the point. He demanded humility, respect and hard work. There's much I owe him.'

Karel de Reus turned up one day. He wore a crude necklace of his own teeth that the senior surgeon had removed. 'I need a list of my personal items,' he said, 'for my will.'

'All of them?' I had watched him successfully bid at successive funeral auctions for a variety of unlikely things and had wondered at his odd taste.

We sat down and he began dictating. The list was long, until at last, he said, 'And to Sunil, I promise my red-buttoned squeezebox.' Then he surprised me. 'And last of all to you, Gerrit, my special pamphlet with all the addresses of Amsterdam's brothels and, to go with it, my copy of Jacob Cats' *Houwelijk.*'

I'd been amused to see him bid successfully for it several weeks ago—a manual on the manners and customs observed in marriage ceremonies. It was brand new, bound in leather covers with a solid silver clasp. 'Have you read it?' I asked.

'Of course not. I bought it to melt down the silver.'

I gave a burst of laughter. 'To pay for your future auctioneering?'

'Of course, what else?' he nodded, his sideways glance bemused. 'What did you expect?'

To be prudent and avoid an auction, I took a similar precaution myself. I wrote,

> *Gerrit de Waal, sailing as oppertimmerman in this ship, in the unfortunate event of his departure from this vale of tears, be it on land or sea, makes solemn dispensation of his goods as follows—to Joost de Vlieger of Zierickzee, sailing in this ship as opperstuurman, The English Pilot and his diary, spyglass and stone and shell. To Sunil Dewaraja of Galle, sailing as apprentice timmerman, his walrus tusk knife and spoon and clothes, as well as all his personal tools of trade.*
>
> *Half of any monies and insurances owing to him*

*are to be shared between his dear mother, Anneka
de Waal, and his grandfather, Laurens de Waal of
Middelburg. Any residues and all remainders are to
be paid to the Orphanage of the Abdij in Middelburg,
the dispensation to be contested by no one.*

*Under the strict instruction of Gerrit de Waal, the
albatross necklace will remain around his neck at the
time of burial. So be it seen to under God, at the behest
of Gerrit de Waal.*

Sunil remained positive, though. No one would wear his
hat of liberty but himself. 'If I die, Gerrit, you must bury me
in it,' he insisted.

As for the red squeezebox, he was already borrowing it
from Karel de Reus and learning to play it, the chants of the
shark sorcerer on Arippu beach at Mannar and the twanging
notes of his thumb-piano his inner-ear accompaniment, he
explained to me.

On 9 December, we sighted the western shore of the island
of Principe through a curtain of fresh rain squalls. I found it
difficult to describe in the journal the pleasurable satisfaction
I felt at seeing land after so long with nothing but with the
empty ocean from horizon to horizon. I noticed many others
experiencing the same positive elation, despite the desperate
straits that the sick among us were facing.

With consistent onshore winds, we made good progress to
Sao Tomé, coasting close to the mangroves until we reached
the settlement on the island's north-eastern corner. Colourful
stilted wooden houses painted in sun-bleached pastels lined
the embankment beyond the long, curving beach. Behind
them, mountains towered upwards, their slopes a patchwork of
intense greens—sugarcane, I assumed, as I peered through the
spyglass, though I wasn't sure, but coconut palm plantations

for certain, with smaller shrubs planted beneath them.

Sunil borrowed the spyglass. 'Cacao plants. At least, I think they are, the smaller trees. They look the same as the trees I saw back in Galewela, but the fruit here is not as big. And, oh yes! I can see vanilla vines… there… and another over there.' He handed back the spyglass, smiling broadly. 'I'm going to like this place.'

I was surprised to make out a French tricolour rather than the Portuguese flag flying above the thick mud walls of what I guessed was the administration compound. The unexpected sighting confused me. *France? What sort of reception are we going to receive from the nation we've been at war with for the past ten years?*

Beyond the compound, I saw a whitewashed wooden church beside a fenced enclosure where I was shocked to count eight African slaves, one clearly a child, squatting in the shade beneath the spread of a fiery red-flowering tree. They wore thick metal necklaces around their throats, a single chain linked to each encircling the trunk of the tree. My thoughts immediately turned to Serafino and Sebastiao. *How would they react to this scene? Are the French extending their slaving operations along the African main-land now? Have they annexed the island from which escape is impossible to use as a collection point for the embarkation of slaves to Brazil and the West Indies? To Guadeloupe, perhaps? Haiti? Or Martinique?*

We anchored line abreast late in the afternoon, opposite the landing. There were steps carved into the limestone cliff face edging the beach leading up to the buildings, where a crowd had gathered. I watched the officers' boats pull in to the jetty.

On his return that night, Joost told me that the discussions had not gone well.

'It would have been easier with the Portuguese in the

old days,' he said. 'But with a French Bourbon now the King of Spain and Portugal, the administrator here fancies the island is part of France itself. He's a self-important petty dictator and he's told us to move on.' Then he chuckled. 'Dirck Blauw is a cunning old fox, though. He saw the Frenchman salivate when he showed him our bill of lading and its mention of Burgundy wine. It's just a matter of further negotiations.'

Over four days of intense bargaining we offloaded several bolts of cloth and a large consignment of the wine we'd taken on board from the *Fortuin* for the French authorities, who allowed the ships to remain at anchor, but in quarantine. Despite the restriction, the senior surgeon visited the hospital and arranged for beds to be allocated to our most seriously sick.

'The hospital is run by Portuguese monks of the Order *de Sao Joau de Deus*, the Order of St John of God,' he explained to me at dinner. 'They refused me at first, but the monk in charge is from a different order. He's a Capuchin, Fra Christoforo. He seems to be a good man and a qualified surgeon, and he has the last word. He is unconcerned that Calvinists will be ministered to by Catholics.'

'Do they have a library?' I asked, as a thought crossed my mind.

'They do, and an excellent supply of medications in their cabinets. The friar is agreeable to me replenishing my stock. At a price, of course.'

'May I come with you next time you visit them? I'd be interested in seeing what books they have available.'

'You're running short of reading material? I didn't think you'd have time for that. I heard Schipper Marinus mention careening and repair.'

'A day here, a day there. He won't miss me.'

'I'll let you know when I'm due to go.'

We were there for four weeks. Both ships were hauled into a narrow, mosquito-ridden creek for a thorough swabbing and careening.

The crews set to scrubbing down the orlop, waist and quarterdecks with vinegar and fumigating them using smouldering juniper berries.

I was allocated a team of twenty soldiers who assisted us in scraping and burning away the skirt of weed and barnacles on the hull and carrying out caulking repairs. Laurens taught Sunil to manipulate the red-hot caulking irons and, with the extra hands working on the hull, we completed the job within a fortnight.

The ships were restocked during the last week. I organised the stacking of the cargo as sacks of manioc and desiccated sugarcane and mangoes and green-skinned oranges suggested by Fra Christoforo as a possible remedy for scurvy were hauled aboard, along with fresh water, firewood and charcoal.

Several sacks of pungent *melegueta* pepper sent a choking smell wafting through the ship, countering the stink of three bony-hipped, long-horned cows hoisted aboard into the ship's waist and roped beside the pig enclosure. Some seamen bought scrawny, multi-coloured roosters with iridescent plumage, whose harsh squawks Sunil's parakeet imitated. Santoso threatened to pluck and cook the bird in the next tureen of chicken soup unless Sunil removed it to his cabin.

When the senior surgeon visited the hospital during that last week, I accompanied him.

At first, I assisted him as he replenished the dwindling medical supplies in his medicine chest from the apothecary in the infirmary. He was able to procure agave resin unguent for ulcers, and cinnamon and caraway seeds for heartburn and bloating and a handful of shrivelled ipecacuanha roots, along with a single sack of dried Peruvian cinchona bark.

'You crush this up and boil it,' the apothecary said, 'to make a potion the Jesuits claim is effective against tropical fevers.'

'Does it work?'

'We swear by it here,' the apothecary nodded, reaching into the back of his cabinet and retrieving two phials containing small amounts of a pale yellow liquid. 'Would you have any use for one of these? It's Gabon viper venom.'

The senior surgeon held it up to the light. 'Interesting. What do you use it for?'

'We add it to strengthen some potions we use for leprosy and smallpox, though we've had little call for it lately and we are about to discard these. It is used in voodoo medicines on the mainland.'

'I doubt if we'll have a need,' the senior surgeon replied.

I reached across for the phial and turned it this way and that. The liquid seemed to have the consistency of mercury. 'Where do you get it from?'

'We have a snake pit here. The Angolares who looks after it is an expert.' He looked up at me. 'I can show you if you like.'

I turned to the senior surgeon. 'If we have the time, I'd like that. After my visit to the library.'

That afternoon we attended when the half-caste Angolares, revered for his sorcery, climbed into the town's snake pit to casually milk one viper directly into a glass phial. That night I wrote a lengthy journal entry.

> *I witnessed today a native who collected the venom of a snake, a remarkable sight he showed to all those gathered there. The snake was the length of my rattlesnake skin, its body of remarkable thickness wound in contortions about the native's forearm. Its scales were patterned in pale brown and purple pentagons, while the belly was*

pale gold. It had two horns and was thereby recognisable.

The native held the monster behind the head, its mouth open against the lip of a phial while teasing the fangs of surprising dimension and thinness and hung with skin webbing from the tissue of its jaw with a bronze rod. The venom slid down the glass, to my mind like yellow mercury.

The native wore no shoes and his bare feet were visible beneath cowhide protectors worn from ankle to knee. I saw he wandered among other reptiles of similar size coiled there, as though under the protection of God Almighty—or some other god of his own belief. I found the docility of the snakes and the native's indifference to them beyond belief.

Furthermore, I visited the monastery library and it was pleasing beyond words to discover there five copies of a simple lexicography of Kikongo words scripted by hand. Fra Christoforo kindly confirmed that they were copied from part of the Vocabularium Latinum, Hispanicum, e Congense, *prepared by the Flemish Capuchin Joris van Gheel in 1652. Novice monks use them to learn the language when they are transferred from Belgium. When I disclosed my connections to the* mulatten *of Middelburg and their need for such a document, he refused my offer of payment and allowed me instead to take a copy as a charitable gift. I could not to my satisfaction express my gratitude.*

I looked forward to sending the copy to Serafino on a return ship when I reached Cape Town. I imagined his surprise on receiving it from me and his elation on reading it. It gave me considerable satisfaction.

On 4 January 1712, we re-embarked the recuperating sick

and set sail. That evening I noted in the journal that we had left behind eight deserters, including three soldiers who had been assigned to me to undertake the careening.

> *It seems they prefer life ashore in a Franco–Portuguese prison rather than risk death aboard the Zuytdorp. Do they sense that we are about to face an impending disaster? Have they already seen enough to deter them from voyaging further?*

I sat staring down at my entry, uncertain how to continue. *Are they right to suspect that worse is yet to come?* I wondered.

Days before we put to sea, with the sickbay so close to my cabin, I had closely observed the surgeons dealing with the first disquieting cases of a strange new fever no one had contracted before. Four of the crew and one passenger, the middle-aged wife of a merchant travelling to Cape Town, reported to the surgeons complaining of nausea, blinding headaches and alternating fever and chills that sent tremors through their bodies.

The senior surgeon was perplexed by the symptoms. The woman appeared severely jaundiced and weak, and he had no treatment for her—but when she soon displayed the same indications as the others, who had collapsed into their hammocks suffering gastro-enteritis, their faeces turning bloody, he treated them all with an experimental antidote, a bitter cocktail of opium in camphor mixed with a dash of wormwood and elixir of vitriol.

At first, it seemed effective. The fever eased and, after a few hours of sweating quiet, when he thought they were regaining their health, the symptoms returned with renewed virulence and more violent seizures.

The woman suffered what the senior surgeon assumed to be a cerebral haemorrhage when she showed evidence of paralysis and lost the power of speech. I could hear her inhuman groans from my cabin before she lapsed into a coma. She died the afternoon we sailed. She had lasted three days.

The senior surgeon was unable to provide us with a diagnosis or suggest the source of the scourge. 'It is not the bubonic plague,' he told us, 'but its virulent consequences are no different.'

The contagion was catastrophic and the carnage haunting. Within a week, I counted forty cases aboard the *Zuytdorp* and I heard there were almost as many aboard the *Belvliet*. Half that number died as we sailed south, their corpses cast into the sea with minimal ceremony—to prevent the disease from spreading, according to the senior surgeon.

The situation was so dire Schipper Dirck Blaauw ordered an emergency change of direction to the nearest landfall on the African coast and we altered course for Cape De Lopez Gonsalvez. There the ships anchored off the island settlement in the estuary of the Ogooue River.

The orlop deck aboard the *Zuytdorp* was soon a charnel house. A dozen corpses were heaped below the aft companionway under canvas for burial ashore. Others died and were left where they lay in their hammocks, to be buried later. The resources, energy and patience of the three surgeons were stretched to the limit.

Schipper Dirck Blaauw, ill himself, was directed by the local village headman to a burial site on an uninhabited upstream stretch of riverbank. Laurens, Sunil and I, amongst others still able, spent the next few days ferrying the growing number of corpses in relays, pulling the boats against the river flood to a series of shallow mass graves we dug in the mud on the bank.

When the chaplain and his two children died, Schipper Marinus Wysvliet instructed me to fashion makeshift coffins for the three using mahogany planks bought at the island settlement's timber yard. We honoured them with full funeral rites in separate graves in the same location on the riverbank, despite Sunil insisting we should have cremated them.

'It doesn't seem right,' he said, as we rowed back down the river. 'Their souls are free now. They are holy and pure, especially the children. They may have achieved moksha.'

'Moksha?' I asked, incredulous.

He released his oar and linked his forefingers. 'Oneness with the Supreme Spirit. No more rebirth.'

'You surprise me, Sunil!'

'We shouldn't leave them to rot in the mud.'

'It's too late now. Better keep rowing.'

OUR CREWS WERE decimated when the ships tacked away from Africa into the gulf on 16 January.

That evening I was standing with Laurens and a few others at the rail after dinner, drinking beer, watching the sun sink into the ocean. A rising breeze was thankfully increasing our speed, the undulations in the sea's surface displaying a growing swell.

We heard the orlop gate crash open and looked round in astonishment at Karel de Reus dragging a body backwards across the hatches with a chokehold across his throat. His victim, whom we couldn't immediately recognise, was flailing his arms and legs, his high-pitched screech suggesting his larynx had been crushed. Before anyone could move to prevent it—although Laurens was the first to react, casting his beer aside and sprinting towards the pair—Karel lifted him to the rail, grunting in animal fury as he fought to hurl his screaming victim overboard.

At that point I recognised the third under-surgeon, his ghastly face caught momentarily in the lantern light. Somehow, he gripped Karel in a desperate attempt to save himself and they both fell across the rail into the darkness.

A solitary wild shout rang out. I leant across the rail to see

Karel's face flashing on the sea's surface before he sank and vanished in the wake.

I ran to the ship's bell and rang it furiously, shouting up at the navigation officers, who roared instructions at the helmsman and the crew on watch. The ship turned and slowed before beginning a laborious tack back along her course, the bell regularly sounding, until Schipper Marinus emerged from his cabin.

'What the devil are you doing?'

When the officers alerted him to the situation, he was enraged.

'Get back on your original course!' he bellowed. 'And make sure you maintain it.' Then he turned to the helmsman. 'You take your orders from me unless I delegate another officer. What was my last bearing?'

'One hundred and sixty-five degrees south-south-east, sir.'

'Right. You don't change that heading under any circumstances without my permission. Have you got that? Especially not for two ne'er-do-wells who choose to fall overboard.'

Later that night, I recorded the death of Karel de Reus. My note was brief and pointed—name, a date.

> *16 January—This night died Karel de Reus of Terschelling, keuken werker, kitchenhand and messmate, in this ship, by drowning, may God rest his troubled soul.*

The next day I stared down and re-read the entry, before picking up the quill to record the story that Sunil told me that morning concerning the circumstances of his death.

> *17 January—Sunil this day informed me in strictest confidence that he had discovered Karel de Reus in the very early hours of 25 October 1711, emerging from the forward chain locker where Sunil at once presumed he had been sleeping or he had relieved himself in the*

heads moments before.

However, to his astonishment, de Reus was not alone. He had in his company one of the young cadets, each with his arms about the waist of the other. The pair promptly dragged Sunil against his will and despite his considerable resistance into the chain locker.

Sunil explained that he was familiar with the penalties for sodomy aboard the ships of the VOC, though he had never seen such penalties enforced. I confirmed that under the 1695 Ordre en Instructie *both recalcitrant parties are to be roped back to back with a plank between them and consigned to the waters with no hope of reprieve.*

Sunil stated that de Reus then swore him to secrecy, under threat of his life.

He stated further that the cadet had next pinned him to the bulkhead to give him an explanation, but with a kiss on the mouth. He had then forced Sunil's hand, which was his right hand, to the cadet's groin, and his left hand inside his waistcoat to his breast. Despite his resistance, which Sunil affirms was violent, he had felt no male genitals but the swell of cleft flesh in the one hand and a woman's tightly bandaged breast and nipple in the other.

Sunil told me he was understandably struck with confusion and disbelief. This shaven-headed cadet was the strongest of the four cadets. She was, in his words, 'a fighter, never to be crossed'. I had often observed him, as I took his gender then to be, almost recklessly sure-footed along the yardarms and powerful in the sheet-handling.

De Reus confirmed she was from Terschelling in

the Wadden Islands, as was he.

I lifted the quill and thought carefully about my next entry.

I had learned the rest of the unfortunate story. She had been struck down by the illness some time before the ships sailed from Cape De Lopez Gonsalvez. Karel, ill himself, had nursed her and shared her agonies, but when she'd died, he'd been unable to prevent the third under-surgeon from stripping her corpse. Karel had turned away at the derisive laughter as the stains were washed away and her unprotected sex was revealed. Then she had been displayed in her indignity to a raucous group of crewmen, her legs stretched wide until the provoost had been alerted and had come below. He'd ordered her trussed and sewn into her bedding.

Shortly after her body had been prepared for burial, Karel followed the third under-surgeon to the deck and, in the vengeful rage I'd witnessed, he took them both over the side.

I dipped the quill in the inkwell and wrote:

> *Despite his barbarous and rebellious nature, I have harboured a certain admiration for the seemingly indomitable spirit of de Reus. I am reminded that he was driven to his insubordinate misbehaviour by poverty and lack of opportunity. Once or twice, when I confronted him in the dokhavn for his defiance of the regulations, this thought indeed crossed my mind—but for the grace of God, there go I.*
>
> *Furthermore, he was from Terschelling Island, as was Willem Barentsz, a man and navigator of great courage and tenacity, whom I hold in high regard. I believe both were carved from the same block.*
>
> *Vale de Reus. The Waterspaniël has drowned at last.*

WE SEPARATED FROM the *Belvliet* in the darkness that night.

We continued on our divergent courses to Cape Town, our last sighting of land the tantalising mountains of the island of Annobon off the African west coast.

One afternoon a week later, I began to feel unwell with a general malaise, mildly aching joints and a slight headache that persisted. The following morning I had a fever, with severe shaking chills alternating with heavy sweating. As the day wore on, the worsening headache was close to blinding. I began to fear the worst.

The senior surgeon, himself showing symptoms, tended to me in my cabin between his other patients. 'Tell me if there are any signs of bleeding,' he instructed Laurens. 'Immediately. If he brings it up or passes it.' He turned to me. 'I've observed that there appear to be two distinct degrees of severity with this sickness. One is milder, the other morbid. It seems milder with younger men like yourself and more severe, if not deadly, for the older ones among us. Although I have observed that does not hold true in all cases. You will recall the children who died.' He looked down at me. 'I pray you are among the more fortunate and, if I have contracted it, that I am also in that group.'

The day after, I was nauseated, unable to stand without debilitating dizziness, and despite eating very little of the food and water that Laurens and Sunil brought to me, vomited and had severe diarrhoea. Laurens and Sunil cheerfully nursed me through all of this. I found their good spirits and humour close to unbearable for most of the time, reminding them without effect that I was extremely ill and likely to die.

On the third day, the senior surgeon came to see me. He was now almost as afflicted as I was, but still able by some miracle to struggle through his rounds. He carried a roemer of steaming hot water in which floated what looked like an unappetising grey gruel concocted by Santoso.

'Do you recall the cinchona bark we obtained at the

infirmary?' he asked. 'This is it, with no additional ingredients. Ground up and boiled for hours. I've been testing it on myself since the day before yesterday. I believe I can sense an improvement or, at least, some slowing of the symptoms. I suggest you try it. Others have. It hasn't harmed them.'

'You trust the Jesuits?' I croaked. 'What are the side effects?'

He smiled. 'None for me so far. If it works, I will give credit where credit's due.'

He placed the glass beside the bed. 'Let it cool and drink it slowly. It is very bitter. If you have any wine, I suggest you add it to the mix. I do, to make it palatable.'

'Now you tell him!' Laurens joked. 'Will beer do?'

'Make sure he finishes it. Down to the dregs.'

That decision by the senior surgeon saved my life and his own, I believe. I drank and chewed each distasteful mouthful for three weeks, the bitter gritty flakes and grounds mixed in wine leaving a tart aftertaste that dried out my tongue and made me gag.

The first time I ventured feebly onto the waist deck during my recovery, I staggered to the rail in roaring westerlies encountered in the lower latitudes. I wondered then if a similar sense of disorientation and depression had driven the second under-surgeon to climb suddenly to the rail in full view of those working in the galley and leap overboard one evening, abandoning the overwhelming number of the sick and dying to the senior surgeon and their own devices. He must have felt powerless to assist so many.

On Wednesday 23 March, we reached Cape Town at last, rounding Robben Island and anchoring in the bay. The *Belvliet* arrived four days later and we soon learned that Schipper Dirck Blauw had succumbed to the fever, leaving Jakob Seinsen in command.

Sixteen

THE DAY AFTER WE arrived at the Cape, the worst cases among the twenty-two men still recuperating were disembarked during the day and transferred to the Gasthuis hospital in the town. It was nightfall when I was ferried ashore with the last of the sick. I was still weak and barely able to walk, but I was sufficiently alert to count twenty-three Dutch ships among those at anchor in the bay as we passed among them.

I assumed that most were part of the homeward return fleet and was surprised and pleased to recognise the *Berbices* among them. I had worked on building her in the dokhavn in 1709 and she was on her maiden voyage. I determined at once to locate someone aboard when I had recovered, to hand-deliver letters and pages from the journal to Mama and Opa, and to give the Capuchin Kikongo dictionary to Serafino. I managed a smile as I imagined instructing the messenger, *'Ask for Serafino. You can't miss him. He's unmistakable. He is the one and only* de Zwarte Prins, *the fisherman from the Kisolongo coast!'*

By the time I shuffled into the ward on the upper floor allocated to the *Zuytdorp* patients, it was full. Half a dozen others and I were assigned to straw-filled mattresses in an adjacent veranda corridor.

One of the Javanese *ziekenoppasser* male orderlies leant over me as he delivered the evening meal. 'Good evening, *juragan*,' he said. 'My name is Hasan. Welcome to our hospital. You are very fortunate to have a bed at all.' He looked down with a beatific expression and then, as though softening bad news, dropped his voice to a whisper and added, 'We have many patients who arrived this week from Stellenbosch and Franschhoek. They are showing the symptoms of smallpox. We have them on the ground floor, which is now full as well.'

He delivered the meals to the others in the corridor and, when he passed me on his return, he stopped his trolley at my feet. He sent me a beaming smile. 'When you are feeling better, *juragan*, I will take you up to the terrace on the hospital roof. There you can sleep in peace under the stars. We have one or two others up there. They enjoy it.'

Later that night, unable to sleep, I crawled to the barred window and peered across what I knew from the town chart was van Riebeeck's Heerengracht canal that ran through the town centre. Pools of water glinted here and there among young oaks planted along its banks and I recognised the rich smell of ripe and drying apricots filling the air in the company gardens, as it had when Mama laid out the tangy slices on trays in the back garden under the late summer sun. I used to help her pick the fruit from the two trees Opa Laurens had planted and espaliered against his workshop wall.

I heard owls call from the spire of the church I could see beyond the oaks. I followed the shadows of a pair gliding across the lines of houses, their roofs terraced down towards the moonlit bay shadowed with the hulls and masts of ships.

The high-pitched notes of flutes and the roar of conversation floated up from a windowless house across the canal, a block of shadow behind a swath of camphor trees. Then I recalled that the town chart had labelled the building the *Loots Logie* prison lodge for slaves.

Sunil visited me the next morning. He rushed onto the veranda, the strap of his red squeezebox slung around his neck. He was carrying my journal on which he balanced a pair of quills and a full inkwell.

'Gerrit!' he said excitedly. 'You're looking well. One night in here has done you good… or you're putting on a show to get out early.' He looked down at the line of patients in the corridor and peered into the ward. 'I don't blame you. This looks worse than Galle Fort Hospital. Take my word for it.'

He carefully placed the journal and inkwell beside me. 'I borrowed these from the *zaalknechten* head nurse's office. She has another set in there. She won't miss them.'

I raised a smile. 'Until she misses them, of course, but thank you for the ham bone. I hope the punishment's not the same for me as it was for Karel.'

'Better write up your journal before she finds out, then.'

He unslung the squeezebox. With a flashing grin, he threw off his hat and danced around it, the instrument wheezing the latest tune he'd mastered. His fingers flew up and down the rows of buttons as he chanted the lines of a Sinhalese song, his reedy nasal voice cut short by a chorus of shouts from the ward yelling for silence.

Later, when he bounded down the stairs and out into the sunlit courtyard, I stood and watched him through the bars as he turned to look back partway across. 'I'll be back tomorrow with my accordion to cheer you up, whether they like it or not. And I'll take care of your share of arrack and Constantia wine. Trust me, Gerrit! I'll let you know how good it tasted.'

When he disappeared beneath the shady oaks, I sat and leant back against the wall. I opened the journal at a blank double page in the back. In a shaft of sunlight filtering through the window, I wrote a letter to Mama and a second to Opa, tearing out and folding the pages.

Then I began recording onto another empty double page the nightmare of the harrowing days after the *Zuytdorp*'s visit to Sao Tomé and Cape De Lopez Gonsalvez.

Each entry on the left-hand page was stark and brief. I recorded the names of the dead who were friends and others whose names I could recall, otherwise I noted the approximate numbers. When the page was complete, I counted up the dead, shocked to discover that since leaving Middelburg, one hundred and twelve among the crew and passengers had died.

I leant against the red bricks, re-reading the names.

The right-hand page is blank, I thought, e*xactly as Serafino and the mulatten designed their gravestone.*

Then I wrote on the blank page:

> *I have recorded here a memorial for the dead, it seems. A column of the names I know and the numbers of the unknown who succumbed to an agonising death. Do my entries reflect the narratives of their lives? Surely not. They are no more than a record of their names before they entered the mystery of the abyss.*

When I'd completed the latest entry, I sat for several minutes wondering whether or not to send the pages to Mama and Opa Laurens. They'd be expecting them as promised, but the news was dire and I wondered how that would affect them. At last, I decided to do so. I carefully tore each page from its binding, rolled them together into a scroll I tied with a loose thread detached with my teeth from the hospital blanket.

I WAS IN the hospital for seven days. I spent the last three nights recuperating on the flat rooftop, sleeping fitfully after the noise in the slave quarters next door had quieted and the dull roar of the drunken conversations of the crews and women in the shoreline taverns was silenced by the visit of the night patrol. Then the whisper of the wind through the oaks and the mournful whistle of the owls lulled me into sleep. And later, woken by the cold wind coming down the mountain, I lay in pre-dawn moments of starlit calm watching the occasional meteorite flare across the sky and picking out the Southern Cross caught in an aerial nosedive towards the South Pole, as though trapped in black glass.

The first evening Hasan led me up and made me comfortable, he pointed out a pair of what I thought were skinks, clicking in alarm as they ran along the parapet wall at our approach. His lantern had disturbed them.

'*Ngisek, juragan,*' he pointed them out. 'Geckos, boss, as you call them. These are the small ones—the dwarves. They are very tame but do not feed them or they will become many and keep you awake with their noise.'

I was alone at first. Then, after an hour, three shadows emerged from the stairwell. As they passed me, in silence and without a glance, I made out two Javanese wearing crimson servants' uniforms, one carrying a roll of mattress and bedding, the other supporting a frail old man I had previously noticed down below in a corner of the ward, lying silently behind a hessian curtain.

They unrolled and prepared the bed before the old man lowered himself to his knees with a gasp of pain and stretched out beneath a blanket. Both servants then went downstairs, one returning minutes later with a pewter mug and a jug filled with what I took for water. He settled a little distance from the old man and sat with his back to the parapet smoking what looked like a thin cigar, its pleasant smoke faintly sweet-smelling. The momentary glint in his eyes above the spark of his cigar as he inhaled told me they were open and he was watching me.

When he also went downstairs for whatever reason, I took the opportunity to crawl across and look down at the old man in the moonlight. I wondered at his hawk-like face, with a hint of Malay about the dark eyes. It surprised me when I saw them half-open, but seemingly peering blindly into an inner distance.

Does he sleep with his eyes open, the lids only partly closed? I wondered.

His face was like a sallow mask framed by threads of silver hair, his skin transparent as parchment and blemished after a lifetime in the sun. A garrotte of what I took for tumorous glands was threaded around his throat from ear to ear.

The old man stared through me at first. Then I saw him focussing and he weakly raised a hand and reached for me. His bony fingers hung limply between us until I understood his gesture and took it in both of mine. The heat of his palm was shocking to my touch and I felt I was looking down at Opa Laurens sleeping on the bench in the apple orchard sunlight, the trees casting a net of shadows over him.

And then the old man whispered, 'I am Simon van der Stel.'

The ex-governor of the Cape! Humbled, I caught the old man's sour breath, heard his chest rattling beneath the blanket and stammered, 'An honour, sir, an honour. I am Gerrit de Waal, oppertimmerman, senior carpenter aboard the *Zuytdorp*.'

I sat beside him, watching as he faded back into sleep, his breathing shallow. He turned from side to side in discomfort, the knotted tumours seemingly strangling him.

A movement in the stairwell distracted me and I saw that the Javanese servant had returned and was sitting in the darkness on the second step watching me. *Has he been there all the time? He must be avoiding the brightness of the moon.* I saw him nod and caught the briefest gleam of teeth as he turned away.

I looked back down at the old man. This was the architect of the Cape, this corpse-like figure struggling against illhealth! This was the governor whose twenty years in office had seen the opening up of the hinterland—the development of Stellenbosch and Paarl and the land van Waveren!

I recalled Opa Laurens telling me stories about the Cape, sometimes reading aloud from VOC newsletters and pamphlets he'd collected at the dokhavn and stored in his library. The old man had developed the company's Tuyn Street Gardens that I'd seen sweeping up the hill behind the hospital. He'd authorised the planting of the oaks that lined the canal and the many vineyards crisscrossing the hills and valley slopes north to Tulbagh and east to Caledon.

Astonished, I looked down, shaking my head. He'd even organised the building of this new hospital… and he'd survived a mutiny across the colony six years earlier, when his son, Willem Adriaan, who had succeeded him as governor in 1699, had been exiled. The coup had threatened to take the van der Stel family down, I recalled, but the old man had taken refuge in his vineyard estate at Groot Constantia and had survived.

Then it struck me with a rush of excitement—*Papa was here in 1694. The old man was then still the governor. Could they have met by any chance? Aboard the* Ridderschap, *perhaps? If they had, would he remember?*

AT DAWN THE next morning, I was woken by the old man calling for water. His Javanese servant had disappeared, I presumed into the ward below. Still half asleep, I crawled across to scoop icy water into his pewter mug.

Grateful, the old man struggled to raise himself and leant back against the parapet wall. He pulled the blanket up around his neck.

'You've done me one favour,' he whispered hoarsely between swallows, 'now you owe me a second.' He looked over his shoulder at the dark immensity of Table Mountain, the glow of morning lighting up the layer of clouds spilling across its face. 'You must help me climb my final mountain. There's one more I have to cross. I must get to the other side.'

I was confused and guessed that he had sensed it when he gave a brief, hacking laugh. 'Not the other side of *life*, my friend. Not Paradise or the other unmentionable place. No *jonge kameraad*, I must get to the other *side*… the south-eastern side,' he gestured weakly across the parapet, 'to *my* paradise, back to my Constantia.'

I was struck by the directness of his glance in the half-light, as though he was momentarily free of pain. 'You must get me out of here and back to the Steenbergen where I can die in peace, where I can watch the sunrise over False Bay,' he inhaled a rasping breath, 'and breathe the richness of my soil.' He was racked by a spasm of coughing. 'I want to feel alive before I die. Tell Franz,' he waved a hand around the parapet, 'tell him I'll have no more of this. *I must go home.*'

The rising sun flushed the distant serrations of the Tygerburg and the hills of Hottentot's Holland, setting alight the quartzite cliffs below the mountain's crest and sending sunlight streaming down its slopes.

As the warmth gradually reached us, the old man explained that his son Franz had brought him to the hospital when he'd been found comatose on the floor of his estate mansion early in the new year. When he'd come to in the hospital ward, it had been resonating to the roar of a late summer storm. He'd listened to the drumming rain and churning sea, he said, his body swamped with spasms of pain before the opiates took effect. And each knell of the Castle bell ringing in the hour seemed to him to signal his impending death.

'I was listening to the sounds of my own funeral,' he said. 'So you understand my need now, to die as I have lived. Not cast aside like this, but in the place where I belong. I have one last destination, Gerrit, and *you*… yes, *you*… will be my coachman.'

He squinted against the brightening sunlight and managed a smile. 'Besides, I have some work for you at the estate. The water fountain. I need a carpenter to finish the carving and to put the pipes in place. I want to see water flow into the pool before I die. I want to drink from it.

'You've given me water here. Now give me water there. The purest water, from Constantia's springs. And it seems I have not one but *two* carpenters at my beck and call. You and the young Tamil musician.' He saw my surprise as he mentioned

Sunil. 'Walls have ears.' He gave a gasping chuckle. 'I may be old, but I am neither blind nor deaf.'

The two Javanese servants appeared and the old man nodded to me as they lifted him and assisted him across the terrace towards the stairwell.

When they'd gone, I remained on the rooftop looking out over the bay. It was 29 March, and I could make out a cluster of some twenty ships in the homeward fleet making preparations for their departure. Sunil had earlier confirmed that the *Berbices* was the flagship for this leg of the journey. He had contacted Theunis de Groot, the ondertimmerman aboard. A carpenter from Veere, I knew him only by reputation, but Sunil assured me that when he'd consigned the letters, scroll and Kikongo dictionary to him, he'd clearly understood his instructions.

When I heard the cannon fire from the ships that afternoon as they sailed, and the return cannonade signalled from the Castle on the Strand, I felt a wave of relief.

THE NEXT EVENING I left the hospital with Sunil carrying my gear. I stepped out into the twilight, glancing up to read over the green door the motto carved into the lintel—*Dit huis, voor zieken opgericht, verkwikt de zwakken*, This house is founded for the sick, it invigorates the weak.

I discovered later that the lintel was the original yellow-wood panel preserved from the first hospital built on these grounds by the founder of Cape Town, Jan van Riebeeck, fifty years before. The words were his.

Heaving a sigh of relief, I filled my lungs in the fresh air and quickened stride to escape the morbid corridors of the hospital and the probing fingers of surgeon Adriaan ten Damme, who had daily prodded my abdomen and inspected my clouded urine as though it was as fine a wine as any from the cellars of the Wijnberg vineyards. I'd overheard him one morning discuss its qualities with the doctor from Stellenbosch, who'd brought in two more cases of smallpox that week from among the Drakenstein Huguenots.

He'd held two bottles up to the light. 'All the samples have the same characteristics. It seems the fevers were caught in Sao Tomé. I'm told by the senior surgeon they anchored the ships among the mangroves there. Look no further. I put it down to the bad air there, no doubt about it, in my opinion.'

'Marsh fever, the Italians call it in the north of that country, I understand.'

'They do. Caused by "mal aria"—bad air, according to them. The symptoms the Italians report are very similar to those described to me by the senior surgeon.'

Sunil and I crossed the courtyard and followed the line of gabled houses down the slope towards Burgstraat. We crossed Greenmarket Square, deserted now, passed the watch house and strode towards the seafront and the boarding houses in the Waterkant quarter. There the street was alive with swiftly passing shadows and the clamour of raised voices.

Open doors led to several smoky, flare-lit taverns among the warehouses. I read their names as we passed. *Het Laatste Stuivertje*, the Last Farthing that Klaas Goelet had mentioned, with its collection of coins; *Het Blaauwe Anker*, the Blue Anchor; *Het Witte Hart*, the White Heart. Further along, music and the roar of voices sounded from the largest of them, a tavern that doubled as a brothel, Sunil told me as we passed—the *Schotse Tempel*, the Scottish Temple.

Beyond the buildings, the sand-swept Strand beside the sea led towards the towering bulwarks of the Castle above the landing, the bell tower over its gateway lit by a signal brazier.

I paused at the door of our lodgings, the *Gouden Eenhoorn*, the Gold Unicorn, to buy a cob of maize roasting on a bed of coals in an iron barrow. It was red hot. I tossed it from hand to hand as I entered the house.

I was welcomed into the warmth of the *middengallerij*, the central gallery, by several tradesmen from the ships, feet up and relaxed, flagons of wine on the tables. The appetising smell of roast lamb filtered from the kitchens and the dining room beyond.

Laurens Voort and Ondertimmerman Alexander Wisse from the *Belvliet* bounded to their feet to shake my hand. Sunil poured me a glass from a grey stone flagon as I stretched out on one of the yellow-wood benches, a zebra skin pegged to its frame.

I toasted my friends as the red squeezebox was tossed from hand to hand. Sunil raced after it, stumbling over outstretched legs. One of the crewmen held it up to an open-flame pipe lantern, threatening to set it alight if he heard another note.

I looked around with pleasure. I took another sip from the roemer of wine, the lamplight gleaming through the scarlet as I swirled it.

As I did so, I tried to visualise the harvest of old Simon van der Stel's vines on the southern slopes of Table Mountain. *Are they carried in reed baskets on the shoulders and heads of vineyard labourers who pour them into ox-drawn wagons at the ends of leafy rows?* I raised my glass to the governor in silent tribute, willing away the old man's fear of dying in his hospital bed. *I will contact Franz van der Stel as soon as work aboard the* Zuytdorp *allows, as I would if the old man was Opa Laurens. I will ensure that he returns to die where it pleases him most—back in the land of the living, where I now find myself.*

THE NEXT MORNING at breakfast I asked Laurens to update me on the seven days I had missed.

'The schipper has allowed us ten days of shore leave,' he said. 'So we have three more days of freedom, counting this one, before we're back in the yoke.'

Then he looked at me, grinning. '*Maar afgezien van de* Schotse Tempel *was het niet allemaal bier en slaapkamers*, but apart from the Scottish Temple, it hasn't been all beer and bedrooms, Gerrit. We've been seconded to work for the local militia.'

'Doing what?'

'Follow me.'

'This will interest you,' Sunil said, as Laurens led us out through the back door to a small open shed in the courtyard. 'Laurens and Alexander have been hard at work.'

There were tools beneath a workbench in the shed. Planks of local yellow-wood leant against the wall and, piled in one corner, lay several carvings of *papegaai* parrots, their wings spread wide. I recognised them as targets the *schutters* in Middelburg used for musketry practice. A handful had been completed and stood on poles at the end of the workshop. They were painted white.

'The local Ensign of the dragoons, Olof Bergh, asked the schipper to replenish his supply. Joost passed the message on to me,' Laurens explained, jerking a thumb towards Table Mountain. 'They took me up to the range to check out the target design. The range is halfway up the mountain. They let me have a shot or two. I enjoyed it, but I discovered I'm no marksman.'

'Neither am I,' I said.

'*They* are, though. They have to be. They've had some lions up the coast prowling around the Salt River flour mills. They took one of the local Khoikoi picaninnies the week before last. They found what was left of him on the beach.' He smiled. 'You both missed the excitement yester-day morning. They shot one of the lions. A big male. It was paraded through the streets. The picaninnies went wild.'

'Where is it now?' Sunil asked.

'It must be in the abattoir down by the Strand. That would be my guess. Olof Bergh told me that if they ever shot one he'd use the scrotum for a snuff pouch.'

Sunil glanced at me, his eyebrows raised. 'Tigers I've seen. But lions, never. You?'

'Two, a long time ago, in a cage in Middelburg. When I was a boy.'

Two hours later we found the carcass hanging from a hook in the abattoir. The hide was stretched on a frame beside it, scraped clean and packed with salt, curing for the taxidermist.

Sunil retrieved several strands of black and golden hair from its mane. When we made our way back past the sheep pens to the Strand, he was busily plaiting his trophy. I watched his fingers deftly twist the ends of the threads into a pair of slip-knots he tightened, then he threaded the bracelet around his arm and adjusted it above his left elbow.

'My Vedda bracelet,' he said, looking back towards the door of the abattoir and removing his hat, 'to give me courage. I thank the lion for it.'

Then he withdrew the remaining strands from his pocket and fashioned a second bracelet. 'The ones we used in Mannar to protect us from sharks and rays were made of elephant hair,' he said as he handed it to me. 'The lion is your Zeeland symbol, so this should be even more powerful.'

Courage? I wondered, as I placed my hand through it and tightened it above my left elbow as he had. *Will I ever need to call on it? Hopefully not, but better safe than sorry.*

Seventeen

17 April 1712
mid-afternoon, Groot Constantia Estate

Sunil reached over my shoulder with a jug of water he had filled from the stream. He refilled my empty pewter mug borrowed from the guest house kitchens, flashes of sunlight corkscrewing through the water as he poured.

Squatting beside the teak statuette, I chiselled the last of the scales in the Triton's fishtail. Shavings lay scattered on the limestone brickwork of the empty pool. I looked up from the carving and reached for the mug. Shading my eyes as I drank, I followed the suspended flight of a pair of rock kestrels hovering high above the Nek, the rocky pass through the ranges behind them that led to Hout Bay and the Atlantic.

I wiped the sting of sweat from my eyes and followed the crest of the hills south-eastwards to the sweep of False Bay and the Indian Ocean. I had first sighted the ocean three evenings before when we'd delivered the old man to the house in a carriage borrowed from the harbour master.

Now the sea was patterned in shifting greens and blues cradled by the curving promontory of Cape Hangklip. Beyond it, a line of distant rainstorms curtained the surface of the ocean beneath a steel-grey sky. I was fascinated, as I had been throughout the two days I'd worked on the fountain. Anticipation surged through me. *It is the horizon we will cross next week.*

I pointed out the kestrels to Sunil as they plummeted in unison, disappearing below the tree line. One of them emerged moments later with what looked like a monitor lizard thrashing in its talons.

I'd been working since early dawn perfecting the features of the teak Triton—the merman fountain. Its shape had been prepared by an Indonesian carver a month before and I had refined the statue's frowning concentration as it blew the trumpet conch shell through which the water was designed to flow. It was pleasurable work after the last two weeks aboard the *Zuytdorp* in preparation for sailing. My fingers were still stained with pitch and tar.

Sunil was backfilling the trench where he'd laid lead pipes connected to the stream. One pipe remained—the last link connecting the stream to the fountain. Jantje, a local Khoikhoi labourer, wrinkled and ancient, and a young Indian slave from Trancquebare, worked alongside him. I listened to their broken conversation, amused by Sunil's attempts at communication which threw the pair into fits of laughter.

I scraped the last of the shavings from a scale groove and set the Triton in place in the arched grotto at the head of the pool. I looked critically at the setting. I ran my hands over the contours of the carving, then dovetailed it firmly into place. I aligned the inlet pipe and the rear of the shell, then locked down the sluice gate.

'That's the work of a *meister* craftsman,' Sunil said, leaning on his shovel. 'Even Varuna would approve.'

'Varuna?'

'Our god of the oceans.'

'King Neptune, you mean.'

I swirled the dregs in my mug and flung the water skywards. I tilted my head, my mouth wide to catch the droplets. For a moment I was a boy again, catching rain falling from the linden leaves beneath a Zeeland sky, sunlight glowing through closed eyelids… till Sunil threw a full jug over me, shouting that it was April after all, and time to celebrate the day of the water Nagas, the Hindu serpent spirit guardians of lakes and oceans, as he and Vesak used to do.

'The more water you splash on those around you, Gerrit, the more water the Nagas will reward you. They bring the rain. They make the rivers flow.' He turned and ran for the stream where he dived into the shallows and sat chest-deep on the pebbles, water churning around him. 'See what I mean?'

His voice echoed over the clearing as he broke into what he later told me was an ancient Vedda incantation to the goddess Indigolla, spinning her silk clouds to trap the rain before she hunted the sacred *sambar,* the spotted deer, following their tracks along muddy paths on the lower slopes of Adam's Peak.

> *'Aeli gigiran pita inda walu katina lama,*
> *Diya gigiran pita inda diya dimana lama.*
> *Naddune dunu diya ata kudu lama.*
> *Riri oruwa pita sakman karana lama.*[33]*

The nasal four-note melody was cut short when I flung a handful of gravel at him. He dived to avoid it. I could see him lying on his back below the surface, his mouth open and exhaling as though he was still singing at the top of his lungs, his silent words bubbling up in foaming spray. Then he emerged and shouted the last two lines of the incantation into the oaks above him.

> *'Yanda enda diya pa man balapiya.*
> *Indigolle devi waediyot suba wiya.*[34]*

---

33 'She is the lady who spins the clouds, who lives within the thunder of the waterfalls. The lady who calms the waters and resides within the water's roar. The lady whose small hand pulls the bowstring of the sounding bow. Indigolle who walks behind the vessel of blood.'

34 'Look at the path along which her watery feet come and go. If the goddess Indigolla appears on the path good fortune will follow.'

He looked at me in triumph. 'She will look after us with the Nagas,' he shouted, 'Indigolla, the barefoot one. Our goddess of the rain!'

I knelt beside the statuette and mixed two bottles of tung oil into a container and applied them to the honey-coloured teak, breathing across my brushstrokes to dry them. I acknowledged Jantje's approving grin, the gleam of the old man's narrowed eyes barely visible in a mass of wrinkles as he smiled. The job was done. The water would flow the next day.

I waved to Sunil, floating spread-eagled on the water, and made my way down the gravel path to the courtyard of the house. The sweep of its front and side gables towered over the peach trees. Green wooden window shutters were latched open against the brickwork revealing a latticework of smoked-glass diamond panes. A labourer balanced on the crest of the roof, lacing freshly dried reeds there, a patch of yellow in the deep tan of the older thatch.

As I entered the gates to the rear of the house, the door to the veranda opened and Simon van der Stel shuffled across it to a yellow-wood bench, supported by a servant.

'You can open the sluice gate tomorrow *mijnheer*,' I called out. 'We've got one last pipe to install and Sunil has prepared it. It will take us an hour or so to connect it to the stream.'

I was interrupted by Ariaantje, a Khoikhoi girl of ten or eleven who peered around the pillars of the gateway and waved shyly at us. She'd been delivering our lunches out to us at the fountain for the last two days. Now she carried a pewter tobacco container across to me in her left hand. I saw Table Mountain etched into the lid.

'*Hoerikwaggo!*[35]' she told me in a confidential whisper, pointing at the etching.

---

35 Khoikhoi name for Table Mountain, 'the mountain of the sea'.

I accepted the container and she indicated that I should open it. Her face creased with pleasure when I prised open the lid and several large butterflies emerged, their wings dusted a velvet brown, two lines of gold and four violet eyelets across each swallowtail. One settled on my shirt-front, deliberately closing and opening its serrated wings before zigzagging erratically up into the breeze, following the others towards the rows of vines. Several ochre-brown pupae yet to hatch lay in the bottom of the container, cocooned among sheaves of grass. A pair of freshly picked, dark red orchids lay beside them, their nectar clearly intended for the adults.

'They are Satyrines,' I heard Simon van der Stel call out. 'They're very common here at this time of year.'

I watched the butterflies scatter like autumn leaves up the hillside. As they disappeared, I remembered our approach to the bay three weeks before when I had lain recuperating on the deck and a swarm of similar butterflies carried far out to sea had struck the *Zuytdorp*'s sails. They'd fallen to the decks and had been trodden underfoot.

When I turned to Ariaantje to return the container, she held my gaze before glancing back at the butterflies. For that arresting instant, it seemed I was peering into the depths of an untamed and primitive innocence. *Such ancient secrets in her dark eyes!* I thought. *Such wildness!* My heart leapt at their spirited beauty as she pointed at the last of the butterflies, delighting in its flight across the vines, before she shook her head, and insisted I should keep the canister.

Then Sunil walked through the gates, the strap to his red squeezebox slung around his shoulder. His wet shirt was wrapped about his waist, the cicatrices shining down his chest. As he approached us, Ariaantje baulked and ran back down the slope to the circle of *matjies huisen*[36] huts where her family lived. A plait of grey smoke coiling up from the centre of one of the huts unravelled in the breeze above the trees.

Simon, his frail arms spread across the back of the bench, gave me a serene smile. 'So you've met Ariaantje? She's a wise one, full of mischief. Watch out for her.' He dipped his head and exhaled a deep sigh, 'You can't imagine how much I'm looking forward to my drink of spring water tomorrow, *jonge* Gerrit. There is none sweeter in this world.'

The smell of fermenting wine drifted to us from the cellars opposite. Through its open doors, I could see latched brass bungs on rows of barrels. There were locks on each latch. *Are they there to preserve the secrets of the old man's success with his wines?* I wondered.

'I see you keep the secrets of your fermenting process under lock and key,' I said, pointing across at them.

'The locks are there to keep the wine in and the thieving slaves and Khoikhoi out,' he replied. 'The secrets lie in the soil and a certain feeling for the vines and the quality of the sunlight. There's no sorcery. The soil makes all the difference. It's the magic of the land I selected that holds the secret. The land.'

Ah, the land. It's always the land.

THE NEXT DAY I woke early to the warning bark of a troop of baboons that came down each dawn to scavenge among the orchards. When I appeared, they bounded warily from the trees and back onto rocks beyond the orchard's walls. A pair of male outriders remained on high ground, sharp-eyed sentries on the alert.

The senior male, a startling loping albino with a flowing white mane, circled the group of foraging females, several

---

36 Transportable domed huts made of curved wood covered in hides
   and grass thatch used by Khoikhoi pastoralists.

jockeyed by chattering young. They retreated further still at the blast of a warning musket shot and regrouped beyond range, shrieking with alarm and rage among the rocks. Their agitated barks echoed as they climbed to the ridge where they fell silent, squatting on their haunches to look down at a pair of yellow hunting dogs baying at the orchard wall.

'You should see them when they're drunk, the *baviaan*,' Simon had told me earlier. 'When the apricots are in season, they eat the fruit rotting on the ground and it ferments in their bellies. They're not quite so nimble then. We easily pick them off. We keep their numbers down to protect the grapes.'

When Sunil and I reached the pool, Jantje was seated on its wall, placidly smoking. A horse he'd been exercising was grazing at the stream's edge, its breath steaming. It shook its head at our approach, the bridle jangling.

The old Khoikhoi removed his pipe and doubled over, wheezing with laughter when Sunil broke into a leaping dance around the pool, his fingers flying across the squeezebox buttons, the horse snorting in alarm.

When he finished and sat panting beside Jantje, the instrument across his lap, the old man tapped out his pipe. He walked over to the horse, the ivory bracelets on his upper arms rattling. He ran a hand the length of its neck and leapt sideways to straddle it, his leading foot edging up over its bare back. He hung there for a precarious moment and then, with practised agility, slipped upright. He grinned at us, his arms crossed. He looked like an ancient centaur bony-naked now, his bullock-skin cloak thrown back and his leather loin-apron awry.

Abandoning the reins, he clicked the horse to a trot. He circled the empty pond as though in some private circus ring, the horse high-stepping to the nudge of his heels. Then he wheeled it up the path and through the stream, his arms outstretched like wings. He ducked beneath the oaks and urged the horse to a canter up the slope between the rows of vines. The leather cloak flew as he disappeared over the crest, the earthy smell of buchu[37] and the residue of his tobacco smoke hanging in the air behind him.

The statuette stood frowning in its grotto. I wiped clear the beads of dew standing out like perspiration. I caulked the pipe joint at the rear of the shell horn and sealed the sluice gate the old man would lift later that morning. Then we ran the last of the pipes out into the stream and backfilled the trench. Sunil raked clear the gravel as the backwash gurgled around the wooden funnel of the entry and I stood back to inspect the assembly and make sure the job was done.

Towards midday, the servants and the young Indian stretchered the old man into the shade of the oaks. He sat watching the final preparations as I checked the overflow pipes leading towards the vegetable gardens behind a hedge of protea.

I bowed, then told the old man that his moment had come. I helped him to the sluice and supported him as he leant across to work the lever on the gate. He grunted with the effort, insisting that he needed no assistance.

Water surged into the pipe and I heard it gurgling towards the fountain. Moments later, it splashed through the horn of the shell—a silver sheet swirling across the base of the pool—to our applause. The old man shuffled to the fountain cornice. He leant across to the flow of water. He ran a hand through it before filling his cupped palms, which he lifted to his lips and drank.

'You have no idea what this means,' he said, wiping his mouth after taking a second draught, 'this simple fountain. It has taken four years to finish. The design is the same as the

---

37 A medicinal herb grown at the Cape and used by the Khoikhoi to perfume and disinfect their skin. Also distilled for stomach and other ailments.

swembad, the swimming pool, in my garden in Holland—in Muiderberg, where I made the best brandy for miles around when I was young.' He scooped another handful of water and sipped. '*Now* you have succeeded, my coachman. *Now* I am home.' He sat back on the wall and I was astonished to see tears streaming down his cheeks, gathering among the tumorous beads around his throat. '*Now* I am ready to die.'

I stood looking down at him as he calmed, before I sat beside him. 'It has been our pleasure to serve you, *mijnheer*,' I told him. 'Our honour… and we thank you for your hospitality.'

I rubbed my hands together, uncertain how to proceed. I looked across at Sunil squatting cross-legged on the grass in front of us. Then I plunged ahead. 'I have not mentioned this to you before, but I am on this journey not only to see the world our explorers have opened up but also for a special purpose. I am searching for my father. I am retracing his voyage. I am repeating it with my own. I hope to discover what happened to him, to find out if he's still alive, or how he died if that's the case.' I struggled for the words. 'In doing so, I believe I'll give meaning to my voyage, if not my life and his.'

The old man gazed at me thoughtfully. 'How old were you when he disappeared?'

'I was ten. I only knew him for the time he was ashore before his departure, when I was eight.'

'How long was that?'

'Nine months.'

'And before that?'

'I was three the time before. I remember very little.' I shrugged. 'If at all.'

He raised his eyebrows and slowly nodded. 'Yes, I think I understand,' he said at last. 'You're following in your father's footsteps, seeking the wisdom you think he would have accumulated in a lifetime completed before your own.'

A brief silence fell as I contemplated his suggestion. *Seeking my father's wisdom? Am I hoping to discover the meaning of his life and thereby make some sense of my own?* I found the thought confusing.

'And you're telling me this because you think there is some way I can help?' Simon broke in.

'Perhaps. Yes, perhaps. He was here in Cape Town in February 1694, when you were still the governor.'

'I see. I certainly was. You want to know if I met him, and if I did, do I remember him?'

'Exactly.'

He gave me a quiet smile. 'Faces I am not so good with these days. Names even worse, in one ear, out the other without my memory interceding. I'm better with the names of ships. I used to see the same ones in the bay all the time. What ship was he aboard?'

'The *Ridderschap van Holland*.'

He looked at me in surprise. 'The *Ridderschap*! How could I forget? The trouble she caused when she disappeared… and the value of her bullion. I forget the figure now, but the VOC considered it a fortune worth searching for. They sent a fleet out two years later. Do you recall the schipper's name?'

'It was de Vlaming.'

'Of course, *Kornelis*! Now him I did meet, under the circumstances.' He frowned as he gazed at me. 'I was on the investigating committee. What were the conclusions we came to if you can call them that? Mutiny? Malagasy Pirates? A storm? A reef somewhere off the coast of Nieuw Holland?'

I looked at him expectantly, my tension mounting. When the silence extended, I asked, 'The *Ridderschap, mijnheer*? Did you go aboard before she left? Did you meet any of the crew?'

He placed a hand on my shoulder and gave me a feeble squeeze. 'I'm very sorry, Gerrit. It was never my practice to visit the flagships when they were in port, although I was often invited to ceremonial dinners aboard. That is the privilege of the *havenmeester*, the harbour master or his delegate. So no, I cannot help you there. To my knowledge, I never met your father. Nor do I recall any adverse reports regarding the crew.'

I felt a crushing disappointment, even though I had prepared myself, suspecting this might be the case.

He squeezed my shoulder again. 'Look, *jonge*, you are young and enthusiastic, with your life ahead of you. What you are doing is honourable, seeking to bring your father back into your life.' He removed his hand and I heard the wheezing deep in his lungs as he struggled to continue. 'Whatever the outcome, make sure you do not allow yourself to conclude that either your life or your search is meaningless. You can take that as the wisdom imparted to you by this old man who is about to die and knows it.'

He gave a quiet chuckle in which I sensed a touch of irony. 'I have summed up my life, as you will when your time comes, and the word you must never use in that context is "meaningless".'

Eighteen

2o April 1712, mid-morning, I was working on the mainmast and was interested to observe the arrival of the *Oosterstein*. I was very familiar with her. The elegant twenty-year-old ship was the grande dame and pride of the Zeeland fleet. She swept in past Robben Island under topsails, a line of crewmen balanced across the mainsail yard furling canvas. She turned as the main and mizzen topsail yards caught the wind from the opposite quarter, the canvas billowing against the masts as she glided to her anchorage.

I heard the whistle of the bosun's pipe calling for the *bij-draaien*—the manoeuvre for heaving-to—and the response of her chanting seamen echoing over the bay. The first of her bower anchors rattled out. As she eased back against the anchor cable, the first two of the white-barrelled cable buoys slung along its length burst to the surface, carrying the hemp rope away from the rocky seabed. She swung slowly into the run of the outgoing tide abeam the *Zuytdorp*, so close I could make out the features of her crew. She returned the shore salute with three cannon shots as the *Popkensberg* and *Zuiderbeeck* followed her in past Robben Island.

Laurens, Sunil and I visited the carpenters aboard the *Oosterstein* that afternoon for news of Middelburg and to talk of our disastrous outward voyage. We learnt, in contrast, that the *Oosterstein* had spent fewer than three months on the journey out and had recorded no deaths.

Paulina Teyssen, a friend of Anneka's whom I'd met several times and who was a passenger aboard, invited us to the poop cabin to admire her new addition to the ship's complement—one-month-old Maria Augusta, born in mid-Atlantic, their *kleine zeemeermin*—their little mermaid. She was awake in a net bag slung to a hook in a cabin doorway. Her hand reached through the mesh and curled around the forefinger that Sunil offered her.

'Her fingernails are smaller than the scales of mullet-fry,' he said in amazement. 'She really is a *zeemeermin*.'

While we were there, Schipper Marinus Wijsvliet and Joost de Vlieger climbed aboard to negotiate with Schipper Jan de Hei for extra crew. The *Zuytdorp* was still short-handed despite a recruiting drive ashore during the past month and the addition of two dozen offenders released from the Stellenbosch prison and Castle cells to serve in the militia in Batavia.

We watched as Marinus sought to convince a group of sailors hand-picked by the schipper to volunteer.

'I need eighteen volunteers at a minimum,' Marinus said. 'We sail the day after tomorrow. I know you're looking forward to your shore leave here, but you still have your sea-legs so you'll be well prepared for another three to four months sailing to Batavia. When we get there, we'll reward you with a salary bonus and twice the period of shore leave you'll be enjoying here.' He looked around the group. 'You can't complain about that.'

One of the group stepped forward. 'You got it right when you said we're looking forward to our shore leave here, and we've only just arrived.' A burst of laughter greeted him when he added, 'We've got more than the last three months' sailing to offload!'

Someone at the rear of the group shouted, 'The last thing we want is to transfer to another ship about to sail and wait for that relief until Batavia.'

'Least of all to sail aboard the *Zuytdorp*,' I heard one of the carpenters call out. 'We've heard about your death-toll and we've been told you were a miser with the rations on the last leg of your voyage.'

'There may be some truth to that,' Marinus said, glancing balefully around the group, 'but we were careful with the food supply in the interests of the ship. We had to survive for five months without wind in the tropics.'

He leant forward and gave the gathered crewmen a belligerent stare. 'As I said, we suffered the calm for *five months*. That situation could have dragged on for longer. We had to be sparing then, but the situation is different now. We've taken on fresh meat and vegetables and rice and herbs, let alone fifteen more sheep we're loading tomorrow. *Hutsepot!*' he bellowed, 'I guarantee you the best *hutsepot* you've tasted since the last one you enjoyed in the *Lui Varken*, the Fat Pig, in Vlissingen.'

'And a full load of dried peas to accompany it,' Joost added drily. 'And the same in beans. Take your pick. You can have either. We may have had no wind before but with that diet, we'll have wind to spare. And if wild oats are to your taste, you can have the next two nights ashore—tonight for an appetiser and tomorrow for the main course. We sail the day after that.' He winked. 'Two nights in the *bordeel* and you'll be itching to get back to sea after those female sea lice put the bite on you.'

Marinus looked round the group expectantly. 'I need eighteen more hands, six from each ship. You have my word you'll be well-treated and well-fed.'

'I heard you had deserters in Sao Tomé,' an old Norwegian seaman at the back of the group shouted. 'What did they know that we don't? That the ship is *ongelukkig*? That she's carrying a jinx?'

'There are deserters in every port,' Marinus said impatiently, his voice sarcastic. 'You know that as well as I do, Noors. The grass is always greener until you find it full of thorns.' He stared at the spokesman. 'You're too old for the *Zuytdorp* anyway, Grandma. *Je bent al te verwijfd*, you're far too effeminate. I need men for my ship, not old women. You can stay on board this ship and work on your Hardanger embroidery.' He looked around the group. 'So who will it be?'

There was a sceptical silence and no show of hands. Schipper de Hei stepped forward to confirm that six of them would be going whether they chose to or not, with six from each of the other two ships. He would select them later that day.

22 April 1712, mid-afternoon

WE STOOD ON the quarterdeck watching a distant cluster of rowdy children on the quayside light fireworks tied to the landing railings. They faintly crackled a smoky farewell to Schipper Marinus Wijsvliet and his officers as they drew away across the bay. Two longboats steered for the *Zuytdorp*, a third headed for the *Kockengen* behind us, her schipper, Hayman de Laver, at the tiller.

I looked down at the movement in the water. The tide was on the ebb. The onshore wind that had chopped the bay all morning had dropped and shifted quarter. The *Breede Raad* had decided to sail before another change in the weather.

We were instructed to sail in tandem for Batavia. The *Belvliet* still required additions to her crew. Schipper Jakob Seinsen was ordered to remain at anchor to wait for the arrival of the next outward-bound fleet with men to spare.

I stood by, as usual, to assist with the operation of the main capstan and the heaving-in of the giant bower anchor. The two sheet anchors were already aboard and the *Zuytdorp* had eased into the streaming ebb-tide against this last cable, her bows facing the cliffs off Green Point. Her topmasts had been greased and raised, their stays firmed. Paired forward staysails were readied, and the main and mizzen topsail yards were partway up, the canvas courses half-unfurled and gently flapping.

The capstan crew ran out the circular messenger rope to haul in the bower anchor cable. They laid it along the forward deck and round the leading rollers on the starboard beam. With three turns around the capstan barrel, the messenger provided a circle of rope to which the main anchor cable would be tied by half a dozen *nippermen* in rotation as it came in. They were lined along the rail ready to follow the messenger down the deck, releasing their ties in succession and feeding the incoming anchor cable down through the hatch into the stowage hold below. One of the cadets spread sand across the decks to prevent them from becoming slippery.

We waited as Schipper Marinus and his officers climbed aboard. They were followed by last-minute additions to the crew. I was surprised to see the unwilling Norwegian from the *Oosterstein* mount the rail and clamber to the deck.

Schipper Jan de Hei must have forced him to take his place among the others, I realised, *despite Schipper Marinus's rejection of him. Perhaps he was only too pleased to see the last of him.*

'If you weren't jinxed before,' I heard him mutter grimly to the schipper as they crossed the deck, 'you will be now.'

The sailors took their places at the capstan bars. At the bosun's whistle, they leant into the first turn, taking up a foot-stamping chant. The messenger rope squealed and creaked as it tightened against the forward rollers and the whelps on the capstan barrel. I ducked beneath the capstan bars to strike at the topmost turn of the tautening rope with a mallet to fleet it up the barrel as it came in. Laurens did the same on the opposite side, kicking the wooden pawls into their slots as the capstan turned, to prevent it spinning backwards.

The hemp anchor cable rode slowly up through the hawse port, spraying seawater under the tension. The sail crews timed the hoisting of the topsail yards to the slow forward movement of the ship as it was hauled towards the incoming anchor. Once the anchor broke free of the bottom, the ship gained sternway on the wind and tide and backed away from the hazardous reefs of Green Point.

The *stuurman* helmsman leant into the whipstaff to turn her and the topsails gently filled as the yards went up, the sailors walking the halliards backwards down the deck. She angled slowly across the wind and tide, gaining steerageway as the great wooden stock of the anchor broke the surface. Two crewmen braced themselves over the side to hook retrieval ropes around the flukes, and the gigantic anchor was winched on pulleys to the cathead-beam. The shank and upper fluke were lashed firmly against the bow as the ship turned south on the run towards the Cape of Good Hope.

The operation over, I revelled once more in the familiar surge of the waves. I tuned in to the timbers as they began creaking and groaning around me with the rhythmic lift and fall of the ship.

Familiar voices, I thought. *Music to my ears!* The raising of the anchor was a symbolic moment, as it had been off Walcheren and in the muddy estuary at Hellevoetsluys. My thoughts raced. *My unmoored future! What unpredictable choices will the ocean I'm sailing towards now present?*

The ship swung onto the plotted course. She rounded Green Point and reached the open ocean, the full sails of the *Kockengen* a quarter *mijl* ahead on the starboard beam. We followed her down the long peninsula in the twilight. The grey crags of the Twelve Apostles passed to port, their lower slopes dark green above cliffs against which intermittent bursts of surf exploded.

When we passed the entrance to Hout Bay, the steep pass of the Nek was visible against the skyline. Groot Constantia was directly beyond it. I went into the forepeak to my cabin to retrieve the tobacco container Ariaantje had committed to my care.

'You admired her butterflies,' old Jantje had told me when he'd spoken to her that day, 'so Ariaantje insists the rest of them are yours.'

I walked to the rail where I lifted the lid. The remaining butterflies emerged, the last one still struggling from its cracked cocoon. I held the container open and they drifted into the wind before the draft along the ship's sides caught them and they fluttered low across the water, rising and falling until lost among the waves.

I picked out the last pupa. I broke the shell apart. The butterfly quivered as it balanced on my forefinger, its wings drying, before it flickered among the sails and emerged leaf-like high above the ship's wake, hovering there until obscured against the background of the hills. 'At least there may be one survivor,' I murmured to myself.

The spectacular weathered outcrop of the rocky Cape disappeared as we surged away from Africa and into the emptiness of the Indian Ocean, as though plunging into a dark and fearful void. Ahead, the faint lights of the *Kockengen* guided us in.

Nineteen

WHEN I CAME OUT on deck at dawn two days later, I saw that the *Kockengen* was several *mijl* directly behind us. The winds were strong and fresh, the deep blue of the Great Southern Ocean a series of rolling, hollow waves that overtook us, crested with foam.

We were under full sail, with studding sails hoisted overnight on yardarms that reached out beyond the ship's beam. Their lower jackyards were so close to the waves as the ship swayed and surged and settled I thought they might catch the surface, but as I held my breath and watched, they lifted at the last moment to skim across successive breaking peaks.

For the first time since the windswept leg down the west coast of Ireland, the *Zuytdorp* was flying, surging down the back of one wave and flinging the seas aside as she sighed her way up the next, a mist of wind and spray sweeping down her decks.

Clearly impatient to reach Batavia and delighted at the advantage of favourable winds, Schipper Marinus Wijsvliet informed us at the morning meeting that he was ignoring his instructions at the Cape to accompany the *Kockengen*.

'She's a handicap,' he bellowed. 'She's only two-thirds our size and far too slow, in my opinion. If we stay with her, four months will stretch into five and we won't reach Batavia until September at the earliest. Besides,' he glared around the gathered crew as though about to justify his decision with an incontestable reason and would tolerate no argument, 'she's an Amsterdammer, not a Zeelander.'

In the silence that followed, the information sank in and I saw concern on some of the faces around me. *We'll be travelling alone,* I thought, *with no assistance to call on if we should need it.*

'What's more,' he went on, 'I'm intending to bypass St Paul

and Amsterdam Islands. We'll change course east-north-east before we reach them. That is earlier than the regulations require at this time of year, but we are allowed to use our discretion. That way we'll reach the twenty-seventh parallel north of the Abrolhos and make our first sighting of Nieuw Holland ahead of time. It will shorten our journey by more than a week, if this weather holds.'

By mid-afternoon, the *Kockengen* had disappeared below the horizon behind us.

For five weeks the weather held. The ship plunged across an expanse of boisterous seas of cobalt blue. The broad, dark clouds of towering storm fronts that we occasionally saw to the south, menacing and rent by lightning, swept towards us but did not reach our latitude, though I sometimes felt the bite of ice on the winds. On an east-nor'-east bearing at last, we sailed away from that ocean of storms towards the welcoming sun.

I sensed a growing expectancy among the crew. They now numbered two hundred; almost half of them new to the ship. I was getting to know an increasing number of them, including three rowdy young deckhands recruited from the Stellenbosch prison cells. They were members of a gang who had vandalised the flour mill and insulted the magistrate there. Sentenced to spend their lives in VOC military out-posts across the Indies, they'd been exiled from the Cape and had joined the ship for Batavia.

'The provost has them under control,' Joost told me one day, when I pointed them out, 'but they are a handful.'

'They certainly have energy to burn. Just as well he has the whip hand.'

'Indeed.'

'You'll have to watch your back,' I said.

He glanced sideways at me, a faint grin as he conceded,

'Frankly, I don't mind them. I'd be glad to have them on my side when the chips are down.' Then his smile widened. 'Have you heard the language they speak?'

'I wondered about that. It sounds like some sort of *keuken taal* kitchen creole.'

'It does, a new Hollandic dialect I can barely follow. And it's interesting, they don't think of themselves as Dutch, but rather as Africans—or *Afrikaners*, as they call themselves.'

'Because they were born in Africa? Or have African blood in their veins?'

'Both, by the looks of one of them… Cornelis Bibault. He's obviously got some Khoikhoi in him. He was telling me his cousin Hendrik was the first to use the word "Afrikaner"… when he was resisting arrest. He was the wildest of them, apparently.'

'Another de Reus, by the sounds. Is he on board?'

'No, thankfully. He was shipped out to Batavia aboard the *Zandenberg* last November.'

'Just as well.'

'So it seems.'

To my mind, the crew was generally cheerful and sardonic and fit, a thankful change from those who had suffered so much before we'd reached Cape Town. What's more, we were surprisingly well-fed, as Schipper Marinus had promised.

The maintenance that Laurens, Sunil and I had carried out in Table Bay meant our tasks were routine on this leg of the journey. Repairs were minor. The topmasts were new, the capstans and pumps had been overhauled, the fresh caulking held and the rudder responded well to the realigned and well-greased whipstaff tiller.

We had time on our hands during each watch, so one morning I retrieved some blocks of mahogany and ebony I'd loaded at Cape De Lopez Gonsalvez. I decided to start carving again and I thought I'd teach Sunil the skills. I'd noted his disappointment at being excluded by Laurens from carving the *papegaai* in Cape Town.

I say teach, but my instructions were barely needed when he proved he was already adept with the tools. He surprised me when he told me that his first ambitious assignment would be, 'A pair of diving goggles, Gerrit!'

I watched him select two small blocks of ebony he carefully measured against the orbit of each eye. 'These will do. Ebony is a hardwood, you said. So they will not rot or let the water in.' He inspected them closely then flashed a smile. 'The goggles I used on the Mannar sandbanks were mahogany, but I like the idea of a black pair.'

About to warn him that ebony would not be the easiest wood to carve, I held my tongue. I recalled the pair of ebony elephant bookends in Leif Morgensen's kunstkamer, which he'd mentioned he'd found in a Buddhist temple workshop in Ceylon. *Sunil is either already familiar with its characteristics or he's going to find out the hard way again. It will be interesting to watch.*

His determined patience, concentration and innate skill intrigued me. His first lens was completed within a week. It slotted perfectly over his left eye, and he took two further days to grind the oval lens from a windowpane he'd borrowed from a consignment in the cargo. He fitted it into a groove in the ebony and tarred it into place. He tested it in his hat of liberty, filled from a keg of drinking water on the deck. Holding the cup-shaped lens to his eye, he ducked his face below the surface. The parakeet screeched and scrambled over his back, blue and green wings flapping and hackles rising, till Sunil threw back his head and flicked the water from his hair to declare the carving a watertight success.

When he'd completed the second lens and connected

both to a headband, Joost came down from the quarterdeck to watch him test them for the first time in a large tureen borrowed from Santoso.

Joost was carrying a five-minute hourglass he showed Sunil when he joined us. 'I've been watching you, Sunil,' he said. 'We didn't believe it when we were crossing the equator on the voyage home. This time we'll prove it.'

Sunil threw him a wide grin, spat into the goggles, washed them out and then pulled them on and adjusted them over his eyes. Peering through the lenses after taking several mighty breaths, his eyes sparkling, he nodded and plunged his head into the tureen as Joost simultaneously turned the hourglass over to begin the count.

'Prove what?' I asked after half a minute, watching the powdered sand filter into the lower glass he was holding in front of us.

'That he swims like a fish,' he replied. 'You see his hat there? We rewarded him with it after we crossed the equator on the way home. We threw him over the side with the others to wash off the lather we'd plastered them in during the shaving ceremony. We had a *shallop* in the water to pick up those who couldn't swim.' He looked at the hourglass. 'That's one minute. Now Sunil—*de kleine klootzak*, the little bugger, he did not surface. We stood looking down for so long we thought we'd drowned him.' He laughed as he checked the timer again. 'One and a half minutes. Imagine the panic. The ship wasn't moving and it was dead calm. The water was so clear it seemed we could see forever through it and there was no sign of his body. Then we found him.' He looked down again. 'Just over two minutes.'

'You found him where?'

'Standing next to us and looking down like we were. He'd swum under the ship and climbed the Jacob's ladder on the starboard side.'

I laughed. 'So what did you do?'

At that point, bubbles erupted from the tureen, but Sunil remained submerged and the surface of the water stilled.

'We dunked him for the second time, of course, and he repeated the feat to prove his point. God knows how deep he had to dive to avoid the barnacles.' He looked at the back of Sunil's head, then at the hourglass as Sunil gradually emerged. He stood panting in front of us, beaming, his chest heaving.

'Two minutes and close on forty seconds,' Joost said, nodding his approval.

Sunil smiled as he hauled off the goggles and pulled on his hat. 'I'm out of practice. I could stay under for longer than that when I was twelve.' He held the goggles out and shook the water from them. 'These are really good. As good as any I've ever worn.'

By the end of May, we knew we were close to making land-fall on Nieuw Holland and anticipated a change of course onto our homeward run.

I listened to discussions around the table at dinner with increasing interest. The frequent topic then was the daily longitudinal dead reckoning. I knew it was averaged each day from the collective judgement of the navigating officers on watch.

'We'll make landfall around the third of June, in my view,' Joost told me late one evening when I asked him. 'At best guess.'

'*At best guess?*' I asked.

He acknowledged my scepticism with what seemed a regretful nod. 'The best you can hope for.'

'That's reassuring.'

He reached out and grasped my arm as I was about to leave. We sat at the table and refilled our glasses after the others had left. 'No need to be sarcastic, Gerrit. It's nowhere near as easy as you might imagine.'

'I know. I'm only pulling your leg.'

Then, as though to justify the procedures for measuring longitude, he explained the intricacies of the calculations. 'We have to take into account the complications of a swinging compass bearing, our drift among winds of different velocities and unfamiliar currents, let alone our inaccurately estimated speed, for God's sake.'

'Relax, Joost,' I tried to calm him. 'I experienced all those problems when I was sailing the *Santiago*.' I broke into a laugh. 'It's nothing new to me. The only advantage I had over you is that I was becalmed beside the orchard.'

'You did not have a schipper the likes of Marinus either, who insists on the traditional convenience of a woodchip floated alongside between the two marks on the ship's side to measure our speed. He even goes as far as to time its progress against the pulse in his throat at sixty beats a minute. Sixty beats a minute!' He gave a snort of laughter. 'What if he has a fever, I ask you? Or he's indisposed and his pulse is erratic? I can't convince him that casting the log with its unravelling line of knots would prove more accurate.'

'What about the moon's transit across the stars. Have you ever tried that technique?'

'On an unsteady deck? When you can't always trust your compass heading because there may be magnetic variations you're unaware of? Out of the question.'

'But have you ever used the method?' I insisted.

'Once or twice, early in my career in northern waters. In the Baltic, yes, I'll grant you it's easier. But the mathematical calculations and the tables are so convoluted, let alone lunar parallax and atmospheric refraction.'

I laughed again. 'You've lost me there.'

'Lost you or convinced you?'

'Both.' I raised my glass. 'Here's to the third of June.'

We were alert and anxious at the prospect of the looming continent. Schipper Marinus, Joost and one other officer were the only three on the quarterdeck who had sighted it on previous voyages, from a distance and further south. Joost told me he'd seen it twice. He recalled on the first occasion a smoke-hazed mirage of low dunes and on the second a line of *vervloekte kliffen*, cursed cliffs, on the starboard horizon, when they'd changed course in the safety of deep water.

He advised me that if we made the turn prematurely, we would experience the nightmare of tacking into unfavourable crosswinds before reaching the Sunda Straits and risked missing the entrance to the straits altogether.

'Get caught up in those winds from the wrong quarter and they'll take us west of Sumatra and halfway to Ceylon,' he said.

Sunil, wearing the completed goggles attached around the crown of his hat, threw his arms out. '*Halfway to Ceylon!* What are we waiting for?'

On 1 June, we faced the first front of a series of storms streaming up from the southwest, sweeping in towards the hidden continent. There were still no signs of land. No birds. No tell-tale streaks of weed or red-brown lines of coral spawn edging the current. We watched the dark lines of cloud swirl across the vault of the sky, obliterating the morning sun and bringing cold gusts of a southerly wind shift that unsettled the flow of waves we had been cresting.

The seas lifted during the morning, surging and hissing viciously across the *Zuytdorp*'s weather beam. Stinging spray drove across the waist deck. The blue of the north-eastern horizon greyed to black and the crew adjusted the rigging before we felt the full force of the gale. The sea was eerily lit in foaming patches of luminous green as the hazed sun glared through the last breaks in the cloud, and then the lashing rain closed in and the winds gusted to a roar.

It was a frantic time for us.

When the gunners manoeuvred the cannons alongside the inside planking, lashing them fore and aft to hooks in the beams, Laurens, Sunil and I fought against the gale to bolt shut the cannon ports and hammer home the chocks beneath the oak wheels of the cannon trucks. It wasn't easy, skidding wind-blown on the greasy decks.

Then we worked in the blinding spray to cover hatch-gratings with canvas battened to the decks, leaving a narrow entrance to each companionway open, a canvas flap allowing egress to one crewman at a time.

We assisted the bosun and two deckhands in disconnecting the cables from the bower anchors, withdrawing them through the hawse ports for coiling below.

At one point, as we sealed the hawse ports, I leant close to the bosun's ear and shouted, 'What if we need the anchors in an emergency?'

'Standard procedure,' he yelled back. 'Schipper's orders. We have the auxiliary anchors down in the rope store if we need them.'

Each of us staggered below in regular turns to check the great wedges at the base of the three shuddering masts, sledge-hammering them back into place as they loosened under the power of the wind.

The pumps were manned and cleared on the half-hour, and the ship's boats were covered in canvas and lashed tight into the davit-slings and to the mizzen rigging. Since it would take time to launch one if a crewman went overboard, we set line to trail astern and ran safety lines fore and aft along the treacherous decks.

Once, when I was crossing the quarterdeck, I heard Schipper Marinus shouting at his officers, 'Scud before the wind! Set one reefed main topsail and a fore-mainsail and staysail. Now!'

When I reached the mainmast ratlines, I looked up through the rain to see that members of the crew sent aloft had lowered and housed the top-gallant masts and were running up the storm-sails. Bracing myself against the rail, I watched them lash rope quick-savers across the front of the straining canvas to prevent them ballooning out and tearing. I checked to see that they'd doubled the tacks and sheets, and saw that they had added preventer stays to reinforce the masts.

The ship immediately responded, running before the wind, maintaining steerage and balance as the set of the sails lifted the bows and deepened the stern. The steady force in the sails eased the shuddering in the ship's frame, justifying Schipper Marinus's decision.

By mid-afternoon, we were in the wild grip of the storm. Driven by screaming winds on a nor-easterly bearing, the *Zuytdorp* ploughed into troughs that burst across her bows.

I took shelter in the forecastle corridor, where I kept watch over the chaos on deck. I realised that spray blasting across the foremast main and staysail and gusting across the quarterdeck must have been blinding the officers in the navigating station, despite the protective storm tarpaulins we'd erected for them.

I could see the two *stuurmen* at the whipstaff struggling to keep the wind on the quarter and the sails trimmed as the swinging staff threatened to hurl them across the deck as the occasional surge caught the rudder and swung the tiller violently across the gunroom below them. I was thankful for their sakes that they weren't able to see the mountainous breaking waves climbing mast-high behind the ship and roaring past as she surged down their backs.

The lookout, sent up the foreyard, lashed himself to the foremast cathead. He sat above the wind-flung spray, shielding his eyes as best he could, but I imagined his view obscured by the curtain of driving rain. *If he were to shout from up there right now, we wouldn't hear a word. His warnings would be drowned out by the wind's roar and the shriek of the rigging.*

For one extraordinary hour at dusk, the rain turned to a thunderous downpour of large hailstones. Stinging ice scattered across the blackened decks, covering them in white gravel as waves of spray washed over them and the last of the light faded.

All who could do so took shelter below, sitting out the storm.

When I went below to check the mast settings, I found the orlop deck stifling with the smell of wildly swinging oil lamps. Thirty of the men were waiting there for the ship's bell to ring the end of the second dog-watch—their signal to take to the decks for the four hours to midnight. I returned up the companionway as the bell sounded.

I called in on Sunil and Gerrit, who were talking in the carpenter's store. When I left them, I heard the sounds of the red squeezebox start up as I opened the door to my cabin. As I did so, the ship heeled wildly to port, echoing to the booming roar of timber screeching across rock. I was flung across the cabin and hurled to the tilting deck that lifted towards me. I lost my footing, spun round as I fell and struck the deck across my back and the rear of my skull.

I blindly raised my hands when I glimpsed the cannon truck tear free. It swung outwards as the ship canted almost vertically, careened in a half-circle across the cabin and its wheel scythed into my right leg. I felt it snap the bones above the ankle and thrust me back towards the door that had slammed shut.

As I slid across the floor, seawater swirled through the fractured planking, engulfing me. Dazed, I did not immediately grasp the situation. *The outer planks will hold.* The contradictory thought engrossed me. *Of course the planks will hold. That's their purpose. That's the way we built them. They are the planks I spent time debarking.*

Then I focussed with extraordinary clarity on water foaming through the smashed yellow pine. My mind froze before a blinding rush of thoughts overtook me, as though I'd emerged from a moment of unconsciousness. *No pain! There is no pain. Yet.* I craned my neck to look back at the outer planking and the inrush of water. *Never mind the timbers. Never mind the ship. I have to get out of here!*

When I sat up and raised my knees with the water to my waist, a searing bolt of pain shot from the sole of my right foot to my groin and I collapsed beneath the water.

Do not breathe in! That thought was a deafening scream that galvanised me into a reflex reaction. My heart raced erratically as I exhaled and propelled myself upright again, as though someone had given me a violent push. For the second time, a horrific rush of pain tore through my leg and took away my breath. The cabin swirled about me and my vision partly faded.

Then I felt the door crash inwards and strike my back. A pair of hands grasped me beneath the armpits and dragged me towards the opening. I recognised the sound of Sunil's voice shouting above my head. Confused and overwhelmed with shock, I could not comprehend his words. Aware that I was out of immediate danger, I felt weak and suddenly nauseated. Disoriented and feeling strangely out of place, I began blacking out as he dragged me through the door.

Twenty

THE SUPERHUMAN EFFORT TO drag Gerrit's dead weight from the cabin took Sunil several agonising minutes, searching blindly for a precarious foothold on the shifting deck as he heaved him backwards.

Gerrit had lost consciousness when they'd reached the passageway. His breath became a rasping moan. Sunil saw the crushed and bleeding flesh of his lower right shin and the distorted angle of his boot. He wedged him against the bulkhead, then reached down and felt the sickening shift of bone beneath his fingers, blood seeping into his palm.

He stood and climbed against the angle of the passage to the door of his cabin, returning with his knife and a short length of rope. He tied it around Gerrit's thigh above the knee and saw the bleeding slow. Then he crawled along the passage onto the waist deck where he clung to a dislodged rail, seeking an escape route for them both.

Waves smashed over the hull above him and swept deep across the deck, carrying wreckage in a swirl of foam. He heard a thunderous roar as the ship slewed across rocks, the explosion of smashing timbers subsiding into an unearthly booming. He felt the bows skid and then hold, the stern swinging with the wind and seas as she broached. He saw the rudder torn away and gigantic waves overwhelm her as she lay on her side, lifting and pounding her across the shelf of rock. Wind and smashing waves drove her towards the towering cliffs he glimpsed through sheets of rain.

From the orlop deck below, he thought he heard the screams of crewmen trapped behind battened hatches and watched in horror as the shadows of the few who made it up the companionway ladders and through the narrow exits were flung aside and swept away.

He clambered back up the sloping forecastle floor past Gerrit to his cabin. He felt a growing calm, as if what was happening was in the normal course of events. He was prepared for what he had to do next.

He opened a wall locker and retrieved his ebony goggles. He slung them around his neck then reached deeper, for his hat of liberty, which he folded into the pocket of his breeches. Laurens Voort, spread-eagled below an iron jack, was beyond help so Sunil stepped into the corridor and manoeuvred his way back down the slant of the deck towards Gerrit and the exit to the waist deck.

This time, between each thundering wave, he saw that the *Zuytdorp's* back was broken. The forepeak decking had split. Beneath him, the orlop deck was a surging flood. The masts were a mass of smashed and tangled rigging angled above the water boiling in the lee. He saw shadows clinging to the spars. High on the poop, he made out a group of crewmen struggling to release one of the ship's boats from its lashings.

Through blinding rain, he saw the precipitous shadows of the cliffs far closer now.

He knew at once what he must do. He turned back down the passage, pausing to check on Gerrit, dazed but conscious. He reassured him that he would be back within moments to assist him.

He worked his way towards the bows. He climbed the short companionway to the heads, where he fought to open the door jammed shut by the wind. The platform of the beak head at his feet was submerged, the sea surging through the gratings. Beyond it, the splintered bowsprit hung at right angles, smashed partway along its length. The farther end was still attached to the forestay and the waterlogged staysail was entangled along its length.

As he watched, the bowsprit parted and the broken end swung wildly away across the face of a wave. It swept out the length of the forestay and slid back to ram the beak head before the inrush of the next wave.

The thick pine spritsail yard that he had lashed to the bowsprit before the storm was gone. He saw the dark shadows of wreckage swirling in the lee and, closer now, the looming cliffs. He clambered back to the store to retrieve one of the canvas carpenter's belts and strapped it on, placing his knife in its sheath. He removed his goggles from around his neck and packed them carefully into the pouch on the belt.

Then he reached into the bamboo cage to grip the shrieking Alexandrine parakeet before scrambling along the passage to release it into the howling wind. It disappeared into the darkness.

He squatted beside Gerrit in the shelter of the forepeak as the sea raged about them. His friend's dreadful injury he could do nothing about. There was no time to apply bandages or a splint. The ship was breaking up. He knew that the forepeak would separate and become engulfed. They'd collide with the cliffs within the hour and, with the storm directing its fury at the base of the cliffs, they would stand no chance in the power of its surge.

He knew the wild nature of the sea during monsoonal storms along the cliffs of Galle Fort Island and they were tame compared with this.

'We have to swim, Gerrit,' he shouted.

'Swim, Sunil? Look at me.'

'We have no choice. You have to trust me. We'll find a landing somewhere. If not, we'll try the cliff face.'

'There are cliffs?'

'There are.'

'So we're not on a reef in the Abrolhos?'

'No.'

'I won't be able to swim. Not in seas this rough. You have to go without me.'

'If I survive without you that will be no survival.'

For one paralysing moment as he looked down at Gerrit, he was back in Galle Bay, hauling his brother Vesak to the hawser of the ship's forward anchor through the red water, where he held on with one hand, horrified to find himself clutching Vesak's upper torso with the other, his head flung back as though his neck was broken. His heartbeat and time itself seemed to slow as he hung there, until Vesak's dead weight and the steep angle of the anchor rope proved too much. His arms numb, he opened up his cramped fingers and let his brother go… and that unforgettable moment of Vesak's death and his guilt at releasing him were seared into his soul.

Then, shocked into action, he crawled rapidly out to the waist deck, where rending timbers screeched in the wind's relentless roar. There was no escape route that way. Across the gulf of surging water, he saw the ship was parting. The gunwales, high on his left, were split as though sawn through.

'This is no time to argue,' he shouted when he crawled back. 'We go together or we don't go at all,'

'We'll both die.'

'So be it. We go together.' He looked down at Gerrit. 'The three of us.' He dragged Gerrit backwards by the armpits to the forward companionway and the door to the heads. 'You, me and Vesak.'

'Four,' Gerrit grunted, grimacing. 'Don't forget my Papa Maarten.'

Sunil leant into the door and it swung open, a surge of water slamming it wide against the outer bulkhead. The platform was deeper now, water foaming through the railings. The stump of the bowsprit reared into the driving rain. He knelt beside Gerrit, who was sprawled in the doorway, locked his arms around his chest and dragged him across the grating.

'Trust me, Gerrit,' he screamed. 'Don't fight me, whatever happens.'

He launched himself across the railing and into the shock of the cold sea, hauling his friend into a thrashing wave that thrust them high and away from the forepeak. They slid down the hollow of its backwash as the next wave roared in. Sunil felt the current swirl around them, pulling them clear of the wreck. He heard Gerrit's scream of pain and it was the remembered weight of Vesak he was fighting to keep above the raging water.

Above them, on the next surge, he saw the smashed bowsprit rolling in the wash, straining at the forestay and swinging towards them, the pale shadow of the torn staysail spread beneath it like a broken wing. He struggled towards it and wrapped his free arm around a frayed sheet.

They floated in the raging water for an hour, drifting slowly southwards on the current, Gerrit slung across the smashed bowsprit that Sunil had hacked free. He fought to keep him above the surface, wrestling his weight upwards as he slid away from the rotating timber when he lapsed now and then into unconsciousness.

Unaware of the passage of time, Sunil harboured his strength, his will concentrated on the effort to save his friend.

The ship disappeared behind them. On their left, the cliffs towered in the storm-dark sky, lit eerily now and then by sheet lightning. The surf thundered and growled at their base, a sweep of white water foaming across rock platforms over which the waves burst.

Then Sunil saw a break in the cliffs. The rock-face angled down towards a streak of sand, hidden as the waves crashed across it, pale as they swirled away. It was a momentary vision, a flash of white in the lightning. At its closest edge, a shelf of rock stretched towards them in the roaring turbulence. Beyond it, the cliffs reared towards the skyline.

Unable to judge the distance and unsure of the strength of the current, he knew that this was their last resort. He grasped Gerrit and turned him over to face the sky, the foam breaking over the two of them. He struggled away from the bowsprit, striking out for the spit of sand across the current.

He was dragged beneath Gerrit's inert form in his effort to keep him afloat, gulping air each time he surfaced. He was no longer aware of the cliffs as he fought to reach them, conscious only of the wall of green water that washed around him as he sank, his lungs bursting, till he emerged choking in the rain and foam, to descend again into the wild green, his body straining towards the distant sand and safety.

His struggle seemed interminable. The alternating wash of the sea and the roar of the wind. The blinding wall of green. His desperate gasp for air and his fight against drowning. He was driven. He felt himself fainting but forced himself to reach for the surface again. He sank into darkness but refused to abandon Gerrit. As he weakened, he retreated into a dazed red world where his heartbeat roared and his arms seemed torn away.

At last, he felt the pull of the inshore undertow as it caught them, sucking them towards the rock platform and threatening to drag them into caverns beneath it. In his agony, he felt that this was one last danger they would not survive. He had no answer to the sea's destructive force and he clung to Gerrit as the waves hurled them towards the shelf.

He saw the shadow of the cliffs loom directly overhead.

He saw the surf burst high around them. He heard the incoherent scream of the wind as they were thrown across the ledge, lacerated by its razored surface, the water surging over them. He clung to the rock as the wave receded. The next wave picked them up and tore Gerrit from his grasp as it drove them beyond the rock shelf to hurl them across the sand. They rolled in the wash as another wave crashed about them, driving them further up the spit.

Gathering the last of his will, he crawled to Gerrit and dragged him beyond the breakers and past the debris and seaweed at the tide line. He stretched him out on the sand in the shelter of an overhang at the cliff face. He listened for his faint breathing, saw the bleeding lacerations and grimaced at the distorted angle of the broken bones beneath the skin above his ankle. When he withdrew his knife and cut the tie above the knee, he saw that the flow of blood had slowed.

Gerrit stirred. Sunil forced himself to his feet to search at the cliff edge, where he found a length of grey driftwood. He snapped it in two and knelt to bind his leg, hacking strips of Gerrit's shirt and trouser leg. The bones ground beneath his fingers as he roughly realigned them and he bound the splints in place as Gerrit groaned before slumping into unconsciousness once more.

His back to the rock wall, exhaustion washing over him, Sunil felt a surge of triumph and relief. He looked towards the summit and at the dark sky beyond it. The pelting rain was easing. He savoured the moment even as he gave himself over to fatigue. He and Gerrit were alive. His strength of will had carried them through.

He scraped two shallow pits, stretched Gerrit out in one and covered him in sand against the biting wind while he lay shivering in the other. Still, he could not sleep. He kept vigil as the storm raged.

Towards morning the rain eased and the rim of the cliff behind him was gradually lit by the pale predawn, though the bitter wind still gusted over the sea from the south-west where further storm clouds were gathering.

When he looked at Gerrit, he saw him conscious and staring at the surging ocean.

'We've arrived,' he said, emerging from his pit and laying a hand on his friend's shoulder. 'Now let me go and find out where.'

When Sunil reached the wreck site, he found a scene of devastation. As he approached across the heath, skirting silver-grey knee-high bushes and shorter russet-coloured shrubs, he saw a dozen or so dazed and exhausted men gathered at the lip of the boulder-strewn cliff above the wreck. Some were standing, others in a state of collapse, staring down at the stricken wreck.

A dishevelled woman in black stood alone to one side, a passenger he recognised, now deeply shocked. She was the chaplain's widow, whose children he used to entertain with his squeezebox before they and her husband died and were buried at Cape De Lopez Gonsalvez.

Most survivors were bleeding from extensive lacerations they'd received when they'd scrambled over the rock platform beneath the summit, across which successive waves now thundered, tossing wreckage and corpses among the rocks.

He joined the traumatised and dispirited group and looked down to see two men clinging to the stays, edging their way across the smashed mainmast towards the cliffs. The second man he recognised. It was Joost de Vlieger, blue-coated and uniformed, his red hair plastered to his skull, a bulging black leather satchel strapped across his back.

Beyond them, he observed another man in an orange

coat teetering on the foremast, who overbalanced and then, mistiming his last-minute leap to safety, fell screaming into a retreating wave that thrust him back into foam boiling from caverns beneath the shelf. His torn body was ejected minutes later to join others rolling among the carcasses of black-headed sheep in the raging surf.

Beyond the ship, a chaos of bodies and wreckage and floating cargo drifted southwards on the current. A strong onshore crosswind was chopping the sea to a maelstrom, its howl rising and falling in the caverns and hollows of the rocky cliff face, but the clouds were dissipating.

When Joost leapt to the shelf and clambered up to them at last, he acknowledged each survivor in turn, before collapsing exhausted on the rocks facing the chaotic scene below.

Then he turned and, looking up at Sunil, gestured at the wreck. 'Gerrit?'

Sunil pointed south. 'He's on a beach down there. He has a badly injured leg. I'll need help to bring him up here.'

Joost nodded. 'We'll need him. Give me time. We'll do it together.'

'The rain won't last. We're going to need water,' Sunil said. He glanced northwards at a gulley fifty roeden beyond them running eastwards at right angles from the cliffs. 'I'll take a look around.'

He made his way towards it and followed the floor inland through windblown stands of stunted trees with narrow, spiny leaves he did not recognise. He splashed through rainwater leaching through the limestone and, a little further in, he found what he was searching for—several seepages from a seam of denser rock at eye level below the gulley's rim.

Just as he and Vesak used to do on the Ulawatte hillside in Galle on their way to school long after the monsoon rains, he cupped his hands and drank. Beyond the dribbling water, he tracked the seam that ran wavelike through the rock wall before curving downwards.

At its end, he discovered a naturally excavated hollow and, at its base, a cylindrical pit part-filled with clear water, four hands across and elbow-deep. Elated, he dragged a loose boulder across it to conceal his find from animals and shelter it from the sun.

When he returned to the wreck site there was no sign of the woman. He saw Joost standing twenty roeden to his left, at the highest point along the cliffs. When Sunil reached him, he looked down and saw her spreadeagled on the rocks below beside the breaking waves.

Twenty-one

I WATCHED SUNIL SCRAMBLE across the scree and up the land-slip where the cliff had fallen away. His shadow disappeared across the summit. For long, dazed moments I fought to bear the waves of pain each time I made the slightest movement. Lying still, covered in the blanket of sand, I watched the red rock-face glimmer into life.

'I can tell you where we are,' I murmured. *'Eendrachtsland!'*

Shivering, fearful, I recalled Opa's prophetic warning delivered beneath the apple trees when he'd called me down to dinner so many years ago. My ship was wrecked and I had landed on the incomplete coastline that had fascinated me, angling across my charts and bronzed globe.

I've completed my voyage on the window ledge. My imaginary landscape has now become real.

The rain drifted momentarily into a fine mist as the sun broke through the cloud and lit the summit of the cliffs. Far to seaward, I saw black sheets of rain in storm fronts moving towards the shoreline and one, struck by a shaft of sunlight, bore on its periphery a sudden double rainbow, the bands of colour wavering ghostlike and then snuffed out.

An omen? A hallucination?

I closed my eyes, stretched out my arms and opened my hands to the sun's welcome warmth. Then I felt a gut-wrench-ing rush of dread. *This dawn is the first on a journey into uncharted territory. What challenges and dangers are in store? Do I have the courage, resilience and will to see me through?*

Gritting my teeth against the pain, I dragged himself from the sand and shifted closer to the cliff face. Leaning back against a rock part-sheltered beneath the canopy of the overhang, I saw my clothing cut away and my throbbing lower right leg crudely bound to splints, inflamed and swollen flesh bulging red and blue between the ties. My left leg was also badly bruised. *Here I am,* I thought, *cut off from my people and marooned as Mama forewarned me so long ago—a sciapod indeed!*

I glanced across the sand as stinging rain pelted down once more in driving wind. Eyes shut tight, I tilted my face, my mouth wide to gather water funnelling from the lip of the overhang. When I opened them at last, I found myself looking directly into the concerned, exhausted faces of Sunil and Joost de Vlieger.

'Good morning, Sunil,' I groaned, 'and Joost.' I attempted a smile. 'Interesting coincidence. *Leuk jou hier te ontmoeten,* fancy meeting you here.'

'Morning, Gerrit,' Joost said. 'Good to see you among the living. It seems we both miscalculated our position. Badly. Now we have a situation. We're going to need you.'

'Ready and willing, *agan.* How many survivors do we have?'

'Fifteen or so. There are bound to be more by the time we get back. Most were caught between decks and must have perished.'

'Any sign of Schipper Marinus? And the other officers?'

'No sign of him or any others.'

'Just us, then. I'm in great shape, as you can see.'

'Well, let's get you up to join the others for a start.'

'Up *there?*' I pointed a forefinger across my shoulder. 'It won't be easy.'

Klaas Goelet was right. These cliffs were *cut by some pagan god in a foul mood swinging his axe.*

They heaved me upright and, supporting me on either side, we began the painful trek. I struggled to hop on my bruised leg and swing my right foot forward with each stride. The pain was virtually unbearable as my blood-flow stabilised when I stood and worse, as the bones ground together with each step.

An hour later, after an agonising climb up the slope and a staggering walk across the heath at the clifftop when I was swamped by waves of pain, frequently dry-retching and on the verge of fainting, we joined the scattered group. They supported me as we peered down at the apocalyptic scene. The broached wreck had broken into three, its shattered main and mizzen masts protruding over the rock-shelf across which successive breakers crashed and seethed, tossing wreckage and corpses like balsa in the boiling cauldron between the smashed hull and the cliffs.

Then they led me to the shelter of a cluster of gnarled trees across which the survivors had earlier tied a square of salvaged sailcloth, another as a windbreak. Three crewmen lay asleep beneath it. Sunil cleared a patch of sand beside them for me to do the same.

As they carefully stretched me out, I grasped Sunil's hand. 'Thank you, Sunil. I will find a way to repay you, even if it's with the life I owe you.'

'No need, my friend.' A characteristic smile spread. 'I did for you what I should have done for Vesak. You have repaid me in full.'

Then his smile turned grim as he gestured at my wounds. 'You may not thank me for what we have to do to you now. We need to reset your leg. It will not heal at that angle.'

He handed me a chunk of wood he'd selected. 'Bite on this.'

LATER THAT MORNING, swamped with pain but with my leg reset and tightly bound, I forced my morbid thoughts away from contemplating the disastrous possibility of losing my lower leg and my chances of dying. I concentrated instead on the dire situation and how we should approach it to survive.

To my mind, Joost de Vlieger was key. We needed a leader. He was shrewd, perceptive and well-seasoned after two voyages to the east. He was respected and reasonably well-liked, but I knew that the absolute authority he enjoyed aboard ship would not extend to these wretched circumstances ashore. He was outnumbered if they refused his leadership, and I did not doubt that he would know this.

Do any among them bear a grudge against him? Dislike him enough to challenge him if he tries taking charge? Not only that, the survivors will soon look for a scapegoat to blame for the navigation errors and abandoning the Kockengen. *We must do something to protect him.*

When Joost joined me and squatted on the sand to find out how I was feeling, it was no surprise when he said, 'They'll get out of hand if we aren't rescued soon and they know for certain they're bound to perish.' He sucked in his breath, shaking his head. 'The *Kockengen* is our only hope, if she sails close enough. The *Belvliet* may be weeks away, and God knows if either of them will see us. We need a signal fire. In this weather, there's no hope of that.' He looked down at me with a sardonic grimace. 'Even if they do, how are they going to get in close enough to rescue us?'

He turned his attention to the few survivors sitting at the cliff edge. The rest, including Sunil, were scavenging among the debris beyond the breaking waves below. 'I can imagine morale deteriorating to such a degree that every man will fend for himself. Think of the deadly consequences. Remember the *Batavia*?'

'I do, and that may be the case in a few days, Joost. But right now I believe you are in personal danger. They'll be looking for someone to blame and then their mood will turn murderous.'

While we were talking, Sunil and one of the survivors clambered to the clifftop dragging behind them a bloated black-headed sheep. Another whooped triumphantly when he appeared, carrying a wooden crate he'd rescued intact from the surf. It was a sealed case of gin which he smashed open to discover several bottles intact among the broken glass. He promptly lifted one out, cracked open the lip and drank. Others joined him.

Joost did not interfere and, by sundown, the situation was spiralling out of control.

'This is also what I feared,' he told Sunil and me that evening, pointing across the carousing drunken group, 'discipline gone by the board! I have no chance of restoring order.'

'You're right. For now.' I looked up at his ascetic face framed by his red hair and unruly beard, his brown eyes intense, his anxiety evident. 'Things will improve when the gin runs out and they settle down to sleep it off.'

'I hope so.' He stifled a cynical laugh. 'Until they find more.'

'Always the pessimist, Joost. Tomorrow will be different. They'll be getting desperate. Is there anyone among them you see as a serious troublemaker?'

He looked across at the group. 'Cornelis Bibault from Stellenbosch, without a doubt. The Afrikaner. See him over there on the left? He for one showed some resentment when I landed. He seemed less than pleased to see me. His fellow Afrikaners have not survived. That may be reason enough. And he has an independence of spirit we spoke of once before, if you recall. You noticed it took special treatment to bring him into line aboard ship. As you said, he's another with the spirit of de Reus. He doesn't mind a confrontation. Among the others, I'm not too sure. I don't know all the soldiers.' He looked down with concern at my swollen leg. 'And you? Your seniority makes you a target also and you're in no state to defend yourself.'

'Less so than you, I think. I wasn't the navigator. So it may be sensible for you to take shelter down at the beach for a day or two. Sunil will give you a call when things improve.'

Joost nodded. 'I agree. In a day or two, it should be easier… at least to reassess the situation.'

'Yes. You have allies among the survivors who were on your watch. I have noted three, including Kasper Meyer, who is influential and trustworthy. And he's a skilled cooper into the bargain. That will come in useful. Among the rest, Pieter Dekker is a good man and Andries Leenders is reliable. You can count on them when they're over the initial shock.'

'And the bottles of gin are spent. After that, we'll only have a brief period, a week or two at most, before they'll be convinced that rescue is unlikely.'

'I agree. You'll need to make the most of the time at your disposal.' I gathered my thoughts. 'I believe they'll soon be looking for leadership and direction. The sensible ones among them, anyway. They know their chances of survival will fall apart without it.'

'And they're accustomed to discipline and following procedure aboard ship,' Joost replied. 'For most of them, their training, work habits and good sense are second nature.'

'Except for Cornelis, as you say. He's the *ongeleid projectiel*, the loose cannon you'll have to watch.'

'You? *We*, Gerrit. You're the other officer here.'

I smiled. 'Alright, we. He's young, and he will no doubt be devious when his words and actions don't dine at the same table. I noticed he had a following among the younger ones on board apart from the other Afrikaners, but I don't see any of them here. That works in our favour. We can isolate him. Find him a distraction to occupy him. The others know it will take effort and organisation to make the best of a bad situation.'

'Very well,' Joost replied, surprising me when he removed a telescope from his satchel. 'This will help you maintain a watch out to sea. The *Kockemgen* should be no more than a week behind us.'

'Surprise, surprise!' I said, turning it over in my hands. 'What else have you got in your bag of tricks?' I looked up at the scudding clouds. 'We can use the lens to start a fire when the sun breaks through.'

'And when the firewood dries,' Sunil said, as he walked across to the drunken group, where he stooped to retrieve two empty gin bottles. He shook out the remnants and shouted at Joost to wait for him. A few minutes later he returned with the bottles filled with water, one of which he handed to Joris, the other to me.

'You're a miracle worker, Sunil. Do you have anything else up your sleeve?' I asked. Then I gazed up at Joost. 'We may need you sooner than you think once thirst and hunger take hold. Things could then go either way.'

I sent Sunil to recall Joost on the morning of the third day. There was barely any wind. The sun was warming us and drying the wood, which the survivors had collected and stacked on the edge of the cliff in a tall pyramid ready for lighting.

Cornelis had surprised me. He'd borrowed Sunil's knife to gut, skin and prepare two sheep now hanging side by side from a tree branch a short distance from the campsite. He'd hung them closer earlier, but clouds of small invasive flies had proved a nuisance. Beyond them hung the outstretched skins.

It had greatly concerned me when he'd sliced and shared the hearts, livers and kidneys, which the survivors had eaten raw. He'd offered me strips of heart and I found them palatable.

When the weather changed for the better that morning, he began cutting finger-sized strips from the muscle, laying them out on a length of sailcloth.

When Joost arrived, Cornelis and several others were down on the rock shelf collecting whatever salt they could find deposited after the storm, to season the strips of meat. Sunil went down to join them.

When Joost addressed the survivors that afternoon, although I sensed the mood was sullen and suspicious, they were not unreceptive. He came well-prepared. He withdrew a chart from his satchel, spread it across a flat boulder and selected a stick to use as a pointer. 'This is where we are, by my calculations,' he began.

'Your calculations!' someone shouted. 'How can we trust your calculations?'

Joost inclined his head in the silence that followed. He gazed slowly around the group, meeting the eyes of each. 'Who said that?' he asked, sounding each word with quiet emphasis. There was no response. 'Who was it?'

For a further moment, no one moved. Then one of the soldiers raised a finger and stepped forward.

'Your name?'

'Bernardus.'

'Bernardus?'

'Herzog. Bernardus Herzog, from Bremen.'

'And your rank?'

'Artilleryman.'

Joost stared at him for a full minute. 'We are in this together, Bernardus,' he said at last. I heard an unexpected empathy in his voice. 'I understand your frustration… and I share it.' He waved a hand around the campsite. 'We are at war, and I'm sure you will agree there is only one way that we can win it—by working together. *Door onze middelen en vaardigheden te bundelen,* by pooling our skills and resources as comrades in arms. Do you agree?'

'Of course.'

'Alright. Now then, you were raising doubts about my calculations. Are you a trained navigator?'

'Of course not.'

Joost pointed down at the chart. 'So if I suggest we are here, you're not in a position to contest my suggestion?'

Bernardus leant closer, as though taking his time to scrutinise the chart. Then he shrugged.

'Then you accept that we *are* here, or hereabouts?'

'If you say so, yes.'

'So why did you call out?' Joost did not wait for his reply. He continued, his voice now clear and authoritative. 'I'll tell you why. Because you believe we officers miscalculated the longitude and we were further west than we believed.' He paused for effect, slowly nodding. 'You are right. We did… and apart from the storm, the wind, the current, the lack of an accurate timepiece, magnetic variation and our inability to truly measure our speed, we have no excuses for it. So I accept full responsibility for these circumstances in which we find ourselves.' Again he gazed deliberately around the group. 'If anyone else has anything to say about it, now is the time.'

There was no response.

'Good. Now we have a war to wage and we have work to do.' Then he used the stick to point deliberately at Cornelis. 'You, I want to congratulate. I see you're already applying the skills you learned at the Cape. I understand the slices of heart went down well and I'm looking forward to the beef jerky you're preparing.'

Cornelis smiled. 'Biltong, *baas*,' he said. 'We Afrikaners call it biltong.'

'Right. Biltong. Keep doing exactly what you're doing. The rest of us will follow your example and apply our skills to the best of our ability.'

Then I saw him smile for the first time before he nodded at Sunil. 'As you know, Sunil here has found us water.' He held Sunil's gaze. 'Well done. We may need more. Would you like to check?'

I watched him spend the rest of the afternoon talking to each survivor, writing up their responses on the back of the chart with a navigational charcoal stick. *What else has he got in that satchel of wonders of his?*

When he showed me his list later, I found he'd appointed five lieutenants and split the group into teams of two or three according to their skills.

'Food and water,' he said. 'Birds and birds' eggs. Fish. The signal and cooking fires. The campsite. Cooking utensils. Flotsam salvaged from the ship. Ablution areas and toilets. Clearing away the corpses. What have I missed?'

'A swivel cannon, perhaps. Gunpowder… if there is any when we can get aboard.'

'*If* we can get aboard. What's worrying you, Gerrit? Wild animals we know nothing about? The local savages?'

'Them too, but more for a signal to add to the fire smoke.'

WE TOOK STOCK the next day.

'There are another two soaks in a second gulley beyond this one,' Sunil pointed northwards when he returned after searching. 'They should last us a month, if we ration the water. Longer if it rains.' He stepped forward as he spoke and indicated the tattered shade cloth beneath which I was resting. 'I suggest we adjust this sail to collect it… and set up all the other canvases we can find.'

The storms had passed inland two days before. Now cold and relentless wind gusts lifted and cracked the billowing sailcloth under a winter sun.

Towards midday, we watched Joost light the signal fire on the edge of the cliff. He soaked a stack of wood and deal and broken barrel staves in linseed oil from a keg washed ashore for fire starters, setting them beneath the base of the pyramid of dead branches the crew had built. Then he wedged a lens from his telescope into the fork in a green branch to focus the sun's rays on a charge of gunpowder from one of two casks scavenged among the wreckage. The explosion was as effective as it was disastrous—the wood in smoky flames, the lens shattered. He designated two survivors the task of building up the fire to signal proportions and others to keep it lit day and night.

'The *Kockengen* should pass the cliffs this evening or early tomorrow at the latest by my estimate,' he told us, 'unless she has already, or is too far out to sea, which may well be the case.'

One soldier discovered a damaged barrel of salted pork with half its contents still intact several roeden south along the cliffs and, further still, two scavengers retrieved a case of mildewed hardtack biscuits dampened by seepage which they laid out to dry.

Late that afternoon, by what seemed an entertaining miracle as the tide rose, we watched Bernardus Herzog and another soldier use ropes and barrel netting to snare a keg of beans and lentils from an explosive blowhole as it surged upwards with the piston-like whoosh of incoming waves at high tide, before being sucked back down like a loose bung.

Joost told me that when he had been down at the beach he had spent his days exploring across the heath and had discovered four intricately woven knee-high nests of sticks. 'They're infested by what look like rats the size of small rabbits,' he said. 'They must be nocturnal. When I disturbed the warrens they scattered and were too shy and nimble for me to catch. They will be something we can think about trapping. I counted about twenty of them. There may be others.'

He stood and gazed southwards along the cliffs. The terrain was rocky, harsh and barren and the vegetation sparse and tangled. The survivors reported that there was no fruit or rootstock to be found, or so it seemed. The seed pods on the stunted trees were green and vile to the taste. Apart from some lizards and Joosts's rats, no other edible animals were sighted.

There were some signs of larger animals though—pellet-like droppings and torn fur were found, caught in the bark of trees in thickets where they appear to have sheltered.

The only birds sighted by Sunil on the lookout for his parakeet were a flock of black and white wrens—or what he took for wrens—that whirred away at his approach, and a solitary kite flying southwards on sunset.

He had earlier noted barnacles, crabs and oysters in the seething surf at the base of the cliffs, and there were clusters of abalone shells visible in deeper water, too difficult to retrieve until the weather calmed.

That prospect excited him. 'I'll be diving for them as soon as I can,' he told Joost and me, removing his goggles from his pouch and shaking them triumphantly at us in his right hand. 'I can't wait to put these to the test.'

During the afternoon, three survivors armed with broken branches shoved and levered several bloated and stiffened corpses back into the sea to be carried away or sink, any earlier grisly thoughts of cannibalism extinguished by the stench.

By that evening, Cornelis had two full legs of mutton roasting in the coals. I was pleased to observe the appetising smell and the prospect of full bellies working wonders on morale. He was marinating the strips of muscle he'd prepared in vinegar one of the survivors had mistaken for wine. He intended coating them the next day in salt crystals scraped from drying pools at the sea's edge before laying them out to cure on a trellis he'd designed, using saplings set up in the shade beneath the sail on which he'd earlier laid them.

'*Coriander!*' he shouted at one point, looking up at us enjoying the mutton. 'I need some. Hey! Have you *aasvoëls* chowing down on my *braaivleis*[38] found any seeds that taste

---

38 Afrikaans 'vultures eating my barbecued meat'.

like coriander?' He gave a burst of laughter. 'My kingdom for some coriander! I need it to spice up the biltong.'

The next day four more dead sheep were found snagged on rocks away from the wreck site, their eyelids and lips ravaged by sea lice, their bellies distended and stiffened legs grotesquely protruding. Cornelis insisted on skinning them for hides and butchering them for any salvageable meat and bones.

TEN DAYS LATER, Joost squatted beside me to discuss our options.

'There's been no sign of any ships, let alone the *Kockengen*. I don't like to admit it, but she must have missed us days ago.' He gestured at the fire. 'Even if she saw our signal during the night, knowing Hayman de Laver the way I do, I'm certain there is nothing on this earth that would convince him to come close enough inshore to check. If I was in his place I'd do the same—sail on!'

'Where does that leave us, then?'

'We have no option except to move the campsite north beyond the cliffs, and the sooner the better. The beaches opposite Dirck Hartog Island provide far better access from the open sea. The *Belvliet* is due here in a week or two, I think, if she hasn't already passed us. She should be in the company of the fleet that arrived in Cape Town before we left. Jan de Hei aboard the *Oosterstein* has the eyes of a hawk and the curiosity of a cat, my friend. If anyone's going to spot us, it will be him.'

I raised my eyebrows. 'Curiosity won't get him far if he has no idea we're here.'

'True, but there's also Renier Hijpe commanding the *Zuiderbeek*.' He smiled drily, pointing skywards. 'You know as well as I do he thinks that God created the sun to shine especially on him. I have no doubt he believes he could walk on water to get to us! All we need is a signal to blow his mind. Any suggestions?'

I gave him a smile that widened to a burst of laughter. '*Grote geesten denken hetzelfde*, great minds think alike, according to Father Cats!' I tapped my temple with a fore-finger. 'I've had an idea up here for some time. A signal so surprising Renier will consider it a message sent to him directly from Paradise and they'll talk about it in Batavia and Middelburg for years to come—a giant kite! We send it aloft and then we explode it.'

'Hah! That's brilliant!' Joost said, as he nodded agree-ment. 'A Chinese rocket. But how would you construct it? And launch it? And set the charges?'

I waved a hand around the campsite. 'We have the sailcloth. We have the ropes. We have the linseed oil. We have sufficient gunpowder left, and we have hands and time to spare.'

'Right, then we should get it done.'

Following my instructions, Sunil and another survivor spent the next two days preparing the necessary parts—intact sailcloth painstakingly cut to the traditional dia-mond shape, one roede long and half as wide; a strong but slender green tree trunk heated in the fire and straightened for the spine, its branches removed and bowed for the spars and lower reinforcing ribs; a three-line sheet unravelled for the ties and the cord, and a long shank of flayed rope for the tail.

They took a further day and a half to assemble the kite, successfully testing it in flight on the strong afternoon breeze to the raucous applause of the sceptical group. Then they applied linseed oil to the body and tail in preparation for impregnation with gunpowder before launching.

'All we need now are the passing ships,' Joost said when he congratulated them on the outcome. 'Are you sure your ignition system is foolproof?'

'We can only use it once,' I replied, 'so it had better be.

We'll know when we sight any sails and launch it into action. We've bowed the spars, so the tail is superfluous for its balance in flight and it will make a perfect fuse once we light it. The kite will fly until the flame reaches it and then, guess what?' I violently clapped my hands. '*Kaboom!*'

'We hope.'

'We know.'

'You've done this before?'

'No.'

'I like your confidence.'

'Trust me. You have so far.'

'Alright then, we'll give it one more week. If the signal fails or we sight no ships in that time, we must move on.'

'Without me.'

'With you.'

'Without. We've discussed this.' I moved my foot a fraction. The pain was searing. The wounds above the ankle were oozing despite Sunil tending to them with heated saltwater. 'I can't be moved and I won't be carried and slow you down. You'll have your hands full carting that swivel cannon you're thinking of using as a signal.'

'Yes, but we're only taking one breech block, so we'll be carrying a lesser load. Why don't we fashion you a stretcher and you join us?'

I shook my head. 'Sunil says he's going to stay. I haven't been able to change his mind. Once I can walk, we'll overtake you,' I gave him a deliberately cheerful smile, 'and get to Batavia in time to greet you when you arrive.'

'That may take months.'

'So be it. I need to heal first or risk losing the leg. Or my life.'

'That's your final word?'

'It is.'

THE WEEK PASSED and, to our dismay, the expected ships did not appear.

On the elected deadline in mid-June, Joost and the group prepared to depart on sunset. They intended travelling under the full moon, he told me, the walk expected to take three days. They left us a selection of supplies, including a bundle of Cornelis's prized biltong, which he had been issuing sparingly, and for which Sunil had developed a surprising craving.

They collected a huge pile of dead tree branches for us to replenish the fire, along with driftwood from the wreck, rarer now, but including one of Opa Laurens's statuettes of the Grecian Sphinx I asked them to detach from the transom and leave within view, partway up the cliff. They also cut a secondary supply of green branches left to dry out.

Baltheser Claasen, one of the German soldiers, presented Sunil and me with a pair of what he called 'sandal-moccasins worn by Roman soldiers' he'd made to measure from Cornelis's sheepskins for everyone who needed them.

'You'd better agree they are a perfect fit,' he said as he handed Sunil his pair, 'and refer to me as a first-class "cordwainer", not a mere cobbler the way these other disrespectful fellows do. Otherwise, I'll commit them here and now to the fire and you and your bunions can go barefoot.'

Sunil tried one on and then the other. 'They are perfect, Baltzer. You are an outstanding cordwainer…Eendrachtsland's best. How are you at making hats? I lost mine swimming ashore.'

'Feet are my speciality, Sunil, not heads.' Baltheser's expression was wry. 'I am obsessed with them. I'm very short, after all, and closer to the ground than most people I know.'

Sunil clambered to his feet and tested the shoes, hopping on alternate legs, raising both hands head-high and waving them in enthusiastic approval before looking down in mock surprise. 'They haven't fallen apart! I thank you for the gift, Baltzer. I will buy you a drink when we meet in Batavia.'

Reclining against the trunk of a tree, I extended a hand to Joost, who shook it in farewell. 'Till we meet again, Gerrit. And you, Sunil. May God be with you both.'

'Name the place in Batavia and we will be there to greet you when you arrive,' I said.

Joost looked down and smiled. 'That's easy. The Hotel Mauritius. Last time I was there they had a Chinese chef working in the Simon Stevin kitchens whose dishes were the envy of the colony.'

'I'll book us a table.'

'For twenty. Even Cornelis will be there if they serve biltong these days.'

We watched the group load up their sailcloth sacks, one survivor carrying glowing embers for future fires flickering in a tureen. Two at the rear hoisted the swivel cannon to their shoulders, a third assisting them.

They faded to shadows as the sun sank into the ocean, extinguished in a crimson blaze, the huge full moon above it glowing like an illusory lantern, bright yellow in the haze. It paled to white and shrank back to size as it rose among emerging stars shimmering across the sky.

Twenty-two

SEVERAL DAYS AFTER JOOST's departure, the weather changed overnight and the sea stilled for the first time to blue-green glass.

When Sunil woke to tend the fire, he walked down to check the sunken shadows of the ship. Seaweed on the rocks beside it was barely moving, the tide on the turn. He had half an hour of motionless water during which to make his first dive on the wreck.

Rushing back to the campsite, he alerted Gerrit to their change in fortunes, took his goggles from his pouch and made his way back to the edge of the platform. The blowholes that had violently spouted spume and foam for weeks now resonated with the wind's haunting sighs as he passed.

He removed his clothes and eased into the water above the dislocated forepeak. His first exploratory dive took him to the beak head and the entrance to the passageway. He remained clinging to the frame for several moments, accustoming himself to the pressure and the novelty of immersion in water far colder than he'd expected, before releasing the lungful of air and stroking for the surface.

Intoxicating pleasure ran through him as he burst back into dazzling sunlight and, gulping a second deep refill of air, he went down again, this time entering the passageway and swimming strongly for the tool store, the door lodged open. Then, horrified, he backpedalled when he saw the pale corpse of Laurens Voort spreadeagled beneath the jack.

He retreated to the surface and trod water as he prepared for a longer dive, this time clawing his way into Gerrit's cabin and scrabbling into a case below his bunk to retrieve his tobacco container. He swam back to the surface with it and climbed to the platform, where he emptied the seawater and checked the contents. Then he made his way back to up the cliff to present it to Gerrit.

'You've been looking for this,' he said.

Surprised by Sunil's early return and beaming at the sight of the canister, Gerrit lifted the lid. 'Eureka!' he shouted, 'I surely have. Well done!'

He removed the spoon and solemnly lifted out the abalone shell, tested the strength of the leather thong and strung it about his neck. 'I should never have taken it off. Who knows? If I hadn't, we may have avoided the reefs. Now I'm fully equipped and ready for action, thanks to you. I'm very grateful, Sunil.'

'Is there anything else you need from the cabin?'

'My stone and shell, you know the ones. They're important to me. My journal, but that will be a mass of pulp. My atlas? No different, I expect, so no. Bring up anything you think may be useful to us. And some clothes, perhaps.'

'What about Laurens? He's in the storeroom.'

'My God, how does he look?'

'Hardly recognisable. He'll fall apart if I touch him.'

'Then leave him. We'll have a memorial service up here for him and all the poor souls.'

The wind picked up and the tide turned as he continued diving, the water shifting uneasily in the passageways, the doors swinging eerily as the surges increased. When Sunil went for his last dive he avoided the wreck. He followed the rock ledges down instead and swam out across the seafloor beyond the forepeak as far as he could, noting the feelers of crayfish protruding from several flat coral formations in deeper water he could not reach. He surfaced carrying three abalone shells he'd dislodged on the way to the rock shelf.

He dressed beside the blowholes, erupting bursts of foam once more as though a lever had been thrown. He'd recovered some carefully selected items—an adze, a hatchet and several canisters emptied of copper nails from the tool store, two sets of spare clothing from Gerrit's cabin, along with his shaving kit in its silver and tortoise-shell case, a set of knives, a frying pan and three iron tureens from the galley, one of them for Gerrit to use as a chamber pot once he was sufficiently healed to squat. Sunil looked forward to relinquishing his daily nursing duties—emptying Gerrit's gin bottle of urine and cleaning away his faeces before washing him down with seawater.

He also brought up Joost's backstaff, which Gerrit had borrowed when Joost had been teaching him to take his bearings and measure latitude. It was now in several pieces, one of which was missing when he handed them over. Gerrit waved a hand up and down the coastline. 'That's nor-nor-west and that's sou-sou-east, that's all we need to remember,' he said as he handed the pieces back to Sunil, who consigned them to the pile of kindling for the fire.

'I couldn't find the stone or the shell,' he told Gerrit. 'They must have washed away.'

'Ah, well,' Gerrit said, disappointed. 'At least you tried.'

'They reminded you of family and home?'

'They did. My papa and my oom. They were also my reminders of man's cultural achievements in natural science and art. I was privileged to have them on loan, but nothing lasts. Now they're back where they belong… in the ocean and the past.' He gave a wry smile. 'So we start again. From scratch.'

Sunil looked quizzically at him, then laughed. 'Natural science and art? That reminds me, I have these abalone to cook.'

He took the shells down to the sea's edge where he shucked, cleaned and trimmed the flesh. He beat them gently with his fist until they were flexible, then thinly sliced them. Back at the campsite, he placed the frying pan on the coals and brought the fresh water he poured into it to the boil.

He added a handful of chopped biltong cubes and shifted the pan on the coals so that it simmered.

'This is my stock.' He looked across at Gerrit. 'Thirty minutes should do it. Then I'll blanch the abalone slices. Have you ever tried it?'

'No. First time.'

'First time for me too, cooked this way. I gave them a good pounding, so they should be tender… but they will be bland. My *appa* used to fry them with ghee, garlic and a pinch of mixed spices.' He raised his hand with thumb and forefingers together to his mouth and smacked his lips. 'Delicious!'

'Anything to fill the gut,' Gerrit replied. 'Were there any sharks down there when you were diving?'

With his back to Gerrit, Sunil was adjusting the pan on the coals. He stiffened and looked around. '*Sharks?* No. Not this time.'

Then he stood, walked across and sat cross-legged on the sand beside Gerrit, gazing out at the ocean.

After several silent minutes, he took a deep breath. 'Let me tell you about sharks,' he said.

EACH YEAR BETWEEN June and late February during the pearling off-seasons, he and Vesak used to work in Galle aboard his *appa's dhoni*[39], taking barrels of fresh water out to the VOC ships anchored in the bay.

The hulk of the *Nijptang* lay on its side in the shallows fifty metres from the water jetty. She had once been used as a pearling boat on the Mannar sandbanks and Sunil had crewed aboard her when he was twelve, the year he'd learned to dive.

She'd been scuttled by a leaking hull. Her masts had been removed. Part of her superstructure protruded at a crazy angle from the water at spring tide, while at the low, her barnacled

---

39 Their father's boat

lower timbers housed battalions of scurrying soldier crabs waving defensive white claws above the light blue armour of their carapaces.

He and Vesak revelled in diving from the water jetty between barrel loadings. They climbed to the topsides of the water cart and leapt high, legs thrashing, into the water. They swam through the worm-eaten hull, along eerie passages among the empty cabins and into the holds. They unsettled the mud and startled shoals of butterflyfish, their massed white and gold triangular bodies parting like string curtains as they stroked their way up the stairwells, through the hatchways and into streaming shafts of sunlight above.

Three years ago, in mid-December, the *Zuytdorp* was anchored in the bay. They were working on the jetty as usual, just below the pump house, helping their *appa* fill the water barrels. They loaded the *dhoni* and sailed out to the *Zuytdorp*.

Sunil rolled the last water barrel across the bottom of the *dhoni* when they were tied up alongside, using his foot to keep it hard up against others lying in the sling, before their *appa* signalled to the crewmen watching from the rail above them. The rope tautened as the men laboured at the capstan to raise the swinging cargo towards the open gate in the railings.

Sunil leant into the *Zuytdorp*'s side to hold the bulging net away, his arms following its upward progress, his feet gripping the rocking *dhoni*'s gunwales. As the barrels cleared his hands, he stepped back into the boat and watched them disappear onto the deck. One of the sailors saluted down to them, then swung back the gate and locked it in place.

Vesak was sprawled out on the front deck. He had one arm stretched out with a fishing line in his fingers. His eyes were closed against the sun. Sunil thought he must be asleep, so he slipped over the side, making sure there was no splash or movement of the boat. Then he swam underwater and tugged on his line.

Vesak jerked wildly into life as Sunil burst from below the bows and sprayed him with a mouthful of water.

Alert now, Vesak walked back the length of the hot deck and then, taking a running start, somersaulted over the side. The sea closed over him and Sunil, with his goggles on, watched him swim to the boat's side, hauling himself out in one fluid movement before sprinting into a second somersault and then a third.

Sunil trod water, adjusted his goggles, and looked expectantly up at the deck rail as the first of the sailors peered down, reaching into his money belt to select a coin.

Their *appa* approached the foredeck to untie the line. The current swung the bow of the *dhoni* outwards and away from them, aligning itself against the *Zuytdorp* in the opposite direction. A full boat length away, it was still moored by the stern line. Their *appa* walked slowly over to untie it, pausing as he always did to give them enough time for their money dives.

The sailor shouted and the first coin flashed towards them. Sunil returned the shout and dived to track it as it swerved this way and that through the water. He followed it down for effect, impressing the crewmen gathering at the rail. When he reached out to pluck it from the water darkening in the ship's shadow, he put it into his mouth and held it in his cheek as he stroked for the surface.

He looked up as Vesak passed him, grinning, with a second coin fluttering before him like a moth in blue-green candle flame.

At the surface, a third coin Sunil hadn't noticed earlier splashed in behind him. He twisted to dive, but it was already deep as he raced to reach it. This was a challenge, his skills tested as he went on down, gathering it in. His ears were bursting as he looped upside-down beneath it, caught it in both hands and swam for the surface.

He burst in triumph from the water waving the coin, which he put in his mouth. He shook the water from his hair as Vesak tilted his goggles to clear them of seepage.

His *appa* told Sunil later that he'd seen the water darken beneath him as a shadow had passed through the space he would have reached with another downward stroke. Then he'd seen a monstrous shark turn and make a closer pass below them.

The pressure of its glide thrust Vesak's legs sideways as Sunil was looking up for the flash of the next coin. The cloth binding of his goggles was tight over his ears. Looking up at the sailors, he couldn't hear their screams but saw them gesticulating wildly and then glimpsed his *appa* shouting as he ran across the boat waving the boathook.

He saw Vesak bring his knees to his chest and sink below him, as their *appa* threw the boathook deep into the water between them.

He tore the cloth from his ears and heard the shouts of alarm as Vesak thrashed his way to safety, clambering over Sunil and sobbing.

The collision tore the goggles from Vesak's forehead and he saw them sink.

He gripped Vesak firmly with a free arm, shocked to hear the panic in his *appa*'s shouts and pandemonium on the deck above.

He ducked beneath the surface as the shark glided across his front. He saw the nictitating membrane sweep in slow motion across the cold and empty lens of its eye, saucer-sized, before the immense barred body swept past, tapering to a broad nicked tail that flicked his brother's legs and the blood poured.

Vesak's scream brought more of the *Zuytdorp*'s crew to the rail as the shark, its broad square nose and tan bars lit along its flanks, turned to come directly at the flailing boys, charging in from the ship's bow.

Sunil caught the boathook that had floated up behind him. He struggled to pull it through the water's resistance to face the shark he could no longer see. He held his other arm around Vesak, gripping his armpit as the shark made a direct charge at the pair.

Its thrashing tail churned the surface and the boathook passed harmlessly over its head.

Sunil was blinded underwater as the jaws tore into Vesak, taking both boys into the side of the ship. Sunil grasped Vesak's other arm as the shark, head shaking and great body thrashing and twisting, towed them out of the ship's shadow and into the sunlight towards the bows. There the blood spread like crimson smoke and Sunil felt Vesak's body lighten as the shark tore itself away.

Sunil hauled his brother to the hawser of the ship's forward anchor where he held on with one hand, horrified to find himself clutching Vesak's upper torso with the other.

From the decks above, the seamen watched helplessly as the shark circled again, the boy's severed lower abdomen and legs entangled in its dislocating jaw, held there by knots of intestines and cloth it struggled to disgorge. It dived slowly from sight, trailing clouds of blood and the streaming russet of Vesak's sarong.

Sunil struggled to climb up the rope, hanging on to Vesak's wrist but his weight and the steep angle were too much for him. His arms numb, he hung, groaning, until he let Vesak go.

He watched his *appa* retrieve the torso before it sank. Vesak's footprints from his somersaults were still a faint wet stain on the timber of the foredeck, his *appa* had told him later.

Shocked, Sunil climbed the hawser to the lion at the fore-peak. He clasped it, shivering and moaning, until two sailors clambered down towards him. The black emptiness in the shark's cold eye, the membrane sliding across it, the brown bars lit along its side swirling remorselessly before him filled him with terror.

He looked down and saw his bleeding ribs exposed, his skin ripped open when the shark had brushed past.

He would never forget the lightness of Vesak's body pulled from his grasp and the unforgettable moment of his death.

'That's the story, Gerrit,' Sunil said, glancing at him, a brief smile of relief as he inclined his head. 'This is the first time I've talked about it without breaking down.'

'My privilege, Sunil. You couldn't have done more for him. You did your best. And never forget—my life you *did* save.'

Sunil stood and gave a whistling outbreath and nervous laugh. 'Time for me to blanch the abalone. You're not allergic, are you?'

'I'll risk it,' Gerrit replied. 'I'm still absorbing the story you told me… and the *Nijptang*! A friend of mine, Klaas Goelet, was the carpenter aboard when she sailed past here in 1697. You may have swum through his cabin.'

'Destiny, do you think?' Sunil asked as he bent to place the abalone in the stock, piece by piece. 'Like us landing on these cliffs and me serving up this abalone?'

LATE THAT AFTERNOON, in shocked disbelief, Sunil sighted unexpected sails on the horizon, the first an unearthly mirage before another two followed closely, line abreast.

'Gerrit!' he screamed. 'Wake up! There are ships!'

Gerrit struggled to sit up and focus.

'What did I tell you, Sunil?' he gasped at last. 'It's the work of the albatross! Get the gunpowder! Prime the kite. We don't have long.'

Sunil splashed the remnants of the linseed oil across the sailcloth and soaked the tail, then he poured gunpowder across both. He unwound the cord to its full length, running it in a series of loops across an open area of heath between the camp-site and the cliffs, its end bound to a boulder at the cliff edge.

He lifted the kite, walked to the lip of the cliff beside the fire, and waited for Gerrit's signal. That took all of twenty minutes, as the ships came straight on before the wind, then jibed away to port to begin their broad reach to the north-west.

'Now, Sunil. Now's the time!' Gerrit screamed. 'Fire away!'

'We need with more wind.'

'It's strong enough. There's no time to waste. Let it fly!'

Holding the kite head high, its ribs bending as the wind caught it, Sunil manoeuvred the thrashing tail across the fire. It crackled into flame and he released the kite, allowing the cord to unravel across both palms, applying pressure as the kite lifted and dipped and shook violently, struggling for height, before soaring majestically across the campsite and powering upwards, gyrating to the left and then the right as he fought to manage the cord.

Dragged slowly towards me as the cord ran out, Sunil released it as the last loop hissed across the sand, giving out an ominous *thwack* as the boulder held. For several tense minutes, the cord hummed like a piano wire before it snapped, sending the kite cavorting wildly across the sky as though attempting to escape the flame ascending towards it.

And then the sailcloth exploded, spitting fire in orange and yellow flames before plunging to the ground, a trail of black smoke marking its descent like a streak of pitch across the sky's clear blue, Sunil leaping and screaming along the lip of the cliff.

To their frustration and despair, the ships sailed on, none responding to the flash of their airborne signal light.

Twenty-three

THE NEXT MORNING, SUNIL took the water canister and made his way to the second pool in the gulley to the north. It hadn't rained for several days, and then only briefly. It was clear the seepages were drying up, so for the past week, he had been refilling the water canister more sparingly than usual.

At the pool, he half-filled the canister and then, on an impulse, he left it there and walked farther up the gulley in search of other pools. He found none, eventually reaching its end, its sides closing in and the floor sloping gently upwards.

He climbed to an exposed grassy clearing and stood among the green thickets at its edge, watching a mob of grey animals similar to those he'd sighted once or twice inland from the campsite. Alerted to his movement or his presence on the wind, he watched them bound away on their rear legs, their thick tails protruding. He was amazed at their hopping action and the length of each swerving leap.

He stepped out into the open to investigate what he took to be a depression at the centre of the clearing, perhaps a water-hole at which the animals appeared to have been drinking. He found nothing but further patches of oat grass and scrub.

As he turned to make his way back to the gulley entrance, he heard voices behind him and froze. Two Indigenous tribesmen, one carrying three long spears across his shoulder and the other his water canister, were crossing towards him, conversing loudly enough to alert him to their arrival. They were naked, their hair and beards wild. Sunil noticed that the warrior carrying the water wore a cape of red animal skin hanging down his back and across his shoulders, strung at the neck.

He could not read their expressions. His first blinding reaction had him back on the Mannar beaches in Ceylon, bargaining with indigenous Vedda tribesmen visiting the pearl divers to sell their carvings and bows and arrows, their moods unpredictable and their appearances as fierce as the two confronting him.

Unable to restrain himself, he blurted a Tamil greeting. *'Vannakam! Vannakam!*[40]'

He backed away as they approached.

They halted three roeden away and Sunil watched the warrior carrying the canister place it carefully in a patch of sand beside him. He reached for a spear from his partner and held the shaft vertically, the glinting quartz barb downwards, barely touching the ground. *'Ngana nyinda?*[41]' he asked, expressionless.

He seemed to deliberately avoid eye contact as he examined Sunil before calmly looking directly at him for several moments, then away.

Sunil took another involuntary backward step, alert to their every move, his heart racing as the silent standoff extended. A minute passed, then two. The warriors continued to look him up and down. Then the first warrior extended his arm, rotated the spear to the horizontal, the barb facing Sunil and the shaft across a shoulder. He gestured across the grassland, sweeping the spear through a half-circle, his frown now menacing. *'Wanthala nyindangu barraja? Gagarrala?*[42]' he asked.

Sunil, alarmed by the aggression he saw in the swing of his spear, stood dumbfounded.

The warrior nodded. *'Ngatha Malgana. Ngathangura nhaganha barraja. Nayiwu nyinda nala yaninyina?*[43]'

Fearing the worst, Sunil ducked, turned and sprinted for

---

40 Hello! Hello!
41 Who are you?
42 Where are you from, which country? To the east?
43 I am Malgana. This is my country. Why are you trespassing here?

the shelter of the closest thickets. As he did so he heard a warning shout and the rattle of spears. '*Hoh! Nyinda wujarnu matharra! Wirra! Wirra!*[44]'

Bent double and zigzagging in desperation, Sunil heard another warning shout. '*Wirra! Gurra bajirri yana! Yugarri! Ngalingu nyindanha ngarrinmanha biladagurru!*[45]'

In the menacing silence that followed, Sunil heard a final warning ring out over the hoarse rasping of his breath as he sprinted on, '*Nyinda gulgathadi?*[46]'

Then, within several roeden of the trees, a single spear whistled overhead, landed ahead of him and slid along the sand. Bracing for the second to pierce his back, Sunil reached the grounded spear, picked it up and turned to face his attackers. Shaking uncontrollably, his chest heaving, he held the spear horizontally in clenched fists in preparation for the confrontation.

The warriors, who had loped after him, took up the same position three roeden in front of him and then, in a simultaneous movement, they swung their spears to the vertical once again, the barbs just short of the ground. The first of them gestured impatiently for Sunil to do the same. Hesitant, he did so.

The first then grounded his spear, stepped forward and gestured to Sunil to do the same. Suspicious that the other warrior maintained his hold on his spear, Sunil waited. The first again raised a hand and pointed at the ground, glaring as he expressed a disapproving hiss. This time Sunil reluctantly grounded his spear.

He saw a nod of approval and the flash of teeth when he stood and, though still harbouring fearful distrust, it struck him that he may have misread their intentions, despite the

---

44 Hey! You, black stranger! Stop! Wait!
45 Stop! Don't run! Stand still! Or we will spear you!
46 Are you deaf?

apparent threat. They had carried his canister of water, after all, and the spear missed him, though by a narrow margin. Besides, the other armed warrior now carried his spear casually across his shoulders, both his hands raised and relaxed across the shaft in the cruciform position, observing developments.

'*Gurra icithayi, ngatha gurra bumanha nyindanha[47],*' the warrior said, stepping forward and, as Sunil flinched for a blow, he reached out with both hands and gripped Sunil by the left shoulder and right bicep, squeezing him as though in a gesture of reassurance or a demonstration of strength, before placing Sunil's forearm against his own for a full half-minute, seemingly examining the skin texture and colour contrast.

Apparently satisfied, he stepped back and inspected him from head to toe once again, bemused. Then he reached up, ran a finger along Sunil's shaven jaw, and pointed at his groin. '*Nyinda wayabandi? Wurrinyu?[48]*' he asked.

When he repeated the question and persisted in pointing at his groin, Sunil took off his shoes, undid the pewter buttons on his calico breeches and removed them. Both warriors beamed before breaking into laughter.

'*T'i! Gutharra kuca warabadi! Nyinda ngugurnu wayabandi![49]*' said the second warrior. His laughter subsided into a wide grin as he stepped forward and took the trousers from Sunil on the point of his spear. '*Nayi naga! Nhanganha wurdbi thumanunyina manda galga wujarnugura![50]*' he exclaimed.

He peered down at them in wonderment, before reaching out to touch them apprehensively. Then, gathering confidence, he released his spear and held them in both hands as he unfolded

---

47 Don't worry, I will not hit you.
48 Are you a man or a woman?
49 Yes! Two big testicles! You are truly a man!
50 Check this out! This is the skin that covers the stranger's backside and his legs!

them, turned them inside out, checked the buttons and held them up to the sun to verify the weave. Satisfied, he gave his partner a triumphant and cheerful shout, '*Hoh! Nayi ngana!*[51]'

Bemused, Sunil watched him sit down, stretch out a foot and insert it into the trouser leg. He stood and pulled the cloth to his thigh. Obviously wary of the feel and watching nervously as his leg disappeared, he hopped comically around them before tearing the breeches off, clearly so relieved to find his leg still intact that Sunil could not suppress a laugh.

Spurred on by Sunil's reaction and the ridicule of his partner, he inserted both feet and pulled the breeches to his waist, struggling with the buttons before Sunil stepped forward to assist him. '*Hier is hoe je het doet*, here, this is how you do it,' he spoke for the first time, with a relieved smile.

The breeches were too large and Sunil tightened the rope belt to hold them in place as the warrior, now highly pleased, leapt around them in a leg-stamping, arm-waving dance.

When he desisted, Sunil donned his shoes and they made their way back to the water canister. '*Baba nyindaguru,*' the senior warrior pointed as they approached it, '*bundu bardiyalu gurra bunduthayimanha marugudu.*[52]' Then he sat and gestured for Sunil join him.

When the three were comfortable, he pointed back at the water canister and then towards the east. '*Ngalingura maya bayirri yan, babamuthagurru. Ngatha ganmanha nyindanha babala barrangga.*[53]'

Sunil shook his head and shrugged, both hands palm up. After pondering for several moments, the warrior said,

---

51 Hey! Watch me do this!
52 There's your water. There's been no rain and it won't rain tomorrow or for some time.
53 Our camp is way over there. We have a plentiful supply of water. I will take you to the water there later.

'*Ngalingu nhanjanu wabagu warabadi wilithi gambanyu yuganga, garla gurrimutha. Nayi nhaga?*[54]'

When Sunil shook his head again, he repeated the question, illustrating his description with exaggerated arm and hand actions and explosive sounds, '*Nganharra nangiyanu nganggu-yanu yuganga marumaru! Pockaa! Pock! Pock!*[55]'

'Ah, that was the kite,' Sunil responded, demonstrating in turn as he spoke. 'We set it in on fire to signal the ships that passed us yesterday.'

He knew that neither warrior understood word or gesture and realised that they would have to return to the campsite for him to demonstrate. He pointed in that direction. 'Come back to the camp. I can show you.'

He stood and lifted the canister, again pointing towards the west. 'Come back to our camp. I can explain the kite. You can meet Gerrit.'

The warriors jumped to their feet, shouldering their spears. The senior shook his head. '*Mirda. Ngali yanmanha warrbathu ngurrala.*[56]'

The other, beaming and still wearing the breeches, told him, '*Marugudu nganharra nhanganha nyinda wilithi jinagabi ngurrala nyindangu.*[57]'

'WHAT'S THIS? THE latest VOC dress code?' I asked, looking at Sunil in astonishment.

Sunil gave me a wide smile as he selected another pair of breeches from the store of clothing. 'You won't believe this Gerrit. A local savage is now wearing them. He didn't have to steal them from my corpse, but I think it almost came to that.'

---

54 We saw the giant white sea-eagle yesterday. It caught fire. Lots of smoke. What was it?
55 We all saw it and heard it yesterday afternoon!
56 No. We'll both get back to camp right away.
57 Tomorrow we'll all see you and the white spirit at your camp.

'You met the local savages?'

'Two, and they surprised me by cooperating in the end. It was the last thing I expected. They carried the water for me. And they told me they saw the kite. They are wondering what it was. They must have been observing us.'

'Were they armed and hostile?'

'Armed, yes. Aggressive, I'm not sure. They were carrying wooden spears three paces long. Barbed with quartz, I think. They threw one in my direction when I was running but missed. Whether that was deliberate or I avoided it, I'm not sure.'

'My God! You ran?'

'Not far. Towards the closest trees. They accosted me out in the open.'

'So what happened?'

Sunil described the incident, pointing out the care with which the warrior had carried his water canister. 'I believe they think I am one of them from some other tribe. I have the impression they are territorial. They made it clear I was not welcome.'

I smiled. 'No permit to travel inland from our anchorage?'

'Something similar.'

'Then we must apply for one!' I raised my eyebrows. 'So what were they like? You said you weren't sure if they were aggressive.'

'At first, I was afraid they were. When they calmed down, I found they liked to laugh, the younger one in particular, wearing my breeches. He was a comedian. The senior one has a strong presence. He carries himself proudly. With authority. I think he threw the spear. He asked the questions. He refused to come back here when I suggested it. I gather he will be bringing others tomorrow.' He cocked his head at Gerrit. 'I'm not sure what they'll make of you, a white man. That will test them!'

Two HOURS AFTER sunrise the next morning, I saw a warrior suddenly appear from the nearest coppice of trees. Alone and unarmed, he was carrying three birds. He was naked, except for a red hide cloak draped around him.

I watched him stride into the camp and greet Sunil, '*Nyinda ngugurnu?*[58]'

He deposited two white and grey banded birds the size of chickens and a large brown-feathered carcass the size of a turkey beside the fire. '*Nyinda bulyarru?*[59]' he asked '*Nhanganha gutharra thanindi barduda. Guga gambaniya.*[60]'

Deliberately ignoring me sitting with my back to a tree beneath the canvas strung across its branches and watching him keenly, he turned to look down the cliff at the wreck. Then he signalled towards the surrounding trees as if summoning others I hadn't noticed in the shadows. Several men appeared, also unarmed. I looked for Sunil's breeches, but no one was wearing them.

Their discussion was boisterous and prolonged until one of them, stepping below the lip of the cliff to the platform, saw the statuette of the sphinx propped against a rock halfway down. I saw him rear back. Its folded wings, scaly tail and distorted features clearly alarmed him. He retreated up the slope calling on the others and pointing. Their immediate silence betrayed their suspicion and I observed them move as one back to the cover of the trees at the edge of the clearing, where they faded into the shadows.

How many others are concealed there? I wondered when I heard the sound of raised voices. *No one has so much as looked at me or acknowledged my presence.*

A short silence ensued, then I saw a tall old man emerge

---

58 Are you well?
59 Are you hungry?
60 Here are two malleefowl and a bush turkey. You can cook the meat.

from the shadows, white-bearded, deeply wrinkled, his sharp eyes deep-set and barely visible beneath protruding brows. His back was remarkably straight, his carriage dignified. His legs were bone and sinew, his stride long. His nasal septum was pierced and parallel body scars were ridged up his abdomen. *Just like Sunil,* the thought flashed through my mind as he approached, *a stairway carved into the flesh that both men have climbed, step by agonising step, bearing the pain before healing over time… as we all do in our lives.*

He walked directly across to me, where he squatted at my level beneath the tree and looked me over, avoiding my eyes except occasionally when his glance was piercing but calm, betraying no emotion. He inspected me closely in silence, checking the weeping wounds and splints on my leg and showing surprise only when he saw the gin bottle half-filled with urine propped in the sand beside me. He stared at it… and then, before I could prevent it, he reached out and felt my genitals beneath the cloth, releasing them at once.

Wordless, he stood and stepped to the other side of the tree trunk against which I was leaning. There he also sat, facing inland, his back turned on me.

No words passed between us. I assumed he was looking directly ahead during the silence that lasted several minutes. Then, in a baritone that shifted effortlessly now and again into a barely audible falsetto, the old man began to sing, his words seemingly a stream of musical sound rather than comprehensible speech. The song lasted and, fearing it may be a prelude to my execution, I tried to pick up cues from the intonation and emotional pitch as to how to respond, to no avail.

When the song ended, the old man was again silent for several moments before he stood and resumed his position beside me. For the first time, he smiled and gestured towards himself. '*Ngatha Kananggadi,*[61]' he said, then pointed at me, his expression clearly questioning.

'I'm Gerrit,' I said. 'Gerrit de Waal.'

The old man's comprehending smile widened. '*Gayirrit! Gayirri! Nyinda gayirri yanmanu… nyinda Gayirrigayirrit!*[62]' He spread his arms wide, gesturing inland and confusing me even further. '*Nhanganha Gathaagudu, ngurra Malganangu uthudujadawana.*[63]'

Then he nodded, as though assuming I'd understood. '*Nyinda bardiyalu jinagabi wilithi, nyinda wiyabandi wilithi yanaangu gayirri wardandula.*[64]' He nodded again, more deliberately, before adding, '*Nyinda nyinamanha narla barrajala ngathangu… yuganga, maragudu. Nyinda wiyabandi Malgana, Garimarangu!*[65]'

He turned and pointed at Sunil, seated at the edge of the cliff watching us. '*Wiyabandi mathara bayirri, Malgana, Barungura.*[66]'

Then he gave a wheezing burst of laughter and waved as he summoned the group concealed in the thickets. Several warriors emerged from the shade and trotted across to him. '*Nhanganha wiyabandi wilithi Gayirrigayirrit! Wiyabandi Malgana mardijithayimanha wurrinyu Banagara!*[67]'

There was a chorus of amazement and a burst of laughter

---

61 I am Kananggadi.

62 Gerrit! Far away! You've come from far away… you are Gayirrigayirrit, Gerrit-from-afar!

63 This is Shark Bay, home to the Malgana people, our much-beloved country.

64 You, you're not a white spirit but a white man who has come from far to the west.

65 You are welcome to stay here in my country from now on. You are a young Malgana man now, of Garimara descent.

66 The young black man over there, he is also now Malgana, of Barungu descent.

67 This young white man is Gerrit-from-afar! He is Malgana now and may marry one of our Banaga women!'

when the old man added, '*Gutiya… bugarra bugarra!*[68]'

Then he shouted at the trees, '*Nhurra nyarlu, gaba warr-buthu, matka atkajadi wanyu. Maruthayinyina.*[69]'

At his signal, two women emerged cautiously from the trees, one of them carrying a hollow gourd of oil. I was concerned when the old man held out a hand and pointed at my wounds. '*Wirda wujarnugura marrigudu, mambu ardandanu marrithayiniyan.*[70]'

The two women, a mother and daughter, it seemed, knelt beside me, one on either side, and inspected the wound. The older woman sent the younger for some seawater, indicating that she should empty the urine bottle and use that.

For a moment the girl looked apprehensive, before she gingerly reached out for it. She picked it up at last, scooped a hole in the sand a roede away and emptied it, before peering through the glass. She seemed mystified by its transparency. She looked over at me. '*Nayi nhanganhanu? Bardalyi?*[71]' she asked.

'*Het is glas… een glazen fles.* It's glass… a glass bottle.' I said, then repeated the word '*glas*' twice.

She gave me a smile and ducked her head before making her way down the cliff face. Within minutes she was back, and they began gently cleaning the wound. Then the younger girl applied the oily ointment. When I bit the inside of my mouth to offset the pain, the girl saw me wince.

'*Nyinda warniyanu?*[72]' she enquired, her voice empathic, looking briefly up at me.

Captivated by her glance, I recalled Ariaantje's dark eyes the moment timidity had turned brazen the first time she'd

---

68 Only one… and very, very old!
69 You women, get over here quickly. Bring the tea tree oil. It's getting late.
70 The stranger's leg is injured. The bone is broken and has not set.
71 What is this? A rock?
72 Did you fall?

handed me my lunch at the water fountain and given me a blazing smile. I saw the same change come over this girl now, her shyness evaporating as she spread the oil carefully across my wound, filling the air with the acrid scent of camphor.

When she was satisfied, she looked back up and, with unexpected daring, reached out to touch the albatross necklace, pointing it out to the other woman. '*Nayi naga nhanganha wilyara banduga*[73],' she said. Glancing shyly at me, she asked, '*Nayiwunga?*[74]'

She looked expectantly up at me, but I had no reply.

After a moment she tapped her breast as though in recognition. '*Ngathangura jayarra,*[75]' she murmured.

Then she reached for the bottle and held it up. '*Glas,*' she said, before pointing again at the necklace pendant. She gave me a delighted smile, leant forward to touch the shell and spoke the word, '*Wilyara,*' then ran her forefinger across the albatross and repeated, '*Banduga.*'

When I responded, '*Schelp* and *albatros,*' and heard her correctly repeat the words, I was back in the timber yards in my imagination, listening to Serafino. *He is right,* I realised, gazing at her. *In losing your language you lose your sense of self, but in sharing it you experience the deepest sense of community...*

---

73 Look at this albatross carved in the shell.
74 What's it for?
75 My totem is the white cockatoo.

Part Three
Tania

2 January 2001

Stefan lifted his fingers from the touchpad and gazed thoughtfully out over the lake. He had reached the end of the unfinished manuscript. It had taken him three days, his progress marked by numerous cuts, corrections and adjustments.

He looked back at the screen and reread the last page. *Crunch time*, he thought. *Time to sort out the ending. No more putting it off.*

He saved the file to a flash drive before closing it, then retrieved and opened another. He checked that the rough draft conclusion he had compiled months ago had flashed up on the screen before standing, stretching and walking out across the lawn to the jetty. He sat cross-legged on the pontoon for several minutes, staring out at Coal Point opposite, clearing his mind.

On his way back to the veranda he paused at the Brunfelsias, leaning in to breathe the musky clove-like scent of the last of the lavender-blue and white flowers that spoke of Tania. A brief rush of warmth ran through him, accompanied by an irrepressible feeling of sceptical uncertainty.

He strode back to the table, sat and began to read:

> *Some members of the Malgana family visited us for several days after that, departing for their camp each evening.*
>
> *The women tended to my leg and began teaching me the rudiments of their Malgana wangganyina language, starting with the naming of our body parts and the things in the natural world around us—the yalgari trees, the bardalyi rocks, the nyiru sea birds, the wirriya ocean, while I responded with equivalent words in Dutch, as though we were playing a game. They found the pronunciation of some words*

tongue-twisting, as did I; and the articulation of the occasional Dutch consonants from the back of the throat had them in fits of laughter.

I came to enjoy their shared light-heartedness and enjoyment of life as we exchanged vocabularies. It seemed we were translating from the illustrated pages of a book that was opening up to us, written in the language of the natural world they were clearly so familiar with and deeply understood.

One day the men took Sunil to their inland campsite with its small water soak and he returned with a full canister and a spear one of them had given him. The next time he visited them to collect water, he astonished them with a gift of five large red crayfish he'd speared.

Then one morning, without warning or words of farewell, they did not return.

They took with them the gin crate filled with empty bottles and all the broken glass they'd collected; the adze and a tureen; a handful of newly minted silver shillings that had washed up on the rock shelf, cast there after one of the cases in Schipper Marinus's cabin must have ruptured; and, surprisingly, three iron barrel hoops that Sunil had spent hours teaching the group of six children to roll and chase. They had taken a great liking to him, especially his occasional energetic clowning. They swam with him and tried out his goggles, sprinted wildly after the hoops, and screamed with laughter as he tried unsuccessfully to somersault and land on his feet from a standing start, a spectacular feat the two older ones could leap into with fluent ease.

Six weeks after their departure, I was leaning against the rough udbi bark of the wind-blasted gurardangu *tea tree. I glanced down at my tarnished spoon, then turned to look inland at the rocky landscape of* barlga *samphire we now realised we could eat, the* bintharru *saltbush and yellow-flowering tangled* ngaya *wattle trees angling upwards to the skyline. Then I saw a shadow detach itself from among the trees. It turned down a faint, meandering path that led across the gulley's boulder-strewn edge towards me, worn by* bigurda *grey kangaroos.*

The shadow disappeared, then reappeared several moments later from the closer trees as Sunil staggered into view under the weight of two canisters of brackish water. He had lugged them from the drying soak an hour away. He placed the canisters carefully under the torn sail canvas roof stretched across the tree branches.

'Almost the last of it,' he panted, his gaunt face shrouded in dark unruly hair. 'Now our troubles really start.'

'We're in trouble?' I smiled.

I thought of that early morning in Middelburg so long ago, the sack over my head, the image of Mama and I smiling at each other in the voorkamer mirror, my face blue-streaked, the canal's freezing water closing over me before I emerged to climb the Maisbaai wall, the crowd of carpenters chanting as I was carried shoulder-high back to the dokhavn, the spoon flashing my name at the world. 'What trouble?'

I stretched my sun-browned, healing leg out in front of me, reached up into the tea tree with one arm to grasp a low branch and hauled myself clumsily upright. I staggered across the clearing. 'Trouble, you think? No such thing. We're right as rain.' I dipped my roemer into the brown water.

'Except it hasn't rained.' Sunil pointed out a solitary cloud, like fading cannon smoke in the empty sweep of sky. 'But you never know,' he commented sardonically.

I grinned. 'Eendracht maakt macht[76],' I said, resting a hand on his shoulder and looking him in the eye. I kicked a toe at the fine sand and stooped to pick up a handful. It filtered through my fingers. 'And this is our Eendrachtsland, where we will come through our beproeving, *our ordeal.'*

As the last of the sand trickled away, I held my other hand in a fist, straightening a finger in turn as I recalled the names of those who'd survived their separate disastrous shipwrecks against the odds. 'Remember Willem Bontekoe and the Nieuw Hoorn? *Remember Abraham Leeman and the* Vergulde Draeck? *Remember Francisco Pelsaert and the* Batavia? *Jacob van Heemskerck? Willem Barentsz?'*

I raised my hand in a fist again and shook it at the sky, 'Especially Willem Barentsz—think of him. He discovered Spitzbergen. He made three separate voyages across the White Sea. He was the first to chart the arctic coasts of Novaya Zemlya. In the end, twelve of his crew returned to Amsterdam even though he'd died and wasn't with them. His spirit got them through. As ours will.'

I raised both fists skyward and laughed. 'Now here we are, you and me. Sunil Dewaraja and Gerrit de Waal!'

---

76 'Our unity makes us strong'; the motto adopted by the Dutch Republic during the eighty-year war of independence against Spain in the sixteenth and seventeenth centuries.

I pointed at the flimsy cover of worn canvas flapping in the evening south-westerly. 'We have ons eigen behouden huis, *our own safe house, and it's far more comfortable without the ice and snow. And besides,' I went on, 'we can't forget that we've now met the Malgana and they have baptised us. You, Sunil of the Barungu and me, Gayirrigayirrit, Gerrit of the Garimara.'*

For a moment, I was seated on my window ledge once again, listening to Opa Laurens as he warned me with uncanny foreknowledge that my sailing skills would take my house-ship into the cliffs of Eendrachtsland when the unpredictable future played its hand.

Stefan scrolled down to the next page. Then he checked his watch. *Half an hour closer to Tania's arrival time tomorrow!* He looked up and continued reading.

Though neither of us admitted to it except in half-hearted jest, by mid-August it was clear we would die of thirst. The last canister of muddy water that Sunil had carried from the drying soak would last us a week.

The next time he made the long walk inland to the soak, he reported that he'd found a dry depression with the arrowed footprints of thirsty birds and the claw-marks of barnka *racehorse goannas imprinted across the cracked mud. Even the reeds around the soak were dead, he said, and rattling in the constant wind.*

'It was exhausting digging, Gerrit. The surface was baked harder than our ship's biscuits.'

He sat facing me in the hot shade of the tea tree.

'Were there any signs of the Malgana?' I asked.

'None. They must have gone south, as they said

they would. To the wilu *river they told us about.' He adjusted the bracelet of plaited lion's mane above his left elbow. He pointed at the canister. 'That is the last of the water. Two days' worth at the most. So where do we go from here?'*

'We must find them.'

'We haven't seen them for weeks.'

I glanced at the sky, the wind trailing fine white streaks of cloud as though dragging its fingernails across the blue. 'They can't have gone far,' I said without confidence. 'We must act now. Our time is running out.'

No blocks of ice to melt, hacked from the crests of icebergs. No snow packed into copper cooking pots to warm over flames on a Greenland hillside. No sparkling streamlet to dive into as it flowed over pebbles down the slopes of Constantiaberg. No pewter mug filled with water from the Triton fountain to fling skywards, the droplets splashing down against our upturned faces.

'We could do with the fountain right now. Do you remember when Simon van der Stel opened up the pipes and let the water flow for the first time?'

'As though it was yesterday,' Sunil replied, glancing at the three notched sticks wedged against the tree trunk.

'I am not ready to die, as old Simon van der Stel was,' I replied. 'We have not come this far for nothing. I agree... they've gone south to the country of the Nhanda they described. That's where we'll find them.'

'They said it was more than three days' walk. There may be no water between here and there.'

'And they said the nearest reliable pool is to the north, at a place they called "Wale" water. We have no idea where that is. Or how far.'

'It's in the opposite direction.'

'Exactly. No point in following Joost that way. We'll head south. We know the river opens into the sea. We can't miss it. It will run across our path and the water upstream must be fresh. Perhaps we can reach it in less than three days if we travel at night in the cool.'

Sunil glanced at the gulley behind us, its slopes covered in dense wanyu mulga. 'In the dark? We'll be fighting our way through bush like that, blind and without water.'

'We have a three-quarter moon this week. That should be light enough. Besides, what's happened to your naga water serpents after all the water we wasted on them?' I asked. 'Perhaps you can sing them another song to convince them to stop playing games with us or call up your yakhina Indigolla.*'*

'No, Jantje's the one we need now,' Sunil replied, gesturing at the limestone ridge. 'That old African Moses could smell fresh water in these rocks and use his magic to conjure up a spring for us.'

'Then we'd better learn to do the same, and quickly. I suggest we make a move tonight.'

Sunil glanced at my leg. 'Are you ready for a trek that far?'

'I'm as prepared as I'll ever be. If not, then I'll die trying.'

Stefan lifted his fingers from the touchpad again, placed his elbows on the table and stared at the screen for several minutes, chin in hand.

What next? He wondered. *Their walk south? Their meeting with the Malgana again, perhaps working in the* ajugawu *yam gardens or building another* marla adumba maya *mud and wattle hut in the Nhanda village they'd mentioned, or digging a second well? No. I need a scene that encapsulates everything Gerrit has lived for, one that reinvents his life, giving it meaning and direction…*

Slowly shaking his head, he saved and printed the document, closed the lid and switched off the laptop.

At dawn the next day, he took a swim and then prepared a quick breakfast. With a slice of toast in one hand for the journey and the printed pages describing Gerrit and Sunil's final days at the campsite to work on while waiting at the airport, he was on his way.

He checked the sky. There were loose clouds about, too high for rain. No wind. He caught the faint smell of ash in the still air, though the fires had been extinguished days ago.

He headed for Toronto and took the back roads around Lake Macquarie through Warner's Bay to Belmont airport. Looking back across the lake at one point, he glimpsed the charred slopes of the hills encircling Mt Warrawalong pitch black against the sky. On a closer hillside, he could make out skeletal stands of scorched trees of Watagan State forest bordering the green.

In top spirits, he had the hire car hood down for the ride and the radio blaring.

He reached the airport with half an hour to kill. He bought a coffee and spread the pages across the table, one ear out already for the sound of the plane, even though the passengers were probably still boarding in Sydney.

Ordering the pages in sequence, he leant over them and began to read, but he found it impossible to concentrate, kept referring to his watch. His excitement and apprehension mounting, he gave up and closed the file. He moved out into the open beneath the eucalypts bordering the runway apron, where he sat on the top step, leaning against the veranda pillar.

Twenty minutes to arrival time!

To distract himself, he recalled the visit that he and Lennard had made to the *Zuytdorp* wreck site the previous August. Lennard had suggested that Stefan would benefit from seeing the place for himself. 'A trip up there will work wonders for you, bro. Give you a first-hand look at the environment. Make sure you bring along your walking boots. The rocks are razor sharp.'

Lennard's father Andy, who ran the sheep station up at Wanamalu, had driven them from Murchison Station to the wreck site in his battered Land Cruiser, grinding along narrow meandering tracks of rock and thick sand used by abalone divers along the cliffs.

Lennard had brought along his translated copy of Amedeo Sala's story describing his survival of the sinking of the Croatian sailing barque *Stefano* off the Ningaloo Coast in October 1875.

'The *Stefano*! How's that for an appropriate name.' He'd grinned as he'd shown Stefan the cover. 'The crew who made it ashore after the sinking were rescued by a local Malgana group travelling across the Exmouth peninsula,' he'd explained. 'Without the Malgana, they had Buckley's. They would all have carked it. And all of them did, bar two. It'll give you an insight into the interaction between the survivors and the Malgana.'

During the second evening at the *Zuytdorp* wrecksite, Lennard had surprised him by suggesting they undertake the walk south themselves. He'd been unusually quiet while Andy had started a fire and made arrangements for roasting 'roo steaks and potatoes in the coals.

'Listen,' he'd said while they were eating, 'it's the twentieth of August today. My bet says Gerrit would have been planning to trek south around this time, if not to the day. In two and a half months, Gerrit's leg should have healed, so he'd have been up for it. They'd have been short on water and up against it… toey as, in fact, to find the Malgana. So why don't we join him? Wander down to the Murchison ourselves? See what they went through.'

Andy had laughed. 'A lot less feral goats then than now, for starters.'

'I'm game,' Stefan had agreed. 'Three days you think it'll take?'

'Around about.' Lennard had pointed at the cloud-filled sky partly lit by a three-quarter moon appearing through the gaps. 'The weather change they promised us seems to be coming in. It may even rain; you never know. I reckon we walk it during the day, get through it quicker.'

'Nah, won't rain, just a lick and a promise,' Andy had said, 'but that's the way I'd tackle it. Eyeball the dugites before they eyeball you and you get bit. I can take the gear and meet you at that dero camp the abalone divers left behind down Coolabinya Gulley way, get a fire goin' so you can get your bearin's if you don't make it before sundown tomorrow night.'

'Good idea.' Lennard had turned to Stefan. 'We should make it to the Murchison by midday on the twenty-third. Sound good?'

'If you say so.'

It had taken them two and a half days. As promised, Andy had met them on the first night after sunset, the fire lit and a meal prepared.

Stefan had surprised himself. While the terrain had been rough—a mix of sand patches and broken limestone—and the gullies running west to east challenging, the heath along the clifftops covered in saltbush and samphire had made for easier going.

He'd revelled in the views, the ocean to their right occasionally lighting up in iridescent greens and blues when the sun broke through, the wind bracing and the crash of breaking waves a constant thunder.

He'd found the going tougher on the second day. It had been rockier underfoot, the gullies more frequent and deeper, the tea trees and wattle denser, their yellow flowers dusting the air, aggravating the back of his throat. But he'd responded to the challenge and had been able to maintain Lennard's pace.

When they'd settled for the night, Stefan was asleep before his head met his rolled-up shirt.

That last day, they'd descended the cliffs for the first time, climbing down to a series of sandy coves between rocky ridges and platforms that ran out to reefs boiling with surf. Eventually, the cliffs had petered out and, for the last few kilometres, they'd found themselves walking in the soft sand of a sloping beach curving away towards the river mouth. They'd turned upriver before midday, Kalbarri Township on the opposite bank.

Andy had been there to greet them, sitting on the foredeck of an aluminium dinghy in the shallows.

'So how'd you go?' he'd asked Stefan.

'Brilliant. Just brilliant.'

'And your impressions?'

'Two words for it. Rugged, but bloody beautiful.'

'That's four.'

'Four then, but I'm not sure Gerrit would've been quite so complimentary.'

'He would if he'd had a fill of the fish and chips we're about to get stuck into,' Lennard had said.

Andy had lifted a paper-wrapped parcel over to them. 'Still warm,' he'd said, as he'd reached into an esky for icy stubbies of Emu Bitter, 'and a coldie to wash it down.'

When Stefan had watched Lennard unwrap the fish and Andy crack the stubbie caps, he'd felt a sense of achievement, a deeply satisfying feeling of connection sweeping through him.

'*Ngatha ngugurnu,*' he'd said. '*Ngatha nala ngurrala nyinanu.*[77]'

Andy had handed him the stubbie. '*Ngugurnu.*[78] Here, get this EB into you and you'll feel even better.'

Then he'd turned to Lennard. 'So you two are goin' to be workin' in Paris on your next assignment, you were tellin' me?'

'Yep, well, I am… I've asked Stefan here to work with me on the project. He has a few things to attend to with Tania before he makes up his mind.'

'It depends,' Stefan nodded.

Andy smiled. 'You'll have to twist her arm?'

'Easier said than done.'

'She's a Yirrganydji woman from Cairns, Lennard tells me. And a dancer. She'd be good value, then. A woman with a mind and a career of her own.'

'She is… I'm hoping we can get back together.'

'I've signed a contract to design a feature for the Quai Branly Museum—part of the landscaping,' Lennard broke in. 'We've got six years before it opens, so there's plenty of time between drinks.'

'What sort of museum?' Andy asked.

'They're thinking of displaying Aboriginal art from around the world. Four continents, excluding Europe.'

'Sounds interesting. What exactly do the Frogs want? A giant green glass Kermit squattin' in a pond?'

Lennard had grinned across at me. 'Now there's an idea. Stick that down in the notebook.'

'Will do. It shouldn't be too technical.'

'The tongue could be a problem.'

'Let alone the fly.'

Andy had laughed. 'No flies on you two bruddas, I reckon. That cenotaph of yours in Freo is the bee's knees.'

---

77 I feel great. I feel at home here.
78 Good.

THE SOUND OF the approaching plane roused Stefan. He leapt to his feet, his heart pounding. He shaded his eyes, scanning the sky as the Twin Otter swung low across the airport buildings before roaring in above the trees, the engine reaching a crescendo as it touched down and bounced into view at the far end of the runway.

It took an eternity to taxi to the apron and glide to a halt. The door swung down and the pilot climbed sideways down the stairs, followed by the first of the passengers.

Tania was the third to appear. Squinting in the sunlight, she raised a hand to shade her eyes, saw Stefan, waved and climbed down the steps. On the bitumen, she turned back to the doorway. She raised her arms to a dark-haired girl of three or four in a green T-shirt and denim dungarees. The child hesitated before reaching to grasp Tania's hands. She swung herself out and wrapped her legs around Tania's waist, her arms about her shoulders. Tania lowered her to the ground and walked towards Stefan, holding the child by the hand.

Stefan's heart missed a beat as they approached. Shock, surprise and the beginnings of elation raced through him. His daughter? The possibility was disorienting and electrifying. He sensed his life changing track as Tania reached the gate.

'Hello, Stefan,' she said as they embraced and broke apart, 'I'd like you to meet Kylie.' She looked down at the girl. 'Kylie, *este e Stefan, sui pai.*' Then she translated, 'This is Stefan, your papa.'

Kylie looked up at him, her dark brown eyes solemn and apprehensive, her black hair ribboned over each ear, ponytails hanging to her shoulders, her skin a deep gold.

'*Ola, Pai,*' she murmured, and when Tania nudged her, she gave a shy, gap-toothed smile, 'Hello, Papa.'

Speechless, Stefan squatted and took her in his arms before releasing her and holding her at arm's length so they could examine one another. He slowly shook his head as he gazed at her and she, confused and timid, looked up at Tania for reassurance.

'You are beautiful, just beautiful,' he whispered, and gently enfolded her in his arms once again.

'It's alright, Stefan. She won't break,' Tania said.

He felt his child's heartbeat against his own and, for one blinding moment, the thought occurred that had Tania hinted four years ago that this racing pulse was beginning to beat deep within her, he'd have passed sentence and insisted she extinguish it.

'Her Portuguese is better than her English at the moment,' Tania said. She placed a hand on his shoulder and he looked up. 'She's the only reason I left you when I did. Having her was a decision we couldn't agree on or forgive each other for at the time.' She gazed at him as though searching for the words. 'I know I should have told you about her, but the timing never seemed right.' She gave him a quiet smile, a mix of apology and relief. 'Now you know.'

Stefan stood and put his arms about her, the confusing possibility striking him that she may have been aware of her situation the last time they'd been at the boathouse and kept it from him. Remorse and concern gripped him as he imagined what she must have gone through in the three months before Christmas.

He took both her hands and then, his voice charged, he said, 'I can promise you this, Tan. Things are very different now. Things have changed.' He looked down, enthralled. 'My God! She's perfect.' He knelt and wrapped Kylie in his arms once more, fighting back tears. 'This has to be our happiest moment.'

Kylie folded into him, and he took the lightest of smiles playing about her lips as her pleasure at the novelty of his closeness.

THAT NIGHT, AFTER Tania and Kylie had retired to the boarding house, Stefan roughly drafted the ending to the book. It had come to him at the airport the moment he'd taken Kylie in his arms and looked up in amazed gratitude at Tania.

> *The two women I searched for were squatting beyond the hill, hidden from the encampment. Keeping my distance, I watched them in the gold blossomed shade of the Mooja tree, blue smoke unfurling from a pile of dried leaves smouldering beside them. They moved closer together. I saw the older woman look down at the squirm of a pale infant, the new-born bilyunu in the leaf-lined hollow of the earth cradle.*
>
> *The younger woman leant back against the rough bark of the trunk. Her legs were spread wide, her hands gripped across her breasts. I made out the blue and scarlet lifeline of the placenta uncoiling from her bloodied vagina like a sunlit sinew to the child's centre.*
>
> *Tense, I watched the older woman reach for the newborn child—is she female?—to lick clean the breathing mouth and the eyes and the quick pulsing curve of rib and stomach, a warm-tongued welcome to this world. Then, teeth bared, she clamped the cord and chewed, separating the child.*
>
> *She lifted her in ancient hands away from the earth-scooped cradle-grave. She stood and held the infant to her withered breasts to feel the heartbeat, the wurduru of another life fluttering against her own, and to breathe the awareness of this new existence deep into herself.*
>
> *I saw her anoint the child with a smear of atkajadi oil and hold her momentarily in the cleansing wisp of smoke before leaning down to pat a free hand in*

the warm ash, the thalaaba *of the fire, using it to powder the child. Then she handed her to her mother, her ngangga, soaked in sweat but smiling weakly at the pitch of the infant's cry that carried to me as she cradled her in an elbow-crook and offered her a dark nipple against which the child rubbed her ash-covered cheek before fastening her lips to it.*

The older woman retrieved the expelled afterbirth. She selected a length which she retained and, with the side of her foot, she filled the birth hollow to bury the rest, scooping back the red earth that would have suffocated the quivering infant had she, the bugarra, *the old midwife, so decided.*

I acknowledged with elation that the child was alive, and I imagined the mother marvelling at the gold of her skin she must have known would darken, and the finest blonde threads of her sparse hair.

The older woman reached up to pick a yellow bunch from the shower of crocus in the tree, then another, placing them in the curved wooden yandi, ready for the mother to lie the infant within it for their return to the campsite. In the flowers, I had been told, was the infant's name and, in her body, was the spirit recalled from its dreaming by the wilithi jinagabi wiyabandi, *the white spirit who is no spirit but a man and her father.*

I witnessed the older woman splitting the length of the placenta and plaiting it into a necklace of ash-covered sinew for the infant; a reminder ring linking her spirit past to her living present. The infant would wear it, I had been advised, as a bracelet similar to the bracelet I wore, during the first days of her life as the others of the Malgana family welcomed her into their circle of awareness in this beloved place of their dreaming, edged by the western ocean and the sleeping of the sun.

They walked back up the hillside towards the campsite, where I, her father, Gayirrigayirrit, Gerrit-from-afar, stood and welcomed her into my sunburned arms.

STEFAN SAVED AND printed the pages. He read them through, then shut down the laptop and exhaled a lengthy whistle of relief. He had finished the first draft. He and Lennard had brought Gerrit to life.

Now Alicia has the task of refining the script. He smiled. *And she can correct all the errors in my Malgana vocabulary and syntax!*

He gazed across the lake and considered Lennard's proposal—that he stay on in Fremantle and assist him in finding another location to re-establish the glassworks and prepare the landscaping installation for the Quai Branly museum. He reached for the phone and dialled Lennard's number at the hospital. He listened as the dial tone rang out and then recorded a message, 'Quai Branly, Ace, I have the answer for you. It's a definite yes.'

About to disconnect, he recalled the first time Lennard had called him four years before and he'd failed to hear the signal when Lennard rang off. He'd listened expectantly to the long silence, only to discover he was waiting for more enlightening words from someone who wasn't there. He looked across the lake and ended his message with cryptic emphasis, 'You've filled the silence for me, bro. I'm grateful.' Then, his expression jubilant, he switched off the phone, murmuring, 'Work *that* one out, my brother, by the time we get home!'

Now Tania had returned, bringing Kylie to him. Their child, who had swum in his company that afternoon, her arms about his neck as he'd towed her through the water. She'd leapt from the end of the pontoon into his arms, her face shining with confidence, her body gleaming!

At the same time, Tania had handed him the gift of an ending to the book.

He stood and reached for the mobile of blue crystal that he, Tania and Kylie had spent time hanging in the boathouse that afternoon. He touched an outer string to set it swinging, its delicate tinkling accompanying the hushed slap of wavelets on the hulls of the kayaks.

As he listened, the final scene of *Three Colours: Blue* came back to him, haunting and obsessive, the sounds of the chorale Julie had completed for her dead composer husband pouring through his mind.

He turned to the lake as glorious voices in crescendo overwhelmed him, 'Though I speak with the tongues of angels, if I have not love, I am become as hollow brass. Though I have the gift of prophecy and understand all mysteries and all knowledge, if I do not have love, I am nothing.'

He walked out to the pontoon and stood contemplating the water. True, Tania had brought Kylie to meet him. And she seemed pleased to see him, appeared comfortable in his presence, appreciative of his interaction with Kylie and her response to him. He saw that she was composed, self-contained and stronger than before. She still had a measure of reserve though, as if she was withholding something of herself from the world, something essential, waiting for her moment.

Has her love for me lessened? he wondered. *Has it leached away?*

The thought alarmed him. He turned and looked back up at the boarding house. Her window was lit, the curtains drawn. He saw a shadow, or imagined it, move across the screen before the light went out.

He stood abandoned on the jetty in the darkness, momentarily disoriented. As he walked back to the boathouse, his senses returned—the strong night scent of the Brunfelsias and the smoky hint of ash, the water shifting and bubbling against the pylons, the play of cold air against his back so that he vigorously rubbed his arms to clear the gooseflesh.

And there, at the clifftop, he saw a figure that detached itself from the darkness and took the first careful step down towards him.

Author's Postscript

FOUNDED IN 1602, the Dutch United East India Company (the VOC) engaged in trade with Asia that lasted for more than two centuries. To achieve this, the VOC built ships, fitted them out and constructed warehouses, forts and harbours across the East Indies, including Japan. Over four thousand often hazardous voyages were undertaken during what is known as the Dutch Golden Age.

One route from the Netherlands to Batavia (now Jakarta) in Indonesia brought vessels dangerously close to the West Australian coast. At least five ships are known to have come to grief along that coast. Among these, the *Zuytdorp* was wrecked on the cliffs north of Kalbarri in June 1712. There were survivors. Did they integrate and settle with the local Aboriginal Malgana and Nhanda clans? Evidence suggests they did, in which case they were among the first Europeans to settle on the continent. Today, some Aboriginal Australians in the area believe their ancestry may include marooned Dutch sailors.

The Life and Times of Gerrit de Waal is a fictional work set in the seventeenth and early eighteenth centuries in Middelburg in the Netherlands and on the north-west coast of Western Australia. While the locations in this story exist and historical and current events are referred to, the storyline is invented.

2019 was the United Nations Year of Indigenous Languages. It has been a privilege to include words and phrases of the Malgana Language, spoken in the Shark Bay area. My thanks are extended to Ben Bellottie of the Malgana First Nations people, Dr Doug Marmion and the Yamaji Language Centre in Geraldton.

About The Author

PETER PURCHASE WAS born and educated in East Africa. Growing up on the Kenya coast, he came into close contact with the evidence of Arab, Chinese and Portuguese exploration across the Indian Ocean.

In his novel *The Life and Times of Gerrit de Waal*, he draws on that experience to describe the rise of the Dutch East India Company during the seventeenth and eighteenth centuries. His writing is motivated by a fascination for the sea and an awareness of issues around Australia's Aboriginal and Torres Straits Islander people. In Gerrit de Waal, he creates a character who shares both passions.

He migrated to Australia in 1963. Working in remote locations in the mining and construction industries in the Pilbara, Northern Territory and Papua New Guinea brought him into close contact with local Indigenous people. He finds their culture, deep-rooted love of country, resilience and unfailing sense of humour inspirational.

Peter eventually settled in Perth. He has a daughter who is a photographer and a son who works in the mining industry.

www.ingramcontent.com/pod-product-compliance
Lightning Source LLC
Chambersburg PA
CBHW070202120726
47909CB00001B/214